Author's Note

'Mere Anarchy' is my fifteenth novel and there is one big thing makes it very different indeed for the fourteen that have gone before it.

It is the first novel designed to raise money for The First Base Agency.

Every penny of profit the book is able to generate will go directly into the charity's coffers. This means that I really should tell you what The First Base Agency is all about.

We are a small independent charity based in Dumfries, Scotland. We like to think we do quite a lot for a small outfit. We punch above our weight if you like. We support families trying to live with a loved one's drug, alcohol or gambling problem. We support veterans battling with PTSD. We support young women at risk of violence as a result of their addictions. We give drug and alcohol awareness classes to over 3000 school kids every year. We hand out over 1000 food parcels a year to people who find themselves in a bad place.

You can find out all about us at www.first-base.org

Life has become very hard since the casino bankers tore the world down, a year ago. We are not unique in this respect. Every charity in Britain is finding the going seriously tough. Maybe every charity in the world. Many funding streams have run dry. The Government is broke. Councils are broke. Grant donating trusts have seen their income from interest and share dividends all but dry up.

Like I said, it's hard.

So how can you help? Well, you probably already have. If you are reading these words the odds are that you have already bought a copy of the book. Thanks for that. The story that follows is of course a fiction. Obviously it is. It is set in 2016 for goodness sake! It is supposed to be an entertainment. I hope when you turn the final page you will feel that you have had your money's worth.

What then?

Well here are a couple of thoughts about how you could help us out.

If you have indeed enjoyed the book then please don't lend it. Instead you might persuade your friends to go to

www.justgiving.com/first-base-agency

Then what happens? Well they can read all about the book of course. And hopefully they will give us a donation. Any donation at all, though £8.50 covers the cover price of the book and the postage.

Then what?

We will e mail them straight away and ask if they would like us to send them a copy. Then we will ask for their 'snail mail' address. If they want a copy, they send us their address and we send them a signed copy.

Simple as that.

Maybe you might be willing to fire off an e mail to those in your address book suggesting they might click on the link to

www.justgiving.com/first-base-agency

Maybe you might be willing to contact all your friends on Facebook or MySpace or Bebo and encourage them to click on a link to

www.justgiving.com/first-base-agency

Even better, you might agree to sign up to become one of our First Base Agents. How does this work? Simple. Drop us an e mail with your name and address and let us know how many books you might be able to sell for us. Maybe it might be five. Maybe it might be ten. Hell, maybe it might be twenty. We send you a package of books. You sell them to your friends for whatever you can get, again, £6 a copy is kind of what we hope for. Then you go online and pay the proceeds on to

www.justgiving.com/first-base-agency

Which of course means that our beloved Government has to throw an extra 35% into the pot.

As I am writing this we haven't sold a single copy. The book has yet to be printed. Maybe this idea will work. Maybe it will crash and burn.

The story you are about to read is not about The First Base Agency. But there is no way I could have written it without working for First Base for the last seven years. This is a story born in what the Tories have come to call 'Broken Britain'. It is about the corners of our country that most of us try to pretend are not really there. The part of town where we would never park our car or allow our children to visit a friend for tea. Where drugs and booze and crime and prison and benefits and ASBO's and graffiti and overdoses and domestic violence and generational unemployment and childhood abuse combine to make up a desperate way of life. How will such places fare in the coming years of austerity? Not well I fear.

'Mere Anarchy' can maybe be seen as a snapshot of how things might turn out.

I sincerely hope not.

What is more certain is that the services we offer at The First Base Agency will attract more and more demand. To continue our work we have to have the means to pay the rent and switch the lights on and cover the phone bills and fill up the food parcels.

I hope that you will find time to help us.

Thanks for reading this,

Mark Frankland
2010

A Glenmill Publication

© Mark Frankland, 2010

The moral right of the author has been asserted.

Glenmill Publishing

Dumfries

Scotland

DG2 8PX

tel: **07770 443 483**

http://www.thecull.com

British Library Cataloguing in Publication Data.
A catalogue record of this book
is available from the British Library.

ISBN 978-0-9551057-7-7

Glenmill logo: Andrew Carroll AKA 'Gizmo'

Printed and bound in Great Britain

Mere Anarchy

by

Mark Frankland

Turning and turning in the widening gyre
The falcon cannot hear the falconer;
Things fall apart; the centre cannot hold;
Mere anarchy is loosed upon the world,
The blood-dimmed tide is loosed, and everywhere
The ceremony of innocence is drowned;
The best lack all conviction, while the worst
Are full of passionate intensity.

The Second Coming
W. B. Yeats

"There's class warfare, all right," Mr. Buffett said, *"but it's my class, the rich class, that's making war, and we're winning."*

Warren Buffett
The New York Times, November 2006

Warren, in case you didn't know,
is the world's third richest man.

GERMANY, MARCH 1945

Something was different.

Rolf Wurtlich could tell as much straight away. But what?

The puddle-strewn road through the forest of pine trees had been just the same as before. As had been the slowly growing stench as they had approached the camp. An all pervading reek of raw sewage and raw despair.

Watchtowers. Barbed wire. Clear ground for one hundred metres to the tree line.

And yet he sensed something different.

That was it. The watchtowers. The watchtowers were empty. And instead of a line of vehicles outside the Hauptbahnfuhrer's offices, there was only one. The Mercedes with the miniature swastika flags on each wing.

Even the car was different. It was no longer gleaming as if it had just rolled off the assembly line. Instead it was smeared with grime.

The main gate was manned by a boy in an SS uniform that looked at least three sizes too large for his shrunken body. How old was he? He looked about twelve but he had to be older than that. Surely? Wurtlich sighed at yet more evidence of the crumbling Fatherland.

This was what things had come to. Boys manning the gates and all the watchtowers empty.

His driver opened the back door and Wurtlich climbed out, stiff after the long drive. The boy from the gate was waiting; looking anxious. Beneath his raging acne the skin of his face was stretched and grey.

"Where is everyone?" Wurtlich chose an off-hand and commanding tone. Every inch the Party man.

A shrug. A shuffle of feet. Had they run out of boot polish? A tiny, beaten sort of voice with an accent from the east.

"All gone sir. Well nearly all. They're coming you see. The British. Can you hear?"

Wurtlich could indeed hear. Pop pop pop. An occasional crump. Small arms fire. Mortars. Tank shells. How far away? Not far. Maybe five miles.

"What about Hauptbahnfuhrer Stuhl? Is he still here?"

"Yes sir. He's inside. In his office. He's . . ."

The boy's voice trailed away. The poor little sod looked as if he was about to burst into tears. This wasn't how it was supposed to be. It was all supposed to be about glory and victory and endless triumph. Not this. Not a thin March rain in a camp that smelt like an open sewer. Not a dismal little clearing in a forest of pine with the British guns drawing closer.

Wurtlich sighed. A wasted journey then. A complete waste.

"When did the prisoners leave?"

The boy blinked a little.

"The prisoners are still here sir. They are in the factory."

Maybe not a wasted journey after all then. "So you still have some guards then?"

"No sir. There's only me sir. And Hauptbahnfuhrer Stuhl."

"Only two?"

"Yes sir."

"And yet the prisoners are still here?"

"Yes sir."

"What are they doing?"

"Working sir."

And suddenly a surge of hope. A sense of triumph in the midst of utter disaster.

"Working you say?"

"Yes sir."

"And no guards?"

"No sir."

And now Wurtlich took the stairs two at a time and burst in through the main door to the administration centre. The reception area was empty. The communications room was empty. The communal room was empty. No matter. Stuhl's door was at the end of the corridor and Wurtlich didn't bother to knock.

Inside Stuhl looked dishevelled. Three days unshaven and a uniform that looked as if it had been dragged through brambles. Empty bottles all over his desk. He fixed on Wurtlich with watery, crimson eyes. And then he laughed.

"Ah. So he returns. The man with the magic potion. Here to save the Fatherland with his chemistry . . ."

Stuhl was on his feet now. Unsteady. Teetering.

"Come on man. Sit down. Have a drink. Take a load off. Let's toast. Let's toast the returning alchemist! Let's . . ."

And then like a punctured balloon he fell back into his chair. Wurtlich didn't bother to hide his disgust.

"You are drunk Stuhl."

This was good for a laugh. "Course I'm bloody drunk man. Can't you hear? They are coming. Almost here now. And then what Wurtlich? How do you think it will be for men like you and me? The Hauptbahnfuhrers and the alchemists? Reckon they'll give us a pat on the back do you Wurtlich? Tell us jolly good show and feed us roast beef? Oh for Christ's sake man drink. Just drink . . ."

"The prisoners. They are still here?"

"Oh the bastards are all still here. Every man jack of them. Good as bloody gold. Up at five and straight to work. They haven't eaten in three days you know. Not a bloody morsel. And yet they still put in a fifteen-hour shift. Not that they are achieving much."

"What do you mean?" There was a sharp edge to Wurtlich's voice.

Stuhl chuckled. "Oh they get up alright. And they go into the factory. Like little stinking commie sheep. But then? Then nothing but shit. Productivity has actually dropped. Oh sure there have been no more escape attempts. No more attacks on guards. No plotting and scheming. But no use either. Worthless. Complete shit. They just stand there and work in slow motion . . ."

"The Hydrapol 5? How long have they been on the Hydrapol 5?"

A shrug. A guzzled swig of schnapps. "Who knows? A while. Maybe three weeks?"

Wurtlich dug into his leather case and pulled out paper and pen.

"The effects? How quickly did you notice a difference?"

Another shrug.

"Pretty well straight away. A couple of days I suppose . . ."

Wurtlich had chosen the camp deliberately. It was a sub camp to a large BMW works. The prisoners fabricated parts for tank transmissions. All the prisoners were Red Army POWs and they had all been captured in the last eighteen months. Wurtlich had chosen them because these were men empowered by many victories against the Wehrmacht in the East. They had tasted German blood and they had seen the once invincible Panzers burn. They had seen the mighty armies of the Fatherland retreat over the endless steppes like a bemused rabble. And so once they arrived at the camp they were militant. Unbowed. Every week there was an escape attempt. Every week

Stuhl would execute prisoners to set an example and it never made a difference. Productivity was appalling. The camp was always on the edge. Which was why Wurtlich had chosen it. Because for Wurtlich it was perfect. His Hydrapol 5 had worked on the rats in the labs. And here was a chance to run a trial on human rats. Communist rats. Rabid, spitting communist rats fat on the thrill of winning.

And now his chubby faced glowed in triumph. "So it worked, yes? It broke their spirit. Made them obedient, yes?"

"Oh it made them obedient alright. Obedient and shit. No work in them you see. Not worth a light. You should see how far I am behind my targets. It would have been the East for me Wurtlich. But not any more. There's no East any more Wurtlich. No east and no west. No more targets . . ."

And then a very strange thing happened. Stuhl's head exploded like a ripe water melon. Wurtlich just about had time to wonder how strange that was when his own head did exactly the same.

Two cautious figures entered the room behind Lee Enfield rifles. An accent from Walsall.

"All clear sir!"

A third figure complete with a peaked officer's cap and a Sam Browne belt. He looked down at what was left of Rolf Wurtlich.

"This one seems rather well fed. A civilian. Might be a good idea to send his case back to the intelligence boys. See to it please sergeant."

Another soldier came in panting with exertion.

"All secure sir."

"Any trouble?"

"None at all sir. Jerry's hopped it. That kid and the driver were all there was."

"Dead?"

"Sir."

"And the prisoners? They're gone as well?"

"No sir. They're all in the factory. 'Bout three hundred of them. Look like Ivans to me sir."

"No doubt they were rather glad to see us."

"Actually, no sir. They're just sort of standing there. At the work benches like. They don't seem bothered like."

"Really. How very strange."

2016

The Prime Minister of Great Britain and Northern Ireland was focussed on sitting very, very still. He was determined to show not so much as a shred of emotion. Were they watching? Probably. They probably had some kind of in-house expert reading his face. For what? Stress? Determination? Chronic, gnawing exhaustion?

Whatever.

As his teenage daughters would say.

Let them watch and analyse. It wouldn't get them anywhere. He analysed himself in the bathroom mirror every morning as the razor moved mechanically across his face. Every morning he watched his skin and hair go greyer and the lines run deeper. In the beginning he had hated the fact that he had to wear make up so much of the time. Now he would feel naked without it.

Sometimes he would watch the footage of himself, Linda and the girls as they stepped into Number Ten. Beaming and waving and all ready to make a better world. The day he reached the top of the pile. The day he was added to the list that included Peel and Gladstone and Disraeli and Lloyd George and Churchill.

And Thatcher.

And Blair.

And now Pendleton.

Oh there was no Empire anymore. Only the Falklands and the six counties of Northern Ireland. And it seemed highly unlikely that he would be required to lead his people into a war with France or Germany. My God though, there had been plenty of times when he had been bloody tempted. There had been times when he had lain awake at night and fantasised about getting the High Command to enter the co-ordinates for Paris and Berlin into the box that controlled the Trident subs lurking deep beneath the Atlantic. Paris and Berlin and bloody Washington DC.

Bastards, the bloody lot of them.

Bastards.

Five minutes into his new home with the famous door with the famous number and they had shown him how to work the box. The ultimate code. In a world of code numbers for bank accounts and web-sites and gym lockers, he was given the big one. The end of history code. And it was supposed to make him feel like he was powerful. All conquering. Mighty.

As if.

The Prime Minister of Great Britain and Northern Ireland. The Chief Executive of Great Britain and Northern Ireland Plc., and from the get go it was clear that the liquidators were already waiting outside the door. By the time he won the big prize, nine years had passed since the casino bankers had tipped the country over the edge. Nine years of borrowing from anyone daft enough to lend. Nine years of crossing fingers and toes and cheques.

And like his predecessors, he had done the brave face thing. Done it bloody well. Oh of course, times are tough. Really tough. But of course Britain will be fine. Britain is always fine. We saw off Napoleon and Hitler and the Red Peril and the IRA. And now we'll see this one off, just you wait and see. Britain will rise from the ashes and resume our rightful place at the top table.

And before he had taken up residence in the famous house with the famous door with the policeman outside, he had probably just about believed it.

Not any more. Not having had the truth stare him in the face for three endless, gruelling years.

Britain was a busted flush.

End of.

As his teenage daughters would say.

And this time there would be no magic fix to stave off the baying creditors.

No more slaves to sell.

No more opium to punt into China.

No more billion cowed Indians to bully into buying cotton socks from Rochdale and cartons of salt from Cheshire.

No more North Sea oil.

No more telephone companies to sell.

No more tax bounty from the square mile of the City.

No more nothing.

Only a country way past its sell by date.

Like Greece.

Like Spain.

Like Turkey.

Like Mongolia for Christ's sake.

A country that had once supplied the whole world with cotton and coal and steel and steam engines and machine tools and medicines.

And now? Now it was Premier League football and a few anorexic celebrities with their estuary English and desperate exhibitionism.

For three years he had done what was expected of him. He had made his telegenic face look right on television. He had done the earnest thing and reassured his people that it would all be OK in the end. Of course it would.

And he had done his best to fly the flag around the world and persuade the creditors that their money was safe.

Like a sharp salesman.

Like a con man in a cheap suit.

And now this. This room with its oil paintings of the old aristocracy in all their finery. Who were the people on the walls? The Duke of this and the Duchess of that. Smug-faced and fat from all their acres. And their slave ships. And their sugar plantations. And their opium deals. And their bloody derivatives. And no doubt their ancestors would all now be skulking somewhere in Monaco or Nassau. The rats who had left the sinking ship as fast as their private jets could carry them once the City Casino had hit the bricks back in 2007.

Bastards.

Who owned the great eighteenth century mansion now? Some corporation with paperwork lodged in a bank vault somewhere. Not the Duke of this or Duchess of that. No chance of that. Maybe oil money. Probably oil money. Oil money seemed to own more or less everything these days.

He had first come to the big house a month earlier. He had been summoned. Ordered. Like he had once been ordered to go to the headmaster's office to be caned. He was the Prime Minister of Great Britain and Northern Ireland and he had been ordered to attend at 10 p.m. sharp. They hadn't actually said not to be late, but it had been implied. Come and come alone. Oh, you can bring your security of course. They can wait outside. But no colleagues or advisors or civil servants or spin doctors. Just you Christopher. And don't tell anyone. What we have to say is for your ears only. Got that? Good. Because it is very important that you do get it. You see, we're in no mood to be pissed about Christopher. OK?

Good-oh.

He could still hear the voice on the phone. 'Good-oh'. The bastard. The arrogant, octogenarian Australian bastard.

Gall.

Lester Gall.

The man with all the newspapers and TV channels and radio shows. The man who made the anorexic celebrities and broke them when they were all used up. The man who boasted about how he could swing a

General Election any which way he pleased. The man who seemed to have bought and paid for half the MPs of the Prime Minister's Party. And half of those on the benches of Her Majesty's Opposition.

And on the phone, Lester Gall had called the Prime Minister 'matey' and told him to attend a meeting at 10 p.m. and to keep it to himself. And when the Prime Minister had agreed, Gall had said 'good-oh' and killed the call without saying goodbye.

Bastard.

And Christopher Pendleton had done as instructed. He had left by the back door and been secreted out of the city and into the rolling acres that had once upon a time been the domain of some great Duke.

And they had made him wait in this very same room with the oil paintings and the high ceiling and the chandelier and the heavy velvet drapes and the Persian rug. And no doubt they had watched him via some carefully hidden camera, and maybe they had chuckled at his weakness.

The Prime Minister of Great Britain and Northern Ireland made to wait like some naughty schoolboy.

Five minutes.

Ten minutes.

Until a door opened and a power-dressed young woman with a perma-tan and pearly, pearly teeth had told him they were ready for him.

They.

The money.

Oil and telecommunications and retail and pharmaceuticals. The men of the super corporations. $20,000 suits and private jets and share options and bulging accounts in banks in tax havens.

Ten of them.

Hard-faced bastards.

Smug-faced bastards.

And Lester Gall in the middle.

"Ah. Chris you old bugger. Look, you best have a scotch matey. Have a bloody big one. Reckon you're going to need it sport."

Matey. Sport. Bastard.

They had a spokesman. More perma-tan and teeth. A three-hours-a-day-in-the-gym-type. No doubt a coming man. Smooth. Deadly.

He ran a power point presentation covering everything the Prime Minister knew only too well. The debt was out of hand. The creditors had decided that enough was enough. The IMF had made draconian demands.

Britain was a busted flush.

Gall listened with a sneer and when the presentation was done he rose to his feet and splashed more scotch into the Prime Minister's untouched glass.

"We're all pissed off Chris. And we're all wondering whether it's worth staying in this shitty little country of yours. We got wind of what the IMF had to say to your Chancellor when he called round with his begging bowl."

The Prime Minister stared ahead. Of course it was supposed to have been a secret, but nothing was secret to these men. They owned everyone. Maybe they owned the Chancellor.

Gall ground on. Strutting the room. Waving his arms. An angry, skinny old man with way, way too much power.

"Seems like it is a pretty up and down choice Chris. You either hammer up taxes or you slash costs. Simple as that. So we decided we best have a little chat. Maybe you might just get tempted to jack up a few taxes. Maybe you might have a go at hitting on the big corporations to drag yourselves out of the shit. Well, you might as well know that if you do, we're off matey. As in up sticks and head for the hills. You're not going to bail yourself out by scalping us matey. No bloody way. It ain't going to happen. End of. Hear what I'm saying matey?"

The Prime Minister of Great Britain and Northern Ireland nodded and stared ahead into space.

"Just so long as that's clear sport. You either cut costs or we piss off. Simple as that. Our people have run the numbers and we pretty much agree with the IMF. 20% Chris. 20% and 20% now. No kicking the bastard into the long grass until the next election is done and dusted. We're talking an announcement within two months and immediate implementation. No spinning it Chris. No spin and no bollocks. It's 20% or we're all off and then you really will be screwed. We've got a few ideas, but really it is your job to decide how you're going to do it. Shit, you're the Prime Minister matey. So we'll leave it to you to make the call. But it's going to have to be real Chris. No trimming around the edges. It needs to be real and it needs to be bloody huge. And it needs to be now. Yeah? This is Price by the way."

Gall nodded to Mr Perma-tan and teeth who had run the power point analysis of Britain's doom. Price nodded.

"Bloody sharp cookie our Mr Price. Oxford and Harvard and the whole bloody nine yards. Hire him as a special advisor. He's the only one you discuss this with. OK? No bugger else. Just Pricey here. And Pricey has access to all our collective resources and quite frankly that is a bloody sight more than your resources. So you kick it around with

Pricey and you find an answer that will make us happy. Otherwise it's bye, bye time. Clear?"

The Prime Minister nodded.

"Is that all?"

Gall smeared a grin across his wizened face.

"Yeah. I reckon that's about it. Not drinking your scotch then?"

"No thank you."

"Fair enough. You might as well bugger off then. We'll see in a month then."

And so he had burned the midnight oil for night after night. Just him and Price who was so high flying that it was scary. They crunched their numbers and ran their scenarios and no matter what Christopher asked for, Price always had it by the next day. The man didn't seem to need any sleep. And his tan never faded. And slowly but surely Price had eased him to finding the right answer. The only answer. The answer that the big money had wanted all along. The only answer that they would be willing to accept.

A month of laying awake at night and just wishing that it could have been someone else's job to own up to the cold, hard truth. Anyone else. Anyone but Christopher Pendleton. Oh and course he had thought about chucking in the towel and resigning. To ride off into the sunset and do a Blair. Write his book and charge top-dollar on the speaking circuit. But he knew in his heart of hearts that such an option wasn't on the table. The big money men wouldn't allow him a sunset to ride off into. There would be no big pay-off like Blair. Instead they would crucify him in the media and make sure that his life would be a prolonged misery. Destiny had decreed that he was to be the one to own up to the fact that the 'Great' in Great Britain was nothing more than an outdated joke.

And now the time had come to present his plan to the men of the big money. It was all just show of course. A silly game. An extra humiliation. Of course Price would have already briefed them in every detail. But they needed to hear it from the mouth of the Prime Minister of Great Britain and Northern Ireland. The horse's mouth. They had deemed that the humiliation was a part of the process.

Bastards.

The door opened and Miss tan-and-teeth ushered in James Hawkes, the leader of Her Majesty's Opposition. Chris wondered if he was surprised. Not really. Not at all in fact. Hawkes greeted him with a rueful smile.

"Hello Chris."

"James."

At noon every Wednesday the two of them tore into each other like rabid dogs at Prime Minister's question time, but whenever they were away from the cameras they got along well enough.

For a few moments the two men stared at the pictures on the wall, not really sure what to say to each other. Pendleton broke the spell.

"So when did they call you in James?"

"Just after you. Or so I gather."

The PM nodded thoughtfully. "They wouldn't what their plans buggering up by a pesky back bench revolt. All party support and all that."

"Quite. Can I assume that you have proposals?"

"Oh yes James. I have proposals."

"Right."

A door opened and Miss tan-and-teeth beckoned them forward.

"Ah Chris. Jim. Just the bloody job. Here. Grab a pew. Drink? No? Fair enough."

Like an aged elf thought Christopher.

Evil elf.

Bastard elf.

"Well no point beating about the bloody bush then. Let's hear it Chris."

The Prime Minister quietly cleared his throat and straightened his tie.

"I will be brief as no doubt Mr Price has already fully briefed you all."

He slowly moved his eyes along the line of faces. The men in front of all the billions. Trillions.

"The demand as you all know is an immediate 20% cut in government spending. This of course is a quite enormous figure. Quite unprecedented. Such a task will require the kind of drastic action only usually taken during a time of war. The actions will be hugely unpopular and public order will be a major consideration. In the light of this I must say that I am very happy that you have brought my honourable friend here."

James Hawes gave a short nod to the room. Christopher ploughed on.

"I have addressed the task at hand whilst maintaining two key principles. In order to stand a chance of maintaining public order, two key elements must be in place. Number one, there must be no cuts in expenditure on either the police or the armed services. In fact, I anticipate extra expenditure. Secondly, and vitally, the government must retain at least an element of moral authority in order to be able keep control. What does this mean? It means we keep the NHS with a few modest tweaks. It means we keep old age pensions and all programmes which help the elderly. We will also maintain public spending on education and public transport as to do otherwise would be to write off the country's future. For the sake of morale, we will also maintain expenditure on many seemingly non-essential programmes such as the Arts Council, museums, libraries etc. This we hope will help to maintain an element of public morale."

He took a sip of water before jumping off the cliff.

"To reduce public expenditure by 20% we will cancel most state benefits with immediate effect. Unemployment benefits, sickness benefits for all but the very most infirm, child benefit, family tax credits, housing benefit, council tax benefits. These savings will come to a great deal more than the 20% target that has been indicated. The savings are made firstly by not only paying out the monies in question, and secondly disposing of the required administrative structure to make the payments. These savings are in fact in excess of 30%. We will therefore be making some changes that will eat up some of the savings. There will be no tax payable on any earnings below £15,000 per annum. There will be no National Insurance payable on earnings below £15,000 per annum. We will abolish the minimum wage with immediate effect."

Another pause. Another sip of water.

"Over the last few years we have heard a great deal of talk about the Nanny State. Quite frankly, this is not a label that I have ever had much time for. That however is immaterial. These changes will herald the end of the Nanny State. Britain will become a much harsher country. Millions of our citizens are woefully ill-equipped to thrive in such an environment. They will be angry and confused and the prospect of widespread public disorder is more or less a certainty. I will have some contingency plans in place to deal with this. These plans are none of your concern. Neither are they the concern of Mr Price. You are businessmen. You live in a world of balance sheets and share options. You have no conception of how to deal with a public revolt. That is my realm. The political realm. And I am afraid it is a very secret realm and none of you are welcome."

He stared out the bloated faces one by one.

"All of you are very impressed by your own power. Understandably so. But don't allow yourselves to get carried away. None of you have the power to make a single phone call to Hereford to summon up ultimate force. I have that power gentlemen. I could make that call and any one of you would disappear of the face of this planet within twelve hours. Oh you all have your silly security around you, but I would dearly love to see them try and take on the SAS. This is my world gentlemen. And James's. Keep out. Order will be maintained in this country, that is all you need to know. That is all you are going to know. This is no place for shopkeepers . . ."

"Now you just wait a bloody minute here . . ."

Gall was jumping to his feet.

Angry elf

Bastard elf.

"Sit down Lester. And shut up. You have your deal. Now you get the terms."

Gall was crimson faced, but he sat.

"I will not allow anyone to starve in this country and if any of you demand it, then you are more than welcome to up sticks and go. Every town with a population greater than 20,000 will have a feeding station. These stations will provide breakfast, lunch and dinner to anyone in possession of the required identity. Essentially this means anyone. They will be the ones who at present are unemployed or signed off sick. The food will be plain but nutritious. It will contain all the required minerals and vitamins. I very much doubt whether anyone in work and thereby in funds would be remotely tempted to freeload. If they do, then they are welcome. All meals will be delivered in liquid form by tankers – porridge for breakfast, soup for lunch and stew for dinner. We will initially make use of the fleet used by milk companies. In time the government will invest in its own fleet. Initially the meals will be manufactured by existing food companies following a tendering process. Foreign companies will not be invited to tender. All ingredients will be grown and sourced within the UK."

Another sip of water.

"I will not countenance any citizen of Great Britain sleeping rough unless it is their choice. We will therefore instigate an immediate programme to construct dormitory facilities in all towns. These will be basic facilities offering a bed with clean sheets, warmth and washing facilities. Once again, use of a dormitory will be available to anyone who requires it. They are unlikely to be particularly happy places. Once again we do not anticipate any freeloading."

Again he allowed his eyes to meet other eyes around the table.

"Our country is about to become a harder place. However nobody is going to starve and nobody is going to have to sleep in the rain. In our new future, even an hour's work will be a thing to be valued. We have a generation who will be quite unable to cope and we will have to keep their bodies and souls together. Maybe for the rest of their lives. Future generations will see the world in a very different light. We anticipate academic achievement to rise dramatically over the coming years as young people channel a fear for the future into better attainment. In time, our country will find its way back onto its feet. Until that time we will have to rule with a firm hand. We are going back to the Autumn of 1940 gentlemen and somehow we must rediscover the spirit of those dark days. I ask that every one of you plays your part in this, especially you Mr Gall. The time for pushing the gaudy wealth of nonentity celebrities and footballers in the faces of the public is over. Up until now it has been merely been distasteful. Not any more. Now such inappropriate nonsense could easily be a trigger for rioting. We are entering a time of sobriety and I expect that to be reflected in the media. I will not tolerate any more of your pathetic celebrity culture. If you cross me on this, then you will be leaving this country and your leaving will not be dignified. The rest of you will be happy enough I am sure. The end of the minimum wage will ensure that your profits will rise dramatically. On your instructions, Mr Price has been insisting on a cut in Corporation tax. This will not be happening gentlemen. You are being granted your pound of flesh. Two pounds is out of the question. I will also require you to make some further changes. No longer will you come in and out of this country on private jets. You can park them in Paris if you like and take the train. I also expect all of you to close any overseas accounts that you might operate. And do not try and hide this, gentlemen. I have a place called GCHQ remember. I can find out when each and every one of you goes for a shit. If you spend more than a fortnight in this country, then you will pay the appropriate rate of tax on any income derived in this country. And that is non negotiable. Bang the table if you wish but it will not make a jot of difference. I am granting you the most motivated, best educated and cheapest labour force in the developed world. That will have to be enough. You will all make huge fortunes. All that I demand is that you do not flaunt these fortunes and that you pay a fair amount of tax on those fortunes. If this idea sticks in your throat, I suggest you buy yourselves some history books and take a look at what happened to the super rich in Russia in 1917. It wasn't pretty."

Another pause.

Another look at angry faces. There was much he had said that Mr Price had not prepared them for.

Well screw them.

"If you don't like it and want to go, then just go. If you are going, then make your announcements in the next month. If I hear nothing, then I will assume that you have agreed the terms I have outlined and decided to stay. The changes I have outlined will be announced a month's time. There is no question of doing so any sooner as many things will have to be put in place."

Now Pendleton turned to the leader of Her Majesty's Opposition. "Can I rely on your support James?"

James Hawkes gave a grave nod. In fact he really felt rather like cheering. It wasn't every day that Lester Gall got it with both barrels and he would have happily laid out big money for his seat in the front row. Gall by now was all out of patience. Up on his feet and looking like something out of Lord of the Rings. A bad something.

"Now you listen here you jumped up Pommie bastard . . ."

Pendleton's voice snapped like the crack of a whip.

"No you listen Mr Gall. You started this thing and I'm going to end it. If you're not happy, then piss off. I'll take you to the door myself with a song in my heart. We don't need you and your scummy rags. In fact we would be a whole lot better off without you. The same does not go for the other gentlemen around the table. They make things. They employ people by the thousand. They contribute. You don't Gall. You're a leech. A cancer. You peddle puerile crap day in day out, and all the while you help dumb down our citizens to drooling bloody morons. So if you want to go, then for Christ's sake, just go. And go now. But if you stay, consider your card well and truly marked. You play ball or I'll personally crucify you. No more celebrity bullshit and no more tax dodging. Are we clear Mr Gall?"

"Oh yeah right. I'm quivering in my bloody boots here matey."

"Do any of your staff break the speed limit in their fancy cars Mr Gall? Do any of your beautiful people carry grams of coke in their designer suits Mr Gall? Do any of your people have child porn on their laptops Mr Gall? Maybe they do, maybe they don't. It doesn't matter you see. Because I can make all of these things happen. I can make them happen to you Gall. I can fill your personal PC up with the worst paedophile images you've ever dreamt of. And then I will sign off on SO19 crashing down your front door and dragging you our in plastic cuffs. And I will personally ensure that every last one of your competitors are waiting on the pavement outside to get the pictures. So don't try my patience Gall. Don't even think about it."

Christopher Pendleton hadn't noticed getting to his feet. He hadn't noticed the rise in his voice. He hadn't noticed crossing the room to stand so close to the media baron's face that his spittle had splashed onto wizened cheeks.

Now he noticed.

Now he saw the naked fear in the watery old eyes.

And he liked it.

Loved it.

He slowly stepped back.

"That's all. You all have a month. If you stay, you pay your share. If any one of you tries to dodge so much as a penny of tax I will wipe you out. I will be issuing instructions to GCHQ to monitor every phone and computer you own. 24/7 gentlemen. 24/7. Stay and you can make a pot of money and pay a more than fair proportion of tax. Cross me and you'll wish you had never been born. Good evening."

And with that he strode out. Taller. Prouder. The Prime Minister of Great Britain and Northern Ireland.

Jason Marsh was in front of the mirror in the Gents and things were not going too well. He was working on trying to look presentable for an appointment with his boss and it was a struggle. There had been a time when mirrors had never been a problem to Jason. Once they had framed a confident young man with good bones and a brash confidence in his eyes. A female favourite at school. An effortless achiever at university. A coming man with his first local paper. Clothes had been at home on him.

And everything had come easily. A move to London and a start with the National Enquirer. The right kind of wife. A son to dote on. A couple of prizes for hard-hitting investigative features. Hard drinking without hangovers. Hard driving without blood pressure. And like a complete fool he had figured that easy street would stretch all the way into retirement.

It hadn't.

His thirties had been a decade of steady decline. His right kind of wife had found her own right kind of man. A City type with the kind of disposable income that a journalist could only write about. The doted on son grew up into a spoilt little git on the back of gifts showered on the back of six figure city bonuses and a stepfather eager to please. Hard drinking suddenly meant crippling hangovers. His hair thinned and his stomach spread and clothes were no longer easy on him. And to cap it all, he couldn't seem to find a decent story for love nor money.

The National Enquirer had changed as much as he had changed. The cold winds of the Credit Crunch had collapsed advertising revenues. It suddenly seemed that most readers chose to read the paper free online rather than shelling out a quid for a hard copy. The offices were emptied out and expense accounts scrutinised within an inch of their lives. And all of a sudden Jason Marsh realised that he had become a dinosaur. Just another lost-looking bloke in his forties, wondering how it was that all his bosses were so much younger than him.

Most of the lads he had cut his teeth with had been put out to grass. Too old. Too set in their ways. Not keen enough on bottles of sparkling water and time on the treadmill. The new breed were cheaper. They wrote stories from the office and sourced everything on the internet. They played safe and never upset the advertisers. They did celebrities and house prices. They railed at terrible teens and patted the government on the back for its anti-terror initiatives.

Most of the time Jason Marsh wanted to scream.

And swear

And smash the place up with a hammer.

But he didn't because the woman who was once the right sort of wife still demanded his half of the mortgage now that her city type had hit the bricks and become a sulking burden.

And life was a bitch.

And he had a gnawing feeling that it was just about become more of a bitch. It had been months since he had turned in any decent copy and he didn't need to be Einstein to know that his name was almost certainly next on the list. A year earlier, Ernie Fletcher had been shoved into early retirement. Ernie was the long term News Editor and he had become something of a Last of the Mohicans figure on Fleet Street. He held a dogged attachment to the idea of newspapers being the bringers of news. He even smoked. Endlessly. Like a bloody chimney. Until he refused to compromise his principles one time to many and they bounced him out of the door. He had always been a mentor to Jason. A father figure. A role model. A supporter. A kindred spirit. A drinking partner.

And now he was no more.

Instead the newsroom had become the realm of Amelie Frenchwood. The dreaded Amelie. Thirty-something and locked onto the fast track like a Japanese bullet train. She had an office wall filled with certificates that informed visitors that she had a brain like Cray computer. She power-dressed and was in the gym at six o' clock every morning. She was more than happy with sparkling mineral water and seemed to live on fruit. At functions she could make a glass of wine last all night. The idea of Amelie smoking was about as likely as Osama Bin laden turning up on a celebrity cooking show. She had never covered a news story in her fast track life, but she could get any advertiser eating out of her exquisitely manicured hands and she knew all about how to tend the bottom line with a devotion bordering on love. She could downsize anyone without batting an eyelid and Jason very much doubted if doing so had ever cost her so much as ten seconds of her beauty sleep.

Within a week they had nicknamed her 'Fridge'. Not that they let on.

The day before the Fridge had sent him an email informing him that she had freed up a slot for him at ten o' clock. To have a chat.

A chat.

What kind of a chat? Would it be one of those 'we all appreciate what a wonderful servant you have been over years Jason but . . .' kind of chats? Or would it be 'I am rather concerned at last month's expenses Jason . . .' kind of chats?

Maybe she just wanted to chew the fat about how things had been back in the good old days when everyone smoked and drank like fish and ate bacon rolls at their desks. And maybe Robert Maxwell would rise up from the grave and convert to Islam.

He was pretty sure it wouldn't be any kind of cosy chat.

And now he was frantically trying to get what was left of his hair into some kind of acceptable shape. It wasn't going to happen. And the creases in his tired suit were not about to straighten out. And the egg yolk on his tie was hanging on with the grim determination of bunch of Spartan warriors in a tight spot.

Ah what the hell.

If the Fridge was about to downsize him, a bit of congealed egg wasn't going to swing things one way or the other. He splashed a handful of water in his hair and forced it down. It would have to do.

He sensed eyes on him as he strode to her door with a confidence he didn't remotely feel. No doubt the new breed were wondering if another nail in the coffin of the good old days was about to be hammered home. They would shed few tears. They resented his awards. They resented his old school credibility. They would shed crocodile tears at his demise.

"Good morning Jason. Please sit down. I am having some tea. Would you like anything?"

"Coffee please Amelie. Black with two."

"Decaff?"

"No thanks. I'll take any caff that's going actually."

A polite laugh. Glossed lips. Designer glasses. Trimmed finger nails. Hair in a tight bun. New breed. New broom.

"So Jason. How are things?"

"Apart from the alimony and my delinquent son, absolutely tip-top thank you Amelie."

Small smile. Neat papers in a neat pile. Papers shuffled by elegant fingers.

"I see."

Jason took a hit of caff and tried to exude confidence. Instead he was acutely conscious of the egg stain on his tie.

"Well, I think it best to be frank. Don't you agree Jason?"

"Absolutely." So this was it. The moment. The scrapheap was opening up its arms to him.

"You haven't been very productive of late Jason. No doubt you have been feeling somewhat insecure. Well of course you have. So many colleagues gone. So many changes. And I dare say you must have wondered at times why on earth you are still with us?"

He shuffled uneasily. "Well. Yes. I suppose I have."

"Of course you have Jason. And why not? Are you still here because I like and respect you? Of course not. I consider you idle Jason. Not a team player. A downright nuisance. And yet I have not yet disposed of you. Have you any idea why?"

"Actually no. I haven't"

She wheeled out a small smile that was straight from the depths of the Greenland glacier. "Your awards Jason. They give us a veneer of credibility. The awards help to remind our older customers that we were once in the vanguard of investigative journalism. And they of course are the customers who still have a newspaper delivered every morning. They are the ones that the advertisers crave. Once upon a time they marched against the bombing in Cambodia and experiment- ed with LSD and listened to the Kinks. Now they enjoy their final salary pensions and never begrudge spending a pound on the newspa- per that has been with them throughout the journey of their lives. They trust us Jason. They like us. We are an old pal. A memory of better days when they were young and filled with hope. And you are part of that legacy Jason. You're a mascot. A keepsake."

"This I gather is you being frank?"

"It is indeed Jason. Now. I am afraid even much loved heirlooms sometimes get shipped out to Oxfam. I need more Jason. Much more. I need you to reconnect. I need you to rekindle the old flames in the blessed hearts of our loyal readers. I need you take them back to the days of their youth when they marched for freedom and wore silly waistcoats from Nepal. Are we quite clear Jason?"

"Yes. I think we are Amelie. Actually."

"Excellent. Now tell me what you are working on."

And all of a sudden hope was alive and kicking and shopping in *Tesco*. And Jason Marsh knew that for the first time in ages he had lucked out.

"Actually, I think you're going to quite like it Amelie."

"Oh I very much hope so Jason. My breath is bated."

His turn for a small smile, although his was Denmark to her Greenland. "Where are all the young rebels? That's the handle. I start by looking at the recent riots in Paris and Lyon. Kids on the street complete with petrol bombs and half-bricks. Tear gas and bloodied heads. The same sort of stuff our lot once got up to back in the Sixties and Seventies and Eighties. So where are they now? And what would get them out and about like the French. I have a pretty decent hook."

"How wonderful. Pray tell."

"A guy who calls himself D-Zed. He is based in Rollerton. Scotland."

"Hardly the centre of the universe then."

"No, but that is the whole point. Rollerton is any town. Every town."

"As in?"

"Population of just over 100,000. Once upon a time it had docks and a couple of factories making carpets and furniture. Now it is a *Tesco* town. You know the score. A High Street full of charity shops and half the population on the sick. Most of those who work are on the state payroll. Council workers. NHS. Cops. Prison guards. Other than that, there is one call centre, three big supermarkets and a bunch of pound shops."

"I see. Now Jason, pray tell me where you interest lies in Rollerton?"

"Well, actually, I grew up there. Sort of."

And now her smile travelled hundreds of miles south to the towering grey waves of the North Atlantic. "Oh how lovely. Jason rediscovers his Scottish roots."

"Well not really, it's just . . ."

"Never mind the why's and the wherefore's Jason, I like it. Love it to bits. I think it is quite super. And I think we should think of going much further than this D-Zed chappie."

"You do?"

"Oh yes I do. I see a series Jason. A hard-hitting series from our award winning feature writer. All about what on earth has happened to all those horrid northern places that got such a rotten deal from

Thatcher. Is there life after dark, satanic mills? Sick note Britain. Sink estates and unemployable youth. Drugs and teenage mums. Jason Marsh revisits his roots. Oh yes, I think it will be quite fabulous."

"You do?"

"Of course I do Jason. Of course I do. And so will our readers. Do you remember that drama series from the Noughties? *Life on Mars*. Yes? Well it was huge wasn't it? So add ten years Jason. Eighties nostalgia is the new black."

"It is?"

"Of course it is Jason. And a person who was twenty in 1980 is now approaching retirement. They are ready to go all dewy-eyed about the CND marches they used to go on. And the free Mandela concerts. And the ten pence pieces they used to put in plastic buckets for poor hungry coal miners. And you know what they do now Jason?"

"What do they do now Amelie?"

"They buy conservatories and televisions and home theatre systems and new kitchens."

"Of course they do Amelie."

"And all the people who sell conservatories and televisions and home theatre systems and new kitchens will be falling over themselves to buy lots of lovely advertising space in *The National Enquirer*."

"How super."

"Absolutely how super. And don't you dare knock it Jason. It gives me a reason to keep you on the team. I will re-brand you Jason. I will see you reborn. Maybe I will even lobby for you to receive another award. You can become one of my very favourite people. You will be able to bask in my glow. Now. Details Jason. Details. This Dee-Z chap. How did you come across him?"

"He was at my school. Rollerton Academy. Four years below me, but we were both there at the same time."

"And now he is a bit of a hellraiser?"

"So I gather. He plays to packed houses."

"Good. Now, I see a series of four or five pieces. Give me a couple of weeks to whet the appetites of our beloved readership. Then we will go one a week for five weeks. Ok with you Jason?"

"Absolutely."

"Which means you will be on the road for a month-and-a-half. And this of course means that we must address the whole area of expenses Jason. I really don't think that my pockets will be deep enough for a swish hotel Jason. Not for six weeks."

"No need. I'll stay with a pal of mine."

"A pal. How lovely. Still in touch after all these years?"

"We are. He's a cop. Quite high up now. Chief Superintendent."

This earned raised eyebrows

"In his early forties?"

"He was fast-tracked. High flier and all that."

"How completely super for him."

"Yes. Super."

"Now Jason, I know that it might be tempting to play the big London reporter when you return to your old patch. You know what I mean I'm sure. Treating comely Caledonian beauties with tattoos and highlights in their flame-red hair to champagne all night. Well not on my expense account Jason. I will run to haggis supper and a deep fried Mars bar and no more. Are we understood?"

"We are understood."

"Super. I simply can't wait Jason. It will be the return of the great Jason. Jason Redux. Happy travelling."

"Thank you Amelie. It has been a pleasure."

"Hasn't it just."

Outside the eyes were all over him again. He gave his step a deliberate spring. Not yet you bastards. Not yet. Still life in the old dog yet. He reached his desk and dropped into his chair. Opposite sat the brooding figure of Tom Grierson who was very much dinosaur number two in the news room. Tom was drumming stubby fingers and looking pent up.

"You all right Tom?"

"Yeah. I'm good. Just wound up."

"Wife or Fridge?"

"Neither. You know how it is when a story is close enough to touch but you can't turn it into a complete picture."

"Story of my life Tom. What you got?"

"Weird stuff coming from Number Ten. Leaks and whispers."

"Like what?"

"Like twice in the last six weeks the PM has headed out in the dead of night. Security only. No staff. No advisors. No diary entry."

"Bit of skirt?"

"Maybe, but I can't se it. Not Pendleton."

"What else?"

"Some geyser called Price. Got hired as a special advisor. Been burning the midnight oil with Pendleton. 2 a..m., 3 a.m. Never talks to the rest of the staff. Comes and goes as he pleases. It's got everyone wound up like clocks."

"Bit of trouser?"

Grierson grimaced. "Surely to God not. Christ."

"So what then?"

"Well that's my problem. I can't get a handle on it. The word is that the lights are still burning bright in the top floor windows of the Home Office at four in the morning. And at MI5."

"An early election?"

"Well, that's the most obvious call. It just doesn't feel that way."

"So what does it feel like?"

Grierson shrugged and took a slug of coffee from a mug emblazoned with the news that he was 'the world's best dad.' "I don't know Jason. I just don't know and it is really starting to piss me off."

"You'll get there Tom. You always do mate. Anyway. I'm off to Scotland. The Fridge is re-launching me. Jason Marsh goes back to the deepest, darkest North."

"You didn't get fired then."

"Not even close. She even gave me the nod to treat the ladies of Rollerton to a haggis supper and a deep fried Mars bar."

"She must fancy you."

"She could barely keep her hands off me."

Jason unhooked his laptop and started packing up what he would need for the road.

"Jason."

"Yeah."

"This thing I'm on. This story. It feels bad somehow."

"Bad?"

"Yeah. Bad."

They looked at each other for a moment and then Jason resumed his packing.

Two days later and Jason felt like he was at the end of a journey around a full circle. Back in Rollerton. Back where everything had started. Back on the streets where the world had once seemed so promising. Where he had seemed so promising. A son to be proud of. A left winger for the school team. An A-lister in the school play. A first-on-the-lister for any birthday party. Grades that guaranteed a choice of universities. Looks and charm and a bright future to walk into.

Now the familiar streets seemed to laugh at him. Mock him. Not that the streets were all that familiar anymore. Oh he could remember where they went easily enough. Where they started and where they ended. He even remembered what most of them were called. His tired car had managed the trek north better than he had expected and he had some time on his hands. So he drove and took on board a new Rollerton. Rollerton redux. Rollerton made-over. Rollerton rebooted. Rollerton minus a heart.

Where there had once been a carpet factory there was now a cluster of prefabricated warehouse units, most of which seemed to be vacant.

Where there had once been a port with fishing boats there was now a half-hearted waterside development of Yuppie flats, most of which were unsold.

Where there had once been a busy high street there were now charity shops and boarded windows and a *Big Issue* seller who looked like he hadn't sold a mag for six months.

Where there had once been a nest of terraces around a textile mill there was now a retail park complete with a smug looking *Tesco 24*. And the car park was full. And the trolleys were full. If you spent more than £50 you could get 5p a litre off your fuel.

Only Greenfield seemed the same. Sixty acres of pebble dash. Sixty acres of sick-notes and dole and single mums and five-bag-a-day smack heads and wannabe gangsters and locked down pensioners. And yet even Greenfield was different. Less shops. More graffiti. More cars. And a sense that any small glimmer of hope that might have survived the Thatcher tornado had finally been extinguished.

A dead zone.

A zone for the living dead.

A zone of daytime TV and cheap booze offers and sexual diseases and illiteracy and knock-off TVs and satellite dishes and memories of the days when people had jobs in places that made things.

Busted up bus shelters.

Overflowing bins.

Clusters of pale-faced kids pretending to be grown ups. Pretending to be tough guys. Empowered by the knives in their pockets. Popping pills to hide from the tedium of their existence.

It made Jason feel tired. Dejected.

It made him feel like a drink.

Ten drinks.

Twenty drinks.

By the time he parked up in Doogie's drive he was flat down. The unavoidable fact was that the full circle of his life had led him back here. A failed man coming home to his failed town. His last chance saloon. And it was hard to get a way from the feeling that Rollerton was all that he deserved. Unlike most, he had been given his chance to leave the pebbledash far, far behind. And he had blown it. And now he was back. The Fridge's in-house mascot tasked with taking rheumy-eyed readers back to the days when they still had some warmth in their bones. Some life. Some hope.

Something.

His phone beeped with a text.

Doogie.

Ten minutes.

Fair enough. And ten minutes later a sleek black BMW drew in behind him and Doogie climbed out. Full uniform and barely an ounce of fat and a full head of glossy-looking hair. The years had been kind on Douglas Jameson. *Six foot two and eyes of blue.* His pal was even still playing football every Sunday morning; a strolling centre half with a tackle like a JCB loading shovel.

Crisp white shirt and shoes that sparkled in the watery late afternoon sun and a smile that was genuine if a little careworn.

"Sorry I'm late. Usual shite."

"The demands of Coppering?"

"Fat chance. I don't do coppering any more. I do budgets and human resources and equality policies. Come on, let's get a drink."

Doogie's house was big and new and ferociously tidy. And rather empty. Angie had moved out five years earlier and taken two teenage daughters, one dog and most of the furniture. Doogie had replaced the basics, but none of the stuff that made the house live and breathe. We are the hollow men. We are the stuffed men. Ditched. Discarded. Surplus to requirements.

The kitchen was new pin-clean and sterile.

"Bloody hell Doogie, you must be a dab hand with a vacuum in your hand."

This brought on a rueful smile. "Nope. I have a lady called Magdelena. She comes from Lvov and she's in three times a week."

Jason raised an interested eyebrow. Doogie caught the drift. They had always caught each other's drift, all the way back to their first week in primary school. "Aye right. She's pushing sixty and dentally challenged."

"A babushka!"

"Aye. A babushka." Doogie splashed scotch into two tumblers from a neatly arranged cupboard. "Good to see you Jace."

"Aye and you. Here's to middle-aged bastards."

Clink. And the familiar warmth took the edge off Jason's drive around the grey dead dreariness of the Greenfield Estate.

"Actually, it looks like I might be here for a while longer than I thought."

"What? In Rollerton?"

Jason nodded. "My boss wants a series of features from her award winning dinosaur. Whatever happened to all those places Maggie screwed over? Terrible tales from the frozen north designed to titillate the retired of the south east."

"She still on your case then?"

"Actually things are looking a bit brighter. She called me a mascot. She hinted that I might get the chance to bask in her glow."

Doogie chuckled and replenished their glasses. He dug twenty B&H from the pocket of his tunic and crashed one to Jason. He took off his tie. He undid polished silver buttons.

"Well you can stay here for as long as you like. I just rattle about the bloody place. I should have sold up years ago when there was still some equity. Now I'm stuck with it. I am the proud owner of plenty of bedrooms that are worth half what I paid for them."

"What about the girls? Don't they come and stay?"

Doogie gave mournful shake of his head. "They come, but they don't stay. They come for a handout and they leave their boyfriends in the car parked up around the corner."

"I guess having a Chief Super for a dad isn't exactly the last word in cool."

"Hardly."

"And Angie's still with the tax collector?"

Doogie's wife had walked five years earlier having come clean about a three-year fling with the man who ran the Council Tax department in the Town Hall. Doogie got to keep the house and the negative equity. And a babushka.

"That she is. They play golf now."

Jason took a pull of scotch. "Jesus. Angie on the golf course. That's a hell of a thought. What about the squash?"

"Oh aye. Squash as well."

"Well she was always concerned that her bum was too big."

"Probably still is."

Jason smiled. "So life's a bitch?"

"And then we die."

Clink.

Doogie peeled off his jacket and tossed it on the counter where

Angie had once prepared low calorie salads with tuna because she was worried that her bum was too big.

"So anyway. What was the thing you were doing before it turned into the whatever happened to the north thing?"

"D-Zed."

Doogie all but spat out his mouthful of scotch.

"What. Ronald Pickup. What the hell is there to write about that little toe-rag?"

"Will our British youth ever take a leaf out of the French book and hit the streets with bricks and Molotov cocktails? What might get them going? Who might get them going? What would it take to light a fire under sink estate Britain?"

"And you reckon Ronald Pickup is your man? Christ Jace, he's just a dickhead. He was always a dickhead."

"I heard that he knows how to draw a crowd."

"Yeah, well that's only because there's bugger all else for the little bastards to do in Rollerton."

Jason grinned. "That's not very PC, Chief Superintentent."

"And it's a mile off the record."

"Fair enough. But he must be doing something. I hear he gets in over five hundred every Saturday night."

"No accounting for taste."

"More to the point, I hear that he gets them to pay three quid each. £1500 on the door. That's not bad for a dickhead. Have you ever been to watch him do his stuff?"

"You must be bloody joking." Doogie looked genuinely aghast at the thought.

"Well I'm going tomorrow night. Why don't you come?"

"Aye right. I'll make a right splash."

"Well go incognito then."

Doogie lit up. "I'll think about it. Another?"

Jason's glass was still pretty well full.

"You're in a hurry."

"Aye. Well. One of those days. Look Jace, the normal deal is still in place, yeah?"

Jason nodded. "Sure. Everything is off the record all the time? Course it is. No need to ask that mate."

"No. Course not. Sorry."

"You look bothered."

"I am bothered. Bloody bothered. Something's not right."

"Go on."

"I got a three line whip to attend a big meeting yesterday. Drop everything and be there at nine sharp. Every top cop in Scotland in the lecture theatre at the police college. There was this suit up from the Home Office and he was as serious as cancer. He told us there would be an announcement in two weeks time and that it would have implications. That was his word. Implications. Public order implications. We are to cancel all leave and make sure we have as many boots of the ground as possible."

"Terrorism?"

"Maybe, but why wait two weeks to announce? Terrorism is always here and now. Terrorism is always do everything by yesterday."

"So what then?"

"I haven't got a bloody clue."

They allowed a silence to settle on the sterile kitchen as the light outside the window thickened into night.

"Before I left, one of the political lads on the news desk told me there was some weird stuff going down." Jason outlined the rumours of the Prime Minister disappearing with no advisors and the Home Office lights blazing through the night.

Doogie grimaced. "On our way back the Chief Constable said something pretty odd. He said that a Home Office email had said that Rollerton was statistically likely to be more affected than most places."

"So what's that supposed to mean?"

"Search me. Anyway we best get ready mate. We've got a date tonight."

"A date?"

"Sure thing. A blast from the past."

"As in?"

"Sally's in town. I told her that you were coming up and she said we should all get together. Dinner and nostalgia and all that."

"Christ Doogie. I haven't seen Sally in over twenty years."

It was nearer twenty-five in fact. Sally Webster had been with them all the way from primary school to sixth form. And throughout that whole time Jason had dreamed of Sally Webster becoming his girlfriend. But instead she had become Doogie's girlfriend in S3 and stayed that way all the way to the day when they had walked through the school gates for the last time. Then Doogie had gone to one university and Sally had gone to another and all the promises of loving each other to the end of time had been rendered null and void. Her parents had moved back down to Norfolk from whence they came and Jason had never seen her again.

"She's an MSP now, right?"

"Sure is. LibDem, though I get the feeling they would rather like to disown her. She's a list MSP, but Rollerton is pretty well the centre of her patch. She does a surgery here every fortnight or so."

"Married?"

"Nope. Divorced. Her hubbie did the secretary shagging thing."

"Sally wouldn't have liked that much."

"She didn't."

Jason chuckled. Sally Webster was a force of nature when she went off on one. Always had been.

"Kids?"

"Nah. Too much of a career woman."

"She was in the council or something last time I heard."

"NHS. Upstairs office and targets. She got pissed off with all the inefficiency and waste and so she ran for Parliament to change it. Now she's pissed of at being in Parliament and not being able to do anything about all the inefficiency and waste."

"She's still a woman on a mission then?"

"Not half. She's like a dog with a bone when representing a hard done to constituent. I've been the wrong side of her a time or two. In an official capacity, yeah. Not great. She made me feel like a Nazi camp guard."

"And you and Sally . . ?"

Doogie shook his head. "No chance. Been there, done that, got the scars. We're just pals."

"Right."

"Come on. We best be doing. I'm grabbing a shower and that. I've got a cab booked for eight."

They had done an hour or so of catching up and Jason was drinking more than was wise. But everything was hard. Once they had all been in the same place. Young people with promising futures. Rollerton's finest. And for a while he had fulfilled his early promise and the awards had been duly awarded. But then he had stalled whilst Doogie and Sally had forged onwards and upwards. They had hit forty at the top of their game. The fast tracked cop and the TV-friendly politician. They were playing in the big league whilst he shambled around and tried to avoid getting shoved onto the scrapheap by the Fridge. More to the point, they both looked like people in their prime. Doogie was still good for a Marboro Man advert in his loose shirt and jeans. And Sally? Well sure, she had put on a pound or two, but they sat easily on her. They had kept the lines from her face which meant that she was still a make up free zone. She wore a simple underpowered work suit that would have given the Fridge the shivers. A white shirt and the same silver chain she once got as an eighteenth birthday present from her adoring granddad. And sometimes she was smiling. And sometimes she was scowling with anger. And sometimes she made her point with vivid hand gestures. And all the time she was animated. Alive. In the fray. In the game.

And with a sickening, lurching feeling in the pit of his stomach Jason knew that he still wanted Sally Webster to be his girlfriend. Because that was just the way some things were. Every year herds of wildebeest slogged it over the Serengeti plains. And every year snow would fall in Lapland. And chickens roosted and dogs barked but pigs had never managed to fly. Especially not in Rollerton.

And now she was doing her serious face and Jason realised that the conversation had run away from him. Slow down Jason. Take a pause. Drink some water.

"Tell Sally what your man said Jace. You know. The PM and the Home Office and all that."

So Doogie had told her about his unexplained meetings. Jason followed suit and Sally's serious face turned more serious.

"There has been some pretty strange talk up in Holyrood. Rumours of stuff in the pipeline from Westminster. Nobody seems to know what. Everyone seems very pessimistic about next year's money. It seems as if things were pretty bad at the IMF."

"Bad enough for them to want me to have boots on the ground in a fortnight's time?" Doogie was doing a pretty good serious face of his own.

Sally shook her head. "Surely not? These things take time. The Chancellor was only out there a month ago. Things can't have moved that quickly. Impossible."

Jason drained his water. "Come on then Sally. You're the politician. What makes Rollerton statistically likely to need all police leave cancelling?"

She shrugged. "Nothing that I can think of. Rollerton is Rollerton. No Muslim population to speak of. No real deprivation. Well. Not on an inner city scale. Off the top of my head, there are only two things that stand out. Percentage of population signed off sick and percentage of the population working in the public sector."

"So any major chop in government spending would have a larger than average impact?"

"I suppose it would when you look at it that way. Take the tax-payers' pound out of the economy and there is barely an economy left. But that isn't about to happen. It couldn't. There would have to be consultation. A notice period. A debate . . ."

Her voice tailed off. And they looked at each other.

Across the table.

Over the three empty wine bottles.

Over the bunched up napkins.

Over the long years that separated then from now.

And they all wondered the same thing.

And they all thought surely not.

The next evening Doogie joined the Jason and Sally in the kitchen with a somewhat embarrassed air. His efforts at incognito ran to an ancient pair of jeans, a T-shirt from the bottom of a half-forgotten drawer and a leather bomber jacket that hadn't seen the light of day since his second year at university. The baseball cap was newly purchased that morning.

Jason chuckled. "Doogie Jameson goes undercover! It's not bad actually. You still look like a copper though."

"Yeah, yeah. And you look like a down at heel hack."

"I am a down at heel hack."

Sally had jumped at the idea of the undercover visit to a night with D-Zed. She'd heard good things about him. He was opening minds. Trying to make the young people who paid out their £3 on the door see the bigger picture. She had scolded Doogie for calling him a dickhead and said that it merely proved that Doogie was just a dreary old copper ready for pensioning-off to a life of fly fishing. She had hit the town and come up with a new outfit that took a decade off. There was a chance that she would just about fit in. She had the look of a presenter on some hip, late night show. A popular lecturer. A doctor for *Medecin sans Frontieres*. Jason gave himself a mental kick and told himself to pack it in and grow up.

"For God's sake, will you two stop being so bloody old about everything. Loosen up. You never know, you might even enjoy yourselves. God forbid."

They saluted.

Simultaneous. They had always managed to be simultaneous.

"Yes Maam." Barked Doogie.

"I hereby promise to be completely down with everything." Assured Jason.

She produced her for the cameras smile. "Splendid. Let's go."

They took Jason's car which was a whole lot less conspicuous than Doogie's Top Cop BMW. On the way they grabbed a couple of drinks in a pub they had once spent their Friday nights in. Then it had been big on darts, dominos and old school Union men from the carpet factory. Now it was working on some kind of country house theme with shelves filled with books. Instead it felt like a cross between a hardware store and an airport lounge. The drinks were overpriced. The lager was flat.

They parked up a few hundred yards from the gig and joined the clutches of young people who were making their way along the pavement. The thin rain of the day had cleared and a panoply of stars sat high above them chilling the air below.

Sally clutched on to Jason's arm.

"You know, I'm really looking forward to this. Aren't you?"

"'Fraid it's all work for me darling."

"Boring old fart."

They turned a corner into a small industrial estate where a queue had formed outside a non-descript looking building bearing the name *Benny Khan's Carpet House*.

"So who's Benny Khan when he's at home?" Wondered Jason.

Doogie knew. "He came up from Bradford a few years back. This was part of a chain. He wrapped it up after the credit crunch when the banks started knocking back HP for Schemies."

"Doogie!" Snapped Sally.

"Sorry Maam. I'll rephrase. When the banks reluctantly withdrew the offer of over-priced credit to the unfortunate inhabitants of social housing schemes who were signed off on the long-term sick as a result of a chronic aching sensation in their little toes."

Jason grinned. "I guess Benny must be chuffed to bits at a bunch of Neds breaking in to trash the place every weekend. How come you lads don't put a stop to it?"

"There's nothing to put a stop to. Benny and Pickup have an arrangement. A lease of sorts. One month rolling. £200 a night."

"Well that's interesting. How's about the council? Health and Safety?"

Doogie shuffled and it wasn't entirely down to the chill of the night. "Pickup is fully licensed."

"You suddenly seem to know a lot about him."

Doogie gave a rueful smile. "I might have run a few checks I suppose. When award-winning journos from the capital visit the frozen north, a copper's nose starts to twitch."

"So he's on the up and up?"

"Yup. Straight as a dye as far as I can tell. No previous. All above board and accounted for. He's registered as self employed. Calls his outfit *Pickup Impact Events*. Paid £321.34 in tax last year."

"Not bad for a toe-rag then." Sally chose the light mocking voice that had earned her decent reviews when she used it to question the First Minister on the floor of the Scottish Parliament.

"Aye well, we can all be wrong sometimes."

"Even Top Cops in the frontline of the fight against organised crime and wicked terrorists."

Doogie decided that to reply would only invite more derision. Instead he lit up having passed a cigarette to Jason. "Is it a London thing not to buy your own fags?"

"I learned the art in Rollerton actually."

"Can we get a fag like mister?"

A cheeky face under a cap that advertised the badge of the *Miami Dolphins*. Before Doogie got the chance to tell the lad to go jump in a river, Sally jumped in.

"Nae bother lads. Here you go."

She crashed Doogie's B&H to five takers.

"Cheers Miss."

"Is it going to be a good one tonight then?" Jason was impressed at how easy she was with the queuing Neds. And then he ticked himself off. Why was he calling them Neds? Just because they were in a queue? Just because they wore baseball caps? Because they were from Rollerton? Because they were about fifteen? Or was it because he had been brain-washed by Lester Gall's poxy rags that had being vilifying teens for over a decade. Sally obviously hadn't bought into the Aussie prick's poison.

"Aye. It's always good here like, ken?"

"He's banging Miss."

"D-Zed's the bizz."

"So where are you lot from then?"

"Greenfield. What about you Miss?"

"Edinburgh now, but I used to be from Rollerton."

"You're too posh for Rollie."

"Oh you think so do you?"

"Aye. You're posh as owt. How come you're here then?"

"Same as you lot. To check out D-Zed."

"Bet you're a cop. Undercover like. Ken like on the tele and that."

Sally gave an affronted look that made them giggle. "How dare you! I'm so upset that I might just go home and have a weep."

They liked that. They liked her. What was there not to like thought Jason.

"Which one of these is your man then Miss?"

"Neither. Do I look like that much of a loser?"

They liked that as well.

"So you're single then?"

"'Fraid so."

"On the pull then are you Miss?"

"Could be. Wouldn't mind a toy boy for the night. Are you single then? Fancy being transported to the kind of heaven you have only ever dreamed of?"

This induced the mother of all blushes and huge merriment among the mates. Suddenly the boy could barely speak.

"Aye. Well. No like. Ken my bird's inside like. You ken . . ."

Sally gave a broken-hearted face and suddenly they found themselves at the front of the queue where Doogie did the honours.

A £10 note. A pound coin in change."

"Expenses?" Asked Jason with a raised eyebrow.

"Obviously. Key research into the habits of the young people in the community."

"No receipt?"

"Top Cops don't need receipts. We're above the law in case you hadn't heard."

They walked into a wall of sound and a blaze of strobe lights. Conversation was a big no and they bought cans of coke from a trestle table stall. Just after ten, the sound seemed to reach up and hit a pitch that bounced the back of the audience's throats. And suddenly a small-looking man dressed all in black appeared on a podium with his arms out Messiah style.

Five hundred voices bayed out his name.

The set was a mix of sound and pictures. Images flashed over a screen with mind spinning speed. Black and white. Colour. War and peace. Riot police and children. Napalm strikes and wheatfields. Martin Luther King and Hitler and Pol Pot. Clips from movies where the sound was gelled into the music. Chaplin. Gone with the Wind. Apocolypse Now. Taxi Driver. Are you talking to me? Are you talking to me? OK? Yeah? A *Coca Cola* can. A *Nike* tick. George Bush. Lord Kitchener. A Zulu warrior. A necklacing on the streets of Soweto.

It seemed impossible for the pitch of the event to get higher, but it kept getting higher all the same. Bodies were lost in the rhythm. Moving like a sea. Perfect rhythm. Perfect harmony. And Jason saw that Sally was a part of it with eyes alight and sweat pouring down her face. Even Doogie was finding it hard not to go with the flow. And Jason decided what the hell. Stuff it. Go with it. Just go.

On and on. Ghandi and *Blade Runner* and *Schindler's List* and factories belching smoke and white tie dinners in baronial halls and top end cars and Eton and punts on the river Cam and pot-bellied babies in the dust and child-soldiers and needles sinking into emaciated arms. Obama and Florence Nightingale and a gas attack in corpse-strewn trenches and cave men clubbing a bear and *Homer Simpson* and *Daffy Duck*.

And when D-Zed spoke his voice blended in with the sound and the images. A part of it. At the centre of it.

> *"So who's popped a pill tonight then? Come on. Let's be having you . . . Plenty then . . . plenty, plenty . . . know what you are, yeah . . . sheeeeeeeeep . . . sheeeeep . . ."*

Lester Gall. Sheep on a Scottish moor huddled in the rain. Christopher Pendeleton. A police line. A collie dog.

> *". . . ever wondered why the cops never seem to bother about Eckies and Ket . . . Well . . .?*
>
> *Ever thought about it? Considered it? Mulled it? Chewed it . . .?*
>
> *No . . . course not . . . coz you're all shheeeeeeeep . . . sheeeeeep . . . baaaaaaa . . . baaaaaaa.*
>
> *They want you popping . . . they want it . . . Lesssssssssssster wants it . . . Lester wants sheeeeeeeeep . . . Baaaaaaaa . . . baaaaaaaa.*
>
> *They want you brain dead . . . They want you dosed up . . . they want you to dance their tune . . . buy their stuff . . . Believe their lies . . . their shite . . . sheeeeeeeeep . . . baaaaaa . . . baaaaaa.*
>
> *So pop those pills suckers . . . pop away . . . dance to their tune . . . stand in line . . . Stand in the corner . . . Stand up – sit down . . . stand up-sit down . . . stand up-sit down . . . sheeeeeeeeep . . . sheeeeeep . . . looooooooooooooosers . . . baaaaaaaaaa.. baaaaaaaa . . ."*

Sally draped an arm around Jason's shoulders and leaned in with in an inch of his ear to make herself heard.

"He's fantastic!"

"I know!"

On and on. An hour. Two hours. Endless. Bouncing the floor. The ceilings. The cranial cavities. The inner reaches.

Until at last it was all over and the lights came on. And Jason felt something that he hadn't felt in years. That end of a weekend night feeling. House lights up. Last dance all played out. Raining outside and reality waiting.

They said little as they walked back to the car. Doogie fired up the engine and became decisive.

"I guess it really has to be a kebab then?"

The kebabs went back home to the house to be microwaved and put on plates. The whisky bottle came out. An old CD hit the deck.

"So?" Sally was fed up with their silence.

Jason wiped his lips clean of chilli sauce. "Like you said. Fantastic. Mind blowing. Best three quid I've spent in ages."

"You didn't spend £3. I paid you in."

Sally gave Doogie a joshing push. "Come on you miserable old sod. What did you make of it?"

"I can't disagree. It was phenomenal. I take it all back."

"What about the stuff about the pills? You know . . . *sheeeeeeeep* . . . what did you make of that? Cops don't bother about eckies because Lester Gall wants his punters all dosed up?"

Jason was only half-joking.

"A fair cop. Come on Jace, what are we supposed to do? Every Friday and Saturday night it is like World War Three out there. If kids want to load up on Eckies and hug each other, that will do me well enough. What do you want me to say? That I'd rather they all tank down the Buckfast and have a slash at my lads with their Stanley knives?"

Jason shrugged. "And Lester Gall?"

"Yeah right. Lester Gall's got nothing to with it. It's just common sense. We get told to nail the smack dealers and the crack dealers. If we happen to nail someone with a sackful of Eckies then we send them down. It's just not a priority."

Sally fiddled with her glass. "He has a point though doesn't he? So long as youngsters scramble their brains with pills and powders, they never get round to looking at the bigger picture. Nixon could have bombed Cambodia for as long as he liked if this generation had been around. They would have figured it was all some sort of an Xbox game. Anyway. What is the view from the Press Room?"

Jason took a sip of whisky. "Don't know yet really. It seemed to me that he was asking them to think, not riot. There was no incitement there. No clarion call to hit the streets to put a few windows through. I'll see what he's like when I interview him. Can you get me an address Doogie?"

"Aye. He lives on Greenfield."

Sally pulled herself up from her chair. "Well I can see that you two are hell bent on finishing that bottle and I'm not joining in. I have stuff on tomorrow so I will bid you good night."

"What have you got on a Sunday?"

"Don't ask."

"Ah come on, don't be shy."

"I really would rather you didn't ask."

"We're asking."

She could tell that she was cornered. "I have been invited to judge which is the best cake at the AGM of the Rollerton Women's Institute. And to give them a talk."

Jason and Doogie never got to hear the bit about Sally giving a talk. By then they were fully engulfed in hysterics. Sally managed what she hoped was a sweet smile.

"Told you I'd rather you hadn't asked. Nighty night."

KENYA, MARCH 1959

Flies and sweat.

Sweat and flies.

Disgusting flies. Disgusting sweat.

All the time. Every minute of every hour. All day and all night. Except at night the mosquitoes would come out to join the flies.

It didn't matter how careful he was when he arranged the mosquito net over his bed. He would tuck in every corner and seal every little gap, but it was never enough. They always came. Fizzing and buzzing and biting and itching.

Sleep was a thing that only ever lasted half an hour at a time. Unless of course he hit the whisky bottle. Hit it and hit it and hit it.

But one morning he had awoken to find his hands shaking and a slippery sickness in his guts. And the oily, slippery sickness had only been driven away by a tumbler of scotch. At which point Gerald Wheeler had realised that it was time to stop.

Already Africa had taken enough of a toll on him.

A bout of malaria that had stripped him to the bone.

A bout of jaundice that had turned him a grey, yellow.

A bout of amoebic dysentery that had all but done for him.

Flies and sweat and disease. And a flat, flat plain that just went on and on and on into a heat shimmering nothingness. Totally empty. Devoid. Parched. Home to spindly trees and cacti and at night the hooping cackling sound of the hyenas.

Gerald Wheeler was a very resentful man. A very resentful man indeed. In his opinion he had been conned by his country. Lied to. Sold a line. And it had gone on for years and years and years.

At the age of twenty-one things had been pretty much fine. He had passed all the tests and become a police constable on the streets of his home town of Wolverhampton. It was a reserved profession and he had been quite safe from conscription papers landing on the mat. There had been no need for him to become a part of the fight to get rid of Hitler. He could have ridden the whole thing out. Instead like an immature, gullible fool he had bought into all the posters that promised a uniform and glory and girls. Like an immature, gullible fool he had changed uniforms and ended up in North Africa where several white hot slivers of shrapnel had shredded a goodly part of his stomach and ensured that he would never really enjoy a meal ever again.

And had he wised up?

Like hell he had. Instead, he had bought into the whole *Brave New World* line that the politicians were peddling. The soldiers who had defeated Fascism could expect a very different Britain to come home to. A better Britain where doctors wouldn't charge any more and nobody would starve. Like a betraying fool he had turned his back on Churchill who he liked, and gave his vote to Atlee who he didn't like. He voted for a Welfare State and fairness and better houses and better food and better everything.

Instead he found that the streets of Wolverhampton had become even darker. Even poorer. Even hungrier. And in the bitter freeze of 1947 his mother had died from hypothermia and he had made up his mind to leave Britain once and for all.

Well, why not?

He was young and single and he had no family left.

He thought Australia.

He thought New Zealand.

He thought Canada.

But like a complete bloody fool he allowed himself to be conned again by yet another poster.

Come to Africa! Walk into a new future! Come to a place of lions and elephants and white sand beaches and fresh fruit and sunshine, sunshine, sunshine.

So Gerald Wheeler had signed on the dotted line and joined the Kenyan police. Now that India was gone, Kenya was the new jewel in the crown. It was a great partnership. Millions of natives, all so very grateful to their benevolent British masters who were bringing schools and courts and roads and railways to their dark and savage lands.

But it wasn't like that.

By the time Gerald's ship made port, the Mau Mau revolt was in full swing. The natives weren't all that grateful after all. They wanted the British out. They wanted some land of their own. They wanted a President of their own. President Truman had told them it was their right. And Comrade Stalin. And the Indians had been given their country back. So why not the Kenyans?

It took only a few months for Gerald Wheeler to realise that he might as well have donned an SS uniform. The British Colonial Government seemed hell bent on aping the policies of the Nazis. All Kikuyu were moved into concentration camps. They were tortured on an industrial scale. Thousands of acres around Mount Kenya and the Aberdare Range were cleared and burned and scorched. Free fire zones. Places where a black man would be riddled with bullets for breathing. For being there. For nothing. To defend property. To protect British interests.

And Gerald Wheeler had done bad things. Very bad things. Things which had kept him awake through the nights. Along with the flies. And the heat. And the mosquitoes. Somewhere along the line he had lost his soul. He had become a monster for the sake of promotion. A better pension. The prospect of a bungalow in Bournemouth. Or Southend-on-Sea.

And it wasn't just him. Everyone was doing bad things. And it wasn't as if the men in charge seemed to mind. Instead they issued pats on the back. And medals. And promotions.

Gerald had been transferred to the holding camps when he had been in Kenya for a year. And he had done more bad things. Many more. And as a reward he had been promoted. And promoted again. And all the while his pension rights quietly accumulated. Until in the end they told him that he was to have a camp of his own. A special camp. Not a large camp. Oh no, not a large camp. Only small. Never more than sixty prisoners. But they were special prisoners. The really, really hard cases. The ones who had fought with Dedan Kimathi in the high forests of Mount Kenya all the way to the bitter end. They were trouble. Unbowed and unbroken and militant.

That was why Gerald's camp was hidden away; hundreds and hundreds of miles away from anywhere on the arid plains up by Lake Rudolf. A place of heat and dust and nothingness where the unbowed and unbroken could be bowed and broken. In peace. In private. Two corporals and a squad of a hundred native guards from Sudan. Guards carefully chosen from tribes who hated the Kikuyu. Guards who liked to call the Kikuyu shit-eating monkeys. All overseen by Gerald Wheeler. Breaker in chief.

And he had done terrible things. Truly, truly terrible things. Amidst the flies and the heat. And no matter how bad the terrible things were, they were never enough to break the men who had hung on in the high forests with Dedan Kimathi all the way to the bitter, bitter end. They were unbowed. Unbreakable.

Until a man called Rogers had arrived all the way from the Home Office carrying six bottles of clear liquid. Rogers was all Eton and Oxbridge and cream suit. He had called Wheeler a bloody good sort and salt of the bloody earth. He had told Wheeler that he was doing a top hole job. He had plied Wheeler with twenty-year-old malt. And he had explained that the bottles of clear liquid were jolly hush, hush. Just about as hush, hush as hush, hush could ever get. Rogers wanted Wheeler to be a good chap and slip 3ml per head of the liquid in the bottles into the maize porridge of the unbowed. The unbreakable.

"And take notes old chap. Copious notes. See if the wogs stop being so naughty all the time. See if they become compliant. Get it all down in black and white. But remember that these notes go nowhere but me. Mmm? All clear old chap. Only me and mum's the word. I'll pop back in two months and we'll see how things are going. OK? Well that's splendid then? Another stiffener?"

It had only taken two days for the unbreakable to be broken. For the unbowed to bow and scrape. When they were asked to get up, they got up. When they were asked to work, they worked. When they were asked to renounce the sacred oath they had taken to rid their land of the British, they renounced their sacred oaths. They were zombie men. Slow motion men. Meek. Compliant.

And Gerald Wheeler was in no doubt that the bottles contained something that was truly, truly evil. But still he made his careful notes. Findings. Observations. All in the same careful handwriting that his old English teacher had once given such high praise for. Not that his notes offered any variety. No problems with the prisoners. No problems with the prisoners. No problems with the prisoners.

In this corner of Hell.

His corner of Hell.

A4 pages of carefully written evil.

For a bungalow in Bournemouth.

Or Southend-on-Sea.

And now there was a plume of dust on the horizon. Was Rogers back already? Unlikely. It had only been three weeks. But when a Jeep and four Bedford trucks pulled up in front of his office, it was indeed Rogers who clambered out.

"Hello Wheeler. Bit of a change of plan old chap. We're wrapping things up here and shipping the wogs out. Then we need to burn the place. Every stick. Come on Wheeler. Let's wet the old whistle before we get started. Come along now. Pop, pop."

"But why? What's going on?"

"'Fraid there's been a spot of nonsense over at Hola." Hola was a bigger camp than Gerald Wheeler's camp. It also accommodated the unbreakable and the unbowed.

"What kind of nonsense?"

Rogers shrugged. "Chaps asked the wogs to work and the wogs refused. Chaps tried to encourage them a bit. All got a tad carried away I'm afraid."

"How carried away?"

"Quite a lot actually. Here you are Wheeler. Chin, chin. Eleven beaten to death and sixty badly knocked about."

"Jesus."

"Yes indeed. Trouble is that the wretched bleeding hearts in the press have got wind of it. There's quite a storm brewing. Questions in Parliament. The whole kit and caboodle I'm afraid. Which is why we need to make quite sure that this camp of yours never existed. So we burn every stick, yes? Every stick."

"Of course."

"Now. Tell me about the magic potion old chap. How's it worked?"

And Gerald Wheeler told him. And gave him the neatly written notes. And Rogers seemed jolly pleased and kept on pouring until the bottle was all gone.

"So what will you do with the prisoners?"

"The wogs? Oh don't worry. They're not bound for a hole in the ground. What sort of chaps would that make us? Good lord no. We'll return them to the place from whence they came. The forests of Mount

Kenya. No doubt they get home in the end. And maybe they'll have some ripping yarns to tell. But it will take a while. And by then all the pesky reporters will have gone back home."

They drained what was left in their glasses and for a very brief moment Rogers lost a little of his perfectly bred perkiness.

"The sun is setting Wheeler. Night is drawing in. We'll all be out of here in a year or two. We'll be out of everywhere. It's what the Americans want you see. What the Americans demand. And what the Americans want, the Americans get. It's all gone Wheeler. Gone never to return."

"What about my notes? Where are they going?"

Rogers offered a conspiratorial grin. "Need to know I'm afraid old chap. Need to know. What I should make clear is that you never actually took any notes. And there never were any bottles of magic potion. And there was never a camp. I presume that is as clear as crystal"

"Yes. Of course."

Already the smoke was starting to pour through the windows of the hut where the prisoners had slept in bunk beds.

Black smoke climbing and climbing and climbing into the burning sky above.

Smoke from a fire that never happened.

2016

Jason found Ronald Pickup's house in Greenfield to be wholly unremarkable. Well, of course it was. What had he been expecting? Pickup when all was said and done was no more than a small town DJ. Imaginative, innovative, bloody brilliant, but in the end locked into a small Scottish town. Was he about to extend his horizons? Maybe. Probably not. Jason's gut feeling was that D-Zed would only ever be a Rollerton craze. And no doubt his star would fade soon enough. Trends would move on and his version of techno would all of a sudden be out of vogue. In fact, was it even in vogue? Did D-Zed's seemingly devoted audience actually listen to a word he said to them? Or did they turn out because it was a place to go? Something to do. Somewhere dry where everyone else was to be found?

He had considered calling first but had decided against. Better to doorstep his prey and give him as little chance as possible to say no.

The Fridge wouldn't like it if D-Zed said no. She wouldn't like it at all.

His first two presses of the doorbell got nothing in response. Maybe not working. Probably not working. Hell, when did Greenfield doorbells ever ring? He gave the door a bang and thirty seconds later a rather bleary-eyed Ronald Pickup peered round a security chain.

"Hi Ronald."

No recognition. No concern either. "Hello."

"Remember me then?"

"Sorry. I don't think so." Tired red eyes. Pale skin. Rather lank hair. The night before he had appeared energised and commanding in his black clothes. Now he was in a dressing gown that looked like a Christmas present from his Gran and he looked like just another bloke about to reach forty in a world that had no time for blokes who had reached forty.

"Jason. Jason Marsh. We were at school together."

"Were we?"

"Aye. I was older mind. Still am. You would have been in S3 when I left."

A small flicker of memory.

"Didn't you become a journalist?"

"Aye. Sure did. Still am in fact."

"OK."

"So are you going to invite me in or what?"

A mildly troubled look.

"Well. Not really. I mean it's quite early and . . . well. You know."

Jason tried on an encouraging smile. "Don't worry Ronald. I'm not some tabloid hack. I'm with *The Enquirer*."

"Oh."

The dramatic eloquence of the night before seemed to have been left in Benny Khan's disused warehouse.

"Bloody cold out here Ronald."

Good manners superseded caution. "Sorry. Of course. Come on in. I'm not really awake yet. Had a gig last night."

"Yeah, I know. I was there."

Jason took in the room. Neat. Clean. Well ordered. Dominated by a corner full of computer equipment ringed around a desk. Pickup seemed surprised at the news that Jason had paid his £3 to join the five hundred faithful.

"Did you enjoy it?"

"Actually I did. Thought it was bloody brilliant in fact."

Pickup blushed slightly, unaccustomed to the level headed praise of a grown up.

"I'm making some coffee. Would you like a cup?"

"Grand. Black and two please."

Jason followed the dressing gown and slippers into a spic-and-span kitchen. Pickup spooned coffee into a filter and set it up in a rather venerable looking machine which soon started bubbling encouragingly. As the jug filled he set up two mugs and a plate of Rich Tea biscuits. Rich Tea! Either this was a very British revolutionary or Jason was barking up the wrong tree in the wrong forest. If the Fridge could see him now she would have a duck fit. There wasn't much in the neat kitchen that gave a flavour of a Che Guevara or a Trotsky. Just a rather innocuous looking guy in his dressing gown. Maybe he could use the dressing gown. Rumour had it that Churchill made most of his big calls whilst paddling about the place in his dressing room. Maybe he had given the nod to the firebombing of Dresden whilst in his dressing gown.

"I presume you are here in a professional capacity Mr Marsh?"

"Jason. Jace if you like. And yes, I am."

"Why?"

"A feature I'm on with. Kids in France are out on the streets kicking off. Kids in Britain are quiet as mice. What is going to change that? Is anything going to change that? Where will the spark come from?"

Pickup gave a somewhat embarrassed smile. "You're not suggesting that it might be me, surely?"

"Why not? You can fill a room and it looked to me like you had them eating out of your hand last night."

"Oh it might have looked that way but I can promise you that it isn't really the case. It's a song and dance act Jason. Lights and sound. Lights and sound. Here."

He passed over a mug of coffee and ushered Jason back through into the living room where a gas fire made things cosy.

Jason sat and helped himself to a *Rich Tea*. What the hell. He dunked. Greenfield had many downsides but at least it was still and always would be a place where you could dunk your biscuit in peace. "I think you undersell yourself Ronald. They were listening. And you weren't exactly telling them stuff they wanted to hear. Losers? Sheep?"

Pickup shrugged. "I just try and do my bit, that's all. I get sick of seeing kids addling their brains on pills and dope. They're all so miserable. Depressed. Drained of serotonin."

"You don't hold with drugs then?"

"God no. I did the whole party drug thing when I was a kid and now I only get by on the Prozac the doc doles out every fortnight."

"Is that off the record?"

"No. Write it if you like. I am assuming that everything is on the record. It's nice of you to ask though."

"Like I said. I'm not a tabloid hack."

Pickup wrapped thin fingers around his cup and looked huddled and older than he should have done.

"Actually, *The Enquirer* is the only paper I read. I never buy it I'm afraid. I read it on line. I might as well admit that I have always followed your stuff. I wasn't being entirely honest at the door."

Jason smiled. "Nobody seems to buy the bloody thing any more. At least nobody under the age of sixty."

"I hope you don't mind my being frank, but I feel your work has gone downhill over recent years."

"Be as frank as you like. And you're right of course."

"Why?"

So who was interviewing who here? "A divorce. A new broom in the office. Too much booze. Too many fags. The cynicism of middle age. I guess I find it hard to believe that the world is going to be changed by anything I do."

"Snap."

"Hey, I'm not having that. You're doing plenty."

"You think so? It might look that way but don't be deceived. I do my bit. No more, no less. I provide some entertainment and hopefully I can be a positive influence without being preachy. I try to persuade a few hundred kids in a small town not to do so many drugs and to think twice about carrying knives. Maybe I have some effect. Maybe not. Like I said, when all is said and done, I'm a song and dance show. And I make a living of course. Nothing very spectacular. But a living all the same."

"Are you married?"

"No. I'm just a sad old geek who stays in with his toys."

"What about the kids? Do they come and see you through the week or is it just a Saturday night thing?"

"Oh yes. They come and see me. Give it an hour or so and they will start to turn up."

"Mind if I stay to meet a few?"

"Of course not."

"So what do you think then? About my piece? What would get the youth of Britain out on the streets and smashing windows?"

Pickup considered this. "It would take a lot. They are very well programmed. Lester Gall has them all exactly where he wants them. They only aspire to what he wants them to aspire to. Pipedreams. A slot in a reality TV show. Their picture in a celebrity magazine. He drip feeds them the idea that so long as they wear the right labels and carry the right phone, then one day it will happen to them. So long as you're thin enough, then it matters not a jot if you never got round to learning how to read and write. And you've no doubt have noticed that most of Lester's celebs load up more than their fair share of drugs. No smack of course, but everything else. He makes it glamorous. Can you think of any of his celebs who don't do drugs?"

Jason thought. He couldn't.

"So the kids pop their pills and smoke their joints and get anxious and paranoid. They daren't go out unless they are clad from head to toe in the gear Lester Gall tells them to wear. They are terrified that their mates will take the piss. And so they spend every penny of spare cash on the stuff he tells them to spend on."

"Mind if I smoke?"

"No. Help yourself." Pickup passed over an ashtray.

"I'm not really sure I buy all that Ronald. You reckon that Gall is actually more or less advocating recreational drugs."

"Of course he is. And why wouldn't he? Lester Gall is a very, very rich man. And all his pals are very, very rich men. The super-rich as we like to call them. The new aristocracy. And it doesn't matter how far back into history you delve, you will find that the super rich always share the same problem. There are very few of them and millions and millions of those who haven't got much. If the millions who haven't got much ever realise that numbers can be made to count, then the super-rich have a problem. They either get out of Dodge quick or get their heads lopped off and their big houses looted."

"St Petersburg 1917."

"Sure. And who is in the front line in any uprising? Young people of course. Hitler Youth. Students at American Universities during the Tet Offensive back in '68. Toxteth rioters in '81. Same old, same old. So it must seem a pretty good idea for Lester and his cronies to encourage young people to smoke their dope and snort their coke and pop their pills. Make them anxious. Drain their self belief. Vacuum away their motivation. It's good old fashioned brain washing. Subliminal of course. Legal. Signed off by the government."

"And so long as Lester Gall is pulling the strings, the youth of today will be meek and compliant?"

"Quite. Have you read *1984* recently?"

"Not recently."

"You should. It has become the here and now. I'm sure Lester must read a chapter every day."

"Which is why you hit them with all those images of rebellion and revolt?"

Pickup smiled. "I try, but it isn't about to happen. I just try to give them the message that it is in their gift to be empowered. They don't have to end up down and depressed and doomed."

"And does it work?"

A shrug. "Maybe a little. It is hard to measure this kind of thing. Maybe a little."

The first of Pickup's acolytes started to arrive soon after twelve and all afternoon they came and went. Jason crashed fags and listened in to them. Hours of can't be bothered and what's the point and who gives a shit. When they were in twos and threes, they talked about who'd battered who and who was pregnant and who got lifted. When they were on their own, they talked about how they were feeling and how their dads were still battering their mums and how their uncle was still on the gear. And as the hours drifted by, Jason found a seeping sadness was crawling through his skin. Behind the labels and the brash electronics they were all so nervous and frightened and insecure. Anxiety masked by sad bravado. And there was nothing about them to frighten Lester Gall. And Jason could get Ronald Pickup's drift. And maybe he even believed some of it. Maybe most of it.

But it wasn't a story. Lester Gall conspiracy theories were not the kind of thing the Fridge would look fondly on. She would tell him about lawyers and courts and lost advertising. And then she would fire him, mascot or no mascot.

A few of the kids told him about a youth drop-in that was open on Tuesdays and Thursdays. They said he should come visit. Shoot some pool and that. And he said he would go. But in his heart of hearts he knew he wasn't about to discover the seeds of revolution on the dreary streets of Greenfield.

His piece would be all about how the youth of Britain were not about to emulate their contemporaries across the Channel. Not even close. And D-Zed was not about to lead a mob through the streets with a red flag fluttering in the breeze.

Which was a shame.

But the Fridge would probably be happy enough.

He thanked Pickup and headed out into the thin drizzle of a

Greenfield night. The sky was uplit by dreary orange. Someone some-where was cooking chips in oil that was weeks past its sell by date. Someone had dumped an old couch on the pavement. Someone had allowed their dog to shit on the pavement.

There was broken glass and graffiti and litter.

It was Rollerton 2016.

And Trotsky and Che were merely faces for T-shirts that nobody bought any more.

Douglas could see that all was not well with the Chief Constable the moment he walked into his boss's office. The Chief was a red-faced man who liked to watch rugby on a Saturday and never missed church on a Sunday. He had come down from the north two years earlier and by and large he was liked well enough by the rank and file. He had never shown any great interest in the political side of his job and was unusually focused on the idea of locking up bad guys. He went out to bat for his lads when push came to shove and tended to give the media short shrift. He was a man who seemed to take just about everything in his stride but now his ruddy complexion had faded,

And his tie was off,

And Dougles had never seen him with his tie off.

"Hello Douglas. Grab a pew. Take a load off. Brew?"

"Please sir. Coffee. Black with two."

It seemed quite an effort for Chief Constable Evans to heave him-self up from his chair to fix the drinks. He didn't talk whilst complet-ing the task and the sound of evening traffic floated in through an open window.

"So how was the fishing sir?"

"There wasn't any fishing Douglas. I'm afraid it was a cover story. Orders you see. And I don't like being ordered to lie to my colleagues Douglas. Not a bit."

What was this? "No sir."

"I was in London, Douglas. Me and every other Chief Constable in Great Britain and Northern Ireland. Every man Jack of us down there on the QT. Say you're are taking a holiday they said. A short break."

And there was a bitterness in his voice that Doogie had never heard before.

"The bloody PM himself turned out to talk to us. Unbelievable. The Scots were wondering what the hell was going on. Whatever hap-pened to Devolution then? Whatever indeed?"

Doogie hadn't the first idea what Evans was on about. Which was rare as his boss was normally clipped and clear. Forever laying out the facts to a court.

"Anyway. I still can't tell you much. Because I am gagged Douglas. Gagged and trussed like a bloody chicken. And I can assure you that this is absolutely no reflection on your trustworthiness. None at all. But I am in a position to give you some elements of the picture. OK?"

"Of course sir."

Evans gave a rueful grin. "Sorry. I'm rambling. I will try and be a little clearer. In less than three weeks the Prime Minister will be going on tele and giving out some momentous news. And believe me Douglas, it will be momentous. I can still scarcely believe it myself. Britain is about to change. Change beyond all recognition. And an awful lot of people are not going to like the changes that are coming one little bit. People are going to be very, very pissed off and there will be a major threat to public order. I can't give you the details yet. Maybe you will have to hear the details from the PM himself along with the rest of the country. We'll see. Maybe they will loosen the gagging order. I have to assume they won't and therefore I can only talk to you in hypothetical terms. OK?"

"Sir."

"When this thing goes live, I expect that a great deal of my time will be eaten up with strategic stuff. I will be off to Edinburgh most of the time. Which basically means that I am going to need a leader on the ground. You Douglas. You're the best I've got. You're young, you're smart and the lads like you. And you can do the press pretty well. Over the next three weeks you need to think about dealing with major unrest on the streets on a daily basis. Major unrest. Big crowds of very angry people. Our orders are zero tolerance. Complete zero. If people break the law, we lift them and we process them. No cautions. No slaps on the wrists. The Government is adamant that the population needs to get the message straight away. Cross the line and you get done. Every time. No exceptions. You will be reading the Riot Act on day one Douglas. And there will probably be TV cameras there to film you reading it. And I very much doubt that the crowd will do as they are told and disperse peacefully. Instead, I expect them to start throwing stuff, which means that every one of the guys on the streets will need immediate access to a full set of riot gear. So check the stocks Douglas. Do it quietly if you can. Use discretion, but do it. And if we are short of kit, get it by hook or by crook. OK?"

By now Douglas was just about incapable of speech. He could only nod. His eyes couldn't help it. They were drawn to the ashtray that had appeared on the desk which contained five dockers. Evans noticed and grimaced.

"Yes, I know. I haven't had one of the little bastards in six years. Well stuff it. Want one?"

"Please."

They lit up and broke a bunch of regulations which Doogie had a feeling were about to be little more than an irrelevance.

"Right. Imagine you are dealing with a street mob, Douglas. You get on the loud hailer and demand that they disperse. But they don't. Instead they start chucking bricks. The orders are that you set an example. You send in snatch squads and you drag out bodies. It will be a boots and batons affair. Heads will be broken and the press will go ballistic. The Government is fully aware of this and they don't give a shit. They want us to go in hard and bugger the whinging. We are to go in like the French. So you break up the mob and you lift bodies. How many? A hundred? Two hundred? And the day before you have lifted two hundred. And the day before that two hundred. OK? As in way, way too many for the holding cells. So here's the thing. The Government wants these people to be properly processed. Booked and held and delivered to the Sheriff. So you need to get your head around the idea of where the hell you are going to put them? And who is going to guard them? And how they are going to stay warm through the night? Or maybe two nights? We might wind up with hundreds in custody. They will all need to eat and take a shit. Are you beginning to get the picture?"

Douglas was. He all but sucked his cigarette right down his throat. "Sir."

"Well these are the things you need to get your head around. Get your nose stuck into a few law books. Play the scenarios in your head. It will help you when the time comes. Get as much sleep as you can as there will be bugger all for any of us when things kick off. We will be looking at no time off for a long, long time. The good news is that overtime will come in wheelbarrows. It will be a miners' strike job for the lads. Can we hold the line? The Government seem to think so. I'm not so sure. If we can't, then they will deploy the army. And I don't want that Douglas. I'll be buggered if we are about to see any armoured cars on the streets of Rollerton. Not on my watch. Not on yours either. We're going to hold the line Douglas. We're going to do what it takes. OK?"

Doogie nodded and stubbed his cigarette. The bad feeling that had been lurking in his gut had just got ten times worse.

"We'll all give it 100% sir. I can't say more than that."

"Fair enough."

Sally was haunting the Parliament tearoom. Eyes and ears open. For two days she had buttonholed fellow MSPs she had barely spoken to before. She had splashed cash on cappuccinos and expressos and herbal teas. Apparently chance conversations accompanied by a bright enthusiastic smile. Fishing. Seeking a hint of knowledge about the dark clouds she sensed to be gathering on the horizon.

And nobody knew anything. Nobody even seemed to suspect anything in the wind. Everyone was business as usual.

Until she talked to McRae.

Jim McCrae.

The maverick.

The dinosaur.

An old school union man from the Eighties. In those days the tabloids had called him 'Red Jimmy'. Page after page of newsprint had dwelt on his exchange visits to East Germany. They said Red Jimmy was on the Moscow payroll. He was a Trojan Horse. When the paratroopers of the Red Army floated down out of the Scottish sky, the press were pretty well sure that Red Jimmy would have been there waiting for them with a bottle of vodka open and ready. But then the Berlin Wall had crashed and the Red Menace had faded into the history books. Jim McCrae got older and started to assume the role of an eccentric uncle. When the Scottish Parliament opened up, Jim duly walked through the door as a Labour list MSP. Not that it lasted very long. He fell out with the Party line within a year and became an Independent. But he didn't fall out with the people of Greater Glasgow. They liked him. They liked his abrasiveness. They liked his God given ability to call a spade a spade. They liked his God given ability to get up the noses of those in authority. And enough of his fellow Glaswegians chose him as their man on the ballot paper for him to return to Parliament at a canter.

Now he was well past seventy, but still a thorn in the side of whichever coalition was calling the shots. He had become a much loved relic. A memory of different times; better times.

He didn't look at all displeased when Sally asked him if the spare seat at his table was free.

"Aye hen. It's free. You going to buy me a cup of tea then? Seems like you've bought just about everyone a cup of tea the last day or two."

"That obvious was it?"

"Aye. It was to me. Probably not to many others though. When you get to my age, your powers of observation tend to improve. You lobbying for something then?"

"Actually no."

Jim raised an eyebrow. "Really? Now that sounds interesting. Get me a brew and tell me all about it."

As Sally collected a tray of drinks at the counter she decided that it would be a pretty pointless exercise trying to bullshit Jimmy McCrae. Instead she laid her cards on the table along with the cups of tea.

"I have been hearing some strange things." She went on describe the meeting at the police college and the PM's unexplained night time outings minus advisors. She told him that she had a bad feeling. And he nodded.

"Join the club hen."

"So you have heard things too?"

"Bits and pieces. Nothing good."

"Will you tell me?"

He slurped at his tea and pushed down the familiar yearning for a cigarette.

"Aye I will. For what it's worth. Because of who I am, well, who I was, people still send me stuff. Stuff they are not all that comfortable with. Stuff that doesn't sit well with them. There has been a lot of that kind of stuff over the last couple of weeks. Buggered if I know what it's all about mind."

"Tell me."

"Ever see that thing from the eighties. You ken, with Bob Peck. All about the secret nuclear state. *Edge of Darkness*. See it did you?"

"Yes. I have the DVD actually."

"Then you'll remember that line from Darius Jedburgh. Remember, the CIA guy in the ten gallon hat? 'To know is to die'. 'To know is to die.' Well I don't know what is going down hen, but I am old enough and wise enough to know that it is nothing good. The State is gearing up to crack the whip. And when that happens, people start to disappear. Or have unexplained car accidents or heart attacks. 'To know is to die.' You seem a nice lass to me, hen. And your heart is in the right place. I've seen that right enough. You get in there and fight for the little guy and that does me well enough. Are you really sure you want to get into this thing? Whatever it is?"

"Quite sure. But thanks for asking."

McRae shrugged and topped up his tea. "Fair enough. I thought you'd say that. Just be careful. Bloody careful. OK. The stuff. I had three visitors to my surgery on Friday and none of them were constituents. They were all lads for the old days who knew well enough not to use phones and email. They came in person and passed me envelopes. The first guy works in a plastic fabrication factory in Coventry. For years they have been laying off and cutting costs. Now all of a sudden they are working 24/7 and overtime is no longer a problem. Ken what they are making? Riot shields. Every police force in Britain is ordering in riot shields and they don't seem much bothered what they pay for them. Visitor number two is a shift foreman in a big food processing place in Lincolnshire. They make tinned soup and stew and stuff. And now they have closed down all the lines for refitting. The tinning plant is all being taken out. Instead product will be made in bulk and loaded into tankers. As in twenty four tonnes at a time. Visitor number three is transport manager for a milk company. He has been told to hire in more staff and pay whatever he needs to. He needs to be ready to run every truck 24 hours a day, seven days a week. So make of it what you will hen. Riot shields and scotch broth moved around the place in artic tankers."

"Christ, I hope nobody is refurbishing the nuclear bunkers."

McRae gave a wintry smile. "I haven't heard of it hen. But there's a storm coming right enough. A real storm."

"Well. Thanks anyway." She got to her feet slowly.

"And be careful hen. Be very, very careful."

She nodded absently.

Riot shields and bulk delivered soup. What the hell was going on?

Christopher Pendleton was feeling pretty good about life. In fact, he had been feeling pretty good about life for several days. In fact he had felt pretty good about life from the moment he had given it to Lester Gall with both barrels. When they had first summoned him to the country house he had been their lackey. Beholden to them. Dependent on their support for money and PR and a chance to get elected next time. They had issued their instructions and he had been every bit as meek as they knew he would be. But then everything had changed. It had changed the moment he had exchanged a nod with James Hawkes. Because as soon as the two main parties were agreed and united, then all the real power moved back to the politicians. The Government. The Prime Minister.

Christopher Pendleton.

He had given them all a month to make their minds up. Stay or go. And they had decided to stay. All of them. They couldn't resist the chance of a labour force in a land of no unions and no minimum wage. Of course they couldn't. And by staying they had doffed their corporate caps to the new order where their influence was all played out.

He had been careful to keep James Hawkes in the loop every step of the way. And when the time came, Hawkes would take a seat in the Cabinet and if the PM's plotting, scheming colleagues didn't like it, then his plotting, scheming colleagues could shove it where the sun never shone.

And Price was angry.

Christopher had delighted in freezing Price out. Right out. Price had been given the job of drawing together all the corporate strings. He had been delegated to work out who would be able to supply the feeding stations and the soup and who would build the dormitory blocks and deliver the food. He had been given logistics, not policy. And he had hated it.

Pendleton saw the resentment on Price's chiselled face the moment he strode into his office.

Resentful and angry.

Well of course he was angry. Pendleton had caught them on the hop. Every single one of them. Out of the blue he had announced a cabinet reshuffle. Holmes had been moved from the Home Secretary to Transport Secretary. Holmes who been seen as the coming man. Young, with a wife who looked good on the tele and the kind of blandness that the media deemed crucial for high office. Well he was gone now. Sidelined to dealing with jams on the M25 and the wrong kind of snow on the railways.

Smug wanker.

Not so smug now. Almost in tears in the cabinet meeting. Unable to comprehend the fact that his smooth path to the top had just run over the edge of a cliff.

And in his place Christopher Pendleton had chosen John Taylor. His man. His man for twenty-five years. Taylor had been the one who had pushed through Pendleton's selection for his first seat. And as a reward Christopher had hired him as his secretary. His right hand man. His minder. His enforcer. Taylor was as hard and uncompromising as the Yorkshire pit village that had spawned him. He did what needed doing. He trod on toes that needed treading on. He scared the living daylights out of just about everyone. Christopher eased him into a safe seat and then Taylor reciprocated and successfully managed Christopher's ascent to the Party Leadership.

And when Christopher had walked through the doors of Number 10, he had made John Taylor his Chief Whip.

And that hadn't surprised anyone.

But when the hit man had been unveiled as the new Home Secretary, it had surprised everyone. They had all assumed that Taylor would always be a backroom man. A player in the shadows. A murky presence. No way would he ever be wheeled out into the light. How could he be? He was ugly and he dressed badly. He spoke with a Yorkshire accent that was thick enough to cut bread with. He was a bachelor. He drove a car that was lucky if it got twenty to the gallon and he had never shown any sign of giving a shit about it.

And he smoked.

In public.

As if that was an OK thing for a politician to do.

And now he was suddenly a member of the big three at the top of the pile under the Prime Minister. Home Secretary. His Majesty's Home Secretary. And His Majesty would be appalled. No doubt he would choke on his organic carrots.

The press were bouncing. It wasn't that they were necessarily all that upset about John Taylor's meteoric rise. No, in fact it was pretty good news for them. They would have hours of fun with the new chain-smoking Home Secretary.

They were bouncing because they hadn't known. Hadn't been given so much as a clue. No leaks. No hints. And they didn't like that. They took it as their right to be tipped off. To be given notice. To be given a sneak peek. Favours for favours. Privileged access.

Well not this time boys.

This time you got to hear at the same time as the rest of the country.

Like it or lump it.

Bastards.

Pendleton marched to his desk and hung his jacket over the back of his chair. He reached for a decanter and fixed a tumbler of malt and drained it down. The he fixed another. And then he turned to look into Price's disapproving eyes. Price of course was a teetotaler. A mineral water man. A five-portions-of-fruit-and-veg-a-day man. And Pendleton knew well enough that he had been hammering the bottle pretty hard over the last few weeks. His wife had yapped on and on and on about it. Well screw her. And screw Price. No doubt he had been sending reports back to his masters. The PM is drinking too much. The PM is becoming volatile. The PM seems to think he is in charge of the country.

Well screw them.

Bastards.

He gave Price a leering grin. "Just live with it Price. Churchill got through a bottle a day right the way through World War Two and he did OK. Well, didn't he Price?"

Price said nothing. He just stared. Malevolent.

"I need you to make yourself scarce now. I have a meeting. John is coming round."

"You should have told us about that."

"Oh should I? And why is that then Price? Since when were you my boss? My line Manager? Since never. That's when. So I suggest you get yourself the hell out of here. But first, I think we should get a couple of things crystal clear. Your role is to make sure that everyone in the private sector are all pulling in the same direction when this thing goes live. You make the feeding stations happen. You make the food happen. You make the dormitories happen. And you make it happen like clockwork. No late deliveries. No running out of carrots. No delays in construction contracts. You lot are always banging on about how bloody superior you all are. Well now it's time to put your money where your mouth is. That is your part Price. And that is all. National Security is none of your business. That is my job and you will play no part in it."

The door opened without anyone knocking and John Taylor came in complete with burning cigarette. His beady eyes latched onto the tumbler in Pendleton's hand.

"That looks a bloody good idea Chris. Ah. You must be the famous Mr Price. Lester's rent boy. What's up with him Chris? He looks like he's just swallowed a rotten bit of fish."

"I've just been pointing out the lie of the land to him. I don't think he likes it much."

Taylor chuckled. "Well that's bloody tough, isn't it? Poor old Pricey. Not so high flying after all. Well, tha' best trot off back to Lester and tell him that we're not doing as we're bloody told. And while you're at it, tell him to piss off from me. Now then. Off you pop. There's a good lad."

Price's sun tanned face was by now white with anger. Karate was one of his hobbies and he yearned with all his heart to try it out on the leering Yorkshireman. But he didn't. Instead he collected his laptop and closed the door quietly.

"Tosser."

The Prime Minister smiled. "I'll drink to that. Come on. Grab a pew. How've you got on?"

"Aye. Not bad. I asked about. Discreet like. And it seems that all roads lead to Dyson."

"Never heard of him."

"That's the whole point. Just about nobody has heard of him. He's a shadows man. Always has been."

"Well shed some light on him for me."

Taylor lit up and sat down and took half a tumbler of scotch in one go. "He comes from old money in Shropshire somewhere. Big spread. Sheep and fat cattle and all that. His dad had a bloody good war by all accounts. Came out a Colonel. DSO. MC. Tanks if I remember rightly. One of Monty's boys. Must have seeded his son and heir more or less as soon as he got back home. Young Sebastian popped into the world in 1945. Prep school. Public school. Oxford. Bit of a lad by all accounts. Could have been turfed out on more than one occasion until daddy intervened to smooth things over. Recruited at Oxford and was supposed to go into MI6 but got siphoned off into more unofficial stuff."

"Unofficial?" Pendleton gave an interested raise of an eyebrow.

"You know the kind of stuff, Chris. All that stuff that's boxed up and locked away for a hundred years. The nasty stuff. The stuff none of us ever likes to talk about much."

The Prime Minister chuckled and thanked his God and maker for the 100 year rule.

"Got to dip his wick for the first time in Aden in 1967. After that it was mostly Ireland. He was a part of several cowboy type ops which by all accounts were pretty successful and completely deniable. Came home in the mid-eighties to do his bit against the miners. Seems to have been involved in the Balkans to some extent. For the last ten years he has been a director of Rutland International. Heard of them?"

"No."

Taylor chuckled. "Good. The less people that have heard of Rutland International the better. It's a private company. Limited mind. Accounts posted and lodged at Companies House and all that. They label themselves as security consultants and 90% of their work comes in from His Majesties Government."

"Security Consultants? So who are they really and why do we give them so much work?"

"They're mainly highly skilled lads who aren't supposed to be needed any more. Ex 14th Intelligence lads from Ireland. Cold War warriors laid off after the Wall came down. A few South Africans. A few Yanks. They do the wet work for us, boss. You probably don't really want to know any more than that. They're very good at what they do and they're bloody discreet."

"So I could ask them to make Lester Gall disappear?"

"And so he would." Taylor clicked his fingers. "Just like that. But it would cost and that kind of thing is hard to keep a lid on. There was some talk that the Israelis paid the lads to disappear Robert Maxwell. Who knows? Probably just a fairytale."

"So why is this Sebastian Dyson the man for us, John?"

"There is just about nobody in the bloody realm with more experience in keeping the lid on. And that's what we're going to have to do, Chris. Make no mistake about it. This isn't going to be no sodding picnic. People are going to be very, very pissed off and we're going to have to come down on them like a tonne of bricks. We'll have to go in hard right from the get go. Hard as bloody nails, and nobody is going to like it much. And that means we'll need the right team of lads up top to make sure everything happens as needs to happen. Dyson had some good thoughts on that part."

"Like?"

"You need to split Cobra." Cobra was the committee that Downing Street convened in any national emergency.

"Go on."

"You have Cobra One which is all down to feeding and housing. You chair it. The business is all about getting the feeding stations up and running and building the dormitories. Then you have Cobra Two which will do all the public order stuff. Dyson had some recommendations. Keep the team small. You, me and him of course. He recommends Parker to represent the cops. It will put a few noses out of joint, but nobody will die."

Parker was Number Two at the Metropolitan Police. Number One would not be a happy bunny. "Why Parker?"

"Dyson reckons he's got the biggest bollocks. Won't go all limp wristed when the riot squad need to pile in."

Pendleton winced but waved his old friend on.

"Then you need to create a new military post. Commander in Chief Home Forces. Give the job to General Lockhead. Dyson knew him when he was a colonel in Ireland back in the eighties. Hard as, apparently. West at MI5 is good enough. And that is enough. Small team and no bullshit."

"Only six?"

"Aye. And I agree with him all the way. Just so long as you get the right six. We're going to need lads who don't flinch, Chris. This thing is going to be a complete and utter bastard for at least six months. We don't want any passengers."

Pendleton pondered for a while. "It will have to be seven. I'm going to ask James Hawkes to come on board as well."

Now it was Taylor's turn to ponder. Not for long. A big grin spread across his raddled face. "You cunning old bastard Chris. Make sure he gets his share of blood on his hands and then he can't get all holier than thou at Prime Minister's questions. Bloody right. Think he'll agree?"

"I think so. Anything else?"

"Aye. Dyson says we need to be ready to roll things out in stages. We need to apply force in steadily increasing doses. These steps will need to be pre planned and it will be up to Cobra Two to press the button each time. And soldiers on the streets is the last resort."

"To bloody right it is."

"He suggests we have a guinea pig town where we try out each step before rolling it out nationwide."

"A guinea pig town. Jesus Christ John. Did he have anywhere in mind?"

"He did. Rollerton."

Pendleton frowned. "That's up in Scotland isn't it? Why the hell Rollerton?"

"There's method in the madness boss. Number One. Statistically, Rollerton has the highest percentage of inhabitants on sickness or dole of any town in Britain with a population of over 100,000. Which means that statistically it has the greatest economic reliance on the tax payer's pound of any town in Britain with a population of over 100,000. Number two. It's in Scotland."

"What has that got to do with anything?"

"Dyson reckons this whole thing will play out worst in the nether regions so to speak. Scotland. Wales. Northern Ireland. The North. Cornwall. They will see it as a London plot and they will kick off accordingly. There will be a Nationalist element to their discontent. If we learn how to stop the rot in Rollerton, then we'll have a template to stop the rot everywhere else."

"Christ John, you make it sound like war."

"Well that's what it's going to be isn't it Chris? Don't stick your head in the sand lad. It's going be down to batons and boots. And let's hope to bloody hell that's all it's down to. If it gets to rubber bullets and tear gas, we're headed for the shite."

The Prime Minister of Great Britain and Northern Ireland answered with a grave nod. "If it gets to rubber bullets and tear gas we're not headed for the shite. We're in it. Right up to our necks."

Taylor stayed until after two.

Two thirds of a bottle of scotch

Detail, detail and more detail.

What would the Americans say? The Europeans? The Commonwealth? The Holier than thou bastard in Buckingham Palace? Should access for the foreign media be restricted? Should they pass new laws to muzzle the BBC?

Details, details and more details.

How to run a police state in the 21st Century.

Feed the masses.

Keep the masses in line.

Keep them back.

At last Taylor checked his watch and heaved himself to his feet. "Come on boss. You look knackered. And half pissed. Get yourself off to bed."

Pendleton nodded and bade his old partner a good night.

But he didn't get himself off to bed. Instead he poured another drink. Stared into more space.

For a while he had managed to feel almost upbeat about what was about to unravel. Part was a pure power kick. He understood that. Telling the smug preening bastards in the media to go stuff themselves. But there was a more. Of course it was going to hard. Obviously. But maybe it was exactly what the country needed. A short, sharp shock and then Britain could get on with becoming a player again.

All his life he had watched the benefits culture grow and grow like a cancer. It was a cancer that drained all the ambition and drive out of successive young generations. They had their parents and grandparents as role models. Why work when to do so would never get you as much as you could wrangle out of the state. The Nanny State. The idiotic state represented by hundreds of thousands of paid lackeys who ticked their boxes and doled out their crisis loans and bedding allowances and Christ knew what else. Culling the benefit culture was just what the country needed, and in years to come history would come to see Christopher Pendleton as a visionary. The man who put the Great back into Great Britain. The man who did what needed to be done. The man who set a drifting nation back on course again.

Of course the poor sods left out in the cold wouldn't like it. They'd hate it. And many would be condemned to spend the rest of their wretched lives sleeping in dorms and eating at the food stations every day. But many others would soon come to see that it was all for the best. The ones in jobs and working. The ones who would see their taxes chopped. The ones who would still have decent schools for their kids and hospitals when they got sick and pensions and care for their mums and dads. And a well motivated police force to keep them safe. Every month there would be more in their pay packets and they would realise just how much they had been coughing up to keep Benefits Britain on the tracks.

But now he wasn't so sure.

He could feel the darkness closing in.

He had no regrets about bringing John Taylor to the top table. He needed him. He had always needed him. But with John Taylor came the hard reality. And the men who lived their lives in the shadows.

Off the maps.

Under the radar.

Men who did bad things that were hidden away for at least a hundred years.

Probably forever.

And now Christopher Pendleton knew that he was being sucked into their world.

And he would soon be the man expected to sign off on bad things.

Bad things and bad men.

And maybe history might well remember him fondly. But of course history would never know the half of it.

But he would. And he would have to live with it.

It would be his cross to bear.

Jason spent a fortnight patiently gathering material. He had discussed a plan of attack with the Fridge and she felt it would be best if he cracked on and wrote the whole series of features before returning to London. He told her that this would need at least a month, maybe even six weeks.

She said that was fine but only after first checking that he was still in accommodation that wasn't about to lead to an eye-watering expenses claim. He assured her that when she eventually got to run her eyes over his claim she would probably climb across the desk and hug him out of sheer gratitude for his frugality. She told him that such an outcome was extremely unlikely.

Jason spent his days on the Greenfield estate and slowly but surely he became an accepted piece of the local furniture. Most days, D-Zed acted as his guide and door-opener. And with each day the two men got along better. They discovered they had much in common despite the different roads they had taken. Jason had headed for the bright lights of the capital whilst Ronald Pickup had stayed home in Greenfield. But they had both come from the same streets. The same school. The same fading light of a town that had lost its reason for being.

Most days Jason simply drove round to Pickup's house and hung out. It was a place where the stories of Benefit Britain came through the door every day. The kids soon accepted him and they were his ticket to finding the tales that the Fridge was so convinced would woo potential advertisers. Twenty-five years after Thatcher's tearful fall, Greenfield was still paying the price of her great rationalisation. Jason was introduced to grandfathers who had done forty years in the old carpet factory before being paid off to a life on the dole. There were fishermen from boats which could no longer catch enough fish to break even as a result of EC quotas. There were families where nobody had done a day's work in three generations. Single mums. Families of eight where any kind of work would be financial suicide so great was their benefit take. Pensioners living a third world existence having had their savings destroyed by the great financial crisis of 2008.

After a week he found another assistant who many years earlier had been in his class. Sheena Cope had been a girl with a future every bit as bright as his back then. A father who had a safe as houses managerial position in the Council. A mother who was an accountant. She was good looking and in the top 10% with her standard grades. Then she picked the wrong boyfriend and things took a nose dive. Dope turned to ecstasy turned to Cocaine turned to Valium turned to Heroin. The wrong boyfriend disappeared off on a five to Barlinnie and her family washed their hands of her. Then it was hostel-land and Hepatitis C and shrivelled veins and gutter-level prostitution. Two weeks before she turned thirty, she was caught with three hundred blue Valium on her person which proved to be the last straw for the Sheriff who packed her off to Corton Vale prison for three years.

Jail turned out to be life-saver. She stabilised herself on a Methadone programme and stuck to it when she was liberated. Against all odds, she never started using Heroin on top of her prescription and instead focused on rebuilding her failing health. Two years of a proper diet and no drink was enough to de-activate the Hep C and by the time she turned 40 life was better if not perfect. Her damning criminal record meant that work was out of the question, but she managed to fill her time with several college courses. At last she got herself a place as a volunteer youth worker at the Rollerton Youth Centre, known to one and all as The Rollie. She was reliable and punctual and worked well with the kids. After a year, she was granted a sixteen-hour-a-week paid position.

For a while Sheena and Ronald had been an item, but it had drifted away. However they still remained firm friends and she was a regular at his unofficial drop ins when she was not working at the Rollie. At first Jason found it hard to get his head around the fact that the woman he was introduced to was really the Sheena he remembered from class. He hadn't aged all that well, but compared to Sheena he was Cliff Richard. She was a stick-thin bag of bones and tattoos. Her face was not so much lived in as trampled on. She had the yellowed look of a sixty-year-old who had nailed two packs a day from the age of thirteen.

But appearances were deceptive. Within the shrunken body was the same bright girl whose future had once seemed so mapped out. For five years she had been fiercely political and she jumped at the chance of helping Jason to expose the long-term legacy of the Thatcher hurricane that had torn through Rollerton so many years before.

Sheena was his ticket to the darkest corners of the Greenfield Estate. The squats where the heroin addicts who had fallen all the way to the gutters of life eked out their desperate existences. The terrible front rooms with much loved decorations where broken mothers gazed yearningly at heart breaking photos of sons and daughters lost to drugs. Fellow Methadone users with stumpy brown teeth who had been deemed unemployable for years and years. Never mind your qualifications. Never mind the person within. Once a junkie always a junkie. Dirty junkie. Filthy junkie.

Removed children.

Grand parents trying to make ends meet whilst looking after the infants of their addicted children.

Zombie-like figures dosed up to their eye balls on huge prescriptions of Methadone and Valium and anti-depressants. Supposedly stable, but in reality dosed to a world of watching hour after hour of daytime TV without taking any of it in.

Days of rain and days of dust.

Flats with no power and stinking piles of takeaway cartons.

Foil on coffee tables pulled from skips.

Needles and needles and needles.

The lower depths.

The mire.

It ate into Jason like a kind of wasting disease. So many faces he vaguely remembered from school now stretched and wrecked by the long years of addiction. A whole generation lost and nobody seemed to have noticed. The drug story had been done to death. It had become yesterday's news. A silent plague that continuously stalked the litter strewn streets and alleys of sink estate Britain.

Here was where Thatcher's children hid away from their bleak reality. The kiss of a needle. The balm of the bottle. Pills and powders and potions. And once a fortnight the magic piece of plastic would draw a few notes at the Post Office counter and life could continue to repeat and repeat and repeat.

A dead zone.

Forgotten. Irrelevant.

An embarrassment swept so far under the carpet that nobody remembered the sweeping.

All over Britain there were towns like Rollerton. Towns that once had a purpose, but not any more. Coal towns. Fishing towns. Market towns. Steel towns. Aluminium towns. Ship-building towns. All over the old west in fact. In Germany and Russia and Poland all the way to the hills of West Virginia and the shores of Lake Michigan. Places the world didn't need any more. People the world didn't need any more. Used-up and washed-up and kept going with plastic cards that produced a few notes at the Post Office counter once a fortnight.

Jason started collecting statistics and doing sums. He added the numbers on the sick to the numbers on the dole. And then he added in the youngsters on utterly meaningless training courses. Then he added in the ones serving out community service sentences. Then he added in the pensioners. And then he added in all the ones overseeing it all. Policemen and prison warders and lawyers living off legal aid. *Job Centre* workers and probation workers and social workers and clerks to the court. Drugs workers and assistant pharmacists.

On and on and on.

Thatcher had deemed it wrong for the tax payer to prop up places that once upon a time made stuff.

Instead she had spawned a new industry that lived off the consequences.

He tried to get his head around the cost of it all. The billions and the trillions. And it was impossible to get a handle on where all the billions and trillions actually came from. For a whole week he tried to find out how much money made its way out of Rollerton in the form of VAT and tax. He wanted to compare it with the amount of cash that came the other way in the form of benefits and salaries care of the state. He asked wherever he could think of asking, but the truth was too well hidden. It obviously wasn't the kind of maths that the Government wanted its citizens to do.

Slowly but surely his feature series started to take shape. He fired drafts down the e mail to the Fridge and the in return the Fridge was effusive and encouraging. And despite himself Jason had to admit that he was on the verge of basking in her glow.

Now he was a month into it and all morning his fingers had been dancing over the keys of his laptop. And when he reread his words, he felt the same way about what he had written as he had once done when he was twenty five and the world had seemed so promising.

He cut, copied and pasted and hit send. A last coffee. A last fag. A shave. A clean shirt and then out for another afternoon in Greenfield. He met Sheena in a Café by the Post Office and after two expressos which came in at a price that would have the Fridge cooing with appreciation, they headed out into a thin afternoon drizzle. By now people nodded to him on the streets. Clusters of bored kids said 'Alright Jace.' A passing squad car gave a friendly beep of the horn.

Sheena was on a one-'til-five at the Rollie and Jason had decided to tag along. He set up his lap top in a corner and tuned out the hammering dance music which was the constant choice of din for the kids who waited on a turn at the pool table. In the corner across from him a familiar scene was playing out. These particular chairs seemed to be permanently reserved for a handsome-looking lad in his late teens. He was there most afternoons dressed from head to toe in pristine designer gear. He lolled on his own personal settee with the arrogance of successful youth. During Jason's visits to the Rollie, there had been at least five different girls nuzzled up to him with adoring eyes. Jason wondered how many others who had shared the hallowed cushions now pushed prams around the cracked pavements outside. It was certainly a busy corner. Kids came and went and came and went and Mr Designer's phone seemed to collect a text every ten seconds.

Jason had kept meaning to quiz Sheena about the young prince, but something else had always come up. Now he determined to bring it up. She came over with two mugs of coffee and perched herself on a stool.

"I keep meaning to ask you about the lad in the corner over there. Mr Popular. What's the story?"

` "Oh you know the story well enough."

"How do you mean?"

"It's the same old story as it was when we were that age. That's Donny Baldini."

"Bloody hell. Seriously?"

"Seriously."

"Is he Freddy's boy then?"

"Uh huh. He's Dot's lad."

The Baldinis had been Rollerton's premier crime family for as far back as Jason could remember. Old man Giuseppe had come to Scotland in the Fifties and opened an ice cream parlour. The word was that he had been straight. In those days there had been money enough in ice cream. Banana splits and Harvey Wallbangers and milkshakes and a jukebox that played The Who and The Kinks and Dusty Springfield.

The recession of the early Seventies took the gloss off the ice cream business and somehow the flare wearing youth of the town didn't want to spoil their appreciation of Led Zepellin by brain freeze. What they did want to appreciate their music was dope and lots of it. They had watched the beautiful people of America on the tele and they wanted a piece of it. Giuseppe's son Franco had been more than happy to replace lost cornet sales with a fine variety of pills and powders. The cops had caught up with him when Jason, Douglas, Sally and Sheena had been in S5 and his ten year sentence had caused a major stir. For them, the demise of Franco Baldini was closer to home than most for his son and heir Freddie was also in their class. By the time Jason had left town, Freddy had already taken on the family business and added Heroin to the menu. Where Franco and Giuseppe had maintained the sunshine of their Calabrian roots, Freddy was very much a son of Scotland. He had worked enthusiastically on his hardman persona from primary school and he chose Al Pacino in Scarface as his role model. Dad and Granddad were disgusted, but dad was locked away and granddad was old. Once he had headed south, Jason had completely forgotten the Baldinis.

"Is Freddy still the main man then?"

Sheen shook her head. "Nah. Freddy's dead. Got a taste for his own goods. OD'd years back when he got home from a stretch in Kilmarnock."

"Poor old Freddy."

"Poor old Freddy nothing. He was a bastard."

There was brittle rawness to her voice which warned Jason off trying to fill in the gaps. Doogie had told him how Sheena had suffered some bad, bad times when she was on the game. No doubt Freddy Baldini had played a part in that. He decided to leave well alone.

"So who's running things now then?"

"Dot."

"Dot!"

Dorothy Baldini had been two years behind them at school and had always been the apple of her doting father's eye. She was very much the pampered Italian princess. No way was she ever about to become Rollerton's Godmother. Surely not? But apparently so.

"Dot's been in charge for years now. She must drive the cops round the twist. Every time I ever got lifted it was all they ever asked about. Come on lass, give us something on Dot Baldini. Anything. Give us something and you can have £20 and we'll let you out. They must have raided her thirty times over the years, but they have never got a sniff. Dot's way too smart for them. I doubt if she will be here much longer. Word is that she's done out a place back home in Italy. Swimming pool, the lot."

"And what about this one? Donny."

"Too full of himself if you ask me. Thinks he's God's gift. He'll probably go the way of his uncle."

"And he's in the business then?"

Sheena laughed. "Good God Jace, are you blind! What do you think he's up to now?"

He shrugged, a little embarrassed. "I don't know. Hanging out I suppose."

"Don't be daft. He's at it. Dealing. And moving stolen goods about the place."

"I haven't seen anything."

"Well he's hardly going to wave a bag of pills about is he? No. Dot's got him quite well trained. He's co-ordinating. That's what all the text messages are about. All over Greenfield there all weens on mountain bikes making deliveries and collecting cash. Here is where he takes his orders and shows a bit of front. He looks after the youth market. Dope and vallies and eckies. Dot keeps him away from the smack and crack side of the business. He's on his learning curve."

"What's he like?"

"Used to be quite a nice kid, but now he's well on the way to becoming as big a bastard as his uncle."

Jason drained his mug and got to his feet. "Reckon I'll have word."

Sheena smiled. "Best of British."

He crossed the room and took a vacant chair opposite where Donny Baldini was flashing off yet another text.

"Alright Donny."

The boy's eyes never moved from the screen of the all singing, all dancing phone that was no doubt the envy of every kid on Greenfield.

"Know you, do I?"

"Nope. But your uncle did. He was in my class."

"Lucky him. Well if it's my uncle your after, you're going to need a Ouija board. He's dead."

"Aye. I heard."

"No doubt from Junkie Sheena. From what I hear my uncle used to sell her alongside all his other products. A tenner for fifteen minutes. Just goes to show how desperate people can be. Don't you think?"

Jason felt himself bristle. But he didn't show it. That would be unprofessional. And he was a frontline investigative journalist. The Fridge had told him so that very morning.

"That's not very nice."

"No it isn't. Does it look like I give a shit?"

The audience liked that. They laughed right on cue, relieved to be back on track. The Ouija board reference had gone clean over their heads.

"I'm Jason by the way. Jason Marsh. I'm from *The Enquirer*."

"Of course you are. The big city reporter everyone seems to be getting so excited about." Still his graceful fingers glided across the buttons of his phone. "Can't see what all the fuss is about myself. You just look like a sad, bald twat to me. But hey. What does it matter what I think? I guess they probably think that you can make them famous. Real celebrities. Pictures in the paper and all that. Dickheads."

"Not very nice."

The phone snapped shut and disappeared into a pocket.

"Is there a point to all this or are we just passing the time of day?"

Jason smiled and made a show of taking a notebook from his pocket. "French kids take to the streets and riot. Scottish kids mope about and sulk. Why do you think that is the case Donnie? What would provide the spark? Or who? Could it be you Donnie? Could you be the man to light a fire on the streets of Greenfield?"

This brought on a smile. Gleaming white teeth framed by olive skin. "What me? How could that happen Mr Journalist? I'm just an unemployed teenager? What influence could I possibly have?"

"Just another loser in knocked off designer gear then?"

That got rid of the smile. "I think it might be time for you to rejoin your junkie pal now Mr Journalist."

"I have my camera with me Donny. Would you like your picture in the paper? Which is your best profile do you think? Left or right?"

"Piss off Baldie. I'm busy."

Back to the phone. Back to the buttons.

"Say hi to your mum for me won't you Donnie."

"Whatever."

By the time he re-crossed the room, Sheena was on her feet and pulling on a coat.

"Fag?"

He nodded. A fag seemed a hell of a fine idea. Outside the thin rain was still thin and the grey streets were still grey. He took nicotine on board and allowed it to sooth his temper.

"So?"

He grinned. "He's not the most personable young man I've ever met. Called me a sad, bald twat."

Sheena chuckled. "Oh dear. I don't suppose he was particularly complimentary about me."

"He wasn't."

They didn't speak for a few moments. Instead they stared down the empty street which was slowly being swallowed into the grey October evening. Soon the street lamps would light up the scene in dreary orange. Another Greenfield day was wandering to a close.

"So what did you expect?"

He shrugged. "I don't suppose I ever expect anything. But it still gets you down all the same."

"Welcome to Greenfield."

"Aye. Welcome to Greenfield."

ADEN, 1967

Lieutenant Hamish McGee was working through his list when the stranger from London came to call. The list was a leaving town list, and it was a list he was delighted to tackle. The Regiment had only been in Aden for a few months, but it already felt quite long enough.

When the Argyll and Sutherland Highlanders had landed, the place had been more or less in open revolt. It had become a trend by now. All over the world the Brits were being kicked out of the places that had once been coloured red on the maps that had adorned the classrooms of his childhood.

No so much red now. A splash here and a sliver there. Now the red swathes of the map denoted the turf of the Russians. The British Empire was breathing its last like a fifty-a-day smoker with TB. On the boat, the briefings had said that it was their job to oversee a smooth transition.

Smooth!

Bloody joke. They arrived to find the locals armed and ready to lop off a few heads. And the bloody suits had issued orders that demanded the Regiment should stay well clear of the Crater district of the city where most of the nutjobs hung out. They reckoned it wouldn't look too good on the tele if the Argyles were seen shooting up the natives so near to independence. Best to stay in camp and keep their heads down. Like good chaps. Don't want to be seen going over the top like the Yanks in Vietnam. Apparently the Prime Minister was quite adamant about that part. The Brits had to be seen to be better. Stiff upper lip and all that.

And the Argyles? Well they would just have to lump it. If a few of them were dropped by snipers and bombs, then that was just tough. Nobody would be too bothered anyway. After all, when all was said and done, the Argyll and Sutherland Highlanders were just a bunch of thugs from Glasgow. Rough and ready types. Eminently disposable.

Thankfully their CO had seen things different. Mad Mitch had more or less told the politicians to stuff their orders right up their collective arses. He had the lads march straight into the middle of Crater with the bagpipes playing all the way. And the towel heads had barely fired a shot. Not one single casualty. Bloody marvellous.

And then 'Argyll Law' had been put into operation. As in 'if you step out of line we'll kick your teeth down the back of your throat'. All of a sudden Crater was nice and quiet. No more snipers. No more bombs. Just a whole lot of well behaved towel heads. And had the bloody puffed up generals given the Regiment a jot of credit? Had they buggery. If they had had their way, Colonel Mitchell would have been dragged in front of a Court Marshall. Thankfully the Press had got a hold of the story and called the boss 'Mad Mitch'. The word was that he had become a hero figure at home. So had the lads. Quite bloody right too.

Enough was enough.

After the re-occupation of Crater, Hamish McGee's company had been tasked to keep a lid on things in El Kabir, a village on the edge of the desert about four miles out of the city. They had been there for three months now and every one of them was heartily sick of the place. Every day there was some kind of incident and already the company had taken seven casualties, though thankfully no fatalities. A routine was now in place. Every day as the heat eased out of the dry desert air, groups of young men would gather into a mob to throw stones at the soldiers. By now the word from London was clad in iron. Show restraint. Show discipline. No more taking the towel heads down the nearest alley for a proper kicking.

The lads were raging. The endless heat and dust and filthy chlorinated water didn't help either. Nor the miserable dehydrated rations which gave a whole new meaning to the word inedible. In theory, the idea behind the god awful food was that it was hygienic. The fact that half of the lads were shitting their guts out all day every day tended to disprove that, but nobody seemed much interested.

The whole thing was a complete bitch. They were expected to sit out day after day in the heat and dust and flies and let the towelies chuck their stones and do nothing in return. Why? Because Harold Bloody Wilson didn't want anyone to think bad of him. Yorkshire prick.

Thankfully the end was now in sight. It seemed that they were to be withdrawn back to the main camp near the docks in less than a fortnight. Then it would be a boat home and the towelies could have their fly ridden shithole all to themselves. The main task now was how to effect a fast withdrawal under the cover of darkness. They would need to offer no clues to their departure because the moment they started to move out would be the moment of maximum vulnerability. Seven casualties was enough. More than enough.

And then his visitor arrived.

A sports jacket and a Panama hat. Where the hell did London find these people? In London probably. Or the Home sodding Counties.

"McGee isn't it?"

"Yes."

"Splendid. Marvellous. Got anything to drink by any chance?"

"Not whilst we're in a combat zone, no."

"No. Don't suppose you have. I'm Dyson by the way. Sebastian Dyson."

"And you are from where?"

This induced a smirking sort of expression. "Now that would be telling wouldn't it old chap. Let's just say I'm from the cloak and dagger side of the fence shall we?"

McGee sighed. This was all he needed. A chinless spook hell bent of his very own version of *The Thirty-Nine Steps*.

"I have not received any orders regarding your arrival."

Dyson gave his nose a theatrical tap with his forefinger. "Well I'm not here actually. Under the radar and all that. Am I right in thinking that the wogs have been getting a tad uppity?"

McGee didn't give him a response.

"Well. That's the kind of picture that little dicky birds have been painting for me. And I gather that orders from on high say that your chaps are not allowed to do anything about it. It really must be awfully trying. I bet your lads are just bursting to knock a few heads together. Isn't politics an awful drag, don't you think?"

"What do you want Dyson?"

"Well. Mind if I sit? Super. The thing is McGee, my people would like to conduct a bit of an experiment and if things go to plan, it might just prove beneficial to you chaps. My information suggests that El Kabir only has one source of fresh water. The well in the main square, right?"

McGee nodded.

"Good. Now. I could do with borrowing one of your chaps who knows his way around making things go bang."

"We don't have anyone like that."

"Naughty, naughty. Of course you have. Sergeant Wilson. I know and you know that Sergeant Wilson is a dab hand at making things go bang."

"So what if he is?"

"This is what we are going to do. Sergeant Wilson will rig up this nice Jeep of mine so that it is ready to go bang. Then we will park it by the well and in the middle of the night, when the whole wide world is fast asleep, we will make it go BOOOM!! With me so far? Triff. Of course everyone will assume that the bomb is the work of naughty, bad towelies, no doubt being paid by Moscow or Cairo or wherever. Now. The key to Sergeant Wilson's big bang is that it will render the well dry. Oh deary me. No well, no water. Lots of thirsty wogs. Now of course that wouldn't do at all. We couldn't have that, could we now Major McGee? Not on our watch. That isn't how the British Empire looks after those under our care. Good Lord no. Of course we will look after the little treasures. We will bring a tanker out from the city filled with lovely fresh water. And we will keep bringing out tankers until our chaps have done what needs to be done to re-open the well."

"Is this all some kind of pathetic effort to generate some positive press?"

"Good Lord no. Heaven forbid. The press won't be allowed within a country mile. OK. Look here McGee, you seem a decent enough sort of chap. Salt of the earth and all that. So I'm going to let you in on a bit of a secret. Well. A lot of a secret, actually. There is going to be little something added to the water. A very special little something. If things work out as we very much hope they will work out, then I rather think you might find that the wogs will lose their appetite for throwing stones."

"Bloody hell."

"Now this is between you and me McGee. Completely and utterly between you and me for ever and ever Amen. There will be no point in you telling any fabulous tall tales to anyone as you will soon discover that I was never here. I simply don't exist, you see, Major McGee? I think it would be much better if you are simply grateful that I can make your withdrawal back to base so much more straightforward. Don't you agree?"

McGee was disgusted by the man and the pit he had crawled up from. But he was long enough in the tooth that there would be no point in arguing the toss. If he tried to kick up a fuss, then his career would be down the pan in the blink of an eye. He knew how things worked well enough.

"Wilson will have the Jeep parked and ready by 21:00. Will you be staying to watch?"

"Of course I will old chap. Wouldn't miss it for the world."

"Well. Just stay out of the way."

Dyson's bang lit up the sky above El Kebir at three o' clock the next morning. The British responded to the needs of the inhabitants a little after lunch time when a tanker filled with 2000 gallons of fresh water arrived in the square. And as the day started to fade to night, the usual mob turned out to hurl the usual stones.

But when riot time arrived the next day, there wasn't a soul to be seen. Suddenly the streets and alleys of El Kebir were eerily quiet. The lads couldn't understand what was going on. McGee sent the word around that it was probably some kind of religious thing. Dyson stayed for three days and took notes. Then he left never to be seen again.

A week later, the Argyles pulled out a few hours after the well was restored to working order. Their night withdrawal was completed with ease and there were no casualties. Many times over the years of the rest of his life, Hamish McGee considered telling someone about the stranger in the sports jacket and the Panama hat and the water tankers that kept the mobs from the streets of El Kebir.

But he didn't.

And McGee and El Kebir and 'Mad Mitch' and 'Argyll Rule' faded into history.

Along with the British Empire.

2016

Sebastian Dyson felt like he knew every inch of the glen spread out below him. And yet he also knew that he could never know it fully. Every day it changed. Sometimes it was sparkling and green in the sunshine of the spring. Sometimes dark and brooding in the Autumn rain. Or crisp and glittering white in the depths of winter. Sometimes framed by a vivid blue sky. Sometimes wrapped in heavy mist.

The heron was back today.

First time in ages. Where had it been? A neighbouring stream that was offering fatter trout? Or maybe it had got lost. Taken a wrong turn somewhere? Or maybe it was a different heron altogether?

The more you think you know everything there is to know, the more you realise you barely ever scratch the surface.

He carefully mixed blue and grey oils to get the right colour from the waiting heron. Just a blur of colour. So very still. Some grey in the midst of all the other greys of autumn. A hunter almost invisible in the fading light.

How many times had he painted the glen? Had to be hundreds. The rough walls of his cottage were crammed with his efforts. None of them were much good. That didn't matter. They weren't about merit. They were his way of draining his mind of poison.

When he had been a young man it had never been a problem. In those days he had been consumed by certainty. For years he had thrashed through his childhood rebelling against everything in his path. Why had that been? He had no idea. It had seemed like the right thing to do at the time.

The memories brought a smile to his lean face. Canings in the headmaster's study. Endless lines to be written out in dreary rooms with lino floors and sunshine and the sounds of cricket easing in through high windows. The troubled expression of his Dean at college. Why Dyson? Why on earth would you want to do such a thing?

Crazy binges. Sometimes in black tie. Other times in back streets. Drugs and girls and driving like a lunatic.

Why? He still had no idea.

Always he had been waiting to be given something that would meet his desires. Drink and drugs and girls and trouble had never come close. Nor sport. Nor study.

And then he had been asked the question and he had said yes without so much as a second's thought. Why on earth had he done that? It hadn't been out of patriotism. Anything but. There had been nothing about Britain that he had ever liked much, least of all its people. His father had been big on patriotism, but he had never liked it when his son had questioned the logic of the emotion.

How much of our land was paid for from selling slaves father?

Smack.

There had been many who had tried to beat the wilfulness out of him, none more so than his father. Old British money had always prided itself on its ability to beat its young into shape. Prep schools and public schools and rugger. Canes and beastings. Ritualistic bullying every step of the way.

Even when he was very young, he had known inside himself that the more they beat him, the more he would make a point of doing the exact opposite of what they wanted him to do.

Why?

He had never known why. The best thing about being old was that he no longer saw the point in asking. Instead he spent more and more time in his Scottish hideaway and sat for hour after hour after hour painting the glen.

The benefit of hindsight told him that the men who recruited him must have seen his lack of patriotism as a major plus point. And his feral wildness. That was why they had kept him clear of the official services. Patriots were funnelled into the Army and MI5 and MI6. The ones like Sebastian Dyson were quietly moved into offices which bore the names of fictitious corporations.

The places where the British practised their dark arts. The Germans and Americans and Russians always used brute force. Sheer numbers. Tanks by the thousand. Artillery barrages that shook the earth. Blitzkreig. Shock and awe. Conquest by uber-power. Sledge hammers smashing nuts into a million pieces.

Not so the British.

Not that strange cold people from their cold, wet island. They would nip away at the edges. Manipulate. A car accident here. A scandal there. Share options. Places on the boards of blue chip companies. Invitations to white tie events. Knighthoods. Disappearances. Divide and rule. Build up and knock down.

And even in those early, early days Sebastian had known that there had always been a place for people like himself. Those with no beliefs. No God and no creed. No love and no hate. Just an unscratched itch. Just a yearning for something beyond the drink and the drugs and the beatings.

And he had done their work. Done it well. With class. With élan.

For years.

In Aden and Ireland and South Yorkshire.

He had erased threats. He had smoothed paths. He had learned the dark arts.

Why?

There never was a why. For it was always a game. The best game on the table. Maybe if life had been different, he might have become a compulsive gambler. Or a crack addict. Or a bungee jumper.

Instead he had signed up to do his country's dirty work.

Quietly. In the deep shadows where there would never be medals or knighthoods. For years there hadn't even been much money. Then they had asked him to join Rutland International and his bank accounts had filled up fast. Not that he had any particular need for money. When his father had died Sebastian had sold up everything the family had taken so many hundreds of years to accumulate and donated the lot to *Medcines Sans Frontieres*.

Why had he done that? Was it guilt? Or was it a whim?

Probably neither.

Old age had brought on a few more questions. They didn't particularly trouble him. Of course he wondered about the point of his life. That was normal. Surely every man in his seventies did that. What had he really achieved? Not a lot really. Not with hindsight. The Union Jack still flew over the six counties of Northern Ireland. The deep coal mines of South Yorkshire were still flooded for a thousand years. The inhabitants of the country's mean streets no longer took to the rich streets to throw bricks and bottles. No more Chartists. No more Jarrow marchers. No more Scargills. Now they stabbed each other over a few square yards of drug territory.

And all of it so a very, very few very rich people could stay very rich.

Not much of an achievement really.

But he had played the game with his eyes open. He had never much liked the men he played it for. Loathed and despised them in fact.

It had been the game itself he had loved. Thrived on. And been good at. The best.

And now they wanted him to take his greatest ever role. His King Lear. His Hamlet. His 1812 Overture. His Sistine Chapel.

The fee he had demanded had been ridiculous. He had expected them to haggle him down to a mere fraction of the sum he had come up with off the top of his head. Instead they had agreed without batting an eyelid. It would keep the young French doctors who worked in African war zones in medicines for months to come. Sebastian rather liked that.

Someone, somewhere must have said that Sebastian Dyson was their man. The only show in town. Pay what you have to. Pay whatever it takes.

And they had. Without batting an eyelid.

Much to his surprise he had quite taken to John Taylor. The bluff Yorkshireman was quite unlike any politician Sebastian had ever met before. Not that he had met all that many. Politicians tended to stay well clear of the world he lived in. They preferred to pretend that it didn't really exist. They wanted everything to be deniable.

Taylor made no bones about things.

And now Pendleton wanted to meet face to face.

Why?

Sebastian had no idea why. He certainly didn't mind. The man was paying the bills after all. No doubt he wanted to take a last breath before plunging into the icy water.

He could hear the distant thump, thump of an approaching helicopter. Once upon a time he might have got up from his seat and gone to meet his visitor. Not any more. The Heron didn't like the sound much. It gave up on the trout it was waiting for and flapped away down the glen.

He heard the helicopter land and waited for them to join him. Only when they were a few yards way did he put down his brush and wipe his hands on a cloth.

Christopher Pendleton stepped up and studied the canvas. Then he compared it to the glen below them. Then he plunged his hands into the deep pockets of his overcoat and stared away into the distance.

"Everyone tells me that you are the best at what you do, Mr Dyson."

"Very flattering I'm sure."

"Well are you?"

Sebastian shrugged. "Who knows. Men in my line of work don't tend to lay out their achievements in autobiographies. People have always seemed to be happy enough with what I have done for them."

Pendleton didn't react one way or another. The weight of what was to come was obviously sitting heavy on him.

"So are we going to be successful Mr Dyson? In your opinion?"

"How do you intend to gauge success Prime Minister?"

"Will we keep the lid on?"

Sebastian smiled. "You can always keep the lid on Prime Minister. Every time. The real question is how much of your soul are you willing to give away to make it happen."

"And how much of your soul are you willing to give up Mr Dyson?"

Sebastian smiled. "I'm not all that sure I ever had a soul to start with Prime Minister. If I had, I dare say sure it withered and died many, many years ago. But my soul hardly matters. You will be the one who must carry the consequences. My part is merely to identify the targets and pull the trigger. It will be you who will call the shots."

The rain that had been threatening all afternoon at last started to fall. Cold and clammy. Soon the Prime Minister's hair was soaked onto his scalp but still he stood very still and stared into the distance whilst Sebastian covered his canvas with an oilskin sheet.

At last Pendleton spoke.

"The broadcast is going out on Wednesday. I suppose you best come down to London on Monday."

"OK. No problem. Have you told the Cabinet yet?"

"Wednesday morning. I'm not giving the bastards the chance to leak."

"And what about me Prime Minister? Will I be official?"

"Hopefully not. We certainly won't be releasing anything to the press. You can come and go through the tunnel. No doubt something will get out though. It almost always does. What will they find if they ask questions?"

Sebastian shrugged. "No much. Bits and pieces if they are lucky. Nothing for a front page spread."

"Fair enough."

More silence. More rain. Night came in closer.

"That's that then"

Sebastian smiled. "I dare say it is Prime Minister. I dare say it is."

A slow hour had passed since Jason had opened up his laptop and taken a seat at Doogie's kitchen table. Most of the time he had managed no more than stare at the screen and smoke. He had taken a stab at a title a few times only to delete and light up another. Already two cans of lager had been emptied, crumpled and thrown in the direction of the bin in the corner. One had missed. One had gone in.

On the table was a pile of paper that represented the results of six weeks of work on the Greenfield estate. Notes and quotes. Material enough for a series of six feature articles. Angry Youth. Life On the sick. Single Mums. Long-term Unemployed. Lost to Drugs. Criminalised and shelved. He had called the Fridge in London and once again he had basked in her glow. She told him that the series was shaping up to be really fantastic. And better still, the advertisers agreed. They were all really, really excited about it. In fact they had hardly haggled at all, so convinced were they that Jason was about to reach out to middle-aged, middle-of-the-road, middle England. The country's largest supplier of garden furniture and barbeques hadn't even bothered to haggle the price at all. They had booked six slots straight off the bat. And it was Autumn!

And then the Fridge had surprised him.

"Give it what you need to give it Jason. Don't worry about shocking anyone. And if you feel the need to tip over an apple cart or two then by all means, tip them over. *The Enquirer* is always at its very best when we tip over apple carts."

"Absolutely Amelie. Couldn't agree more. I'll crack on and get tipping."

An hour had passed by and he hadn't tipped over a thing. This was unusual for Jason. As a rule of thumb he could snap open his laptop and nail a story in no time at all, pissed or sober. So why not now? Well that was clear enough. It was because he had started caring again. Lots of people had mucked in and helped him. Doogie, Sally, D-Zed, Sheena, loads and loads of residents of Greenfield, young and old. They had trusted him to tell it as it was. Not to judge. Not to sneer. To explain their reality. To make those who lived lives in luckier and easier places understand.

So no pressure then.

He popped another can and lit another cigarette. Come on Jace. Just crash it down on paper and worry about it later.

SO WHAT WILL IT TAKE FOR OUR YOUNG TO REBEL?

'All summer our TV screens were filled with images of French youngsters battling it out with riot police on the streets of France. Bricks and bottles flew in one direction. Rubber bullets and tear gas

came from the other side. Broken glass and broken heads. Masked faces and helmeted heads. Cars on fire and sirens wailing. Through it all, the streets of Britain remained normal and quiet save for the usual Friday and Saturday night mayhem that has become such a British tradition.

Why?

Are we so much better off than the French? No.

Are our youngsters so much happier with their lot than their French counterparts? Hardly.

Are our policemen more ferociously effective in maintaining order? Maybe more effective, but hardly more ferocious.

So why?

And what would it take for the youth of Britain to take to the streets and start to tear the world down with their rage. Sometimes we are told that this kind of thing simply isn't the British way. Oh the French can get a little hot-headed at times. And the Italians. Even the Americans. But not us. We're above that kind of thing. But is hasn't always been that way. There were times during the Chartist agitations of the Nineteenth Century when the big houses were in danger of burning like torches. Captain Swing and the Luddites. The General Strike. Notting Hill and Toxteth and Handsworth and Brixton. Orgreave.

And then thirty years of nothing. So have our youngsters all been turned into sheep? Compliant? Obedient? Slaves to corporate labels and the latest electronics? Well, the man who calls himself D-Zed certainly thinks so. More than this, he tells them so. Loudly. Every weekend. And five hundred youngsters turn out rain or shine to hear him berate them for their compliance. They even pay £3 each for the privilege.

OK. So who is D-Zed? Where is D-Zed? What is D-Zed?

To answer the question of what it might take to get the young wrapping scarves round their faces and hitting the streets, I decided to take a journey back to my own roots. Rollerton in Scotland. Once upon a time Rollerton had factories and fishing boats. A workforce. An identity. Civic pride. Now it has all disappeared. Now Rollerton has become a Tesco town complete with a high street of boarded windows and charity shops. The people of Rollerton don't work in factories and on fishing boats any more. Those that work have jobs in supermarkets or with the Council or with the NHS. Those who don't work are on the dole or signed-off sick. If they are young, they are corralled onto meaningless courses which keep them clear of the official unemployment figures.

Here is Rollerton's new claim to fame. No town in Britain with a population of over 100,000 has a higher percentage of its citizens drawing their living from the state. If anyone were to take the tax payer's pound out of the Rollerton economy, then there would be no economy left.

Rollerton today bears almost no resemblance to the place I grew up in. It has lost all its pride. All its reason for being here at all. It was never great, but now it has become dismal. Ground down and living off hand outs from the rest of the country.

So how do the young of Rollerton feel about this? Does it make them angry? Do they meet in each other's rooms to plan an uprising? Hardly. At weekends they get plastered and a higher number than in most places take all the pills and powers they can lay their hands on. They spray graffiti and set wheelie bins alight and sometimes they stab each other.

But rebel? I don't think so. I came up here to see D-Zed. D-Zed is actually an ex-schoolmate of mine. Ronald Pickup. Ronald is now closing in on forty and he still lives on the Greenfield estate where he grew up. Every weekend he rents an old carpet showroom and puts on his unique show. It's all about images and lights and film. Trance Dance with a message. The place is always sold out and the atmosphere is electrifying. The first time I went along I was accompanied by two friends – a senior cop and an MSP. Three middle-aged professionals in a sea of sweating kids. And I have to admit it was brilliant. The years dripped away and we were completely lost in the throng as D-Zed berated his audience for being Lester Gall's little sheep. Baaaaaa! He hit us with pictures of Mandela and Malcolm X and Che Guevara and the riots of '68. On and on it went, and after a couple of heady hours anything seemed possible. Paris in 1848. Berlin in 1968. The campus at Berkely.

But as we hit the cold, damp streets it all drained away into the dismal Scottish night. For six weeks I have been asking D-Zed's young followers if they might ever put his words into action. Fight back. Demand more. And all they do is shrug and say dunno. What's the point? Can't be bothered.

Ronald puts on a hell of a show, but he isn't even close to rousing his followers from the stagnant pond of apathy that is Rollerton.

There is a youth centre on the Greenfield Estate. The locals call it the Rollie. Every day a young man sits in the corner and co-ordinates the sale of pills and powders and stolen goods. He wears the *kind of designer clothes you see on the tele. He's smart, good-look-ing and the girls just love him. Apparently they all want to be his bitch. More to the point, he represents the third generation of Rollerton's premier crime family. I won't mention his name because his mum has the means and the bottle to sue and then I would get sacked and never complete my series of Rollerton features. He knows who he is. Everyone in town knows who he is.*

Maybe if this young man ever decided to raise a mob, then things might get a little exciting. He has the required charisma. If you look hard enough, it is possible to see a faint echo of Che.

But will he?

Of course not. Why would he? There money is pouring into his designer pockets and there are still plenty of Rollerton lovelies to impregnate.

And D-Zed? Well his audience stumps up their £3 a head and they certainly hear him. But they don't listen to him. They like the pictures and the lights and the sound. The message is of no interest.

So the message to the Establishment from the dreary streets of Rollerton?

Feel safe.

Feel very safe.

Jason Marsh.
November 2016'

He sat back. He opened up another can. He lit up another cigarette. He re-read and wished he might have been able to say something different. But what else was there to say?

There wasn't about to be a rebellion in Rollerton.

He made a couple of changes and hit 'send'.

By now it was past ten and he was about to go and watch some TV when his mobile rang.

The screen told him that the incoming caller was the Fridge. Working late then. Now why wasn't he surprised about that?

"Jason. It's Amelie."

"Hi Amelie."

"If you would like to go out and do something really silly on expenses I promise to sign the chits. Terrific Jason. Really terrific."

He smiled. "Am I free to bask in your glow then Amelie?"

"Absolutely. You bask away. And treat yourself Jason. Surely Rollerton must have a massage parlour with dreamy Latvian girls."

He chuckled. "Not really my scene boss. I think I'll catch the ten o'clock news instead. Maybe I'll splash out on a haggis supper later on."

"Well throw in a deep fried Mars bar from me. Really Jason. This is excellent work."

"Glad you approve Amelie. Let's hope the advertisers feel they are getting the requisite amount of bang for their buck."

"Oh bugger them. Sometimes we can be reporters Jason. Not often. But sometimes. Keep it up."

Once the call was killed he studied the blank screen of his phone with interest. Maybe the Fridge had a few hidden depths he hadn't noticed. He decided to skip the news and head straight out for the haggis supper.

LIVERPOOL, 1988

Sebastian took in the faded grandeur of the high-ceilinged bar and felt suddenly tired. Tired of himself, tired of the endless dirty games, tired of one dark corner after another. Many of those he had once shared a dormitory with at Eton were now hoovering up the new millions to be had in the resurgent square mile of the City of London. They were living in the gaudy, glitzy light of the new Thatcher miracle. Britain had gone from busted flush to tawdry rich in a blink of an eye. Well at least some of Britain had. The suburbs of the South East had never had it so good. House prices were rocketing and the Middle Classes were wearing brogues and baggy cords and sending their offspring to public school.

Sebastian had spent little of his time in the leafy highways and byways of the stockbroker belt. These were not the kind of places where the Realm had needed defending. The wealth of the land had been firmly re-directed from the have nots to the haves. From the North to the South. From the nether regions to the centre. At the heart of things, a pampered few snorted Cocaine and drove Audi Quattros. On the edges the Peasants had done their level best to revolt. In Ulster and Liverpool and Scotland and South Yorkshire. Sometimes the beaten towns and cities had blazed. For days at a time the pavements were coated in broken glass. For weeks at a time South Yorkshire had been run almost as a police state. There had been many who had hoped to become the next Trotsky. And over the years Sebastian and his fellow shadowmen had been tasked with quietly knocking them down. Honey traps and forgeries and set ups. Dark and dirty deeds that left men and women all broken up and humiliated and wondering just what had happened to them.

By now he knew that his name had become something of a legend in the darker corners of the State. Dyson, the man who gets it done. How? Oh, best never to ask how old boy. Just forget it ever happened and hope to hell that all the papers made it to the incinerator in the basement. He was never invited to meet his betters in the panelled offices of Whitehall. Instead he took his instructions in dingy bars and restaurants. Men who met him would forever look over their shoulders to make absolutely sure nobody was listening in. For to seek the help of Sebastian Dyson was always the last resort of desperate men. Men who were in a corner. Men who had got themselves into a hole. Men who had inadvertently opened up a can of worms. At which point a discreet word would be passed in a club or on the golf course or at the races. Ever heard of a chap called Dyson? I gather he deals with this kind of thing. Reputed to be very discreet. How? Oh you never ask how old boy.

Belfast and Londonderry and Liverpool and Sheffield and Glasgow. Men with gleaming eyes and donkey-jackets on picket lines. Women dressed in the colours of the rainbow at Greenham Common. Pale, hard faces in smoky clubs on streets where the kerbstones were all painted the colour of the Irish Tricolour. NUM Shop stewards in battered old Cortinas with bald tyres. Militant Tendency members with bookshelves stacked high with the writings of Trotsky and Liebknecht. The enemies within.

Sebastian would patiently find their weaknesses. Their addictions and perversions and corruptions. And if they had none of the above, he would create them.

In the end they would all fall from grace. Shattered, frightened faces caught in the flicker of flashbulbs. Frantic denials. Raging anger. Tears. Humiliation. And then a lifetime of utter obscurity.

It had been many years since Sebastian had found any joy in his work. At first the sheer darkness of his art had given him a buzz. Not any more. Now it was simply what he did. From time to time he considered moving on to something else. But what else was there to move on to? And would he be allowed to move on to that something else? Or would people become nervous that he was about to have a mid-life crisis and become some sort of a loose cannon, desperate to unburden his tortured soul to some fearless hack from *The Guardian* or *The*

Washington Post or the *Berliner Zeitung*? No, that wouldn't do at all. Nobody would be ready to risk that. Dyson knew too much for that. The Realm would be under threat. So it would be a car accident on a quiet country road somewhere. Everything would very mundane and dull. A few lines on page seven of a provincial paper. A middle aged man who must have tried to take a corner too fast.

At times the idea had a certain appeal. But never for long. Sebastian wasn't bored enough to crave death. And so he carried on.

This time the venue was a bar in Liverpool's Adelphi Hotel. Every elegant pillar and chandelier spoke of the time when the world's goods had beaten a path to the great port on the grey Mersey. Slaves and sugar and cotton and spices. Now the docks were all empty and brooding and the city had become a national basket case. *I can do that, giz a job.* A city of loser's alleys.

Anderson stood out like a sore thumb. He had tried to make himself blend in with jeans and an M&S golf jacket. But the ramrod straightness of his back made the effort worthless. He scanned the bar with the eyes of a man trained to assess a landscape for potential ambush sites. He clocked Sebastian and strode across the space with purpose.

"Dyson?"

Sebastian nodded and waved a lazy hand at a chair.

"Hello Anderson. Drink?"

"No thank you. I'm fine."

"Jolly glad to hear it."

Anderson's hard eyes flashed with annoyance at Sebastian's tone. He sat. Very stiff. Not so much as a shred of ease.

"Tell you who I am did they?"

"Actually they did. And then I filled in a few gaps myself. Like a run-down?"

A nod.

"Born and bred Lincoln. Daddy managed a bank for Barclays. Mummy stayed home with her little treasures. Dismal little public school. Modest A levels and a place at Newcastle. Bursury from the army. Modest degree. Modest at Sandhurst. Six years with Royal Signals. Into at SAS at the fourth attempt. Rather good in the Regiment. Transfer to 14th Intelligence. Lots of undercover stuff under hedges in East Tyrone. Promoted Colonel and given the job of running the Forced Research Unit. Been there three years and not covered yourself in a great deal of glory from what I can gather. Now listen my dear chap, there is something I am simply dying to ask."

By now the look on Anderson's face was one of seething anger. Sebastian guessed the man was itching to try out one of the kill in thirty seconds with bare hands drills he had picked up at Hereford.

"What?"

"Who on earth came up with that ridiculous name. I mean, I ask you. 'Forced Research Unit'. Even our beloved cousins from Virginia wouldn't go that far. It is straight out of *Monty Python*."

Now Anderson took a deep breath. They had warned him that Dyson was a flippant bastard. In truth there had been times when he had wondered himself which grey-faced bureaucrat had come up with the name. It certainly wasn't a name that was intended for public consumption. The unit had been set up as competition to MI5 in the endless turf war between the soldiers and the spooks. For years the army had been frustrated at the ineptitude of the spies who were supposed to get under the skin of the various terrorist groups of the Province. In the end the brass had decided to do the job themselves and they had duly established the Forced Research Unit to attract and run infiltrators and informants. Suitcases of used notes had exchanged hands and there had been one or two modest successes. Then things had got out of hand. Badly out of hand. And now the shit was about hit the fan in a big way.

"Would you like me to brief you or would you like to continue with this childish crap?"

"No need for a briefing old boy. I learned how to do dot to dot at the age of five, actually."

"What is that supposed to mean?"

Sebastian smiled his very best and most annoying smile. "Patrick O'Leary? Am I warm?"

Now Anderson's face flared into an impressive scarlet.

"Who on earth told you?"

Sebastian chuckled. "Nobody told me you bloody fool. I read the papers. Quite the thorn in the side isn't he, our Patrick. A starred First in law. A real high-flier. A handsome face ready made for TV. Lovely wife. Lovely kids. Pals with every journalist on the Emerald isle. Always available for a quote. Always there to defend any Bhoyo caught with an Armalite or a pipe bomb. And annoyingly good at it too. Like a dog with a bone when it comes to digging out cases of naughtiness on the part of the gallant officers of the Royal Ulster Constabulary. Mmmm? Getting warm am I? And then his good pals from the Provo Army Council tip him the wink that a few of their chaps have been whacked in rather suspicious circumstances. So

Patrick rolls up his sleeves and starts digging. Why were there never any roadblocks? Why were known vehicles given safe passage across the city? Why were areas cleared of policemen and soldiers at the very time the dastardly deeds were done? It really isn't the sort of thing we want on the early evening news is it? Especially when the speaker is such an articulate sort of chap with such a lovely wife and such a fine face for the television. I expect your seat is getting a tad warm Colonel Anderson. Because if you start to read between the lines, it seems like someone is deliberately feeding names and addresses of IRA players to charming individuals in the UDA and UVF. And not only giving the names. Clearing the way as well. Free passage across town. All the way there and all the way back again. Very, very naughty indeed. No doubt you have already tried to persuade your Loyalist pals to make Patrick's face a tad less easy on the eye, but even they are not that stupid. And so in your moment of panic and desperation you let out a cry for help and lo and behold, here you are. Am I close?"

Anderson nodded. "Close enough."

Sebastian lit up a Rothmans and sipped his coffee. "OK. Now the problem is that our gallant lawyer is running for the city council and over the next few weeks he is going to be playing to packed houses all the way. Lots of exposure, lots of cameras and lots of hints at murderous collusion between the security forces and the Loyalist death squads. Not very good at all. And what on earth will they say about it all in Washington? All those Congressmen from Boston who like nothing better than to sing Danny Boy over a jar or two of Guinness?"

"OK. So there you are. They said you might be able to do something."

"I dare say I can. Nothing else is there?"

"Yes there bloody well is. You will have to run everything by me. Step by step. I have overall control."

Sebastian chuckled and finished his coffee.

"Don't be so silly. I will make your problem go away Colonel Anderson. That is all you need to know. Nice meeting up and all that. I very much doubt if we will meet again. Cheerio."

Two weeks later Sebastian walked into a small grocers store in one of the better areas of West Belfast. It was a minute before five and Jimmy Donald, the proprietor, was about to turn the sign in the door from saying 'Open' to 'Closed'.

"That's OK Jimmy. Carry on. Pull down the blinds and shut up shop as usual. You and I need to have a little chat in private."

The shopkeeper froze rather dramatically. Well that was understandable. One of the IRA's prime sources of funding came from robbing shops and banks. But it was clear that Jimmy Donald was having trouble with the accent. Few of the local Provies tended to speak with the dulcet tones of the English public school system. In which case…

Sebastian had tracked the older man's thought process carefully and it was now clear that he was about to kick off. With a sigh he a drew a gun from his coat pocket and aimed it just above Jimmy Donald's belt.

"Now, now. No need for alarm. Believe it or not I have never shot anyone in my life and I don't intend to start now. But of course there is a first time for everything. So why not be a good chap and get the kettle on? Back room, yes?"

Jimmy was now ready to do as he was told. They moved into the back room where the Irishman clicked on the kettle as per instructions. With shaking hands he fixed two mugs of tea whilst Sebastian looked on with a small smile playing on his lips.

"Any biscuits?"

There were biscuits. Rich tea.

"Now isn't this all very civilised Jimmy? Please, do sit. That's it. And feel free to smoke. I expect you are more than a little nervous. Right. Time to cut to the chase. Your country needs a helping hand Jimmy. I dare say you are not particularly inclined to offer the required assistance. Sadly, not many are in this nasty little town. Which is the whole point I suppose. But it wouldn't be a good idea at all not to do your bit, Jimmy. Not a good idea at all. You see, if you don't play ball, things will get rather awkward. If you don't play ball I will make sure that the word gets out that Jimmy Donald is a true friend of the Queen. The word will seep onto the streets that Jimmy Donald is passing on solid gold, triple-A intelligence to the servants of the Crown. Maybe it will be believed, maybe not. But it doesn't really matter either way, does it Jimmy? Because I know and you know that the Bhoyos can't afford to take any chances right now. Kneecap first and worry about it later, mmm? Ouch. And I don't imagine that trade will be all that brisk either. There is hardly likely to be a queue at the door to buy tea and biccies from the hobbling tout. No Jimmy, it is an outcome that does not bear thinking about. Far better to play ball, don't you think?"

By now the older man's head was bowed. Sebastian sensed tears of helplessness. Was there a nod of consent? There probably was.

"Right. That's all sorted then. The good news is that the service your Queen and country requires is very straightforward. No risk Jimmy. No risk whatsoever. Every Friday evening Patrick O'Leary visits this establishment on his way home from work and purchases a bottle of Jameson's whiskey. Like clockwork, as they say. The two of you pass the time of day and off he pops. Agreed? Good. So. In my bag here I have four bottles of Jameson's. These are the bottles that you will sell to Mr O'Leary over the next month. Extra profit for you Jimmy. These are on the house so to speak. In fact there is also £1000 in the bag for your troubles. And that is it. O'Leary comes in. You sell him the whisky. O'Leary goes out again. Now that isn't too bad is it? Now you must remember that for the next month everything is bugged Jimmy. Home, shop, phones. And we will be watching your every step. Understand?"

A miserable nod.

"Excellent. That completes our business for the day. Lovely cup of tea. Allow me to convey the heartfelt gratitude of Her Majesty for your co-operation. I'll be off now. You don't mind if I use the back door do you?"

Sebastian unbolted the door onto the alley at the back of the shop. He paused just before stepping out into the early evening rain.

"Don't even think of playing the hero Jimmy. It really would be an appallingly bad idea."

And with that he was gone. There were no bugs. No surveillance. In fact nobody other than Sebastian had any knowledge of the four bottles of Jameson's which had been ear marked for Patrick O'Leary. But of course Jimmy Donald didn't know any of that. He sold the Whiskey and hid the cash in the storeroom. He fed it into the till little by little until it was all gone. And then he did his best to wipe the whole thing from his memory.

A month later Sebastian slipped into the back of the community centre in Ballymurphy where Patrick O'Leary was billed to make a speech that promised to cause uproar. The Republican Press Office had been dropping hints to any journalist they could get to listen for three weeks. You don't want to miss the big O'Leary speech. He's going to lift the lid big style. He's going to dish the dirt. He's going to make the Brits squirm. And Sebastian could see that the fourth estate had taken the bait. There were three film crews and a host of eager faced reporters chewing through cigarettes and pumping each other up. The hall was filled to well beyond the health and safety maximum, but health and safety officers tended not to make waves in Ballymurphy. O'Leary was sitting at a table up on the stage with his wife. They were without doubt a handsome couple. But things were clearly not quite right. There was a slackness to O'Leary's usually chiselled features. He wife was whispering urgently in his ear but he gave no sign of hearing her. A small bald man was at the lectern giving it to the Brits with both barrels. After each sentence he punched the air and many in the audience followed suit. By the time Sebastian took his place at the back of the hall, the warm up act was more or less done.

"So with no more ado, I give you our very own Paddy O'Leary !!!!"

Everyone was up, feet stamping the wooden floor. Someone started up with 'The fields of Athenry' and soon the whole hall was a wall of fervent sound. At first O'Leary made no move to get up. Maybe he was milking the moment. Timing after all was everything. But then it became clear that he was showing no sign of getting up at all. The singing faltered as the crowd took in the weird vacant look on his face. His wife nudged and in the end hauled him to his feet. He stood up and seemed to have little idea of where he was. The bald man eased him forward to the lectern. The singing faded to silence. An uneasy silence. A horrible silence. And endless silence. And Patrick O'Leary just stood there and stared into a million cubic metres of space. Soon there was shuffling. Murmours. A hum of discontent. Until Mrs O'Leary could stand it no more and eased her husband away from the limelight.

And Sebastian Dyson slipped away into the night unnoticed.

2016

Jason knew he was being childish. Really childish. But there was no getting away from the fact that he felt like falling into a deep sulk. For the first time in years he had at last managed to produce a piece of work that was decent. More than decent, bloody good, even if he said so himself. Well, at least he wasn't alone in that respect. The Fridge had been effusive. She had been full on encouraging and impressed and he had enjoyed basking in her glow. Now he wanted more glow to bask in. The piece had run that morning. A note on the front page pointed readers to page 21 where the first instalment of a ground breaking series of features was waiting for the reader. And there it had been. A full page with a bleak photo of the Greenfield Estate. He had checked out the online page and found that there was a long and growing column of comment, most of it positive.

He had been out in the cold for many years but now he was back. The wanderer had returned. The mid life crisis had been stopped in its tracks. The prospect of redundancy had been pushed back a few months. He felt like the comeback kid. He felt twenty years younger.

He felt like celebrating. In fact he was in the mood to paint the town red. Doogie had been away with the dawn. He always seemed to be out of the house at some ungodly hour and by the time he made it home he was quiet and sullen. Maybe a thrash around the pubs would do him some good. It had taken Jason ages to get him on the phone and when he did at last make contact he came up against a brick wall. Sorry mate. No chance. Up to my eyes I'm afraid. Sorry mate, haven't seen it yet. Alright is it? Good man. I'll try and grab a moment to give it a read. Have you heard by the way? The Prime Minister is making some sort of announcement at six tonight. I guess we'll finally get to hear what's going down. See you when I see you.

Sally was even harder to track down. When she came on the line she was edgy and anxious. She hadn't read the piece either. The whole Parliament was in a lather about the PM. Nobody had a clue what the hell it was all about. No way she could get away. She kept saying that she had a bad feeling. A really bad feeling.

He threw a cigarette into his mouth and dialed up the office and got hold of Tom Grierson.

"Bloody hell, it's the blue eyed boy. How's life in the Caledonian wilderness?"

"Not bad mate. Look. What's the score with the PM. Everyone up here is in a right old lather."

"It's the sixty-four-thousand dollar question. I've been at this bloody game for twenty years and I have never known a secret to be so well kept. Not only is nobody saying anything I get the distinct feeling that nobody actually knows anything. Whatever the hell it is, Pendleton is keeping it locked down. No doubt having John Taylor close by has a lot to do with it. I can imagine Taylor ordering summary executions in the Number Ten bunker for anyone getting leaky. How's about you? Heard anything?"

"Nothing really. My mate is senior cop and he is burning the candle at both ends. Something's certainly afoot. All overtime cancelled and all that. I have another mate who is an MSP up in Edinburgh. She has been picking up some strange bits and pieces."

"Like?"

"Requisitioned milk tankers and bulk orders for riot shields."

"Yeah. I've picked up some of that."

Jason docked his cigarette. "There was one more thing. The Chief Constable told my mate that Rollerton was statistically likely to be more affected than anywhere else."

"Why the hell is that?"

"I haven't the foggiest. I figure we'll just have to wait and see what Pendleton has to say."

"Figure so. Nice piece by the way."

"Cheers Tom. Call me if you find anything out, yeah?"

"Wilco. Speak soon."

Three o'Clock. Three hours until the Prime Minister would put them all out of their misery. Suddenly he had no wish to stay in and watch the broadcast on his own. He grabbed his coat and headed out to find Sheena.

Christopher Pendleton checked the clock in the mirror. Twenty minutes to go. Time for deep breaths. The make-up woman was all but done. Not bad. The bags under his eyes had miraculously disappeared and the blotches on his skin were well hidden. He looked OK. He certainly looked a whole lot better than he felt. When had he last felt this nervous? Never. Not for his maiden speech in the House. Not for his key speech at the Party Conference when he was running for the leadership. Not for his first Prime Minister's Question Time. Not when he had paid his first visit to the White House. Those had all been times when he had got a buzz out of the nerves. He had prided himself on thriving on pressure. Not now. Now he felt like he had a stomach full of hyperactive eels. Christ he needed a drink. Not that he was about to have one. Every word he was about to speak would be picked over and analysed. Any hint of a slur would be jumped on. He would have a drink later when he at last made it back to the office. That relief was many hours away. Immediately after the broadcast he was due to meet the cabinet. They were already assembled and John Taylor had told him that they were a very, very pissed off group indeed. They would hear about the new Britain at the same time as sixty-five million other citizens. If that wasn't enough, they were about to have the leader of the opposition sit in on the meeting. The thought of it made his lips move into a grim smile. They would just have to lump it. He would tell them that anyone who was not happy with the new world order could resign there and then. Deal with it or piss off back to the back benches.

Once he was done with Cabinet he would be straight into the Cobra meetings. Cobra One would be all about getting the dormitories and feeding stations up and running as soon as possible. The tireless Price was adamant that all was on course. Well, they were all about to find out.

Then it would be the first meeting of Cobra Two. Every instinct in his body told him that the thing would be won and lost in that room. Seven men tasked with keeping the lid on. Three politicians, a soldier, a cop and a spook.

And Dyson.

In the end the whole thing might well come down to Dyson. Christopher had not been able to get any handle on the man when they had met. Instead he had been chilled. There was something empty about the man. No passion. No zeal. Nothing. A coldness. A sense of darkness.

"OK sir. All finished."

"Thanks."

He stood and straightened his tie. A door opened and Taylor marched in.

"All tarted up and ready boss?"

"Ready as I'll ever be. How are the Cabinet?"

"Bitching their heads off, but they get over it. You still set on not using the teleprompter?"

"Yes. I'm better doing it straight."

Taylor shrugged. "Your call boss." He pulled out a packet of B&H and lit up.

"Give me one of those John."

Taylor's face was a mask of shock. "Never knew you smoked."

"I don't. I haven't had a fag since I was sixteen. But stuff it. Desperate times and all that."

The nicotine blurred his vision for a moment and then it hit the spot. One of his better calls.

"How long?"

"Ten minutes."

"Christ."

Later in the months and years that followed the dropping of the Pendleton bombshell, the broadcast was to achieve a Kennedy assassination status. Everyone remembered clearly where they heard the words. And who they were with. And how the world changed in a moment. In the majority of cases these memories were not entirely true. The British public had lost any semblance of awe and respect for its leaders many years earlier. The days when the country would hang on the words of Churchill with bated breath were long gone. Of course a special announcement from the PM was unusual. Not an every day event. But that did not make it particularly interesting for the majority of the population. It would probably be something about Europe. Or the banks. Or the war without end in Afghanistan. Boring.

It was only when the mobile phone network lit up with the news that the millions sat up and took notice. Then they rushed to the nearest TV to catch the broadcast on the ever revolving roll of the news. And then they slotted their memories into place. So most remembered exactly where they were when they watched a re-run of the speech. And who was there with them. And how the world had turned.

Jason and Sheena had made their way round to D-Zed's humble flat where a cluster of Rolly regulars had moaned long and loud when they had changed the channel from *MTV*. Doogie watched in the Chief Constable's office with a number of senior officers. Sally watched in her office in the Parliament.

At six o'clock, a formal voice informed the audience that there was to be an announcement by the Right Honourable Christopher Pendleton MP. And with no more ado, there was the man himself. Dark suit. White shirt. Sober tie. What else?

"Good evening. You know, I have been a politician for over twenty years now and throughout the whole of that time I have heard one complaint over and over again. Why, oh why, will you politicians never tell it as it is? Why do you have to spin everything? Why will you never give a straight answer to a straight question? Sound familiar? It certainly does to me. So. Maybe today is the time to change the habits of a lifetime and do as you all ask. Basically I am going to do my best to tell it straight.

Here goes. My fellow citizens, it falls on me as your Prime Minister to inform you that we are broke. There you are. Hopefully that is straight enough for you.

'Has this just happened? Have the bailiffs been called in this afternoon? Of course not. This is a moment that has been coming for many years. The problem is that my predecessors and I haven't been able to bring ourselves to own up to it. So when did it happen? Hard to say. Probably sometime in the mid 1970s when we had to go cap-in-hand to the IMF for a crisis loan. That was the moment when Britain revealed itself as a shadow of its former self. Things would have had to change in a big way had we not found a huge oil well under the North Sea. The oil got us out of jail and kept us out for twenty years.

By the late eighties things were getting tight again and so we sold off everything we could to raise cash. British Telecom, British Airways, British Gas, millions of council houses. In accountancy terms, we realised our assets. And then of course in the nineties those very clever people in the City of London seemed to have found a way of making money out of fresh air. We all thought that we had found the Holy Grail. Millions and billions flowed out from the square mile and we all suddenly felt rich. The value of our houses went through the roof and there seemed to be an endless stream of people ready and willing to let us use or homes as cash machines. Heady times indeed. And then of course in 2008 the wheels came off. With hindsight, that was the moment when we really hit the bricks. We should have said so. We should have been honest. Instead we pretended that everything was going to be fine. We promised that there were good times around the corner. And we maxed up the country's credit cards and hoped for a miracle.

'Well. There is no more credit and there is no miracle in sight. My fellow citizens, the time has come to stop pretending. It is time for some cold harsh reality.

'Before going forward, I am going to go back. It is time to be honest about Britain. For a while in the eighteenth and nineteenth century we were pretty good at making stuff. We were the first country to have an Industrial Revolution. We made steel and trains and cotton and ships. We were the workshop of the world. We invented things and we were market leaders. The problem was that it didn't last for very long. And if we are to be honest, and quite frankly we might as well be, we have always been rather too fond of easy money. We love to talk up the great days of Empire. But we don't like to look at that closely about how we made our fortunes. The bottom line is that we have always been a bunch of wide boys. We had a navy that excelled in piracy. We sold slaves by the million. We peddled Opium. We conquered countries and drained them of their resources. And most recently we pretended that we could make money out of fresh air. One way or another, we have managed to keep the balls in the air for hundreds of years. Well. As Prime Minister it falls on me to tell you that the balls are no longer in the air. They have fallen to earth. The good times are well and truly over.

'So what does it mean? What is our real situation? Not good I'm afraid. Not good at all. In a nutshell, we are living beyond our means to the tune of 25%. Now when you here the number 25% it really doesn't sound all that bad does it? Maybe the best way for you to look at

this is to compare it with your own personal situation. Let's say there are two of you and you both work. Let's say you have £3000 a month coming in after tax. And then let's say that you have £4000 a month going out. Well something has to give hasn't it? For a while you can live of credit cards and re-mortgage the house and borrow from family, but in the end the moment of truth is going to arrive. There are only two long term fixes. You either get your income up to over £4000 a month or you cut your outgoings to £3000 a month. Well, we would all love to get a 25% pay rise but it doesn't happen all that often. For most of us the only way to fix the problem is to cut costs. You can maybe imagine how things would be if I were to announce the kind of tax rises that would be needed to boost Britain's income by 25%. It would be a catastrophe. Businesses would leave. In fact anyone who could leave, would leave. In my opinion it isn't an option. It isn't going to happen on my watch.

'Which means that we are going to have to cut costs. I will go back to the household income example. How do you cut £1000? It needs much more that cancelling Sky TV and buying value beans. It needs something big. Get rid of the cars. Sell the house and buy a smaller one. Big stuff. Well that is the choice that I have been faced with making. For too many years politicians, myself included, have tinkered around the edges. We have never dared own up to huge hole we are in. It is no good any more talking about efficiency savings and cutting a few bits and pieces here and there. Those days have gone. Now we are in a situation that demands something big. So what is the equivalent to getting rid of the cars or selling the house and getting a smaller one? There are four big areas where the Government spends your money. The NHS. Education. Pensions. And the DHHS. I will take them one by one. Like almost every British citizen, I am fiercely proud of the NHS. It is something that defines us. The right to be healed when we are sick without worrying about how we can pay the bill. Maybe a future Prime Minister will be willing to sacrifice the NHS. I am not.

'Number two. Education. In my opinion to cut spending on Education would be much akin to national suicide. All over the world there are people willing to work for a dollar a day. They are skilled people who can turn their hands to almost anything. We can't begin to manage on a dollar a day. We can't begin to manage on a dollar an hour. Or a pound an hour. So we have to be smarter than our competitors. And that means better educated. And that means that by hook or by crook we have to keep up our standards. We need to

improve them. It is our only long term hope. So I refuse to cut the Education budget.

'Number three. Pensions. Well, I say once again. Not on my watch. We work all our lives and we pay our taxes. We trust our Government to put money aside on our behalf to keep us going when we are too old to work any more. We give this money on trust and I am not willing to break that trust. To take away pensions would be pure and simple theft. I may be many things, but I am not a thief.

'And so we get to the DHSS. Benefits. The safety net that was put in place back in the 1940s. There are some who might argue that this was the moment that Britain started out on the long road to the bankruptcy we now face. You have to be a very rich country indeed to be able to afford the kind of all embracing comfort blanket that we have offered our citizens for over seventy years. Well we are no longer a rich country and we can't afford it any more. So my fellow citizens, today it falls on me to announce that there will be no more benefits in Britain from the end of this month. There will be a few exceptions. We will support those who are chronically ill, either physically or mentally. But it will be very few. All other benefits will cease. Jobseekers allowance, sick pay, housing benefit, council tax benefit, child benefit, tax credits, everything. This represents a truly massive saving. Well over 30%. It is enough of a saving for me to double the amount we can all earn before paying tax. The saving is twofold. First there is the money we save by not paying benefits any more. Second there is the saving we make by no longer having to employ people to administer the payments.

'OK. Time for a deep breath. I have said it. It is time for some more detail. Next month a huge number of our citizens will no longer have any income. They will no longer have their rent paid and so unless they can find a source of income they will become homeless. Are we willing to see shanty towns spring up on the edges of our cities and towns where hundreds of thousands of British citizens shiver and starve? No we are not. As of tomorrow a massive construction programme will get under way. We will build dormitories. There will be dormitories in every town in Britain. These will be places that are safe and warm. They will provide a bed for the night and a chance to wash and use the toilet. There will be no means testing. If anyone needs to sleep in a dormitory, then they can. I do not pretend that these will be pleasant places, but I give you a pledge that nobody in this country will have to sleep out in the cold and wet if they do not want to. We will also be opening feeding stations which will serve three meals per* *day. Once again there will be no means testing. Anyone who wants a free nutritious meal can receive one. My pledge is therefore a simple one. Nobody will go cold and hungry. Everybody will have a bed for the night. Nobody will starve.*

'There will be some other changes. At the end of the month there will no longer be a minimum wage. Every hour of work will count and millions will no longer pay any tax. I will redirect a large proportion of the money we are saving to building houses like we have never built houses before. Over the coming years we will build millions. Planning regulations will be drastically rationalised and rents will be fixed at historically low levels. This will have the effect of dragging down rent levels and house prices across the board. I believe this is a thoroughly good thing. It will mean that anyone who gets a job will be able to comfortably afford somewhere to live. The days of children having to stay at home into their thirties even when they have jobs are over.

'Our country is about to become a tougher place, no doubt about it. But we will also become much better motivated, less complacent. Our money will go much further. Hard work and enterprise will be much better rewarded. Maybe we can learn how to make things again. I know that these changes will not be well received by many. Many will be angry. Very, very angry. Many will be ready to riot and take the law into their own hands. To any of you who consider walking that road, I must give you fair warning. This country is not going to descend into anarchy. Law and order will be maintained no matter what it takes. I give you all this pledge here and now. I will do whatever is necessary to maintain law and order. Whatever is necessary.

'There is no point in pretending that the next months and years are going to be easy. But let us all remember that we have been here before. In the dark winter of 1940 nobody gave Britain a ghost of a chance. But we defied all the odds then and it is my belief that we can defy all the odds again. For many this will seem like the end. I believe that in years to come this day will be seen as a beginning. It is going to be a long hard road, but one day we can become all the better for walking it. I thank you all for listening. Good night and good luck."

Even the boys from the Rolly had been reduced to silence. At first they had kept their moaning about the switching off *MTV*. Then they had given surprised approval at Pendleton's new 'tell it as it is' style. And then slowly but surely the weight of the words coming out of the screen drained their bravado. By the time it was all over a heavy silence hung in the room.

"Did I just hear what I think I heard or am I dreaming?" Sheena's voice was a small as Jason had ever heard it. His own voice wasn't much bigger.

"You heard it. Christ. No wonder the whole thing has been such a secret."

"What does it all mean Jace?" One of the lads. A thin, pinched face and a tight frown.

"I suppose it means what the man said. Come the end of the month there will be no more benefits."

"Like none."

Jason shrugged. Pendleton seemed to have made it all horribly clear.

"What will it mean for my Ma, Jace?"

Jason had visited the boy's mother as part of his single mum research. He had gleaned the bare facts of her situation. She was a single mother of four living in a house provided by a social landlord. Her GP produced regular sick lines confirming that she suffered from depression. Sick pay, housing benefit, council tax benefit, child benefit . . . After they had talked, he had added them all up and concluded that in reality it would be impossible for her to find a job that would be worth even a quarter of what she was receiving from the state. Now all of it would soon be gone. Reduced to nothing.

"It doesn't look good. Unless your mum can find a job in the next fortnight, then all of you will have to move into one of the new dormitories, assuming they can get them ready in time."

"What's a dormitory?"

"It's a big room filled with beds. You'll have seen the kind of thing on DVDs showing army camps."

"So we won't be able to stay in our house?"

"Not unless your Ma can find a job."

"But my Ma has never had a job."

And therein lies the problem, thought Jason. In the course of a few televised minutes the boy and his mother and millions of others had had their lives turned upside down. This wasn't a pay cut. This was a nemesis. They were about lose everything and be reduced to little more than refugees. Christ. Doogie's words jumped into his mind. Rollerton would be statistically more affected than any similarly sized town in Britain. Now it made sense. A horrible sense. Jason had just spent weeks seeking out those very same statistics and he had come up against a brick wall of bureaucracy. Well the statistic was easily enough worked out now. As of a couple of weeks time, it would be a big, fat zero. The changes would hit Rollerton like a runaway truck.

"What the hell is going to happen to Greenfield?" D Zed was no longer the tyro who strutted his high tech stage on the weekends. His lovingly constructed business was about to crash and burn. No longer would his young audience be able to tap up their parents for the £3 entrance money. The taps were about to be switched off at the mains. No gigs, no income. Then there would be no fall back benefits and the rent would be unpayable. Then a dormitory. Just a middle-aged bloke in a dormitory.

Jason tried to compute the problem. "From what he said they will be chopping rents down to the bone. There are loads of youngsters out there who are still living with mum and dad even though they have a job. Assuming they keep their jobs, they will be able to afford to rent a place. I guess there will be enough of them to take all the houses that come free."

One by one the youngsters got up and left. Their heads were spinning with the news. They needed to go home to work it out. To come to terms with the new reality.

D-Zed made tea and the three adults half-watched the frantic analysis on the TV. The experts were agog. It was the biggest social change in the history of the country. The economists worked things through. For those in work the higher tax thresholds would mean a decent pay rise. For the working young it would mean the chance of getting a place of their own. House prices would crash. 'Buy to Let' would collapse. The green belt would be history. It looked like a boom for business. There would be a desperate potential workforce and no minimum wage. Britain would become uniquely competitive within the EU. There would be a big increase in inward investment. Companies would be queuing up at the door to re-locate to the UK. But it was soon agreed that all of this would depend heavily on one big thing. Could the Government keep the lid on? Would there be mass unrest among the losers in Pendleton's New Britain? The experts soon reached a consensus. If the lid stayed on, then the changes could well herald a significant economic upturn. If not, then the country that prided itself on never succumbing to revolution might well be about to join the club.

"No wonder they told Doogie to cancel all overtime for the foreseeable future."

D-Zed lit up and shook his head. "Know what, that Pendleton is one clever bastard."

"Why do you say that?" Asked Sheena.

"For once we seem to have a politician who has mugged up on his history. This is all about revolution. I've done my homework on revolution for my gigs. Come on Jace, you've been doing the same. What will it take for British kids to hit the streets and start putting windows through? It's why you're here, yeah?"

"I suppose it is."

"So come on. Think it through. What is the key thing to a successful revolution? And what is the key thing that will make a revolution fail?"

Jason shrugged.

"The middle classes stupid. Unless you get the middle classes on board, then you revolution will fizzle and die. Middle Class means cops and soldiers. Whoever owns the cops and the soldiers rules the roost. Lenin and Trotsky spun their Revolution, but in the end the only reason it worked was that the middle ranking cops and soldiers came on board. Hitler got that. He pandered to the needs and desires of the middle classes every step of the way. Well, look at it. How are the middle classes going to feel about this? Oh they'll agonise about the cruelty of it all, but in the end they will do their sums and feel pretty good about life. There will be a few quid more at the end of the month and schools and hospitals are still free of charge. Their kids will be able to afford a place to live and their mum and dad still get their pension. Cops? Well they are about to take a trip to overtime city. This is going to be another Miner's Strike for them. Army? Just imagine the queues at the door of every recruitment office in Britain. They're about to get the pick of the litter like never before. The poor will have a rage, but they will find no allies. So yeah, Pendleton's no mug."

"Bloody hell."

The Chief Constable clicked off the TV and clapped his hands.

"So there we are. No more mystery. All out in the open now. Gentlemen, I am sure you have started to work things through. The powers that be have worked out that Rollerton is statistically the most affected town in Britain with a population of over 100,000. Our citizens are going to be beyond pissed off. Thousands are about to be made homeless and moved into dormitories. The dormitories by the way will be built on the site of the old carpet factory. Work starts tomorrow. The feeding station will be in the park. Again, work starts tomorrow."

Doogie shook his head. "Bloody hell boss, how the hell do they think they can put up dormitories by the end of the month? That's just ridiculous."

"They seem quite bullish about it. I gather that to start with the dorms will basically be king size tents that can sleep 300 each. There's a whole bunch of them coming in from China. The permanent dorms are prefab affairs. China again. Apparently they will slot together like giant Airfix kits. Mind boggling really. Anyway. That's not our problem. Our game is all about keeping order. So as of now I want every man we have out on the streets. On foot and in car and in uniform. I even want CID and admin people in uniform and out there. We need to send out a message. Here we are and we're going nowhere. My gut feeling is that the shit won't hit the fan straight away. People will be numbed. They will find it impossible to face the reality of what is happening. Things will kick off at the end of the month when the money stops and the only way to eat is to go to the feeding station. Then people will start to rage. We can expect shoplifting on a massive scale. And that is something we absolutely cannot allow. We need to send out a rock hard message from day one. Get caught nicking and we'll come down on you hard. Really hard. Then we will move on to the really tough phase. The eviction phase. Thankfully it isn't going to be our job to turf people out. The security companies have that gig. They will be recruiting from nine o'clock tomorrow morning and there will be no shortage of applicants. It won't take people long to realise that any kind of job will be like gold dust. The new rents for social housing are looking like being somewhere in the region of £30 a week. The new bottom line will be that if you can get just about any kind of job then you will have a place to live. In most cases at least one family member will get something and the rent will get paid. It's amazing what human beings can achieve when the chips are down. But there will soon be plenty who will have nowhere to go but the dormitories. The security firms will have the task of getting people out. Our job will to be to maintain overall control. The bottom line is that if anyone kicks off, we lift then. No special cases. We do it ten times out of ten. We lift, we process, we prosecute."

By now the eyes around the conference table were wide. The head of CID spoke up.

"That's all well and good boss, but where the hell do we put everyone? We've only got twenty holding cells. That won't even scratch the surface."

The Chief tuned to his second in command.

"Doogie."

Doogie cleared his throat. "I was given the task of coming up with a plan of how we can handle, hold and process large numbers of detainees. It's not great I'm afraid. We will use the football ground. It is the only place with the facilities we will need. Obviously it can seat up to 10,000 people, though we don't anticipate it being anything like that. Obviously it has toilet facilities and catering options. And it is secure. A football ground is designed to make sure that nobody can get in without paying. That means that it is easy enough to make the changes required to make sure nobody can get out. The conference rooms will be converted into temporary courts which will ensure we can process people quickly."

"Jesus Doogie, that's the same as Chile in the 1970s."

"Like I said, it ain't great. Obviously, that's where I got the idea. There is one big difference. We are not about to start torturing anyone and if we get things right we will be able to get people in, processed and out in a matter of hours. When all is said and done there really isn't anywhere else. I gather most forces across the country will be taking the same line."

"What about the match?" A concerned Rollerton Thistle season ticket holder.

"Everyone is processed and out by 5 p.m. Friday afternoon. That leaves the stadium open as normal on Saturday. Then it's business as usual from Sunday morning."

Head of Community policing Jenny Nish was far from on board. "Look, am I the only one here who is wondering just what the hell we are doing here? Think about it Douglas. You are talking about detaining British citizens in a bloody football stadium. Have you any idea how that sounds. Well I know how it sounds to me and it isn't good."

Doogie banged his hand down on the table. "Do you think it looks any better to me Jenny? Christ, I've thought through every scenario here, believe me. So tell me what we are supposed to do? Do we allow every pissed off little toe rag in Rollerton to run riot because the PM has sent us back into the Dark Ages? Or maybe we stand back and turn a blind eye whilst half of the Greenfield Estate descends on *Tesco* and clears the place out. Is that what you suggest? None of this is our doing. More to the point, there's not a dammed thing we can do about it. Our job is to do as we are bloody well instructed."

"Oh we'll only be following orders will we? Jesus Christ! Now where have I heard that before?"

"Wrap it up. Both of you." The Chief Constable had decided that enough was enough. "Let's not get off the page here. We're coppers, not social scientists. Our job is no different from yesterday. We take our instructions from democratically elected politicians and we carry out those instructions. End of story. There is a very simple solution for anyone who is not comfortable with those instructions. Resign and for

Christ's sake do it quickly. The next few months are not going to be easy. No point pretending otherwise. The upside is that the lads are going to rake in OT like never before. The downside is that a large percentage of our fellow citizens are going to hate our guts. We will catch the blame because we will be the faces in the front line of this thing. Bricks and bottles with get thrown and heads will be broken. And no doubt the press will we waiting on any case of the lads losing their cool and piling in too hard. All of which means that we stick together like glue. Anyone who is not on board needs to leave and leave now. Am I 100% clear?"

Nods.

"Jenny?"

"Very clear sir."

"Good. Now let's get out there and show some uniforms."

Dorothy Baldini snapped off the huge wall mounted TV and took a thoughtful sip of wine. It was good, the best the old family estate in Calabria had produced in years. The rich taste brought images of low dusty hills and olive groves. The hum of crickets and the kind of wall to wall blue sky that you never saw in Rollerton.

It seemed that Christopher Pendleton had helped her to make a decision that she had been toying with for many months. Work on the villa was all but complete. The pool was tiled and ready for filling. The furnishings from Milan were all delivered and unpacked. The family was ready to receive the Scottish wanderers back into the fold. In truth, she could have made the move six months earlier, but business had been so very good. It was never easy to walk away when such spectacular chunks of cash were rolling in. In her heart she knew well enough that she had put away enough. More than enough. Life was not expensive in Calabria. With yet another miserable, wet Rollerton winter on the horizon she had almost reached the moment of decision.

Now the moment had arrived.

Dorothy Baldini was sharp. She had needed to be sharp to maintain her place as Rollerton's number one supplier of Heroin for so many years without being caught and shipped off to HMP Corton Vale. Now she could see that the good times were over. What percentage of her weekly takings came from money paid out by the state? 60%? 70%? Impossible to say. A lot for sure. And now all of that money was going to be withdrawn. Her customers would be driven to unprecedented levels of desperation. They would try and steal anything that wasn't nailed down. But who would buy the stolen goods? The majority of money laid out on knocked-off items also came from the state. Those on benefits never bought their kids *Nike* trainers from *JJB*. They bought them from blokes in pubs who had in turn bought them from desperate junkies. All of that was about to change. The shops would hire in more security than ever before and it would be cheap enough to hire. No minimum wage and a desperate work force. Her customer base was all of a sudden a busted flush.

It was time to go.

Donny was up in his room. Preening himself no doubt. He would certainly find Calabria a shock to the system. No way would he be strutting around like he did in Rollerton. The elders would soon put him in his place. It was high time the little sod learned some respect. She picked up her mobile phone and texted him to come down.

Five minutes later he strutted in, a walking clothes dummy for a selection of American sportswear corporations. That was another thing that would have to change. The kids in Italy would laugh themselves silly at his ridiculous garb. They would go to Milan and dress him properly.

"What is it?"

"Did you watch the news?"

"Some of it."

"Did you understand it?"

A silly shrug. Idiot. "S'ppose."

"The game is up Donny."

"How?"

"Where do you think all the money we make comes from?"

"Punters. Who else?"

"And where do they get it from?"

"Parents. The Brew. Whatever."

"There is no more Brew, Donny. The Brew is history. As of the end of this month our punters are stone broke. No money, no trade. We're off."

"What!!"

"That's right. Away from this miserable hole. We're going home Donny."

Now the pretty-boy face was twisted up and angry. "It may be home for you but it isn't for me. No way am I going to that shithole. No way."

"Oh really? So what are you going to do Donny?"

"Staying here. That's what I'm doing. Business as usual. There will always be money to punt. Always."

She smiled to annoy him. Just like his grandfather. Just like his uncle. All such tough guys and barely a brain cell in sight. Was it worth arguing? Probably not. The little sod was stubborn as a mule. Maybe it would be better to go back home without him. He would only be an embarrassment. Leave him to learn the hard way. No doubt he would wind up doing a few years. So be it. Then he would return home less cocky. More mature. More respectful.

"It's up to you. I don't care much either way. I am off next week. If you want to stay, then stay. I will give you some money. And I will pay the rent on this place. The money is a one off mind you. Don't be ringing me and begging for more because it isn't going to happen."

"How much?"

"£20,000."

"Fine. Is that all?"

"Yes Donny. I do believe it is."

"I'm going out then."

"Off you go. You go and be a big fish in this little pond of yours."

"What's that supposed to mean then?"

"It means what it means. You have no class Donny. You are a sad little toe rag who likes to strut about and shag everything that moves. I really don't like you very much, son or no son. I suppose that makes me a bad mother. Well guess what? I can live with it. When you grow up and learn some home truths you can come out to Calabria. Until then, I wish you luck. You'll need it."

For a few moments Donny stood stiffly bunching and unbunching his fists. Then he turned and left with a slam of the door. Dorothy poured another glass of wine, closed her eyes and smiled at the thought of sunshine, fresh pasta and tomatoes that tasted like tomatoes.

Christopher Pendleton slumped into his leather swivel chair and blew out his cheeks.

"Thank bloody Christ that's done with."

Across the desk the leader of the opposition gave an understanding smile.

"Can I gather that you dear colleagues in the Cabinet were less than amused?"

"You could say that. I'd get more respect wearing a West Ham shirt in the home end at Millwall."

John Taylor did the honours with the whisky decanter. Next he pulled cigarettes from the pocket of his rumpled jacket offered one to the PM with a raised eye brow. It was duly snatched and the proffered light accepted. Hawkes chuckled. "That's the spirit. Come on John. Pass one over here will you?"

"You as well?" Christopher was amazed. Hawkes never seemed to be off the TV cycling here, there and everywhere.

"Yup. Cracked about a fortnight after being elected party leader. It seems to be par for the course. They say that Obama was on forty a day by the end of his second term."

All three took deep swigs of Scotch and long pulls of nicotine. The PM squeezed his eyes shut for a moment to savour the joint alcohol and nicotine rush, then he leaned forward.

"So John. What do you think? Will they all stay in line?"

Taylor issued an icy smile. "Oh the bastards'll stay in line all right. They all know I've got fat files on every last one of them. One call to our beloved Lester Gall and I can have any of them hanging by their bollocks. Don't worry about any of them Chris. They'll bitch and twine, but nowt else. They all like their Ministerial salaries far too much to do owt else. They'll stick."

Hawkes shook his head. "Lovely games we all play aren't they. Party Unity thanks to secret lists of indiscretions. How was Cobra One?"

"Well. As much as I hate to say it, Price has excelled himself. It appears that everything is well on target. We have three ships full of prefab dormitories inbound from Shanghai. They'll dock in Felixstowe, Liverpool and Glasgow in a week's time. *Wimpy, McAlpine* and *Barratt* will start training their guys next week. The cargo of tents is due in three days time. All the food companies are up to speed and we have enough ingredients ordered up for the next two months. Nothing will be perfect of course. It never is. But it seems like we will hit the ground running reasonably fast. Have you been watching the pound?"

"Sure have. It's jumped like a kangaroo. The money men seem to have liked what they have heard. Nothing like kicking the poor to get a bump in the currency."

"Excellent. So the talented Mr Price called that one right as well. I might even have to start being a bit nicer to him."

"Do that boss and you can have my resignation." Growled Taylor.

"Oh well. So much for that plan then." Pendleton drained his his glass and docked his cigarette. "Right then. Cobra Twos?"

They made their way down to the bowels of the building where the other four members of Cobra Two were waiting.

Commander Parker of the Met reported that as yet there was no sign of any civil disturbance anywhere in the Realm. West from MI5 confirmed that all potentially problematic groups were now fully watched and bugged. General Lockhead confirmed that the TA would start a two week intensive riot control training package within a few days.

Then all eyes turned to Sebastian Dyson who lolled indolently in his chair, dressed down in faded jeans and a venerable Aran sweater.

"We won't see much in the early stages. I predict mass denial. People won't really believe anything is going to happen. It is beyond their imagination. They will hang on to the hope that something is bound to turn up. We will only be able gauge the extent of any problems where the Giros fail to land. Have you finalised your housing policy yet?"

Pendleton nodded. "We have. We'll announce tomorrow. As of the first of next month all social housing will rent out at £25 per week for two bedrooms going up to a maximum of £35. We will crash a new law through capping private lets at £50 a week for two bedrooms going up to a maximum of £100. The boffins reckon it will cave property prices by at least 50%."

"Any concerns about that?"

"Not really. The banks will hate it, but they have it coming to them. Middle England will squeal but they'll get over it soon enough. It will free up a huge amount of cash for consumer spending as young professionals who rent find a few hundred quid extra in their pockets at the end of the month."

Dyson nodded.

"And the experts still predict a big exodus from North to South?"

"Yes. We will try and keep up with it by sticking up as many Dorms as we can right across the capital." Price had predicted that the young would make their way to London and the South East to take advantage of free food and accommodation and a better chance of work. The theory then ran that they would send money home to enable their families to pay the rent. The model was based on the behaviour of the 700,000 young Poles who had descended on Britain early in the century.

Again Dyson nodded. "Let's hope it pans out that way. The more young men we can drain out of the worst hit areas, the less angry young men there will be to throw bricks at policemen. Subsidised rail fares, yes?"

"All done. They'll be able to get to London for less than a tenner from anywhere in Britain."

Sebastian drummed his fingers quietly on the table whilst Pendleton bummed a cigarette of his Home Secretary. "Couple of other things you might want to run by some of your bright young things. Not especially Cobra Two. Just thoughts really"

"Fire away. We're open to anything and everything."

"OK. Why not find a few really hip, geeky types to fire up some sort of quasi underground internet campaign. Simple idea. Britain is the new black for backpackers. Come to Britian, stay in a free dormitory, eat all your meals for free. We can become a magnet for gap year students from all corners of the earth. It will cost us pence per day to house and feed them and they will all come with wallets full of cash from mummy and daddy to inject into the service sector. It would have to seem very unofficial. If it appeared like a tourist board campaign it would lose all its cool."

Taylor gave the table a cheery thump. "Consider it done. Like it Dyson. Like it bloody plenty."

"Well, that's terrific John. Next. Pile cash into expanding the number of university places available for foreign students and build lots and lots of dorms and feeding stations near to every campus. Then we basically play the same sort of cards. Come to study in Britain where you and sleep and eat for free. You still pay fees of course, by the million."

More pleased nodding.

"Last. Bit sensitive this one, but what the hell. You crash through an emergency bill offering all companies a halved rate of tax if they can prove that over 90% of their workforce carry British passports. Another bill will make it quite legal for make any member of staff redundant in order to reshape the workforce in order to achieve the reduced tax rate. Obviously this is an unashamedly Nationalist move and it will play well with van-man Britain. Of course it will be against every EU rule in the book and every one of our fellow members will scream in anguish. They will take steps and maybe even throw us out altogether in the end, but that will take years and years. And whilst we get our lawyers to stall the thing every step of the way, we will match jobs with our own nationals. In the end it will cause many less genuine problems than any kind of protectionism. Countries are not overly concerned if we keep their citizens away from our jobs. They only get really jumpy if we keep their goods out."

The PM took a long, long draw on his cigarette. "Start the process of leaving the EU? Interesting. It will play well in the right wing press, no doubt about that. Is that your thinking Sebastian?"

"Partly. Obviously it gets as many into jobs as possible and therefore enables them to find the money they need to rent property. That in turn frees up space in the dorms for tourists and students who in turn will bring cash into the economy. The main idea is to pull the rug from under the feet of the far right groups before they get the chance to make political capital out of the new situation."

Pendleton smiled. "Not bad. Not bad at all. Leave it will us. What about law and order?"

Sebastian shrugged. "Suck it and see really. We can try and second guess how things will play out, but we won't really know until people find there is no Giro in the system. All we can do is to make sure we have as many policemen available as possible. We will need to ensure they are mobile and ready to be deployed around the country at short notice. They must be properly equipped to deal with civil unrest."

"Where will you be working from? We have plenty of office space if you need it."

"No thanks. Actually, I'm off to Rollerton."

"Rollerton."

"Absolutely. As I explained before, If things are going to kick off anywhere, they will kick of in Rollerton. It is our guinea pig town. In Rollerton we will employ trial and error and find out how far we need to go to keep the lid on."

The idea of a guinea pig town sent a small shiver through the Prime Minister. It had an unpleasant resonance with the kind of thing that once upon went down in Stalinist Russia. But he had brought Sebastian Dyson to the table with his eyes open.

"OK. I understand. Make sure you keep us in the loop."

"Will do boss." Dripping sarcasm. Forever the bad boy of the class finding an edge to skate close to.

"Jason! How is my absolute favouritist dinosaur?"

"Good evening Amelie. Working late I see. Ever the driven modern woman."

"We all have to step up to the plate in these thrilling times. Tomorrow morning as the larks begin to trill, the middle-aged of middle England will be looking to our venerable newspaper to tell them what our PM has said is going to mean to them. Will they still be able to afford that super new conservartory they saw in the advert next to that super piece of old school journalism from Jason Marsh?"

"A heavy burden Amelie."

"Heavy indeed Jason, and it is a burden we must all share."

"Ah. Now that is beginning to sound like work."

She chuckled, never happier than when the chance came to drive her troops forward.

"How very perceptive. I'm afraid that I am about to drive you forward Jason. There will be little time for romantic moments in the doorways of chip shops with flame-haired lovelies."

"Mind if I ask you a personal question Amelie?"

"I expect that I will mind Jason, but since your stock of brownie points is quite high right now you may ask away."

"I am beginning to wonder if you have some deep-rooted lesbian tendencies with a particular fascination for Scottish ladies with red hair. They do seem to come up a lot."

"What a wicked thought Jason. Wicked, wicked, wicked. A wicked thought that deserves punishment and I am going to punish you with work. Lots and lots of it."

"Shouldn't have asked should I? Go on then. Give me the worst. My notepad is ready and my pen is poised."

"Right. Well obviously the little talk Mr Pendleton has had with us all this evening has changed quite a lot of things. Basically Jason, it means that your series of features are all about a world that is about to end in a few weeks time. Which means that we need to squeeze it all in before D Day arrives and the giro cheques as consigned to the filing cabinets of history along with ration books."

Jason chuckled. "'Filing cabinets of history'. Not bad Amelie. At times I think you are wasted as an ice queen who downsizes people and woos the makers of conservatories."

"Oh I am a woman of many talents. So. I am going to need the five remaining features in the next ten days. And it is going to be completely super. A last look at a disappearing world through the eyes of the intrepid Jason Marsh. Like a documentary about an Amazonian tribe who have lived the same way for thousands of years in the week before the logging trucks arrive. With me?"

"Always."

"An achievable deadline?"

"No problem Amelie. I'm a front line journalist remember. I smoke, I drink and I thrive on deadlines."

"Of course you do Jason. That is why you are such an asset to this newspaper. But there is more."

"Somehow I thought there might be."

Now it was her turn to chuckle. "A comment you made a week or two ago came to mind as I listened to our leader tonight. Something your policemen friend mentioned. If I recall correctly, he had been told that Rollerton was statistically likely to be the most affected town in Britain by the coming changes. And your MSP friend wondered if this might have anything to do such a high number of Rollerton's population either being on benefits or drawing their living from the state."

"That's right enough."

"Well, you need to dig a little deeper Jason. How many unemployed? How many in receipt of housing benefit and about to be evicted and pushed into dormitories? How cold is the cold wind going to blow in Rollerton? Talk to those who are about to feel the icy blast. How do they feel? What are their plans? Will they go quietly into the night? I am going to want something every day if possible. A countdown to the New Britain. And of course when the new situation unfolds, I will still need daily pieces about how Rollerton looks when the brave new world arrives. Did you ever watch *The Wire* Jason?"

"Yes. I did the whole box set in a oner."

"Me too. Anyone who watched seventy hours of *The Wire* felt like they knew West Baltimore almost as well as they knew their own town. Just like they once felt that the *Boys from the Black Stuff* took them into the very heart of Thatcher's Liverpool. I want you to make our readers feel the same way about Rollerton Jason. I want them to wake up in their cosy commuter belt homes and turn straight to the Rollerton page as they sip their Fair Trade coffee. I want them to be concerned for the place. I want them to feel anxious for the poor souls who are freezing in the cold north wind."

"You want the thing to have legs."

"Absolutely Jason. Like an investigative journalism equivalent to a soap opera. I want Jason Marsh's very own *The Wire*."

"And with a bit of luck, all the conservatory companies will book their ads in multiples instead of one at a time."

"Of course they will Jason. You are catching on fast."

"Well in that case, I suppose there is only one question left to ask."

"Ask away."

"Will I get the chance to bask in your glow?"

"Oh absolutely you will. In fact you can start basking this very minute like a sleepy crocodile on an African rock. I am giving you a pay rise Jason. 15%. I'll even give you a little more elbow room on your expenses. Let's say deep fried Mars bars five times a week?"

Her words hit him like a line of speed. This was completely out of left field. To his complete and utter amazement he realised that he had just been motivated. It was an emotion he hadn't experienced for many, long years. He suddenly felt worthwhile, valued, talented, capable, once again the promising lad who had headed south like a modern day Dick Whittington all those years earlier.

"Bloody hell Amelie."

"Now I am going to require a little more class than that Jason. But seriously, well done. You deserve it. My gut feeling is telling me that your time has arrived. Maybe the time for this paper has arrived. Once the penny drops about what has actually been said and done this evening, our country is going become a much more serious place. The comfort blanket has been pulled. Our fascination with celebrity and flim-flam comes from too much time spent in front of daytime TV watching mindless crap. People are not going to have that time for daytime TV any more. I doubt whether they will have TV rooms in the new dormitories. The people of Britain will be spending their days trying to get away from the edge. Jason, we are leaving the era of gossip and entering an era of news."

"Christ Amelie, that was almost Churchilian."

"Believe it or not Jason, way back in the days when I used to work all night to get my starred first, I harboured dreams of being a reporter who would change the world. Those were the days when I had glasses and spots. I never saw myself as a person who would spend her days smooching with people who made conservatories and balancing the bottom line by downsizing people. But this paper has been around for over two hundred years and it was my job to keep it breathing. We have been in a holding pattern Jason. Circling the airport patiently waiting for our time to land. Well that time has come Jason. Now we will be able to balance the books and make profits by selling papers and advertising instead of relying wholly on advertising. I feel my teenage self, emerging from the shell. I think it is time to shake the tree again, don't you Jason?"

"Absolutely Amelie."

"Jolly good. Well, get out there and shake it Jason. Shake it as hard as you can."

He sat for a while smoking and staring into the clean, desolate space of Doogie's bachelor kitchen. Amelie had ripped down the wood and revealed the trees. *The National Enquirer* had been at the heartbeat of British life from the middle of the nineteenth century. Through war and peace and the collapse of Empire, it been an ever constant thorn in the side of the establishment. Only in the last two decades had it become becalmed and marginalised in a dumbed down Britain where the mass of the population had been rendered docile by the celebrity pap peddled by Lester Gall and his cronies. Sales of newspapers had been one the slide for his whole career at *The Enquirer*. An air of resigned doom had become ever present in the newsroom. They had all been much more concerned about who would be downsized next rather than digging hard for a scoop. What was an old fashioned news scoop worth anyway when all anyone seemed interested in was who the latest Big brother non-entity was shacked up with? And Jason realised that he had pretty well gone with the flow, intent on nothing more than hanging on for another month and then another month after that.

Now the game had changed.

In the course of the most stunning ten minutes since Churchill had promised to fight on the beaches and the hedgerows, Christopher Pendleton had rendered the age of celebrity obsolete. Amelie had grasped it in a heartbeat. It was a new day. Once again the people of Britain were about to be hungry for news. Real news. The news that the politicians and their big business backers would fight tooth and nail to keep hidden deep in the shadows. People would return to the old questions. What does it all mean? How will it affect me and mine? What kind of country do I live in? Is the future dark or sun kissed? Do I fight or play along?

A slow smile spread across his face making him suddenly look younger even though there was nobody there to see. He snatched up his mobile and for the next twenty minutes he begged and cajoled his way to a conversation with Sally.

"Hello Jason. I'll have to be quick. Bloody mayhem here."

"I'll bet. Let's meet for a curry. I can be up in Edinburgh just after midnight."

"Look Jason, I'm really sorry but . . ."

"No buts Sally. We need to have a curry. We really need to have a curry. Believe me."

"We do?" The tone of her voice had turned at the sound of the new and unfamiliar tone in his voice.

"You find a place and call me with an address. OK?"

"I suppose so."

"Great. See you there."

"Jason?"

"Yes."

"You're not about to make a pass or propose or something are you?"

He smiled. "Tempting, but no. Bigger fish to fry."

"OK then."

Two hours later and he found a yellow line to park up on fifty yards down from *The Bengal Tiger*. Sally was inside in the waiting area browsing her laptop and sipping a glass of chilled water.

"For one sir?"

"No, I'm meeting someone. Pint of lager would be pretty good though. Good lad. Hi Sally."

He joined her and yearned on a cigarette even though he had worked his way through the best part of a packet on the road to the capital. Sally cocked her head and appraised him.

"There is a worrying gleam about you Jason."

"To bloody right there is."

"I rather like it. It takes me back to different times."

"It is easy to forget the whole concept of being young at heart when you turn into a sad middle-aged git. OK. Questions. Are you in politics for the money?"

"Of course not."

"So why?"

She frowned at this unexpected inquisition. "Look Jason, I don't know where all this is going but . . ."

"Just go with me a while Sally. I don't think money ever had anything to do with it. Not you. You always wanted to make a difference."

"I still do."

"And do you? Make a difference?"

"I do my best."

"But you are just a Lib Dem MSP in a devolved Parliament on the edge of everything. You do what you can but what you can do isn't all that much, right?"

"Thanks."

"It would be nice to have the chance to do more, right?"

"Of course it would."

He took a long swig of lager and grinned. "Well we have the chance. Big time."

There was something about him. She couldn't quite put her finger on it but it was certainly there.

"Go on."

"The world has changed tonight Sally. You know that. Who with half a brain doesn't? But it has also changed in a big way for me. And it can for you. Maybe Doogie too."

"You're losing me Jason."

"Yeah. Sorry. Look. Let's order up some grub first."

Two chicken Madras. Pilau rice. Papadums and naan bread. A move to a table in a deserted restaurant.

"I had the most amazing conversation with my editor tonight."

"The Fridge?"

"The one and only. She knocked me clean into next week. Here's the gist. *The National Enquirer* has been about since Gladstone and Disraeli. Once upon a time we used to keep the government honest. We used to lift the lid on things and expose what need to be exposed. And then slowly but surely Lester Gall managed to turn the people of Britain into mindless illiterate morons only willing to cough up 30p for their daily dose of tits, celebrity and football. Well those days are gone as of this evening. Hard news is going to be the new black, as Amelie says. The good people of Britain will once again look to *The National Enquirer* for the truth. They will crave an independent view like a junkie craves a bag of smack. We will be able to pay the bills by selling papers, not advertising. Amelie sees the moment is right to be radical again. There will be money in digging the dirt and printing it."

Sally dunked a piece of papadum in the mango chutney and chewed. "I can see why this has got you going Jason, but where am I supposed to fit in?"

"Simple. You are there to represent your constituents, yeah?"

"Obviously."

"And the majority of those constituents are in Rollerton?"

"Well, not quite a majority, but a lot."

"Remember what Doogie said. That stuff about Rollerton being statistically the most affected town in Britain with a population of over 100,000? And you could only think of the percentage of people on benefit or working for the state. Well you were so bloody right. Rollerton is about to be hit by the hurricane like no other town in Britain. Amelie has seen it. She wants to make Rollerton a daily event. Big and bloody bold. She wants me to show how it all plays out. Think about what that means Sally. Let's try out a couple of assumptions. There is no way Pendleton would have done this without the consent of Gall and his big business cronies. Which means that 90% of the media will go into overdrive to give everything the most positive spin they can. Hell, this whole thing is like a dream come true for big business. No more minimum wage and a hungry workforce who will do just about anything to avoid a night in a dormitory. The bastards will be slathering at the prospect. And beyond all the spin will stand *The National Enquirer*. Can you see?"

"Yes, I can see."

"Remember when we were eighteen? Remember all those nights when we talked about everything we were going to do? You and me and Doogie. Daft kids with big dreams. Well, our moment has come. Think about it Sally. I have an inside track into Greenfield on the back of my features. You are on the inside of politics and Doogie is a senior cop. And all three of us are in Rollerton where the hit will be the hardest. To cap it all, we have a carte blanche to give us the best platform to tell the truth. Can you see what an opportunity we have?"

She had given up on the idea of eating. Every sensible instinct in her was itching to reject Jason's new zeal out of hand. But the sensible instincts were being shepherded out of the door by big tattooed bouncers with crew cuts and hard eyes.

"I can see."

"So you're in?"

"I'm in."

He waved over the waiter and ordered up champagne. "I have just been given a 15% rise and had the shackles taken off my expenses account. Might as well make hay whilst the sun shines."

"Just one thing Jason."

"Go on."

"Remember I told you that I had a talk with Jim McRae?"

"The maverick? Old leftie warhorse from the Eighties?"

"The very one. He said something to me. He warned me about going into the dark corners of the state. He said that bad things tend to happen to anyone who sticks their nose where it isn't welcome. Car accidents, Stuff like that."

"And what did you say?"

"I said it was a risk I was willing to take. I still am. But it is different for me than it is for you and Doogie. No kids. No dependents. Just me. You need to ask yourself the question Jason. If we do this, there is a good chance that we won't make it to the other side in on piece. We might not make it to the other side at all. I have already made the decision. You need to make it as well."

Jason leaned back and stared at the ornate ceiling. In his bubbling excitement he hadn't even come close to considering any of this. He spoke his thoughts aloud.

"Maureen's man is makingna fortune in the city again and to be honest my son seems to hate my guts. Maybe he will grow out of it, maybe he won't. He doesn't seem to need me as a dad and he certainly doesn't rely on me for cash. There is plenty of life insurance. So sod it. I'll take my chances. What do you think Doogie will say?"

She smiled. "Our beloved Doogie will need some working on but we will break the bugger down in the end. Where do you want me to start?"

"I have been trying for weeks to get some facts about exactly how much government cash flows into Rollerton in the form of benefits.

And how much it costs to run the offices that pay them all out. I haven't got anywhere. The whole thing is buried a mile deep. You should be able to dig it out. Let's start by sussing out exactly how much is about to be taken away."

"Sounds logical enough to me. I should be able to get hold of that."

"Perfect. I am going to revisit a few of the folk who helped me with the features and take a look at how they see the new world that is coming."

"I read your piece by the way. Well done."

"Thanks."

"It seems that the old Jason is back with us."

"And the old Sally."

"The old Sally never went away. You just never got round to calling her."

He gave an embarrassed shrug and lifted his glass in apology.

"Us?"

She smiled.

"Us."

Sebastian marked the page in a well thumbed copy of 'Crime and Punishment' and laid it down on the bed. His eyes had a promising tiredness about them. Maybe he might sleep tonight. If he did, it would be a bonus. He never slept much. For years he had learned that the last seconds that divided sleep and wake were the time when his conscience would twitch. It was never much of a twitch. More often than not it was barely noticeable. But it was enough to wake him back up. Then he would choose something to read and patiently wait for the relief of weariness to come around again. Dostoevsky had become something of an old friend. He had never discovered what the Russian master had done, but he knew in his bones that it must have been something bad. Every page carried a familiarity with the dark corners where Sebastian had lived out his days. Russians were world experts in searching their souls. For a while Sebastian had tried to take a leaf from the Russian playbook and find sleep through alcohol. It had never been real sleep. More like a kind of oblivion which would bring no rest and a sickness in the morning. Over the years he had come to the realisation that the human body required barely any sleep. He was forever tired but still able to function perfectly well.

What time was it now? Just after one. Outside a strong wind had blown up and a mean autumn wind was splashing rain onto the window. Around him the room was the last word in bland. An American inspired chain hotel with as much character as a tin of beans, every room identical to the next all the way from Detroit to Darwin. A place for travelling salesmen and secret affairs. And the colourless men who defended the Realm.

He smiled at the bleakness of everything and snapped open his laptop. There was free WiFi. There was always free WiFi. By now the online editions of all the papers would be posted for the day. *The National Enquirer* was the third on his list and the front page jumped at him.

ROLLERTON – THE TOWN WHERE THE STORM WILL HIT HARDEST.

Interesting.

A short paragraph explained that inside the paper on page 8 award winning reporter Jason Marsh would start an ongoing series of features covering the fortunes of Rollerton, the small Scottish town where the Christopher Pendleton's new dawn would feel the coldest.

He clicked the link.

'Most of you will never have been to Rollerton. To be honest, there are not too many reasons for anyone to come to the town. The fact that it has no Tourist Information office pretty much says it all. It is one of those names that most people know from half listening to the Scottish lower league football results. Rollerton Thistle 1 – Cowdenbeath 3. Why is there a town here at all? Well, first and foremost, Rollerton is by the sea and once upon a time a fleet of fishing boats would sail out to catch cod. They still do. All three of them. Fifty years ago the town also enjoyed a modest reputation as being a place where carpets were manufactured. Not any more. A trawl through the archives makes interesting reading. In 1937, 72% of the male population of the town were employed either as fishermen or carpet makers. The balance was made up of shopkeepers and teachers and policemen and soldiers. Oh, and there was a high percentage who were unemployed looking pale and hollow-faced in their cloth caps. It was never a rich place. It has never produced pop singers or authors or TV personalities. It has no statues of famous sons and daughters. But it was OK. Just another place where people worked long hard hours and made ends meet.

'Not any more. Everything has changed. For a start, almost 50% of the population of the town does no work at all. Some are at school or college. Others are retired. Others are signed off sick and others are at least on paper seeking work. Of the 50% who do work, an extraordinary 78% receive their salaries from the tax payer. They are policemen and social workers and bin men and nurses and bureaucrats and soldiers. Many of these jobs of course are the best paid jobs in the town, which means that 84% of the money the people of Rollerton earn comes from the tax payer. Take away the public pound, and there isn't much left.

'After a long and frustrating search I have learned that six times more money flows into Rollerton in the form of salaries and benefits and pensions than meagre amount that flows out in the form of PAYE and VAT and customs duty. It is a pretty well kept secret and one that has been pretty well kept for many, many years. There is no getting away from the fact that places like Rollerton have been completely subsidised for years. Are the people of the town to be blamed for this? Hardly. They never asked for the Chinese to be able to make carpets so much cheaper. They never asked for a succession of decisions in Brussels to render the Scottish fishing industry obsolete. It was hardly their fault. It was just how it was.

'Rollerton hasn't made any sense for half a century. It has just been a town where 100,000 people happen to live. It's only real industry is the state – hospitals and schools and a prison and pensions and benefits.

'That was the world that was – a world that ended on Friday evening. The gravy train is about to draw out of the station, almost certainly never to return. Some of the jobs provided by the state will be safe – the policemen and the teachers and the bin men and the prison warders and the doctors and the nurses. Others will disappear, the ones that manage and distribute all the benefits as the bureaucracy of the Welfare State is dismantled and closed down. Our investigations suggest that this will mean an extra 700 or so bodies joining the ranks of the unemployed. Then we need to think about the few retailers that are left on a High Street that is already dominated by boarded-up windows and charity shops. How many will survive when so many suddenly find themselves with no disposable income whatsoever? Not many. Will Rollerton still be able to support three supermarkets when so many no longer have the wherewithal for a weekly *shop? Almost certainly not. If two supermarkets close, then another 300 will join those who are headed for the dormitories and the feeding stations. And what of the pubs and cafes and Rollerton Thistle?*

'Over the coming months the town is about to change beyond all recognition. Those who can leave, will leave. The young and the qualified and the ambitious. But most will stay. They will have nowhere else to go. The ones who never learnt to read and write or to do anything much at all. The ones who learned about how to max up on benefits from their parents and their grandparents. Then there are those who are chronically addicted to drink and drugs or completely tied down by broods of children that once generated cash but are suddenly a millstone.

'How will it all play out? Nobody really knows. Rollerton will be taking a step into the unknown over the coming months. It is shaping up to be a long, cold winter. The new dormitories, which are going up all over the town as I write, seem likely to be oversubscribed. What will happen to all the empty properties? Will huge swathes of the town come to resemble those empty, boarded up suburbs of Cleveland Ohio that came to epitomise the sub-prime crisis of 2008? Possibly. Probably.

'Economists with lots of letters after their names seem to think that the Pendleton agenda might bring a degree of greatness back to Britain. London and the South East are set to boom on the back of cheap, desperate labour. School children might start to achieve, for to fail will mean a life of dormitories and free soup and porridge. But it is very hard to see how the new dawn will be anything but icy for Rollerton and all the places like Rollerton. We will be watching in the weeks and months to come. We will try to show how the picture at ground level begins to take shape. Will Rollerton adjust? Will the town actually survive at all? Or will it slowly be drained of all meaningful life?

'We are about to find out.

Jason Marsh
Special Correspondent

Sebastian sat back from the screen and smiled. Jason Marsh. The man had written a piece about Rollerton on the day of the announcement. It had been a little lost in the news storm that had followed the PM's broadcast. What had it been about? Something about what it would take to put youngsters on the streets like their contemporaries in Paris and Marseilles. He seemed to remember that it had been pretty good. He would go back to it. And he would make a point of finding out a little more about this Jason Marsh.

He stood, stretched and paced. There was a bigger picture here. No chance of sleep now. He pulled on an anorak and a woollen hat and headed out into the wet night. Time to walk. Time to think. Time to kill the empty hours.

It was *The Enquirer*. Once upon a time *The Enquirer* had always been in the vanguard. In many ways the paper had been a constant throughout his own strange career. It alone had questioned the brutal tactics of the Argyles in Aden back in '67 when the rest of the media had trumpeted the exploits of Mad Mitch. It had always been sniffing around the cracks and corners of Ulster and the Miners' Strike and the campaigns in the Middle East. But over recent years it had become somewhat half-hearted. There was no money to be made from selling serious news printed on paper. It had toned itself down to what advertisers were still willing to invest in.

Was this a change?

Maybe it was. And if it was, it was pretty smart. There would be a new hunger for real news. That was suddenly clear enough. Whoever was at the helm was a sharp cookie. Ahead of the game. He would have to find out who that person was. And how extraordinary that *The Enquirer* had zeroed in on Rollerton just as he had. In a way they were united, joined at the hip by a seemingly random statistic. The town over a 100,000 statistic. As ever, it pleased him to discover that something that at first glance had appeared to be entirely random was in fact entirely logical and predictable. Someone out there in the night had chosen to watch the changes that were about to come through the lens of Rollerton. Just as he had. He sensed something of a fellow traveller and felt pleased.

His mobile phone trilled from a deep pocket.

"Yes."

"Dyson?"

"Yes."

"It's Taylor."

"Hello Taylor."

"Seen *The Enquirer*?"

"Indeed I have."

"Should we be concerned?"

"On the contrary. We should be extremely pleased."

"Why's that then?"

"Whatever is about to happen will be accelerated. Rollerton is about to get more limelight than it has ever enjoyed in its nondescript life. People are forever the same when they find themselves in a spotlight. They act up. They perform for the camera. They are desperate to please. Whatever is about to happen will merely happen more quickly. That in turn will give us more time to react. More time to meet whatever challenges as may come. Better still, we will be able to quickly gauge public reaction. *The Enquirer* is offering us a perfect sounding board. A focus group on a massive scale. Don't worry about it Taylor. It is a boon."

"Aye, well. If tha' thinks so."

"I do think so Taylor."

"Speak soon then."

Over and out. Just the sound of the wind whistling by a set of traffic lights moving from red to green and then back to red.

Bexx was feeling edgy. All the talk of what they were about to do with her benefits was winding her up something rotten. She had even started trying to watch the news. And she hated watching news. News was boring crap. News was posh bastards from London looking down their noses. But now all anyone seemed to be talking about was the bloody news. In the pub and at the *Bingo* and in the *Spar* shop. News, news, news. It was doing her head in.

She rummaged in her bag and pulled out the wherewithal for a spliff. Before starting to roll up, she snapped off the news and trawled the screen for something less boring. After thirteen hops she landed on some American show where a tearful husband was getting it with both barrels from his wife and mother-in-law for shagging his secretary. More like it. Stuff the news.

The sound of somebody being cut in half by a machine gun was piling out of the front room where her two youngest sons were camped out on the Xbox.

"Switch it down you little bastards. I cannae hear myself think in here!"

Nothing.

Little sods.

She pulled herself up and stomped to the door. "Listen. You either switch that down or it goes away."

"That's shite Ma. It's only good when it's loud."

"I don't give a shit. Just switch it down or I'll batter the pair of you."

Two resentful turned backs. A finger on the remote. An easing of the volume. Better.

She resumed her seat at the kitchen table, lit up and inhaled. Nice. That Donny Baldini was a proper little Dago git but he didn't half punt some decent weed. The adulterous husband was now crying his eyes out and the studio audience were baying for his blood. Soft prat. Served him bloody well right. They should pin him down and let his missus kick him in the bollocks, so they should.

A tap at the back door.

"Who is it!"

'Alright Bexx. It's Sponge."

Sponge the Junkie. They had been in High School together. Back then he had been a skinny nerd who was big into trance dance. Then he had walked the familiar Rollerton road from dope to eckies to smack. Pondlife, but useful pondlife. She opened up the door to find him looking like a drowned rat in his charity shop anorak. How old was he? Same age as she was, duh. Thirty-one and he looked sixty. A bag of shivering bones with the stump brown teeth that only a decade of Methadone could bring. Not that she had any great room to talk. When he had once been a speccy nerd, she had been blessed with big tits and a small waist. No shortage of dates back then. It had been her golden era. They had beaten a path to her door in their baseball caps and pimped up little cars. Her first ween had thickened her waist and numbers two, three and four had turned her to blubber. Now she tipped the scales at fourteen stones and gave the mirror a wide birth. When Darren, her eldest at thirteen, threw a wobbly because she wouldn't give him a fiver to go out, he would get in her face and call her a sad, fat cow. She couldn't argue really. Not that she gave a shite. There were still plenty of Friday night blokes eager enough to jump on board given half the chance.

"You alright Bexx, yeah?" Wheedling little bastard.

"Aye. I'm right enough."

"Any chance of a wee cup of tea like? Freezing my bollocks off here like."

"Go on then. In you come."

He hunched himself onto one of the chairs and eyed her glowing joint greedily. "Any chance of a wee toke like?"

"Piss off. How many sugars?"

"Four please Bexx. You're a bloody star like."

She plonked a mug in front of him and spilt a bit on the stained table top.

"What you got then?"

He took a slurp whilst managing to wolf down a digestive at the same time which meant he spat some soggy crumbs as he spoke. Items started to emerge from his carrier bag.

"Got some sausages. Couple of packs of bacon. And gammon. Nice bit of gammon. Lovely like. Fiver the lot, right?"

"Fiver! You mad or something? Two quid. Take it or leave it."

"Two quid. Ah come on Bexx. Two quid's shite."

"Two quid's all your getting. I've heard nobody's buying much. Everyone's saving in case they get kicked out next month."

His grey face creased into an expression of concern. "You dunnae think they'll really do it do you Bexx? Kick us all oot like?"

"Will they hell. It's just the usual politician shite."

"Aye. S'ppose. You cannae manage three quid?"

"Two and count yourself lucky."

"Aye alright then." He pocketed two pound coins and pondered the long hours of frantic shop lifting that lay ahead before he could get himself a tenner bag.

"I'll be off then."

She ignored him, lost in the dope and the next televised victim from America.

More infidelity. More screaming accusations. More baying for blood from the studio audience. Her brain slowly dissolved into joints three and four to such an extent that she barely noticed a return to full volume in the front room.

However it was not an entirely contented fog. The cannabis was unable to remove the shiver of unease that had settled on her in the days following that jumped up pratt Pendleton appearing on the tele. Everyone seemed worried about it. And now even Sponge was worrying. Some of the women in the Spar seemed to really believe that everyone was about to get their money stopped. Not just some of it, all of it. And not just that. They were going to have to pay their own rent too. It was ridiculous. How was she going to manage to pay rent with four weens and that? Anyway, she was sick. Her doctor agreed. Every month he signed her off and doled out the Prozac and the Valium. There was no way they would be allowed to take money off a sick woman with four weens. Somebody would put a stop to it. Obviously they would.

Slowly her soggy brain registered more knocking at the back door. Christ. Like Hyde Park bloody corner. Probably Sponge back from another round of thieving. But it wasn't Sponge. It was Sheena and the reporter bloke from London.

"Hi Bexx. Got a minute?"

"Aye, hen. Come on in. Just watching tele so I am. Want a cuppa?"

They took seats at the kitchen table where a half smoked joint smouldered in an ashtray. Bexx was all slow motion as she did the honours with the tea, finding it hard to remember where the sugar was even though it had been in the same place for ten years. "Have a toke if you want Sheena hen."

"No thanks. All done with that now."

"What? Even a spliff like?"

"Done with all of it hen."

"What about you? Like a toke do you? Sorry. Cannae remember your name"

Jason smiled and shook his head. "It's Jason. Once upon a time. Now the problem is that it would get me writing even worse shite than usual."

Bexx shrugged, somewhat confused. It wasn't like it was smack or anything. She deposited mugs in front of her guests and started the job of working her way through a pack of Maryland chocolate cookies that she had picked up the day before as part of a £2 carrier bag deal from Sponge.

"So Jason. What do you make of all this nae money shite they'll all talking about?"

"That's why we called actually. To get your thoughts on things. See what your plans are?"

Bexx spat out a disgusted batch of crumbs. "Plans! How's the likes of me going to make plans? I've got four weens to look after and I'm sick. I cannae make plans."

"But you're going to have to make some pretty big changes."

"Like what?" The shiver of unease was back.

"Well, have you got any savings?"

"How do you mean?"

"Money put by. In the bank. A back stop for a rainy day."

Another shower of amused crumbs. "You must be joking. How can the likes of me save money? I'm not some stuck up bitch with a fancy job. I'm trying to raise four weens here."

"So no plans then?"

The warm glow of her three morning joints was all gone away. Instead, a gnawing, chewing paranoia wormed its way into her guts along with the Maryland cookies.

"What plans should I be making then?"

"Well I suppose the big question is whether or not you feel you might be able to get a job to pay the rent here. Or do you think you will all have to move into one of the dormitories?"

"A job! Are you kidding? How can I get a job? I'm sick. I've got four weens. I cannae manage a job with four weens. How am I supposed to do that then?"

Jason crashed fags around the table. "They announced yesterday that all schools will be open from eight until eight. Basically you can drop the kids early in the morning and they can be looked after for up to twelve hours. It frees you up to work."

"But I'm sick. I get depression."

"That will be up to you. You will need to weigh up what makes you most depressed. Working and being able to stay here, or killing time all day in one of the dorms."

"So I'm supposed to sleep in a room full of Neds and junkies? And ma weens!"

"Actually no. They say there will be family rooms. You will all have a room of your own."

"What, all five of us?"

Jason nodded.

"But they cannae do that."

"They can do what they like. They are the Government."

Now the paranoia was chewing through every inch of her. "So if we get nae money how are we supposed to eat?"

"The food station. They promise three hot meals a day to anyone who wants them."

"And clothes and that for the weens?"

"Clothes banks."

"I'm not dressing ma weens in any charity shop shite."

"Actually I gather the childrens' clothes will all be new. From Cambodia I think. They will double up as school uniform."

"And what about me?"

"Hopefully you will have enough clothes to keep you going until you get a job."

Suddenly it registered with Bexx that this wasn't paranoia any more. This was real and it was coming and it was an almost unimaginable nightmare. Suddenly her brassy voice was much, much smaller.

"Why are they doing this to me? What the hell have I done?"

"They're doing to everyone Bexx. Nobody has done anything. The country has just run out of money, that's all."

"But how can a country run out of money?"

"It happens. And it has happened to us. It is going to be a very different world I'm afraid."

There were tears now. Helpless and desperate. She had been putting her head firmly in the sand at the *Spar* shop and down the pub. Playing the could'nae give a shite card. Playing the what a load of bollocks card. But now it dawned on her that there might not be too many more cards to play.

"So when's all this going to happen?"

"You will get your last payments next week. They will give you a month's notice on the house. Then you either find a job to pay the rent or you'll have to go to the dormitory. Or move in with family of course. Or borrow from family."

"Are you kidding? All of us are the same. We'll all be in the poxy dormitory together. The whole of bastarding Greenfield will be there. Then what? Are they just going to leave all these houses empty to become shooting galleries or what?"

"Probably not. The new rent will be about £30 a week. The waiting lists are full of people who are working who have been wanting a house for years. They just have never managed to get enough points to be considered a priority. Most are still living with their parents or sharing flats in the town. Now they will easily be able to afford the rent and get a place of their own."

"That's not fair. What makes them so special? They don't even have any weens or nothing."

"It isn't about fairness. It's all down to money. They have jobs, they can afford the rent. Simple as that. It is how things are going to be from now on. Anyway, look. I have a draft of the article we talked about. I changed all your details like we discussed. I'm calling you Jen and saying you have five kids. Nobody will know it is you. Would you like to read it over?"

"No. Just so long nobody kens it's me like. Did you come up with any cash?"

"I did. £300. Maybe it would be a good idea to put it to one side and use it pay up some advance rent. It will give you a couple of months to try and find something.."

"Aye. Maybe." She counted the money twice and pocketed it.

MERE ANARCHY

THE VIEW FROM ROLLERTON
By special correspondent, Jason Marsh

JEN

'Ever read any Jane Austin? Or Charlotte Bronte? Or Thomas Hardy? Maybe. Set text for an English lit 'O' Level? Whatever. Bet you've watched a mini series on the box. Assuming you have either seen or read, then you will be more than familiar with the story of one of the female characters in the story having a thoroughly good match arranged for her. You know the kind of thing. Squire Engleby is interested and he has 200 acres with good shooting and a settlement of a hundred guineas a year. A hard-faced mother will bully her tearful daughter into the wedding despite her head over heels passion for a penniless cavalryman. This kind of thing once upon a time went all the way to the top as the royal houses of Europe interbred with each other to forge alliances and build territory. It is nothing new and it is isn't all that long since it was the height of respectability. Daughters followed the same path as their mothers and grandmothers.

In a way, Jen is no different. She never knew her dad. He was a great unknown. A one night stand when her mum was seventeen. Jen was the middle one of three and there was no dad for any of them. Mum never worked. Instead she reared her brood care of the state. The family never went short. They were housed and there was always enough in the coffers for food and a house and clothes and nights out for mum and an occasional holiday in the sun. As Jen grew up she was never around anyone who actually worked. Instead the lessons she learned were how to max up on the many benefits on offer. She saw school work as a waste of time and her mum wasn't about to disagree. Her raw intelligence ensured that she managed to learn to read and write reasonably well, but that was about it. She was generally considered to be a bonnie lass and there were always plenty of local lads eager to have their wicked way. Like mother like daughter, Jen first fell pregnant a few weeks after her sixteenth birthday. How did mum feel about this? Was she distraught that her daughter would be tied down by motherhood and unable to go to college and start a career? Not at all. Mum viewed her daughter's young pregnancy in the same way that those Victorian matriarchs once viewed excellent matches with landowning squires.

Had Jen avoided getting pregnant where would she have been

129

now? Maybe she would have a job in a supermarket or a high street shop. What would that bring in? Maybe £160 a week after tax. Maybe just about enough to pay the rent and council tax on a small flat, but that would not leave her a lot for herself. Instead Jen followed the family tradition and pursued a far more lucrative career. By the time she was twenty-seven her brood had grown to five and the cash was rolling in. Right now she receives almost £400 a week. There is no tax and all of her rent and council tax tabs are all picked up. Best of all, there is no requirement for her to do so much as ten minutes of work to earn the cash for Jen is signed off sick with depression which spares her annoying visits to Job Centre Plus and gives her a comforting base of free prescription Valium and Prozac. Jen makes her £400 a week go a long way. Sometimes she visits the local supermarket or Spar shop for provisions, but not often. Every day she receives home deliveries care of a helpful Heroin-user who we will call Rolo. Rolo receives shopping lists from Jen and he fills them accordingly. Jen pays him about a third of the marked price for what she buys. A £20 bag of stolen shopping will change hands for £6 or £7. It is a well established routine. Rolo gets the list, nicks the stuff, sells it to Jen and races round to the nearest dealer for the next tenner bag. Then the process repeats and repeats and repeats. Jen's kids are dressed from head to toe in top end designer gear. They have fancy phones and every electrical goodie the market can offer and all of it has been supplied by the gallant Rolo at a third of cost. Not surprisingly there is always plenty of disposable income left over for treats. Jen works her way through an average of £40 of cannabis every week and goes out at least three nights. When she hits the town, she likes to dress up and live it large. An average night of double vodka and cokes, a club, a Chinese takeaway and a cab home will run to £60 or £70. So no problems there then.

Well, you all know what is coming next. In less than a week's time the gravy train will be pulling clear of the station. Jen is about to see her income drop from £400 a week to zero. The good news is that the rent on her house is due to fall by over 50% to £30 a week. The bad news is that this will have absolutely no impact for Jen as she has never paid a penny of rent in her life. So what are her options? Well the obvious answer is to get out there and find a job in order to pay the rent and put food on the table for the family. If the job is only enough to cover the rent, then they can eat at the nearest feeding station. Will this happen? Well, Jen has never had a job and so the idea is rather alien and there will be ferocious competition for the few jobs Rollerton has to offer. I wouldn't bet the mortgage on her finding anything. A much more likely outcome will see the whole family decamping to one of the family rooms in the nearest dormitory. No more designer clothes, no more takeaway food, no more living it large up the town, no more daily payments for Rolo. It is going to come as one hell of a shock to the system for Jen and all the hundreds and thousands of other Jens all over Britain. Life will bring new and demanding challenges – a long, hard rocky path to find work and enough money for a house of their own. Maybe she'll make it, maybe not. How will she take it? I suppose we are all about to find out. Jen and her children are very used to a very comfortable standard of life and it is all about to be taken away. Will they meekly accept their family room, free meals and zero income? Or will they and many, many others lose the plot and hit the streets to burn the world down? We will all have to watch this space.'

Sebastian finished reading the piece for the second time and then laid the paper to one side. He could have read the thing hours earlier online, but he had preferred to get out into the rain early and walk a couple of miles to a musty newsagents shop. He had chosen a dingy café by the bus station as a place to digest the news whilst he sat at a table by the wall. Just another anonymous figure. A retired guy in an anorak that had seen better days, sipping tea from a chipped cup.

It was time to walk again. He pulled on his woollen hat and a settled his bill at the counter. Outside a couple of seagulls were being buffeted by the brisk wind and an empty crisp packet bounced along the pavement. What passed as a morning rush hour in Rollerton barely filled the streets. A few buses. A few agitated parents taking kids to school. Delivery vans. A few aimless wanderers killing time.

Without really thinking about it he had been drawn to the harbour front. Grey waves rumbled half heartedly into the concrete. A couple of rusty looking fishing boats bobbed and idled. Three hardy sea fishermen hurled their heavy hooks way, way out.

Jason Marsh had added pictures to facts and figures. Was Jen the woman's real name? Probably not. It didn't matter. What mattered was the distance she was about to fall. It wasn't a case of having to readjust. It was a nemesis, pure and simple. For her whole life she had seen money magically appear from the wall. Lots of money. Enough for a surprisingly comfortable life. He started doing a few mental sums. Six of them in the house. At least five bedrooms. Rollerton was hardly a hotspot for soaring property prices, but a five bed house would still be at least £150,000. A mortgage of £1200 a month or so. Say £15,000 a year plus Council Tax. Call it fifteen grand for ease of reckoning. Plus twenty grand in disposable income. £35,000 in total. How much would you have to earn to get £35,000 after tax? £50,000 at least. Why on earth would a young woman keen to have a full purse choose a minimum wage job on the tills at *Tesco* when she could pull in fifty grand a year for doing no more than breeding children? Why indeed? Sebastian smiled at the Victorian analogy. He liked that. In fact he was getting to like this Jason Marsh character. There was no reverence about the man. Sebastian hated reverence with a passion. Marsh had it on the nail about the big question. How was Jen going to take her fall from grace? And her kids? Would she take it on the chin and be meek and mild? Unlikely. She would be seething mad. More to the point, she would not be on her own. The dorms would be filled with people who had lost everything they had assumed to be theirs by right. Very, very pissed off people.

So really there was no question about whether or not they would kick off. Of course they would kick off. They would not be remotely interested in talk of shrinking tax revenues and the spiralling cost of keeping an aging population. All they would see was the money from the wall that was rightfully theirs had been taken from them. Not only would they kick off, but they would do it in big numbers.

OK. Fair enough. They had already planned for this. The police had been instructed to deliver the letter of the law ten times out of ten. In Rollerton plans were in place for the football ground to be used as a processing centre complete with a makeshift Sheriffs court in the corporate lounge. That was all ready and waiting. But Sebastian now saw that the plans were far from complete. They had plans in place to arrest, hold and process. They could get an offender all the way to the Sheriff's domain very efficiently. But then what? What about punishment? What would dissuade the likes of Jen from doing whatever they had done again? There was the rub.

He wandered his way to an internet café for a half hour browse. He took some notes. Then he drove his car five miles out of town to an old deserted airfield where once upon a time Lancaster bombers had rumbled off the runway to head across the North Sea to blitz Germany.

He stood and smoked and after a while he smiled.

Yuri Bonderenko finished Jason's article and then neatly folded the paper and laid it down. Interesting. And according to his very own tame professor, entirely accurate. The room was one of the hotel's so called executive suites. It could have been anywhere on planet earth. Tokyo. Frankfurt. Denver. It happened to be Glasgow Airport. And like all similar hotels it was as bland as a piece of bread. But it suited Yuri well enough. It oozed a kind of sterile anonymity. Nobody noticed anyone or anything. Everyone was passing through: looking forward to being somewhere else. Or not.

It had been almost ten years since he had taken control of Scottish operations. It had been a fine move. He liked Scotland almost as much as Russia. In fact, now that he had become hopelessly addicted to the game of golf, he probably liked it even more. For the last five years he had lived in a spectacular lodge on the shores of Loch Lomond and life was better than good. A remarkable outcome for a boy born and raised in a crumbling tower block on the outskirts of Tver. Had he not been so smart, no doubt his career would have been a grinding factory job in his home town. Years of vodka and cabbage and a slow death from some industrial disease. But he had always been smart and it had been duly spotted at an early age: they had been good at that back in the Soviet day. They had fast tracked him to an academy in Moscow and from that point on his career had been in the fast lane. First university, then a stellar rise in the second directorate of the KGB and then when the Soviet State had imploded, a move into the top echelons of one of Mother Russia's most successful Mafias.

They had given him the job of looking after their interests in Scotland back in 2006 and he had settled with ease. For a while he had considered it a temporary posting. Yet another step on the ladder that had carried him so far from the smoke stacks of Tver. But after a couple of years he decided that here was the place to end his days.

Business had been spectacular. Slowly but surely they had come to dominate Scotland's hugely lucrative drugs trade. They worked far away from the day to day grind of the streets. They were wholesalers who sold consistent, grade A product which was always delivered on time. Mid-level dealers from Inverness to Berwick-upon-Tweed soon came to appreciate the first class service they received. They also learnt that it was a suicidally bad idea not to pay their bills. Organised crime in Scotland had a long and distinguished past and the locals were never shy about breaking a few heads. But when it came to clinically vicious violence they were light years behind the men from the North. Yuri was soon as feared as Stalin had once been in his homeland.

The business had diversified over the years. Imitation cigarettes from Kaliningrad were a significant earner. As were the massage parlours filled with trafficked girls from all over the former Eastern Block. But Heroin was the real money spinner. Heroin moved out of the north of Afghanistan and thence on a series of trucks to Poland for the final leg. Heroin produced cash by the lorry load to be laundered through a host of businesses and then salted away into a variety of banks. The profits were constant and huge. The top men back in Moscow were delighted and Yuri got to live the life of the super rich. Not that he was particularly ostentatious. He kept himself pretty well to himself. He fished. He played golf. He had a season ticket at Parkhead and he was a regular at charity dinners. Everyone who met him tended to like him. He was good company and was adept and playing the part of the larger than life Russian bear. As far as the world was concerned Yuri Bonderenko was a consultant to the Russian energy industry. Nobody really knew what that actually meant, but it explained his lavish lifestyle.

Now he was but a few months shy of turning sixty and the kingpins at home had happily agreed to his request to retire. All that was left of his long and successful career was to keep the ship on an even keel and make sure that all was well for his successor. And then the right honourable Christopher Pendleton had turned the world upside down. Yuri's heart had sank as he watched the broadcast. So much for an easy wind down to a life of golf every day. The world was about to become a very, very different place. Three hours after the PM had wound up he had called his tame professor.

Jeremy Huntly had come to Yuri's attention in 2012. One of his larger Glasgow customers had mentioned with some amusement that he had a £50 a day smack client who was a professor of economics at one of the city's universities. Yuri's interest had been pricked and he had requested a meeting which had duly taken place.

A deal had been agreed on. The professor received free heroin in return for being on call to offer Yuri economic advice as and when he needed it. The Glasgow dealer had been compensated generously for his lost custom.

Over the years Yuri had come to value Huntly's advice and the academic was seldom far wrong in his reading of the intricacies of the black economy. When Yuri had called for an assessment of Pendleton's new world, the professor had asked for a week. Now Yuri had listened carefully to Huntly's considered two-hour report delivered in the blandness of his executive suite.

It had offered little cheer.

The analysis had kicked off with an examination of average customer profiles. An average Scottish heroin user was consuming £30 a day for product each day: just over £200 per week. About 75% of customers were signed off on the sick and therefore getting paid just over £200 per fortnight. Few invested much of this on food and basics, they certainly seldom paid rent arrears or fines preferring instead to serve out a week or two in jail to clear their dues. The bottom line was that just about 100% of the sick pay received by his customers was being used to pay for his product. Logically this suggested that once the sick pay and all other benefits were removed his customer base would have 50% less income to spend with him. Not a happy conclusion and one which more or less guaranteed a 50% decline in sales. Ouch. Next Huntly had examined where the remaining 50% of the money came from. A certain amount was begged from family, but his analysis suggested that a clear majority of the families who sired Yuri's customers also relied almost entirely on benefits for all of their disposable income. Not much chance of them filling the hole then. Shoplifting next. The removal benefit cash from the economy was about to have a profound effect on the high street. There would of course be some who were about to be clear winners once the new changes were put in place. The young, working single citizens of Britain were about to be handed a fat tax break and the opportunity to rent their own place for peanuts. The bad news for the high street was this group over recent years had moved most of its spending online. High Street shops were disproportionably reliant on customers receiving benefits who tended to buy with cash rather than making purchases online. Many of the outlets on the High Streets of Scotland had been hanging by a thread for years. The new dawn would almost certainly herald their demise. This would mean that there would be many, many less places for Yuri's customers to steal from and the shops that survived would be much better guarded as the lack of a minimum wage would make security much cheaper. There would of course be a sharp upsurge in burglaries, car crime and muggings, but a clear majority of Heroin users tended not have the natural inclination for such drastic crimes. The police would be waiting to pounce and all known heroin users would be watched carefully. Huntly had no doubt that the police would be carrying out exactly the same analysis as Yuri was undertaking himself. It would be major priority to come down like a tonne of bricks on anyone embarking on a career of burglary or mugging.

The bottom line was that the heroin industry was about to go the same way as coal, steel and shipbuilding.

Other recreational drugs offered a little more hope. The newly-enriched ranks of the working young would have more to spend in the weekend pubs and clubs. However job security was about to become a great deal more fragile. Work meant a nice flat, decent clothes, a car, holidays and a status. No work meant dorms and feeding stations. Huntly guessed that an increasing number of the working young would avoid the risk of drugs if they felt that a conviction might put their job at risk. Overall, the professor felt the impact of the new order would be marginally detrimental for sales of product other than Heroin.

So long as the law stayed the same, the outlook for the massage parlours and lap-dancing clubs was bright. Here the average customer tended to be in work and therefore a majority of such customers would have more to spend.

The final part of the report was all about whether or not Pendleton would be able to make the new changes stick. Early indications suggested that he would. The world's money markets had been impressed and the pound had inflated in value. Those who would be hit hardest represented a significant minority, but a minority all the same. The majority would ultimately have little sympathy for their plight. For years there had been growing levels of resentment to those who lived their lives on benefit. Already the tabloid press was majoring on the 'serves them right' approach and opinion polls suggested that most of 'Middle Britain' tended to agree. There would of course be rioting and unrest in the most deprived areas but it seemed the appointment of John Taylor as the new Home Secretary heralded a new hard line approach to law and order. Huntly expected the line to hold, and were that indeed to be the case, then there was little hope that Yuri's drug income in general and heroin income in particular would ever return to previous levels.

Yuri asked if major unrest might make the changes unravel. Of course. But it would have to be big. There was a clear determination at the highest levels of Government to make the new regime stick.

So there it was. The professor's analysis had more or less mirrored Yuri's own thoughts. All in all, he had chosen a pretty good time to retire. He would duly make his report to Moscow and he had no doubt that his London colleague would be saying much the same. Maybe they would simply consolidate the UK operation and put everything under Pavlov. On the surface it seemed a sensible idea. It was what he would do. The UK was about to become a backwater. It would no longer need two men at the helm. Maybe they would even suggest early retirement. If they did he would pull their arms off.

A tap on the door brought him out of his reverie. A vast-shouldered minder opened up and allowed room service access to Yuri's temporary world.

"Just there is fine. Mikhail, you can give five pounds."

The waitress who was herself just a fortnight off the plane from Riga set down coffee pot and sandwiches with a nervous smile. She instinctively sensed Mafia and wanted out of the room before they could bundle her off to some massage parlour.

Yuri tried and avuncular smile. "Don't worry. You are safe. A tip. That's all. You can go."

She went and he poured coffee whilst Mikhail resumed his station by the door.

How strange that Jason Marsh had chosen Rollerton as his base. Yuri had never visited the town but it sounded like a miserable kind of place. A bit like Tver but with the sea. And yet Rollerton had always enjoyed a special status with him for Rollerton meant Dorothy Baldini. Yuri had taken to the stately dealer with the dark Latin eyes from the get go. The woman had class and demeanor. And brains of course. Plenty of brains. Like Yuri she saw what they both did as mere business. She never showed any signs of the pathetic strutting gangsterism that so many of his customers were so enamored with. They all watched far too much American TV. They were ignorant and illiterate and had no understanding of the depths of life. He found most of them small and tiresome and worthy only of contempt. But in Dorothy Baldini he had found a kindred spirit. They had spent time together, sometimes organising their meetings to co-inside with the ballet or a play by Chekov. He had felt a pang of sadness when she had called to say that she was leaving. It wasn't unexpected of course. She had been talking for some time about a return to the warmth and quietness of her native Calabria. The Pendleton announcement had merely firmed up the date. Luck had it that her flight was on the same afternoon that he had booked his executive suite at the airport to meet with Huntly. He had implored her to drop by to say goodbye and she had agreed.

Another tap at the door and this time it was her. She smiled and took off her coat and accepted a proffered coffee.

"So Yuri. I suppose this is it."

"Yes, of course. All things come to an end. But for you a new beginning I think. Let's hope a good beginning."

"I'm sure it will be. And you? Business will be hard I think."

"For sure. Very hard. But there can still be profit. For me it has little matter. Soon I retire and then it will be golf every day. Your son. He is not with you?"

She gave a rueful smile. "No he isn't. The young fool thinks he can stay on and enjoy business as usual. The young are always such idiots, don't you think?"

He chuckled. "We were young once. You still are."

"But I was never an idiot. I can't imagine you were either."

"No. Maybe not. Times were different for us. Will he still want to buy?"

"I expect he will. May I ask a favour Yuri?"

"Of course. You know you can."

"No credit. I have given him the house and £20,000. I dare say it won't last very long. He will soon wake up to the reality of the new world. And then I expect a call. I would hate the little fool to get into any debt and . . . Well. You know."

"Of course. I will consider him to be family. I will watch over him. You must have no fear. And in return maybe we can go to the Opera in Milan from time to time. And eat pasta."

She smiled. "I would love that. And I am very grateful."

He waved her thanks aside. "There is no need. I am here for one more day. You can tell him to come and see me. Tell him tomorrow at 2 o'clock. It is good?"

"Very good. Thank you Yuri."

She checked her watch and finished off her coffee. They stood and embraced and Mikhail did the honours with the door. Yuri had thought about asking if her son had been the one in Jason Marsh's first piece from Rollerton. He felt sure that he had been. But in the end it mattered little. No doubt the boy would be yet another strutting little fool, but Yuri would be true to his word.

12.56. Four minutes until Moscow were due to call. Time for a piss and some water splashed on his face. For forty years his every move had been governed by grey men from Moscow. Soon he would get the chance to be his own man and the day could not come soon enough.

Twenty minutes and the idea of golf every day held an even greater appeal and yet it looked a long way away. The voices on the conference call had harked back to his days in the Second Directorate. Remember the old days Yuri. If we didn't like how things were going in a country, we would make some changes. Like Hungary. Like Czechoslovakia. Shit, we should have gone in hard in Poland and East Germany. We're back in the same place Yuri. These changes are against our interests. These changes are going to cost us money. So we need to see if we can stop these changes in their tracks. And we are pretty lucky really because our man in place is Yuri Bonderenko. Maybe we better put the whole retirement thing on hold for a while whilst you find a way of resolving this local situation. You want resources, we can give you resources. Pavlov will be doing the same kind of thing in England. Sure, it's a long shot. Sure the chances of success are slim, but we are going to try anyway. One year Yuri. One year to see if you can tear this thing down. Then we will talk about retirement again.

Another year. A year to achieve the impossible. Did the fools not realise that the Soviet Union had crashed and burned a quarter of a century ago? But there was absolutely no point in trying to argue about it. Arguing wasn't allowed. It never had been. Not under the Tzars. Not under the Bolsheviks. And not under the rule of the Mafia. A good Russian did as he was told and kept his mouth shut if he didn't want a bullet in the back of his head.

Some things never changed.

Dorothy was having telephone frustrations of her own. For over an hour she had been trying to get through to her son and now her flight was about to board. At last. A voice at the other end.

"Yeah."

"It's your mother."

"So?"

"I need to be quick. My flight is about to board."

"So be quick then."

She gritted her teeth and forced herself to stay calm.

"I have just met with Yuri. I have told him that you intend to keep things going. He has agreed to see you at two o'clock tomorrow. I will text the details."

Silence on the line now. Obviously this was not what the little sod had been expecting.

"Now Donny for once in you life I suggest you listen to some advice. Yuri isn't some jumped up Ned out of a scheme. Yuri is Premier League. He won't be impressed by attitude. If you want to be smart you get an early train and buy a suit in Glasgow. Get a decent haircut. Put on some shiny shoes. Try for once in your life to show some class. Some respect. And when you meet him I suggest you shut up and listen. Then maybe, just maybe, this stupidity of yours might just stand a chance. Do you here me?"

"Aye. I hear you Ma."

"Good. I need to go. We'll speak soon."

"Thanks Ma."

For a moment she stared at the phone in astonishment. Had he just said thanks ma? He had. Good Lord. Wonders never ceased.

For one of the very few times in his short life Donny Baldini actually did as he was told. He was out and about in Buchannan Galleries just after nine the following morning and by the time he arrived at Yuri's airport hotel he was gangster chic.

A burly Russian waved him to a chair whilst an even burlier Russian minded the door.

"So you are Donny. Your mother is a great woman. You know this I hope?"

"Yes I do."

"Coffee?"

Donny hated coffee but he accepted regardless. He didn't want to look like some spotty kid. They settled into their coffees.

"I think these clothes are not normal for you? Is correct?"

Donny nodded.

"Then this is very good. You show some respect and respect is important. It shows you have brains. Too many men forget that brains are important. All they care about is face. I don't need face. I can buy plenty of face. You see Mikhail here?"

Again Donny nodded.

"Mikhail was Spetsnaz. You will not know Spetsnaz. They are like your SAS. Mikhail fought in Chechnya. I expect you do not know Chechnya either. It is very bad place. In Chechnya, Mikhail was a killer. He killed many, many men. Close up and from far away. He was professional. Perfect. Now he works for me. So maybe you can see that I do not need face. Mikhail can give me face. I can have the best face in the world. Understand?"

Donny didn't really understand but he nodded anyway. He certainly knew that the big guy by the door looked like an eighteen stone nightmare on legs.

"Your mother is a smart woman. She understands that the good times are over. There are about to be big changes. And if these changes are set in place there will be little business for you and me. So what do we do? We can be smart like your mother and catch a plane out and retire. But you are not on that plane Donny. You are here with me. Does this mean you are not smart? Maybe. But maybe it means you are a fighter. And I like fighters. So. Maybe there are things we can do here. You and me. Maybe we can make a fight. Your mother has given you £20,000. I know this. It sounds much, but it is only little. You can keep your £20,000 Donny. Instead I am going to give you free product to sell."

Donny tried to keep his face impassive. This was all heading way out of his understanding. Yuri smiled.

"Confusing? Sure. Very confusing. Maybe I can make it less confusing. It is really very simple. If these new changes are put in place everything is finished for men like you and me. So we need to try and stop these changes, OK? Here is what I think. We can make experiment. We can call it the Rollerton experiment. Suddenly everyone knows Rollerton I think. They read about Rollerton every day in *The National Enquirer.* So everybody will be watching Rollerton to see what is going to happen to all those people with no jobs who need their benefits every week. Will they accept it or will they make trouble? And if they make trouble, how big can that trouble be? We need very big trouble Donny. Very big."

Yuri poured himself more coffee and crossed a tree trunk leg.

"Do you know methamphetamine Donny?"

"Not a lot. Never seen it in Rollerton."

"No. It has never been here in Scotland too much. In other places it is very big. In America and Australia and Thailand. Hitler's scientists invented it for the Nazi paratroopers. They wanted a drug that could keep men awake for a whole week and make them fight like Berserkers. Oh they were crazy. Very, very crazy. They crazy all the way to my home city Donny. They were so crazy that they killed twenty million of my people. Twenty million! Think about that Donny. Four Scotlands. It is why some people in America call methamphetamine Nazi Crank. There are other names of course. Always plenty of names. Crystal Meth. Yabba. Many. I have a new name for us Donny. Our very own brand. Just like America I think. They love their brands. And I think we can launch our new brand in Rollerton. Our brand will be called Anarchy. You know what is Anarchy?"

Donny shrugged. He was pretty sure he knew what anarchy was but he didn't want to make a fool of himself.

"Anarchy is crazy. Big crazy. Anarchy is the world on fire Donny. On fire. Methamphetamine is more addictive than Heroin and Crack Cocaine. We can make it in laboratory. There is no need to grow any plants. Already I have asked about this. It is no problem. There can be a lab in Kaliningrad next week. We want Anarchy, no problem. We can buy plenty of Anarchy. We can buy all the Anarchy we want. So. How much? In America an addict can get a hit for two dollars. Two dollars! So cheap. Even cheaper in Thailand and Cambodia and Vietnam. Maybe 20p. Nothing. In Rollerton one hit can be free. OK? But wait. How can you make money when you give this Anarchy away? Easy. I pay you money. I pay you £10,000 every month for giving away Anarchy, OK? Very nice. Very good. So maybe you don't bother to give away this Anarchy and only pretend? Not a good plan my friend. A very bad plan because Mikhail will be with you to make sure that you earn my money. Understand?"

Again Donny nodded.

"So. At first free is no problem. And they will love Anarchy. It will be cool. When we have many who love Anarchy too much we can make them pay. Maybe one pound. Maybe two pounds. And then they will discover that they need their Anarchy more than they need air to breathe. What will they do? They will do anything. Anything that you tell them to do Donny. And I will tell you what to tell them. Understand?"

"Yes."

"And it is good?"

"Yes."

Yuri smiled and pulled himself to his feet. He took some chilled vodka from the mini bar and poured two glasses.

"So. Now we are comrades. We drink."

They drank.

The Cobra Two meeting was already well established by the time Sebastian made his entrance. He was still all dressed up as a bone weary Rollerton pensioner. Charity shop anorak and thin synthetic trousers. His appearance won disapproving glares from the soldier, spook and policeman. Taylor grinned. Hawkes nearly grinned. Pendleton was indifferent as he waved Sebastian to the spare seat that had been spare ever since their first meeting on the evening of the broadcast.

"So. We are honoured. Anything to report?"

The PM's expression troubled Sebastian. There was barely hidden triumph. The man was basking in the mainly positive reaction from the media and the money markets to his big move. Idiot. What else were the media about to do? They had set the ball rolling after all. And the big money men were always going to rub their hands with glee at such a concerted effort to shaft the poor. Worse still was the vague glaze across his eyes. The muffled edges around his speech. The man was drinking. Sebastian took his seat and thrust his hand deep into the pockets of the anorak.

"Nothing too much. I presume everything is still calm?"

Taylor grinned and lit up. "More than bloody calm lad. Positively placid. The buggers are taking it on the chin. Barely a whisper of bother the length and breadth of the Realm."

Sebastian nodded. Bored. "As expected then."

"Well you might have been expecting it lad, but the rest of us were bracing ourselves for some major kicking off."

"It isn't time yet. The winners are counting all the extra money they will have and the losers have their heads in the sand. There is mass denial. All their lives these people have seen magic money come out of the wall once a fortnight. It is cast in stone. They have no concept of where it comes from. No thought about how it is afforded. It just comes. Like the rain and snow. It is their inalienable right. Oh sure they have heard what you had to say but it means nothing. They don't believe a word any politician ever says. That is also an article of faith. It has washed over them. They have no comprehension that a politician can stop their magic money. For them it would be much the same as a politician claiming he can change the weather."

"So what are you saying?"

"Kick off time will come when the magic money fails to materialize and the bailiffs arrive at the door. When the reality sets in. The first enforced meal at a feeding centre. The first night in the dorm. That is when the penny will really drop. That is when people will start to get angry."

The PM's expression became more morose as he digested the sense in Sebastian's words. He had allowed himself to believe that he had got away with it. Now he realized that such optimism had been hopelessly premature.

"Have you anything new Dyson?"

"Actually I have. We need to think more about punishment."

"Punishment?"

"Indeed. Crime and punishment. Thus far we have made contingency plans with regard to crime. There will be more crime of course. Lots of it. There will be public order offences and a great deal of petty theft. We know this. We have made plans. Maximum police presence and zero tolerance. Most towns have decided to use the local football stadium as a holding and processing centre so that the system can be fast tracked."

Taylor made an impatient sort of noise. "Old bloody news Dyson. Been there, done that. What's new?"

"What's new is what's next. Punishment. OK. We find Joe Bloggs guilty of half inching a loaf of bread from the *Spar* shop. What then? Fine him? He will probably have no money. Jail him? The prisons are already bursting at the seams and we haven't even started yet. Community service? It wouldn't even start to cope. So what do we do? What is the deterrent?"

Hawkes leaned back in his chair and ran his hands through thick hair.

"I presume you have some recommendations Sebastian."

"I do. I'm working on Rollerton as a case study. Three miles out of town there is an old Second World War airfield. I recommend that we fence it in and build dormitories to hold a thousand. On the old runways we place pallets of bricks. Blue pallets will hold a tonne of bricks and red pallets will be empty. A Sheriff or Magistrate can then issue sentences of tonnes of bricks. A stolen loaf of bread from a *Spar* shop, first offence, let's say ten tonnes. The convicted offender is removed directly from the court to the detention centre where he or she shall stay until such a time as they have moved ten tonnes of bricks from the blue pallets to the red pallets. A forklift will place ten red pallets stacked with bricks in a line and a line of ten empty blue pallets opposite. Once the prisoner has moved all of the bricks from the red pallets to the blue pallets they are free to go. Maybe they will complete the task in a few hours and leave that very day. Maybe they will become militant and refuse to undertake the task in which case they will stay. In the end they will find that the only way out of the centre is to move the bricks. If they find themselves back in front of the Sheriff or Magistrate again they will receive a sentence of twenty tonnes. Then forty. Then eighty. And so on and so on. It is cheap. It can be put together in a hurry and people won't like it much. It isn't particularly brutal. Bricks are not heavy and we will issue thick gloves. Instead it is demeaning and boring. Spirit crushing. Devoid of glamour. A cheap, cheerful and effective deterrent. If you are nervous it can be tried out in Rollerton for a week or two. My recommendation is that you give instructions for a Rollerton detention centre to be constructed now so that it is ready for business when everything goes live. Get Price and his merry men to prepare a contingency plan for the programme to be rolled out nationwide if required."

The colour had drained from the PM's tired face. "You can't be serious."

"Oh he's serious all right." Nodded Taylor. "More to the point, he's right. There has to be punishment boss. There has to consequences. And those consequences have to be quick and cheap. Best of it is that these centres can start dealing with the petty crime we have anyway. All the little bastards who set wheelie bins on fire and spray graffiti everywhere. Christ, if we play our cards right we can empty out the prisons and save a packet. Good lad Dyson. Bloody good lad. Tha's earning tha' shilling."

There were a few objections raised but not many. Ten minutes later it was agreed that a detention centre would be constructed on the old airfield outside Rollerton and plans put in place for similar centres to be built in every town in Britain. Anyone who refused to take the medicine that was coming would pay in tonnes of bricks.

For the seventh time in two days Jason and Sheena thumped away at paint peeled door that had become all too familiar. The small front garden was home to a sodden sofa, a variety of litter and oddly enough a rusty 'No Entry' sign. It wasn't a high end property. In fact it was the lowest end that the Greenfield Estate had to offer. Jason was just about to give up on the idea permanently when the door creaked open to reveal a careworn face that was as grey as the damp evening.

Sponge's eyes flickered with relief when he saw it was not someone about to give him a kicking for an owed tenner. An eager smile revealed a row of stump brown teeth.

"Hi Jace. Sheens. Come in like. Sorry. Hang on, let me get this shite out of the way."

Dark inside. No electricity. Was there ever any electricity? Was there ever a day when the option of £10 spent on a power card prevailed over the next tenner bag? The lounge was like an indoor landfill site. The kitchen was much the same but at least there was a little light thanks to a flicker candle on the table.

"Sorry about the mess like, I've been meaning to tidy up but you know . . . anyway. Here. Have a seat. I'd offer you a cup of tea but . . ."

They all sat. Sheena could see that Sponge was rattling his head off and a host of unwanted memories washed through her.

"Rough day Sponge?"

He sort of hugged himself. Like a carrier bag of desiccated bones. "Aye. Not good like. Polis took me in all afternoon. Bastards. They kept me till after five so I missed my Methadone."

She tried an encouraging smile but knew it was pointless. Been there, done that . . .

Jason lit up and passed the packet over the Sponge who dug hungrily for the rare pleasure of a ready-rolled smoke.

"How's the story then Jace?"

"Coming along. I have a draft with me if you would like to read it?"

"Nah. It'll be OK like. What are you calling me like?"

"Nate. Like we said."

"Aye. That's right enough. So we did. Should have remembered that."

They had talked about it a week earlier. In a former life Sponge had actually been Nathaniel Peter Clarke care of a pair of Born Again Christian parents. It had been a very long time since anyone had addressed him by any of those names. Sometimes people in the *Job Centre* or the doctors. Never on the street. The years of heroin had morphed him into Sponge and the days of being Nathaniel Peter were as far gone as the Bronze Age. Even so he suggested Nate instead of Nathaniel. Just to be on the safe side.

He wrung boney hands and summoned up the nerve to pop the life of death question.

"Jace. Ken how you said there might be a pound or two . . ."

"Sorted. My editor agreed £300."

The thin grey face transformed. Suddenly there was hope. More than hope. Near certainty.

"But." Sheena's voice was firm.

Back to desperate anxiety on the back of a single three letter word. "Aye?"

Sheena smiled. "It's OK. Don't panic. You're going to get a sorter. But I have put my foot down. I hold the cash, OK? You come to me once a day and I give you a tenner until it's all gone. We're not having you top yourself on our cash, fair enough?"

"Aye Sheens. Fair enough like. Just so long as I get my sorter the now, like."

Jason leaned back and then changed his mind as the chair made alarming noises. "Just a few more questions if that is OK."

"Aye. Nae bother Jace."

"You told us that on average you use three bags a day, yes?"

"Aye. More or less."

"So about £200 a week."

A shrug. "S'ppose. Never really add it up. Too depressing."

"And you are on the sick?"

"Aye. Get depressed and anxious and that."

"So you benefits are what? About a hundred a week?"

"Aye."

"So they pay for about half your habit?"

A shrug.

"And to make up the balance you shoplift?"

Embarrassed shrug. Jason checked some notes. "You told us that you are banned from most shops so now you mainly steal food and sell it around the estate. In fact I think you said that your customers give you shopping lists?"

"Aye. I get about £3 for every tenner's worth. Hard grafting like."

"No supermarkets though? No chance of getting in there?"

"Nah. They all know me. I get kicked straight oot."

"So you must be pretty concerned about all the changes that are coming?"

"What changes?"

"Did you not see the Prime Minister's broadcast?"

"Nah. Nae Tele like. Nae power even if I had one. Heard about it though. They're saying something about cutting the Brew and that?"

"Not cutting it Sponge. Stopping it."

"Aye but I'm on the sick like. They will'nae cut the sick."

"They will. They are doing. Next week will be your last week. Housing benefit too. You get a month's notice then you will have to pay your rent yourself."

"You're having a laugh."

Jason shook his head and docked his cigarette in an old Coke can.

"How am I supposed to pay rent?"

"Get a job."

This almost brought a laugh. "Aye right. Like anyone's going to gi' a job tae the likes of me. So where am I supposed to stay?"

"The new dormitory. You've probably seen it going up at the old carpet factory. There will be a feeding station right next door."

Sponge frowned and tried to clear his head of the swirling misery of withdrawal. "So I get no benefits and nae hoose, right?"

"Right."

"Jesus."

"Tell me Sponge, are most of the people using kit in Rollerton on the Brew?"

"Aye. S'ppose they are. There's one or two like. You ken, who have jobs and that. But not many."

"So it would maybe be fair to say that about half of the money spent on Heroin comes from benefit payements?"

"Aye. When you look at it that way it will be. Bloody hell. I wonder if that's why Dot's legging it to Italy."

"What was that?"

"Dot like. You ken. Dorothy Baldini. Punts out almost all the kit in the town. Well she's left. Gone back to Italy. Has a house out there, so they say. Got a pool and everything. Her son Donny's staying like. He's a little shite."

Jason smiled. Another story wrapped with a neat bow. He leaned back enjoying a wave of satisfaction.

And then his chair fell to pieces and the frontline journalist found himself on the deck next to an empty milk carton.

THE VIEW FROM ROLLERTON
By special correspondent, Jason Marsh

NATE

Nate doesn't have much of a life. In fact what he has is barely life at all. It is an existence. Every morning he wakes up in a wreck of a house that hasn't seen a power card in months. Maybe he will light a candle. Or maybe he will head straight out of the door. Every day is a re-run of the same drama that has played out for the last fifteen years of Nate's life. Every day by hook or by crook Nate strives to come up with the £30 he needs to buy three 'bags' of Heroin to top up his Methadone prescription. The methadone is enough to drive away the gnawing demons of cold turkey, but it does nothing to mask the relentless misery of his plight.

Nate is every inch one of the urban ghosts of the twenty-first century. He might weigh eight stones, but I doubt it. He is a walking twig and his veins have retreated as far away from the needle as they can get. His face has twenty more years on the clock than it should have and his teeth are a row of brown stumps. He carries the physical and mental scars of umpteen beatings. He has active Hepatitis C and a host of other ailments. Some might say that Nate is a dead man walking. Few would disagree.

Maybe it is worth taking a peak at the economics of Nate's life. He has a house of sorts which is paid for by Housing Benefit. One top of that his sick pay gives him about £100 a week. His Heroin spend averages £200 a week. The maths are therefore pretty simple. The Tax payer pays for half of his habit. To make up the balance he steals to order. He has a roster of clients who give him lists of household basics; food and cleaning materials mainly. He can't use any of Rollerton's supermarkets to fulfil his order book. They wised up to him years ago. Instead he works the corner shops and Spars. A tin of beans here. A bottle of washing up liquid there. On a good day he will manage to steal £90's worth of goods and cash them in for the £30 needed for three bags of smack. On a bad day he gets lifted by the police before he has the chance to pinch so much as a pint of milk. Those are the worst of days. The boys in blue are only too aware that the chemists close at five o clock and so they hold him until ten past. No Methadone, no Heroin, no nothing. Just a long, long night of sickness and shivering.

Like I said, an existence. Not a life.

So what now for Sponge and his 300,000 fellow travellers in Britain? Well the house will go for sure. Nobody is about to employ Sponge. Not with a criminal record that runs to ten pages. So he will be headed for the dormitory. Maybe that will be for the best. At least there will be heating and light and clean sheets. And the feeding station will give him the chance of three meals a day. Of course half of his weekly Heroin money will be taken away in one go. What of the other half? The shopping lists? Well that will probably go the same way. Those who give out the lists are all on benefits themselves and will no doubt be joining Nate in the dorm. Even if there are still customers ready and able to pay for his stolen goods, it is hard to imagine he will find the stealing itself achievable. Without customers on benefit most of the smaller shops that Nate steals from will soon close down. Those with jobs and cars do their weekly shop at the supermarket. Those on the Brew walk to the corner store and pay more for their beans on toast. The retailers who will survive in Christopher Pendleton's Brave New World will be the large chains. The ones with the cameras and the security. The ones who keep Nate and his fellow addicts out on the pavement.

So. It seems likely that no matter how hard Nate tries he will struggle to come up with anything remotely close to the £200 he spends on heroin. Well Nate, I'm sorry to say it, but three cheers to that. It means you move into a warm, safe dormitory and eat a well-balanced diet. You will have to manage on your daily dose of methadone which is licensed, clean and supplied by trained professionals, not criminals. Your health will improve and your mind will clear. Whether you like it or not, it will be the best thing that has happened to you in years. Maybe you will even rediscover the person you used to be.

So who loses? Interestingly enough, it is the illegal drugs industry. There are well over a thousand Nates in Rollerton and they all spend £10,000 a year on heroin. 1000 x 10,000. As in a turnover of ten million a year. Ouch. Now that is really going to hurt. Little wonder then that our local drugs baron left town a few days ago. She jumped on a plane and flew to the sunshine of Italy to retire to the sumptuous villa she has built ready for a rainy day. As Nate says, it has a pool and everything. The lady in question has taken a long look at the writing on the wall and she hasn't liked the words.

So Mr Pendleton, it appears that you are about to enjoy quite a bonus. Did you plan it? Who knows. I am sure you will say that you did. Who cares really. If you manage to land a heavy blow on the organised criminals who have wrecked Nate's life and the lives of thousands like him, then this journalist for one isn't about to complain.

When D-day arrived it wasn't much of a D-Day at all. The Giros of Great Britain Plc, were not programmed to land on a single day. The system wouldn't have been able to deal with such an avalanche. Instead the computers that called the shots had everything spread out over a fortnightly cycle.

For several weeks the media had counted down to the first day when the taps would be closed off, and when the day arrived camera teams were duly waiting and ready at post offices the length and breadth of Britain. And people turned up of course. Because no matter how many times they heard it on the news it was still overwhelmingly hard to believe that it really could be true. How could it be true? Nobody could really take away their money. Surely not.

So they queued patiently to slip their cards into the machines at the counter only to discover that it was true after all. Nothing. Zero. Zip. And then with pale anxious faces they told the reporters outside that they didn't know how they were going to manage. And ever present in the background were police patrol cars with their engines idling.

There were some incidents of course. In Barnsley a group of thirty women hurled bricks at a post office window. A man in Cirencester refused to heed a police warning to shut up and go home and instead launched a one man assault on a squad car. The anchor teams in the news studios waited for news of civil unrest across the country and none came. Just small flashpoints here and there. Other reporters were stationed ready for the 7.00 a.m. opening of the feeding stations. About 60% of the planned stations were open on time and ready for business. The same design was replicated from Inverness to Penzance. A large oblong marquee about the same size as a football pitch. Long aluminium tables with matching chairs in long precise rows: enough to seat 500 a time. A serving area not unlike a motorway service station. On offer was porridge, one bowl of, toast, two slices of, jam, butter, tea or coffee. Gleaming kitchens steamed with vats of porridge. The staff were decked out in crisp green uniforms which only a week earlier had rolled off the line in a sprawling factory in Northern Cambodia.

On the morning of day one business was hardly brisk. The shuffling, grime-faced, long-term homeless were predictably enough the first to arrive. When interviewed they gave the new stations the thumbs up, particularly the huge gas heaters which warmed the tents. Groups of intrepid student types also arrived in force, keen to notch up a new experience. MPs and council leaders dutifully turned out to give their nod to the cameras. But few of the huge tents were more than a tenth full.

By mid-morning the cameras were invited to film the arrival of articulated milk tankers which docked with stainless steel vats and pumped in thousands of litres of soup ready for the lunch shift. Press releases were issued explaining that each vat held sufficient soup to serve a thousand customers and that it would take an average of fifty-two minutes for the contents to be heated to the required temperature. Bread rolls were delivered part-baked on trays ready for a seven minute stint in many-shelved ovens.

By and large the media was impressed with what they saw. There was much talk about how efficient and clean everything was. Some registered a degree of disappointment that so little of the new kit had been made in Britain. The huge tents and all furniture had rolled off containers from Shanghai. The precision boilers and ovens had made a much shorter journey from the Ruhr. At least the plastic bowls and cutlery were from Birmingham.

And by and large those who turned out to be fed gave a half-hearted thumbs up to what they had been served. Ok but plain was the general consensus. Enthusiastic government nutritionists bubbled on about how perfectly balanced the new diet was. They promised that the mix of fat, carbs and protein was absolutely tip top. The TV teams who filmed the factories where the soup and stew was prepared were duly impressed by the stunning amounts which could be churned out in double quick time. A precisely calculated blend of minerals and vitamins was introduced to the mix once all the food ingredients were blended and fully cooked. The state boffins predicted that the diet the people of Britain were about to eat was going to be the healthiest imaginable. They had measured every nutrient down to the last gramme.

Many arrived at the centres to watch from the street. Fascinated. Nosey. Not yet ready to step inside the tents themselves. Not ready to believe that they would ever have to. Others stood and watched the dormitories being slotted together by tough little Chinamen in hard hats whilst the newly-recruited local workers watched and learned. The speed at which the new dorms took shape was a source of wonder to those who watched. Work was of the round the clock variety as the supercharged Chinese teams worked a six day cycle – twelve hours on, twelve hours off. Government spokespeople promised that by the time the one month notice periods were up, at least 70% of predicted dormitory capacity would be built and ready.

The extraordinary changes in Christopher Pendleton's New Britannia were a magnet to news teams from every corner of the globe. As the nuts and bolts were slotted into place for the cameras, a genuine worldwide debate was sparked off. By and large the liberal commentators were united in their abhorrence at what was happening. They likened the British PM to Stalin and Pol Pot. They warned that he was ushering the world into a new and dark time where the poor would be treated little different to animals on a factory farm – housed in basic warm conditions, fed a scientifically calculated diet to maintain their health, and punished with an electric cattle prod should they dare to step out of line. The story played differently according to where it played. The conservative right of the American heartland lionised Pendleton as a new visionary. The Russians also liked his style well enough and some went all dewy-eyed with fond memories of the days when Comrade Stalin had made their Rodina a country to be feared. The Chinese basked in the glow of global awe at the machine-like efficiency their guys brought to slotting together the dormitories. The Germans liked what they saw, particularly the brand names on the stainless steel kitchen equipment, but were a little embarrassed to say so for the world had once upon a time heaped similar praise on one of their high profile leaders for his fabulous new autobahn system. Only the French were openly derisive, but nobody really took them all that seriously. Within weeks Christopher Pendleton's face was front page the world over. His approval ratings at home were OK, but as far as the rest of the world was concerned he was the new man.

An octogenarian Harvard professor of economics pretty well summed up the feelings of the watching world in an interview for CNN. "You know what, the Brits used to be pretty good at coming up with new stuff. Railways, steam engines, telephones, the computer. They have been sleeping for a while, but it looks like they've just made comeback. It kind of looks like they've figured out a way to deal with poor people. Do I think that other countries will jump on this new band wagon? You bet your bottom dollar I do."

MERE ANARCHY

The moment of truth arrived for Bexx on the Thursday of the first week. She had actually given a few minutes of thought to Jason's suggestion that it might be a good idea to use his £300 to pay some up front rent. But the weens had been blagging her for a new Xbox for ages and there were some amazing deals on shoes in New Look and one of the girls had arranged a big night out in Glasgow...

Whatever.

It got spent. It always got spent. And as a result as she made her way to the Greenfield Post Office on a cold but bright morning her purse was hardly bulging. In fact her cash reserves that morning ran to a somewhat unpromising £6.73.

Her earlier bravado was by this stage long gone. All week the TV had carried pictures of people just like her going into Post Offices and coming out again looking confused and beaten. Part of her had wondered whether it was worth bothering at all. But a habit was a habit. For the whole of her adult life she had been making this fortnightly journey to draw down her money. And it was her money: nobody else's. She was entitled. Just as her mother had been entitled. It was something as certain as autumn sliding into winter.

There wasn't much of a queue inside. Two people in fact. One weighed and sent a package which apparently was for a son serving in Afghanistan. The next was clearly a pensioner who put his card into the machine and cash duly emerged.

Her turn.

The semi-haggard look on the Postmaster's face was enough to tell her what was about to happen. But she followed through anyway. Number in.

Nothing.

Not a penny.

Only a fortnight before it had been over £800. And now it was nothing. Instead she had £6.73 in her purse and a chilling realisation settled into her guts.

£6.73 was supposed to last her for the rest of her life. She exited the shop in a daze and drifted back home. No point pretending any more. The people on the tele had been right after all.

Once inside she undertook a hasty stock-take of her cupboards. Thankfully Sponge had been more desperate than usual and she had reaped the benefit with a few spectacular carrier bag deals. There was a reasonable amount of cereal and tinned food. The fridge had a couple of pints of milk. The chest freezer was about half full. So how long? She had no idea really. There had never really been a need to learn the art of food budgeting. Maybe a week? Maybe even less. Much more pressing was the cannabis/cigarette situation. The packet of fags on the kitchen table was down to twelve and she knew exactly how long that particular stock was about to last. It would be gone by the early evening, assuming that she kept the packet in her pocket to stop her two eldest, Darren and Kylie, from picking her clean. Her dope stash was hardly any more healthy: enough for three or four spliffs maybe? Five if she made them skinny. A day's worth at best.

And £6.73 in her purse.

And then no more.

Not ever.

Sponge was finding life even harder. In just a few short days the world seemed to have changed out of all recognition. One by one his customers were dropping off and they were not being particularly nice about it. A simmering bad mood had settled over the tired, grey dwellings of the Greenfield estate. One by one their cards were becoming worthless. Pound by pound the cash was draining away. It didn't matter if he offered goods at a tenth of their ticket price he was still told to take a hike. What point was there in offering a carrier bag of shopping for a pound if the punter hadn't got a pound and wasn't about to get one any time soon? No point at all.

That said, it was getting harder and harder to come up with a carrier bag of goods to offer to sell. Every day saw the shops he favoured getting emptier and emptier. These were the shops who catered for the budget customers of the town. A whole lot of burgers for a couple of pounds. Great value just so long as you give reading the label a wide berth. Cheap goods meant slight security which in turn meant relatively easy pickings for Sponge and his like. Now everything had changed. The shops were all but empty and all of a sudden there was security everywhere: guys who had read the writing on the wall and realised that £2 an hour was going to be the difference between paying the rent and heading for a dormitory. The town's three giant supermarkets were almost as busy as ever. For the majority of their customers little had changed. The weeks and months to come promised more in the pocket at the end of the month as the Pendleton tax breaks kicked in. These great palaces had always been hard for Sponge to get into. Now it was impossible. Security had been trebled. On the three occasions he had tried to get in he had been stopped a good thirty yards from the front door.

To make things worse his appearance was worsening by the day. He hadn't managed to buy a tenner bag for three days and the shivers were upon him. A glance in the mirror in a town centre gents revealed grey skin coated in a clammy sheen of sweat. Christ. No wonder he wasn't allowed within ten yards of a shop door. He might as well have been wearing a T-shirt saying 'Rattling Smackhead.'

As he trudged wearily to the Post Office his legs felt barely able to function. The half-mile walk seemed like a trans Siberian trek and in his heart of heart he knew it was pointless anyway. By now the whole of Greenfield was agog with shared horror at the new reality. The money machine was no more. The train had drawn clear of the station. The last lifeboat had disappeared over the horizon. For almost two weeks barely anyone he knew had got any money. The money machine now only worked for pensioners and really, really sick people. Sponge had been to see his GP and begged to be considered really, really sick. Instead the woman had tapped at her computer and told him in no uncertain terms at all that he wasn't all that sick at all. She had pointed out that he was lucky enough to have a prescription for a daily dose of Methadone. His best idea would be to focus on stabilising himself on his medication. And then she suggested that he should also try hard to pay three visits a day to the new feeding station in the park. The food was very healthy and nutritious. He should take advantage of the excellent diet on offer and build himself up. Then maybe he could consider some sort of work . . .

He had felt like smashing her neat office to bits. He had felt like putting her head through the computer screen. Instead he had burst into tears.

And now he had a feeling that he was about to experience a last throw of the dice moment. There was no conceivable reason why his card should work when everyone else's had drawn a blank. But he was driven on by the desperate illogical hope of the long term addict. Maybe the GP had taken pity and deemed him to be really sick after all. Or maybe there might have been a computer error. Maybe there was a God after all. Whatever. He knew he would never settle until he put his card into the machine and asked the question.

The *Spar* shop that housed the supermarket was strangely quiet. A sign over the counter politely informed customers that the store was to close at the end of the month. The owners thanked everyone for their support over the years. It had not been a decision that had been hard to make. The first week of the new era had seen takings collapse by over 60%. There was a villa waiting on the Costa Del Sol and a lovingly gathered pension fund providing a ticket to the sunshine.

The postmaster gave Sponge a mildly contemptuous look as he fumbled in his pocket for his card.

"Not a lot of point"

"Aye. Well. Might as well try like."

He tried. The card failed. He had no requirement for stamps. His legs ached like they had been hammered by a team of Iranian secret policemen wielding iron bars.

He started crying again.

Outside the sunny autumn morning seemed to mock him. He was a man accustomed to the very depths of despair but the way he felt now was on a whole new level. Heroin was the only thing in his life. Everything else had been cashed in long ago for the opiate love of his life: family, health, friends, self respect, comfort, everything. And now the perfection he craved every second of every day was being taken away from him. There were no shops to lift. No punters to fence stuff to even if he lifted anything. And not even the chance to join the rattling ranks of the once a fortnight 'Giro Junkies'. Just nothing.

He had a fortnight left of his notice period for the house and then he would be turfed out unless he could come up with £30 a week. It might as well have been £30,000. Not that he cared much. It had been many years since his house had been anything other than a barely habitable tip. He hardly ever had money to get the power on and any stick of sellable furniture had been cashed in years earlier. Now he camped in a flea ridden sleeping bag on the floor of the back bedroom. A candle. A spoon. Some kitchen foil. A scattering of litter. His worldly goods. In comparison a place in the new dormitory would seem like the Hilton.

There was no getting away from the fact that in many ways the smug bitch of a doctor had been quite right. The warm bed and the hot water to wash in and the three meals a day were things he hadn't known for a very long time. Well. Except when he was in prison of course. Part of him knew he should be feeling a sort of optimism at the prospect of these unaccustomed comforts. The problem was that none of it mattered. Only Heroin mattered. Nothing else. It was the only thing that made life remotely liveable and now he couldn't imagine how he would ever know its kiss ever again.

"Yo! Sponge."

He looked up to see the handsome features of Donny Baldini framed in the window of a black Mercedes. The cocky little Dago bastard. Who did he think he was? Mummy's boy. But there was no mummy any more. Dot had flown away.

"Come here a sec."

Sponge obeyed. Sponge always obeyed a Baldini. He was hard-wired that way.

"Jump in."

Sponge opened the back door and sank down into a leather back seat. Donny looked him up and down and shook his head with a small mocking smile. Up front the driver was a stranger. A very large stranger with a neck like an oak tree. He watched Sponge in the rear view mirror with washed out grey eyes.

"Shit man, you look like the walking dead."

Sponge stared at the seat in front frantically trying to remember if he owed Dot a tenner from way back when. "Aye. Things haven't been so good like."

A smile of pearly white teeth. "Life's a bitch, eh Sponge?"

Sponge tried to shrink into himself and stare hard at the leather headrest in front of him. A phone trilled and Mr Oak tree neck picked up. He spoke quietly. What the hell was it? Polish? Russian? With every passing minute Donny's man in the front was morphing into some kind of Bond movie bad guy and Sponge was increasingly unsure that he could trust his bowels to behave themselves.

Donny was still regarding him with those spectacular teeth.

"Well Sponge, life might just be about to look up." He reached into the seat pouch and pulled out a carrier bag full of colourful pills. "I'm going to be launching a new product over the next few weeks. Anarchy. It will cheer everyone up a bit in these dark times. Get a bit of a buzz about the place. Ken what I mean Sponge?"

"Aye."

"So. Businesses need to take the long view. I know that people are hard up right now. People are playing safe and saving. This is why I need to get the market kick started. Ever been in a supermarket when some old bag is offering the punters a free sample of something?"

"Aye."

"Well that's what I want you to do Sponge. Get yourself out and about a bit. Collar the kids. Let them have a free taste. And make sure you promote the shit of the thing, yeah. Anarchy is the business and all that. The shiny new ride in the theme park. You can do it. You'll be great. I want you to get out there and get some hype on the streets, OK? And if I like what I see, you get three bags a day. Uncut by the way. 40% pure just as it was when it arrived in town. We'll give the freebies out for a week or two and then you can start punting for cash. Not much like. The price will match the economic realities. Maybe

30p a pop. And you get three bags a day for your trouble. OK? Happy?"

"Aye." Was this real? It didn't seem real. It seemed like he was probably still asleep. Three bags a day of uncut smack for giving away free drugs? Unbelievable.

"Now Sponge. Important stuff. The gentleman in the front is called Mikhail, OK? And Mikhail is a bad man. He is the worst man you have ever met. He is a bad man who has done very bad things. And should you so much as whisper where you got this bag of sweeties, he will do very bad things to you Sponge. He will do such bad things that you will wish you had never been born. There is a simple reason why I am choosing a woeful, piece of shit toe-rag like you to launch my new Anarchy brand onto the market. Wanna know why Sponge?"

"Cos you dunnae want anyone to ken it's you, like."

"Give the man a prize. Because I dunnae want anyone to ken it's me. Absolutely right. And if anyone should ken it is me, then that it will be down to either you or the other losers I have out and about. And you have no idea how completely disposable you are. So if you should find yourself in there with the boys from the drug squad, you say absolutely nothing. And I will see you right. If you serve some time, I will make sure you get your three bags a day. But if you so much as breathe my name then I will have Mikhail take you apart piece by piece. Are we understood?"

"Aye Donnie. Nae bother like. I would'nae grass you up like."

"Excellent. So we have an agreement. Here is your bag of sweeties to give out. Here are your three bags of smack. D-Zed is doing his stuff tonight. Make sure you are out and about. It can be our big launch night."

Sponge sprang from the back of the car with renewed vigour. He had all but given up on the idea of ever knowing the taste of Heroin again. And now an absolute miracle had happened and he had three bags of pure in his pocket. Maybe there was a god after all.

Sebastian had given the D-Zed gig long consideration. He had been fascinated by Jason Marsh's descriptions in *The Enquirer* and all day he had been trying to come up with a way of getting himself into the old carpet showroom as a spectator. Much to his annoyance he had drawn a blank. Whichever way he looked at it, a balding old bloke would stand out like a sore thumb in the midst of such a youthful throng. And Sebastian Dyson had been very careful never, ever to stick out like a sore thumb. So instead of paying himself in for the gig itself he parked up his hire car on a side street that ran up a low hill and afforded a decent enough view of *Benny Khan's Carpet House*. His binoculars from the old Zeiss factory in Jena brought the activity in the street below him into sharp focus. Earlier enquiries had revealed that ticket prices had been dropped down to 25p to reflect the new circumstances of Rollerton's youngsters. Sponsorship from *The National Enquirer* and the local police force subsidised the event sufficiently for it to go ahead.

Sebastian wasn't really sure what he expected to see. Not that this worried him a great deal. He had learned many years earlier that 90% of time was wasted. But you could never get to the 10% that was fruitful unless you sat through the wasted hours. The street started to fill with young people about an hour before the doors were due to open. They waited in small groups. A raggedy-looking figure appeared who seemed rather out of place. Sebastian put down his binoculars and picked up a camera complete with long zoom lens. He zoomed in on the new arrival and fired off a few shots. A hatchet-like face with the stumpy brown teeth of a long term addict. A chancer? A drifter with nowhere else to go? The raggedy man approached a group of six and engaged them in conversation. Shrugs. Interest in something. A transaction. Hands reaching out and collecting. But no sign of money being passed in the opposite direction. Interesting.

Over the next forty minutes Sebastian watched the same process repeated many times until the man had become something of a Pied Piper figure surrounded by a group of upwards of thirty. And still there was no evidence of any cash changing hands.

Conclusion? The man was giving something away. It seemed that way. More to the point, the youngsters seemed keen and eager to receive what he was giving out. So keen in fact that they were soon queuing up to take whatever it was.

Very interesting.

Jason had been more than happy to use a chunk of his newly buoyant expense account to sponsor the D-Zed gig. He felt indebted to Ronald Pickup. The nights at Benny Khan's had been the start point of the journey that had taken Jason from the scrapheap to the main stream. Amelie wasn't merely happy with him; she was ecstatic. Sales of *The National Enquirer* were breaking records. Online hits were doubling by the fortnight. And Jason Marsh was slowly but surely becoming something of a household name. Over the last few weeks things had happened that he had never dreamed would happen in a million years.

He had been on a *Question Time* panel. He had been on the *Today* programme. He had been interviewed by *Time Magazine*. And Amelie had actually admitted that the time was coming when it would be she who would bask in his glow. Had the old Jason Marsh so much as hinted that he wanted to pay out over £1000 to sponsor an eclectic night of teenage trance dance in a small Scottish town she would probably have had him sectioned. Now she signed it off as if it was a cup of coffee. If Jason wanted, Jason got. It was hard not to let it go to his head.

For most of the afternoon he had wondered if there would be a new mood amongst the crowd who gathered to listen to D-Zed. Would they now take his messages more seriously? Were they finally about to become more like their French counterparts? By now, many of the D Zed regulars had already moved into the dormitory and Jason was in no doubt that there was a growing well of discontent. For a fortnight he had listened to their bitter complaints. The biggest shock to the system was the time they had to get up. Many had left school at 16 and were accustomed to lying in until well after noon. Now the bright lights snapped on at 7.30 a.m. and beds were cleared. Many had been accustomed to tapping up their mums for a few quid to go to *McDonalds* or a bakery for burgers or bacon and tattie scone rolls. Now they moaned endlessly about the porridge and the vegetable soup. Jason had noticed that many of the most voluble complainers had less spots on their faces by the day as their new healthy diet started to clear out their pores. Not that he mentioned this. Instead he did the frontline journalist thing and simply listened.

It had also been interesting to witness how many of them became ever more animated and articulate as their days were no longer filled by a succession of joints. Few could afford cannabis any more. Instead of spending hour after hour getting stoned in front of daytime TV or games consoles, they were out and about in the fresh air of the late autumn. Colour was appearing on faces. Minds were sparking into life. They were like old toys with new batteries. There was no doubting the fact that they were becoming increasingly angry.

Already the vacated houses of Greenfield were being re-allocated to working young people who had been living at home with mum and dad. Groups of evicted youngsters instinctively made the journey from the town centre dormitories to their old hanging out places on Greenfield. For a while they had been allowed to do so, but there had been incidents of smashed windows and cars and now the police turned them away from what they consider to be their home turf.

Already Greenfield felt like a different place. Gardens that had been home to wrecked settees and piles of litter now had swings and barbeques. Windows and doors were re-painted. Pitbulls were replaced by Labradors. At the weekend parents visited in well polished Volvos. Suddenly there was less litter everywhere. Outside the *Spar* shop groups of chatting young mothers with prams replaced groups of smoking teenagers in hooded tops. It wasn't Greenfield any more.

And those who had been born and raised there became resentful at their changed circumstances. They poured abuse at their parents when they could no longer give out ten-pound notes to buy some peace and quiet. They hated the fact that there was nowhere to plug in their Playstations. They lacked the means to top up their mobile phones and suddenly finding the price of a bottle of *Buckfast* was as unlikely as buying vintage champagne.

In an article the previous week Jason had wondered if the sudden lack of cannabis might be enough to propel disillusioned youngsters onto the streets. Maybe the drug had been one of the main reasons that the disaffected youth of Britain had preferred to zombie out in front of reality TV shows rather than battle with lines of riot police.

As soon as he joined the back of the crowd Jason could sense a new mood. The music was washing over the crowd in towering waves of sound but the crowd was reacting in a new way. Instead of a slow unified rhythm it was clear that groups were forming. Heads were pushed close in to each other to make shouted conversation possible. A couple of familiar faces came and went with oddly glittering eyes. Things were already very different. There had always been electricity around the D-Zed nights but this was something new. This was the like the untamed, lethal electricity of a sheared power line, thrashing and jerking in the wake of an air strike.

He registered a tap on his shoulder. Sheena. Sheena looking strained and concerned.

"Something's off!"

Jason nodded vigorously. "I know! Let's go outside for a minute!"

There was respite in the cool of the forecourt.

Jason lit up two cigarettes and passed one over. "Any idea what is going on? What is with the groups in there?"

"Youth teams. It is the FCNS and the LAYT."

Jason nodded. So called Young Teams had been around back in his day. All over Scotland youngsters aped the antics of their contemporaries in Glasgow. Most of the time being a part of a Young team involved spraying initials on walls and having photos posted on social networking sites. Every now and then there would be short, vicious fights, usually where the victims were outnumbered at least 5 to 1 by their assailants. For years two such groups had vied for supremacy on Greenfield – The Fenchurch Crescent Nutting Squad and the Lawrence Avenue Youth Team. It had been a thirty-year war fought out with spray cans and V-signs. Plenty of threats and occasional follow up. Busted noses, ASBOs and stolen mobile phones.

"They seem pretty agitated in there."

Sheena sucked hard on her cigarette and nodded. "There are some new pills kicking about. They say they are called Anarchy."

"Anarchy?"

Sheena shrugged. "Never heard of them. Could be anything from Ecstasy to Anadin Extra. You know how it is. There are always new brand names kicking around. What is odd is that they are being doled out free of charge."

"Free?"

"A few of the long-term wasters are dishing them out. The story is that they are free tasters."

"And the kids are taking them?"

"Come on Jace. What do you think?"

He nodded. It was one of those do bears shit in the woods questions. The kind of lame question to bring a frown to Amelie's fair brow.

"Here." She held out a bright orange pill that could easily have contained a high dose of vitamin C. "I blagged this of Sponge. Took some doing by the way. The wee sod was a shifty as hell. Wouldn't tell me anything. Maybe you can get it tested?"

Jason stared at the innocuous looking pill in the palm of his hand and didn't quite know what to make of it. He pulled out a tissue, wrapped and pocketed. He was about speak when the front door crashed open and a brawling mass of youngsters spilled out onto to the forecourt.

In a matter of seconds the peace of the night was shattered. He took Sheena by the arm and retreated to the relative safety of a long disused loading bay. Members of the two youth teams poured out of the building and threw themselves at each other with the kind of ferocity they had mouthed off about for years. The level of violence was extraordinary and already there were writhing bodies on the ground. A blade glinted in the orange light and a spray of blood spurted from a pale cheek. Twisted faces with veins standing proud. Punches and kicks and head butts. Howls of battle and screams of pain.

"Jesus H Christ . . ."

Sirens coming in fast.

Flashing blue bursting through the dull orange. A squad car. Two officers climbing out and registering shock at the mayhem in front of them. One on a radio. The other looking confused. Shocked. Scared. Indecisive.

Suddenly the two uniforms were noticed by the melee and the mood switched. A brick arcing through the chilly night air and turning the windscreen of the squad car into a spider's web. The sight inflamed the crowd. Pointing fingers. Howling threats. More bricks now. Many more. And bottles and cans.

The cops hesitated and then dived into the car and shot backwards down the street in a full on Holywood reverse. But the driver would never made the stunt team. In less than thirty yards the car was wedged against a lamp post and the mob was swarming like angry ants.

A door open now.

The female officer was dragged out by her hair. Pale terrified face. Huge, bulging eyes. Boots and fists and blood lust. More sirens now. Lots more.

The crowd around the wrecked car melted backwards to a patch of waste ground offering a rich supply of half bricks and the kind of general detritus perfect for throwing.

An ambulance arrived at high speed and the paramedics worked frantically to get the unmoving body of the police woman strapped onto a stretcher whilst other officers tried to shield them from the rain of missiles. Car after car after car until the tall figure of Doogie arrived to take control of the lunacy. A line of charging officers protected by a wall of shields raced at the waste ground and finally the mob seeped away into the night leaving a collection of groaning bodies down on the ground.

Jason felt like he was hyperventilating. Never, ever had he witnessed such inexplicable brutality. How long had it all taken? It seemed like an age but his watch told him that it had all been less than half an hour. He took the orange tablet from his pocket and stared at it as if it was about to attack him.

"Are you going to give it to Doogie?"

He shook his head, feeling rather ashamed. "What kind of journalist would that make me?"

Sheena shook her head with a look of mild disgust. He brushed it aside. "What the hell do you think it is?"

"Give me a fag will you? Thanks. I have a pretty good idea. Ever heard of Nazi Crank?"

"No."

"Methamphetamine. Crystal Meth. Yaba. It has been causing mayhem for years in the States and Australia and New Zealand. In Thailand they have even deployed the army into areas where the stuff is rife. The Germans invented it back in the Thirties. When the Generals were planning how to make Blitzkrieg work they told the scientists that they needed something that could keep their Stormtroopers awake for a week at a time. On top of that, they wanted something that would make men behave with total aggression. To attack anything with no fear. The boffins came up with Methamphetamine. Lots of British and French soldiers spoke of being attacked by men who seemed barely human. They said that the German shock troops were like berserkers. Completely crazed and devoid of fear." She shuddered slightly. "It all went pear shaped in 1941. By this time many of the assault troops had been gubbing the pills for over a year and they had well and truly lost the plot. One of the side effects is massive paranoia. One night a battalion on the road to Moscow got collectively freaked out. They were convinced that they were surrounded and fired off every bullet and shell they had. Just like that. They just fired at nothing until they had no ammunition left whatsoever. When a platoon of retreating Russians turned up the next morning the whole German battalion had no choice but to surrender. That's when the High Command withdrew the pills and half the army went into withdrawal."

"How the hell do you know all this?"

She shrugged. "My college course. Sites on the internet. Who knows. Maybe most of it is just urban myth. It took years for the stuff to turn up on the streets. Wherever it takes root there is hell to pay. It is cheap and cheerful and as addictive as Crack. We have been lucky. Crystal Meth has never really got a toehold here. Maybe that has just changed."

Doogie leaned back in his chair and stretched his arms at the ceiling. Time? Jesus. Ten-past-one. What time had he clocked on? Seven. Eighteen hours and counting. Most of his day had been spent up on the Greenfield estate where a full scale investigation was underway to try and get under the skin of what had happened at the D-Zed gig. He was still a little rattled by the scene that had confronted him when he had arrived to take control of the situation. What the hell had got into the kids? There was a wildness about them he had never seen before. It had almost been like they had gone beyond fear. His line of baton crashing officers had been forced to go in unbelievably hard to finally disperse the rioters. Once a semblance of calm had been restored the damage had been unbelievable. Four torched cars, including one squad car. A WPC in intensive care with a suspected fractured skull. Three stab victims, one critical and umpteen cracked heads.

What on earth had kicked it all off? As ever, squeezing intelligence out of the estate was like pulling hen's teeth. For two days clues as to what went down came in dribs and drabs. It had started with a gang feud as The Fenchurch Crescent Nutting Squad and the Lawrence Avenue Youth Team had squared up inside the carpet warehouse. The fight had soon spilled out of the main doors and onto the car park. Then as soon as the squad car had arrived the mob had turned on his officers. There had been quite a bit of talk about the dormitory kids hitting boiling point as a result of early mornings and no fast food. Fair enough. The dramatic change in lifestyle was always going to be a shock to the system. But to lose the plot so completely? It just didn't sit right. There was something else. There had to be.

He clicked onto the internet and brought up *The National Enquirer* site to see if there was anything from Jason. He hadn't seen his journalist lodger since the night of the riot. *The Enquirer* Home Page carried a loud and large Jason Marsh link. "Mayhem on the streets of Rollerton." Doogie sighed and hit left click. The headline which sat over a picture of the post riot detritus outside Benny Khan's made him frown.

Nazi Crank sets the streets of Greenfield alight

Doogie's frown deepened as he worked his way through the piece. Jason described the strange mood at the D-Zed gig and the sudden inexplicable descent into violence. He touched on the long held gang rivalry and painted a horrible picture of the attack on the squad car. Why? Absolutely, thought Doogie. The $64,000 question. The next paragraph annoyed him intensely. Over fifty cops had done door-to-door for two whole days and drawn blanks. Now it appeared that Jason had dug the dirt. The article described how a few of the town's long term addicts had been seen outside the gig handing out free orange pills to any youngsters up for giving them a go. The new pills went under the new brand name of *Anarchy*. The intrepid reporter then revealed that he had acquired one of the pills and the paper now had a full laboratory analysis.

Nazi Crank. Methamphetamine. Crystal Meth.

Shite.

The next two paragraphs were pretty much a rehash of the potted history Sheena had given on the night of the riot.

Shite and double shite. Doogie had attended enough police drug conferences to know all about what happened in towns where Crystal Meth got a hold. Two years earlier he had spent two days with the Pittsburgh Police Department and seen it at first hand. It hadn't been a pretty sight. The tough American cops had left him in no doubt that the drug was a game changer. Meth addicts never went meekly into the back of the van. Not ever.

The article finished with a question.

'The fact that this most dangerous of drugs has suddenly appeared on the streets of a small Scottish town is alarming enough. However, more alarming still is the fact that it was handed out to youngsters free of charge. Free drugs are a rare thing indeed. Nobody gets a beachside villa in the Caribbean complete with speedboat by giving the stuff away free. And yet someone, somewhere seems to have decided to do exactly that. Of course we are all well enough used to getting free sample. Companies use sprats to catch mackerel. And there is no doubt that anyone addicted to Crystal Meth is a fat mackerel indeed. But is there really that much business to be had from the teenage audience at a D-Zed gig? These were the new Dormitory Kids complete with empty pockets. Hardly the most promising of markets. So maybe the idea behind the free pills wasn't merely about a product launch. Maybe the idea was to pour petrol on the growing flames of rage. It seems like a lifetime ago that I penned the first of my Rollerton features. In that article I described my first D-Zed gig. I wondered what might drive British kids into the kind of full on riot their French contemporaries were so accomplished at. Well, maybe we found the answer the other night.

Nazi Crank.

Doogie finished the article and was sorely tempted to put his computer through his office window. For two days his lads had assured him that they had no stone unturned and come up with fresh air. More to the point he had reported as much to the Chief Constable. And now his lodger had apparently answered the question. He was in two minds about to do with Jason. One part of him favoured the straight forward and simple approach of wringing his old friend's neck. A more caring part favoured the less drastic action of water-boarding. Maybe he would put his firearms skills to the test and kneecap him. Time? Almost one thirty. Hopefully the bastard would be tucked up in bed and fast asleep. Hopefully he would have his mobile switched on and by his bed.

Payback time.

Doogie reached for his own mobile with a black heart and made to speed dial. His fingers were halted by the ringing of his desk phone. What now? Nothing good, that much was for sure. Nothing good ever prompted a call at one thirty in the morning.

Shit.

"Jameson."

"Douglas Jameson?" A gravel toned Scottish twang. North and East. Aberdeen?"

"Yes."

"Frank Parker."

Doogie didn't know Frank Parker from Adam but there was a hard authority about the man on the other end of the line which made him play it safe.

"Am I familiar with you?"

"Maybe. Probably not. I'm in the Met. Number two. I worked a while with your governor up in Glasgow. He tells me you are a decent copper."

Now Doogie was on the page. Parker had the reputation of being a champion of no nonsense old fashioned police work whereas his boss was all personal grooming and smooth sound bites for the media.

"What can I do for you sir?"

"Working late?"

Doogie chuckled. "Aren't we all? I daresay you're not at home in front of the tele."

"Aye. That's right enough. Have you heard of Cobra Two?"

Doogie frowned. "Only what I have read in the papers. Cobra Two does law and order, right?"

"Right. We keep the lid on. Well that's the plan anyway. I represent the police."

Now Doogie remembered. There had been some gossip when Parker got the seat at the table ahead of his boss.

"Right."

"Your man says you can be trusted. Correct?"

"He has never had reason to say otherwise."

"Good. I need something. It is low level but I need you to do it yourself, OK? Don't delegate it Douglas."

"OK." What on earth was this all about? Parker had obviously sensed a jaded suspicion in his tone.

"OK. I know. Cloak and bloody dagger and calls in the middle of the night. All the usual bollocks. I can promise you that it pisses me off as much as you. Sodding Dyson."

"I'm sorry?" Doogie was surprised at the weariness in the man's voice.

"Sebastian bloody Dyson. It's the new order Douglas. Dyson says jump and we jump."

"Who is he?"

"Christ knows. He's flavour of the month with the PM, that's for sure. He's from out of the shadows somewhere. Until he turned up at Cobra Two I had never heard of him. Tried running his name and drew forty years of blanks. He's one of those, yeah?"

"Sorry, but you've lost me . . ."

"He defends the Realm, Douglas. He works in the shadows. And anything he does doesn't even make the hundred year rule. With me?"

Douglas was. He had come across similar characters every now and then since the War on Terror had been launched fifteen years earlier.

"There has been no mention of him in the press."

"Course there hasn't. He sits at the table but he isn't really there. We never know whether or not he will attend. Most of the time there is no sign of him. And then I turn up at a meeting and there he is. Scruffy bastard with a right cocky smile. Anyway. He's my problem. He wants somebody identified. I'll e mail you a photo. It's not bad. Christ knows who it is and why he is of interest to Dyson. Quite frankly I don't want to know. I suggest you take the same approach. The guy lives in Rollerton and he looks like a waster to me. Just get me a name and address and forget all about it. I'm hoping that you might be able to I.D. the toe-rag yourself. My gut tells me that the less people involved in this thing the better. I've e mailed you five images. Can you open them up?"

"Sure." Doogie hit the requisite buttons and a crisp image appeared on his screen.

"OK. I know him. Goes by the name of Sponge. Long term addict. Low level. Pond life to be honest. What the hell does this Dyson want with him?"

"No idea and I have no intention of finding out. Can you e mail me his details?"

"No problem. Ten minutes."

"Good job. Send it. Delete it. Forget it. OK?"

Doogie felt suddenly chilled. "OK."

"Good lad. Get yourself home and pour a large one."

Dead air. Doogie duly pulled Sponge's details and sent them out into the ether. What the hell had he just done? He had obeyed the orders of a senior officer. And it made him feel like he needed a shower.

KENYA, 2006

Everything was red.

Not exactly blood red. More like dried blood red. It wasn't very often that Sebastian felt a touch of warmth enter his soul, but this was one of those times. He had taken a path from the main Lodge which took him to the top of the rocky outcrop that gave some shade to the water hole below. It was busy down there. The cool of sunset had brought strolling groups of animals across the plain for an evening drink. Zebra. Elephants. Gazelle. Now they had their heads bent low to lap up the thick, muddy water. Right by the water hole was a long viewing window that gave intrepid tourists the chance to shoot close up photos from behind the safety of two inches of unbreakable glass. White-jacketed waiters with huge smiles were no doubt serving ice cold drinks and club sandwiches.

Sebastian had never been much interested in animals, wild or otherwise. He preferred the solitude of his viewing rock. And what a view it was. The volcanic emptiness of the Tsavo West game reserve stretched out in front of him. How long was the view? It had to be over fifty miles. Fifty miles of silent emptiness. Millions of years earlier, some monstrous seismic event had left the ground strewn with sharp, red rocks. Almost a desert. Utterly unyielding. Uncompromising. Un-everything. A place that human beings could never dream of taming. Man had left few fingerprints here. A deserted road. A few telegraph poles, obsolete now in the digital age. And the sumptuous lodge complete with a pool and chalets with perfectly-thatched roofs. Not a lodge for backpackers. Not even a lodge for well-heeled package tours. It was a place for those with serious money. Each of the ten chalets was available only to those able to afford $2000 a night.

It was a tiny enclave of outrageous luxury in the midst of the African wilderness. Far, far from the madding crowd. Odd that he should find himself in Kenya. Years earlier he had read the ultra-secret account of the first use of Hydracol 5. Half a century had passed since those first Mau Mau guinea pigs had been tamed. To the best of his knowledge, that had been the only time that Hydracol 5 had been used by anyone other than himself. But he didn't really know that. Maybe there had been other times. And other men like himself. Grey men.

Had he made some sort of subconscious decision to come here to Tsavo? To bring Hydracol 5 back to Kenya after so many years? To turn the wheel full circle? Maybe he had.

His latest journey had started in deep leather armchairs in a discreet London club. A foreign office type. All public school good manners and Oxbridge cufflinks and old world charm. Tea and crumpets and a quietly ticking clock. The man had been silver haired and as smooth as polished marble. He had poured tea and quietly outlined the spot of bother that they hoped Sebastian might be able to help out with.

BP had found rather a big oil field off the West African coast. Luckily enough it lay in the territorial waters of an old friend of Britain. Not the nicest of chaps in the very strictest sense of the word. Deplorable human rights record and fat bank accounts in the Cayman Islands whilst his subjects got by on a dollar a day. Or didn't get by. But a loyal chap all the same. Had a decent little army equipped with British kit and trained by Tim Spicer's lot. Had a place in Surrey and the son and heir at Harrow. A season ticket at Stamford Bridge no less. Bit of a rough diamond, but all in all, a thoroughly good egg.

Sebastian had sipped his tea, ignored the crumpets and waited for the man to cut to the chase. It didn't take long. The thoroughly good egg with the rat infested torture cells was more than happy to cut a deal with BP. Not a problem. For $50 million in his Caymans Account and a guarantee of ongoing weapon supplies, he was more than happy to sign on the dotted line. The deal was an oil man's dream. A big, fat long term cash cow that would keep the share price up where it needed to be. Best of all, there were no environmental requirements and no provision for improving the lot of the country's mainly illiterate citizens who were rubbing along on their dollar a day.

In short, all had appeared to be tickety-boo. And then a certain Dominique Ferrer had turned up to place her Gallic spanner firmly into the spokes. Dominique was an oil man's nightmare. She had the looks of a catwalk princess and the eloquence of a barrister. Her husband was Jules Ferrer, a fixture in the Arsenal midfield and the

French national team. They were a media darling couple. No big-hitting charity event was complete without their stellar presence. Jules enjoyed huge sponsorship deals to market designer clothes and jewellery and cars, whilst Dominique used their celebrity status to go out and bat for the poor. She was a cameraman's favourite when she turned up in the shanty towns of Africa in her designer bush wear. The TV adored her, especially when she gave her French passion full vent. And she had given it to BP with both barrels. How dare they steal the resources of such a poor country like some modern day robber barons? Where was their environmental responsibility? Where was their sense of decency? Had anyone else said any of this, they would have been met with utter indifference. Nobody cared what went down in tin pot countries that nobody could find on a map. But lots of people cared about Dominique Ferrer. She was a A lister. She was a *Hello* Magazine regular. She mattered.

Talking about her seemed to give the man from the Foreign Office a headache. His handsome features creased with distaste. It was all very tiresome. But sadly it was symptomatic of the modern world. Good old Clive never had any such difficulties in India. Nor Cecil Rhodes in Africa. For a moment the man had stared into space and reflected on how things had been once upon a time. Then he had straightened himself and asked if Sebastian might possibly have been able to help out. And he promised that Her Majesty's Government would be eternally grateful if he did. And he also promised a cheque with many, many noughts.

Sebastian had taken his time and done his reading. And then he had given the man from the Foreign Office some proposals to take to the big wigs at BP. They should suggest a meeting of all parties. Somewhere discreet, far from the prying eyes of the media. And it should be somewhere in Africa, on the soil of the continent that stood to benefit from the riches off its West Coast. All parties would sit around the table and thrash everything out. There would be to the big hitters for BP. There would be President and his entourage. And there would be an environmental team headed up by Dominique Ferrar. The luxury game lodge in the midst of Tsavo's wilderness would surely be perfect. Discreet and sumptuous, and of course BP would be more than happy to pick up everybody's tabs. Of course they would.

The proposal was duly agreed by all. Arrangements were made and Press releases released. When they arrived, the chalets were allocated. Four for the President and his people. Three for BP and three for the environmentalists. There would be three days of meetings interspersed with game drives through the bush. It was a perfect place for an accord to be reached. For hands to be shaken. For a new way to be found. And on the fourth day the party would move to the Nairobi Hilton to tell the world's media that they had all become the very bestest of friends.

The fridges in the environmental chalets were well stocked with fresh juice from South Africa and sparkling mineral water from the glaciers of Switzerland. In Dominique's chalet there was an abundant supply of her very favourite tipple: pomegranate juice. And Sebastian made sure that every last bottle carried a hidden dose of Hydracol 5. By the second day, the righteous anger seemed to have drained out of the environmentalists. The President was delighted. BP made offers and the environmentalists agreed to all of them. They were disinclined to say much. They merely nodded and signed where they were asked to sign. The only disappointment was that on the third afternoon Dominique was far too listless to appear by the pool in her tiny bikini.

And now the deed was done. There would be a last celebratory dinner and by the time the sun set on the next African day the world would have heard all about it. There would probably be some speculation that the fair Dominique was not quite her usual self. Might there be a baby on the way? Or maybe Jules might be playing away? The threadbare nature of the BP concessions would be lost in the small print. And then the circus would leave town and move on.

Sebastian lit a cigarette and smoked absent-mindedly. By now there was only half a sun on view. Red. Blood red. Staring back at him with an air of malevolence as it departed the scene. Once upon a time he had enjoyed a rush of triumph when the deed was done. Not any more. Now he felt almost nothing. Instead of triumph there was only a sense of self disgust. Sleep was becoming harder to find. What had he just achieved? A despicable tyrant was about to salt away $50 million. The oil company directors would make a similar amount on their share options. And a couple of million people would continue to eke out a semblance of life on a dollar a day. Children would continue to die of dysentery and malaria. Sewers would remain open. Schools would remain empty of books and the torture rooms would keep up a brisk trade.

All because of Sebastian Dyson and his potion from hell.

The sun was gone now.

Night was coming. Night was always coming. He ground out his cigarette and got to his feet. Somewhere out in the gloom a hyena cackled.

Sebastian Dyson felt tired and old.

But there would be no sleep.

2016

Yuri collected a coffee from a service station franchise and took a seat by the window. Outside a line of high sided wagons were shaking slightly as a hard wind roared down the grey valley that funnelled the motorway south. All around him snatches of conversations seemed to be focused mainly on the weather outside. How cold it was. How miserable. The British never ceased to amuse him with all their weather talk. Too hot, too cold, too everything. What did they know about weather anyway? Maybe if they ever had any real cold weather they would stop talking about it. He stirred in some sugar and re-read the latest Jason Marsh article.

There was no point in pretending that he wasn't annoyed. He had hoped to be able to quietly launch Methamphetamine onto the streets of Scotland. The goal had been to stay under the radar. A covert operation like in the good old days when the cold war warriors from the KGB had destabilised countries across Latin America and Africa. Instead this Jason Marsh had caught a whiff of the truth on day one. Infuriating and downright unlucky. But Yuri had learnt enough in those very same good old days that few plans ever stayed on track. For a while he had considered shelving the idea and finding some sort of alternative. However a long night without sleep had drawn a complete blank. His instincts told him that is was going to be vital to strike hard and fast against the new order. Already Pendleton was being feted as a visionary in countries right across the globe. Few people had recognised the huge underlying well of discontent there had been across Middle Britain at the concept of working long hours to pay high taxes to support people to do nothing at all. In the new age of political correctness, many had been fearful of voicing their resentment too loudly. Hating the scrounging poor was not really an acceptable position to take. But now it had become easy. Now it was arm in arm with being patriotic in a time of need. Britain had linked the idea of hammering the idle poor with the old Blitz spirit of the autumn of 1940 and the whole world had been impressed. Doubting voices were few and far between and not many were interested in listening to them. For the first time in years the ordinary working man felt empowered: important: like what he thought, did and said was valued and listened to. Mr and Mrs law-abiding, hard working, middle-income, middle-of-the-road were feeling pretty good about life. Their taxes were down and their children could afford to have a place of their own. Sure the dormitories were full of fellow citizens who didn't know what had hit them, but at the end of the day it served the lazy bastards right. Christopher Pendleton's approval ratings were through the roof.

So Yuri knew that he had to stick with the plan, especially as the voice on the phone from Moscow was getting colder with every passing day. Only a few months earlier he had been counting down the days to a blissful retirement. Now he was worried that the next few months might well bring a bullet in the back of the head.

He looked up and saw Mikhail and Donnie Baldini working their way across the room. Mikhail had an expresso whilst the wannabe gangster carried a tray laden with burger and fries. Yuri wiped any trace of concern from his face and waved them to empty seats.

"So. Donnie. We have made a good start I think."

Donnie shrugged and took a huge bite at his burger.

"OK. But a start is only a start. You have done well and I am pleased. There is money in your account. Good money. Now we must step forward. OK?"

A nod.

"Good. In a war it is important to find the weakness of the enemy and hit it hard. I have been looking for this weakness. Do you understand supply lines Donnie?"

A shake of the head.

"OK. It does not matter how strong your army is at the front if the supply lines are weak. Soldiers need food and ammunition. Every day. Every single day. With no food and ammunition and re-enforcements, even the strongest army is weak. My country learned this in Afghanistan. Our soldiers were the best. The Red Army is always the best. But our supply lines were weak. The enemy attacked our convoys and in the end we could not get food and ammunition and reinforcements to the men at the front. So we lost. Supply lines are where this Pendleton is weak. Right now he is big hero. He says everyone has a warm place to sleep and food to eat. OK. But what if there is no food to eat? What then? What if these dormitory people are hungry? Then they will start to get a little crazy. Then they will attack the shops and this *Brave New World* is not so brave any more. So Donnie, this is what you can do. You can give out many pills. Many. I don't care how many. You can do this for two weeks, OK. In two weeks people will need these pills. They will do anything for these pills. They will kill their mothers for these pills. Then you can tell them there is only one way to get more pills. They must attack the feeding stations. And they must attack the re-supply tankers. For sure, the police will do everything to stop this, but they will not expect how crazy these pills will make everyone. You can make this thing happen and there is more money. Big, big money. So. It is good I think?"

Another nod. Another bite. A loud slurp of Coke.

"Aye. Nae bother."

Sebastian had also been impressed by Jason's reading of the D-Zed riot. He had watched things go crazy from his vantage point up on the hill. There seemed little doubt that whatever had been handed out to the kids had sent them onto the rampage. Some internet research backed up Marsh's theory about methamphetamine. But why? And who? It had been immediately clear that the first step would be to find a road into whatever was happening and to that end he had e mailed Parker one of the photos he had taken on the night. The answer had come back the next day. Nathaniel Peter Clarke AKA 'Sponge'. 31 years old. A long list of petty, drug related crime. Five years of Methadone and twelve short prison sentences on top of an endless list of unpaid fines and un-served community service. The police, DHSS and NHS files told a story of years and years of hopeless Heroin addiction.

It was obvious enough that this rather aptly named Sponge was well and truly at the bottom of the food chain. So what would Pendleton's new world mean for him? Well, the records showed that he had never once paid any tax which suggested that a regular job would be completely out of the question. His school records were more or less a blank sheet of paper. More than likely completely illiterate and innumerate. So. No more house, no more benefits and off to the dorms. Police mug shots showed a face ravaged well beyond the man's years. Sponge wouldn't have looked out of place in a pair of striped pyjamas. Hollow slack eyes, sunken cheeks, stumpy brown teeth and the yellow hue of a hepatitis carrier. It would be hard indeed for anyone looking like Sponge to get into the shops to steal anything.

Conclusions? Easy enough. If ever there was a man who was likely to do just about anything to secure a fix, it was Nathaniel Peter Clarke AKA 'Sponge'. Therefore if anyone was looking for a sucker to dish out free methamphetamines, then Sponge would be their man. So who might that be? Well, the fact that they knew Sponge, were no doubt able to pay him in heroin, and had access to a bountiful supply of free Methamphetamine pills strongly suggested the illegal drugs trade.

Why?

The big question. The important question?

In the end it took Sebastian over four days of brain wracking to get there. And when he got there it amazed him that it had taken him so long. The answer was the same as the answer had always been the same before. It would be down to money. Unwittingly Christopher Pendleton had dealt a huge blow to the illegal drugs industry. For goodness sake, Jason Marsh had said as much in one of his articles. At which point Sebastian slapped himself on the forehead and laughed out loud. Marsh had given his man the name Nate. As in Nathaniel. As in Nathaniel Peter Clarke. As in Sponge. They were both looking at the same sad and sorry guy.

And there it was as clear as crystal. How many Sponges were there across Britain? Thousands. Hundreds of thousands. And these half-noticed figures would pay over every penny of their fortnightly benefit money to their nearest dealer. Like Marsh had said, benefit money made up over half of the turnover of the drugs trade. And then there was the proceeds from shoplifting which were now going to collapse as there were going to be less shops and better security. The drugs industry was staring down the barrel of financial meltdown and surprise, surprise, they were not about to take it lying down.

The next logical step was an easy one to take. The drugs industry would go to more or less any lengths to stop the Pendleton plan from becoming permanent. They needed to stop it before it took root. How? They needed to sow the seeds of chaos: a chaos to overwhelm the comfort of the majority. How? Marsh had it again. The very same chemical formula which had once turned the German Stormtroopers into crazed berserkers as they had rampaged through the Ardennes forest all those years before.

Sebastian realised that it was time for him to start earning his corn. He picked up his mobile phone and called Atwood.

Jason had been putting off paying a visit to the main Rollerton feeding station. In many ways there seemed to be little point. The media was filled with images of smooth running operations from Inverness to Penzance where smiling residents tucked into a superbly balanced and healthy diet. Some articles focused on the new sense of community that was emerging. For the first time in years the young were sitting shoulder-to-shoulder with the old. In the London stations there was a definite sense of vibrancy as the tables were dominated by young people who had taken up the Government's subsidised rail fares to head for the suddenly booming capital. The evening before he had received an email from Amelie pointing him to a particularly glowing four-page special in one of Lester Gall's papers. Her message as ever was short and to the point. "Is this really true?"

MERE ANARCHY

He knew where she was coming from. As the new order had unfolded, it had become crystal clear that Gall was its main cheerleader. The Australian was using every one of his numerous media platforms to paint a picture of a spectacular new Britain where the ambitious young finally had the chance to chase their dreams. It was no surprise that the London feeding stations and dorms were upbeat places. Young people from all over the world were flocking to the capital to take advantage of free food and accommodation. Already there were reports of a growing consumer boom. Pubs and clubs and coffee houses and retailers were reporting record takings. It seemed like there were jobs for everyone as foreign workers found it almost impossible to either find or hold employment as companies took full advantage of the spectacular tax breaks on offer for 90% British workplaces. And of course free food and accommodation and a high tax threshold meant plenty of disposable income to spend in the pubs and clubs and coffee shops. Gall painted a glowing picture of win, win, win.

Jason was pretty sure that the Rollerton centre would be a rather different place. There were no eager youngsters getting off the train in the quiet railway station. The Rollerton dormitories were filled with people from Rollerton. He had already posted a feature on how the keenest and the brightest had taken advantage of subsidised travel and headed south. Some were sending money home to help their families stay in their homes. Others were simply living life to the full. Rollerton had been a dismal enough place before the changes. Now it was even worse. Already most of the smaller shops had closed down: only the giant supermarkets on the edge of town seemed to be doing any business. Those who had work stayed clear of the town centre which was filled with the disaffected who had been stripped of everything they had taken for granted. The policy of emptying out the dormitories by 9.00 a.m. had caused the most complaint. The council had quickly made the decision to keep the feeding stations open for 24-hours-a-day to ensure that people had somewhere to go to stay dry. Tea and coffee were on tap and soon the stations were constantly full with the newly dispossessed.

Jason arrived a little after 10. The breakfast shift was over and a clutch of smokers stood outside the tent working their way through cigarettes. Inside almost every seat was taken. Maybe there was something of a sense of community in that the sense of smouldering discontent seemed to be all pervasive. He counted twelve uniformed police officers dotted around the tables. Doogie had told him that the constant boredom was causing fighting which meant a round the clock police presence was a necessity.

177

He spotted Bexx sitting alone on the third table from the door. Every last inch of her body language spoke of fuming anger. He took a deep breath and made his way over to her.

The body language was telling no lies. Bexx felt like she had died and entered hell. Her new life was little better than a constant torture. She missed just about everything. She hated being driven from her bed at 7.30 a.m. Christ, the last time she had got up at that time was when she had been six. She hated the cramped family room where the five of them would fight like cats and dogs as the kids grudgingly got ready for school. She hated the endlessly healthy food and craved a bacon and tattie scone roll. She hated the smug faces of the women behind the serving counters who doled out the porridge and soup. But more than anything else, she hated having no money. It was like an open wound. Every minute of every day she craved nicotine and cannabis. Her hair was getting lanker without the lacquers and dyes that she had used for so many years. Every morning her face seemed fatter and greyer in the mirror now that she had run out of make up. Every morning the kids would beg her for money and the moronic cretins seemed incapable of getting their thick heads around the fact that she didn't have any. Worst of all was the fact that there was nothing to look forward to any more. No buying a new outfit for the weekend. No weekend in anything but the fact that the calendar said so. No hitting the pubs and clubs. No getting pissed up on double vodka and coke.

No nothing.

Up at 7.30. Argue with the kids. Eat healthy crap. Hang around until lunch. Eat healthy crap. Hang around until the kids returned and to the cramped family room. Eat healthy crap. Watch TV. Row with the kids. Crash out.

Again and again and again and again.

Some of the women had started selling themselves for cigarettes and the chance of a night out. Already newly established pimps were doing the rounds and signing up recruits. Many newly empty Greenfield houses had been converted into knocking shops and the word was that business was brisk. One day when her nicotine craving was driving her bananas she had approached one of the pimps and sounded him out. He had laughed in her face. Did she seriously think anyone was about to lay out good money to shag a fat cow like her? Aye right. She had retreated to the toilets to hide and cry. Her efforts at job-hunting had met with similar humiliation. How were her reading skills? How were her maths skills? How were her IT skills? What work experience had she had? What training had she had? Did she have references? No, no, no, no. Bexx had only ever learned one skill. She had followed a well-established family tradition and bred children. Why on earth would she have done anything else? Breeding children had won her a house of her own and £400 a week. Who in their right mind would piss about on computer courses to win the chance of a place behind a checkout machine? But now the pigeons had all come home to roost. Jobs were like gold dust in Rollerton, even those that paid £1.50 an hour. Hell, even those that paid £1 an hour. Even £1 an hour was enough for a pack of fags a day. But nobody was showing any interest in Bexx. Her complete lack of a CV ensured she was permanently at the bottom of the list.

Barely a month had passed since the family move to the dormitory and already it seemed like a lifetime. Minutes felt like hours and hours felt like millennia. A week earlier she would have said that it was impossible for anything to get any worse. But things had got worse. Miles worse. Something was up with her Darren. He had always been a bit of a handful but now he had gone clean off the rails. It was like he was possessed or something. Most nights she never saw him at all but occasionally he would return to the family room late at night wild-eyed and wired up. Obviously he was using something. She guessed some kind of speed. But how the hell was he able to afford it? Crime obviously. She tried to tackle him but he would just fly off the handle and storm out. Two nights earlier he had completely flipped and pinned her against the wall. She had been completely unable to get him off her. It was like he had the strength of a man twice his size. He had pushed his face close in to hers and splattered her face with spit as he shrieked at her. The abuse had been savage and she had wet herself with fear. As he registered the smell of her urine his face had contorted in rage and he had hit her. Hard. Hard enough to drop her to the floor like a sack of potatoes. The door had slammed and he was gone. The other kids had been almost catatonic with fear. She had hurried off to the bathroom to change her knickers and patch herself up. It had taken hours to get the younger ones down but she had not been able to sleep at all. What should she do? Should she go to the police? All her life she had abided the local rules that outlawed grasses. Was she going to grass up her own son? Obviously not. But if not the police then who? There was nobody. Not a single soul in the whole world. In the end she had decided that the problem would probably sort itself out. If Darren was behaving like this with the family he was no doubt behaving the same when he was out and about. He would be bound to get lifted sooner rather than later. It was surely only a matter of time.

Best to leave it be. But all the same she was terrified about what would happen when he eventually came back.

A few of the other women in the dorms seemed to be having similar problems with their older sons and daughters. Most put it down to the fact that they had no money or anything. Others agreed with Bexx and were convinced that they were on something. But nobody had a clue what it was.

The day before she had decided that enough was enough. What was she supposed to do? Spend the rest of her life eating vegetable soup and killing the dead hours with a constant stream of free tea. No way. It wasn't right. None of it was right. She wanted some make up and something to get her hair right. She wanted something decent to eat. She wanted some chocolate. She wanted a bottle of vodka.

The time had come to stop wanting and start getting. She had tried every avenue available to her and drawn a blank. Nobody was willing to give her a job. Nobody was even willing to cough up a fiver to use her body. Now it was time to get onto the front foot. All day she had done the rounds. Table by table she had engaged former neighbours from Greenfield to sell her plan. The plan was utterly simple. They would meet up at an appointed time on the *Tesco* car park. They would collect trolleys. They would enter the store and fill the trolleys. And then they would break out. So long as there were enough of them, what were the security going to do about it? Sure, some would get caught but most would get clear. And if they were to get caught, then what was anyone going to do to them? They all had kids to look after, right? So what then? A fine? Community service? What the hell could make things worse than they already were?

At first she had been nervous about approaching other women with her big idea. But not for long. Within minutes she knew that she was pushing at an open door. Most of them were in exactly the same boat. They were past caring. A month of dormitory life had been enough to have them ready to try anything and the hell with the consequences.

Now Bexx was preparing herself. If everyone came who said they would come then there would be more than thirty. A force to be reckoned with in anybody's book. Thirty totally pissed off women from Greenfield on the bloody warpath. Got help any pound an hour bastard in a security uniform who dared to get in their way.

"Alright Bexx."

She hadn't noticed the reporter approach her.

"Christ, you jumped me there. I was miles away."

"You looked it. Mind if I join you?"

"Not here. Let's go outside. If you've nae got any fags on you I'll gouge your bloody eyes out."

They stepped out and Bexx all but sucked her cigarette down to the butt on the first draw. She held the smoke and then let it out in an enormous cloud that climbed quietly up towards the drizzly grey sky above.

"Holy shite, I needed that?"

"Gagging, right?"

"Too bloody right. I have'nae had a fag in three days. It's a complete bastard."

He passed her his all but fill pack and for a moment he thought she was about to burst into tears.

"Thanks Jace. You're a diamond."

They decided to walk. Bexx chain-smoked and brought Jason up to speed on her dismal existence in the dormitory. They stopped for bacon rolls and he bought her a full carton of cigarettes whilst absorbing the grim facts that were such a far cry from the enthusiastic pictures painted by Gall and the rest of the media. He said little. When she explained how her oldest son had gone completely deranged and given her a black eye he held her for a while whilst she sobbed onto her shoulders. They stopped off in a pub and she knocked back four double vodkas to restore herself. And then something of the old Bexx reappeared.

"Could have a story for you this afternoon."

"That would be good. Tell me more."

"Cannae tell you much. Just be at *Tesco* for 2.00 o'clock, OK? If you get a decent story you can pay me, right? I'll leave it up to you. You've always played straight with me. You've saved my life this morning. I was about to lose the plot. Needed someone to talk to. I had no idea before that there was nobody there you know. I always seemed to be yapping on to someone or another. But they weren't really pals. Just people. I dunnae even get a chat with Sponge. Christ, things must be bad if I'm missing that little Junkie toe-rag. Anyway. Stuff it. You get yourself to *Tesco* this afternoon, OK?"

"You're not telling me any more than that?"

"Nah. That's your lot. Take it or leave it. Look, I need to get moving. Thanks for all the stuff like. And I'll see you later."

She seemed re-energised as she jumped up from the table with a new sense of purpose and strode out of the pub. Jason shook his head. The wonders or alcohol and nicotine. How would he manage without either? Not all that well. Especially if he was forced to spend his days in the general desperation of the feeding tent. He hadn't had a great deal of time for Bexx when they had first talked. Her sense of entitlement had grated on him. What kind of a crazy system would reward someone so outrageously for nothing other than getting pregnant and delivering children into the world? Just about everything about her lifestyle had annoyed him. The stolen goods, the way she humiliated Sponge on a daily basis, the utter lack of discipline with the children, the endless daytime TV, the gossip, the appalling food, the constant fug of cannabis. But now he found himself feeling terribly sorry for her. After all she had only made choices according to the system as was. The options had been clear enough. Get work and struggle to get by, or avoid work, have kids and live well. Who was he to get all Victorian about it and say that the likes of Bexx should have opted for a third of the income for doing the right thing? And now it was all gone and she had literally nothing. No wonder she was on the edge of being completely broken. He wondered what kind of desperate scheme was about to be hatched at *Tesco* in an hour's time. The chances were that it would be a long way from the utopian New Britain of Lester Gall.

But the chances were that it would be a story. And Amelie would never forgive him should he not be there, all ready and waiting with pen in his hand.

Terry Phillips had been counting down the last minutes to his break. This was a thing that happened like clockwork every four hours and the last five minutes were always the longest as his brain cells started to anticipate a hit of nicotine. He kept telling himself that it was a really good thing to be working in the non-smoking environment of *Tesco*. He had worked it out. On average he worked 45 hours a week. One average he smoked four cigarettes per daytime hour. Which meant that being smoke free in *Tesco* saved him 180 fags a week. Or nine packets. Or £70. And that wasn't to be sniffed at. Not the way things were these days anyway.

Terry was almost forty and the security gig in *Tesco* was his first job. He had never really considered work before. He had got into the habit of lying in bed until the middle of the afternoon in his late teens and despite many resolutions, he had never got out of it. Every now and then he would have a brief spurt of job hunting but it never came to anything. With no qualifications and no CV there had never been much of a chance. Instead he had picked up bits and pieces of cash collecting debts for a local loan shark. He had been pretty good at it.

He had been a creature of the local gym for many years and he had no qualms about dishing out a bit of stick to those who fell behind on their payments. He always had enough in his pockets for an endless supply of black market fags, body hugging designer clothes, an array of tattoos and occasional visits to Ibrox Park. Life was OK. Not brilliant, but OK.

And then everything changed.

Suddenly he had no flat, no benefits and his loan shark employer had no customers any more. Luckily enough a pal from the gym got him a start as one of the new security guards at *Tesco* and Terry found himself doing something that only a few weeks earlier he would have deemed completely and utterly out of the question: working 45 hours a week for a lousy £1.50 an hour. He hated it with a passion but he wasn't about to give it up. Every morning he saw the hungry eyes of fellow smokers in the feeding tent and there was no way he was about to join them in their constant craving.

Outside the afternoon was sunny and bright with a hint of winter. He lit up and inhaled deeply.

Better.

The second drag was less frantic and he cast bored eyes across the car park. And immediately his eyes became less bored. There was something up. Fifty yards from where he stood a group of over forty women had gathered. Not just any women. These were women he knew well enough. These were ex-Greenfield women. Dormitory women. During his time as a collector he had come down heavily on over half of them. The thing that prompted him to take one last ferocious drag and then dash back into the store was the fact that every one of the women was armed with a shopping trolley. Full size. And they all seemed to wearing their game faces. Intent.

He found the head of security by the customer services desk.

"S'cuse boss. Got a sec?"

"Sure. What's up?"

"I reckon we might have a problem. I was just outside on my break and there's a bunch of women gathering out there."

"And?"

"Aye. Well, I ken most of them like. They're all ex Greenfield. In the dorm now. None of them has any money. Yet they're all gearing themselves up with full size trolleys. Must be over thirty out there."

The man in charge of keeping the shelves safe furrowed his brow. There had been e mails from head office about this. Already there had been raids in stores across the country. He dug around his memory bank to retrieve the protocols that had been put in place to cover this kind of eventuality. That was it. The in-house lawyers had gone through all the small print they could find and concluded that it would reflect badly on the company's 'every little helps' image if they were to bar entry on the grounds that potential customers might not have any money. Instead the recommendation was that all such customers should be monitored closely on the cameras. It was also recommended that an early call to the local police should be made. Were there to be any kind of mass breakout then the decision as to whether the store security should intervene was to be at the discretion of the man in charge. If it seemed likely that some kind of unseemly brawl was going to break out, then the breakout customers should be allowed to leave the store where hopefully the police would interdict.

What else? He was sure there was something else? Yes. That was it. All duty customer services managers had been on a training course. What was it? Buggered if he could remember. Something about diffusing problematic situations. Who was on today? Barbara. He gave himself a grimacing sort of smile. He would enjoy watching the stuck up cow trying to talk down a bunch of wired up women from Greenfield.

"Barbara. It's Barry. You best get down here. Looks like we're about to have a problem."

Done. Cop shop next.

Bexx checked her watch. 2.10. How many were they? Well over thirty. Plenty. Any stragglers would just have to catch them up inside.

"Right. Let's get on with it. We go in in twos and threes. We fill up and meet at 2.25 near the entrance, right? Let's make sure all our watches agree. I've got 2.11, OK?" She felt thoroughly pleased with herself. This was like some movie about a SWAT team getting ready to storm the bad guys. Get in there.

"Let's do it then."

She waited until the last group, feeling completely hyped up as her troops entered the store in small groups. OK. Showtime.

A tap on his office door brought Doogie's head up from his paperwork. Not that there was any paper. Just columns of figures on his computer screen. Budgets and overtime costs. Book balancing. Accounts whipped into shape ready for inspection. Whatever the hell happened to real police work?

"Come in."

Jeff Harrison. Twenty years served and counting down the days. Desk bound now and sneaking surreptitious looks at estate agency websites advertising retirement properties on the south coast.

"Could have a bit of a problem boss."

"Go on."

"We've just had a call come in from *Tesco*. They have a group of upwards of thirty-five filling trolleys like there's no tomorrow. One of their people is pretty sure they are all ex Greenfield. In the dorm now."

"Women?"

"Aye. All of them."

Doogie got to his feet with a sigh. "Bloody marvellous. Get on the net Jeff. Instigate Operation Harvest."

Operation Harvest. It sounded like some half forgotten action from Vietnam. A new protocol that had landed on his desk from on high. Over the last week there had been several attempts at mass theft in supermarkets up and down the land. The idea always seemed to be pretty much the same. Groups of mainly women would fill trolleys and then look to ram-raid their way out of the store. There had been some CCTV footage at the regional meeting he had attended a few days earlier. The tactics would have done Rommel proud. Frantic dormitory women would close ranks and then make a charge using their heavily laden shopping trolleys as battering rams. Maybe someone, somewhere had studied the old Blitzkrieg tactics that had torn a gaping hole in the Anglo-French defensive line in the spring of 1940. The charging trolleys and screaming women made up a formidable offensive force. In Stoke an over brave security man had been literally stampeded at the doors of the store and was now laid up in hospital with a broken arm and concussion.

Police and store management had met to devise an appropriate response.

Operation Harvest.

Doogie had hoped that he might get lucky and not have to press the button in Rollerton. Well, so much for that. Operation Harvest wasn't the most complex of deployments. A call on the radio to all patrolling offices simply stated 'Operation Harvest Tesco Two.' This was essentially a mobilisation. Every patrol car within two miles of the named store would now drop everything and deploy to the car park. Every mobile female office within five miles was similarly mobilised. The role of the store was to negotiate and no more. To buy time for the police to gather outside on the car park. If a breakout charge took place, the security were under instructions to back off and allow the charging group out of the store and onto the car park where responsibility for the incident would pass to the police.

Once he was in his car Doogie got the store on the line and spoke with the head of security.

"Where are we up to?"

"Looks like they're more or less done filling the trolleys now. They seem to be gathering."

"How many?"

"More than thirty."

"Happy days. Well, you know the drill. Hold them in place for as long as you can. We're on our way."

"Aye. Will do."

Bexx surveyed her troops. It really was one hell of a turnout. All the nerves she had felt earlier were well away. They were a force to be reckoned with. No doubt at all about that. It was clear enough that they had been noticed. A small clutch of security men had gathered by the front door. That jumped up bastard Terry Philips was there. Tosser. He had once slapped her around in her kitchen for a £50 cannabis debt. She would enjoy smacking him with her trolley. And if he went down he was getting one right in the bollocks. No doubt about that. That was a s sure as night following day.

All around her were determined faces. Nobody looked like they were about to bottle it. They were unified. They were raging angry and they had nothing to lose. For weeks they had been humiliated: turfed out of their houses and left penniless in the dorm. Well. Enough was enough. Time to teach the bastards a lesson.

She was about to issue the order to charge when a large woman waddled out in front of the massed ranks of trolleys. The wrong side of fifty with bleached hair built up on top of her head like a wedding cake. She took up a position ten yards from where they stood and crossed her hands in front of her lap like a footballer in a wall facing a Brazilian free kick. A carefully cleared throat and then a posh voice with the kind of tone a Primary School headmistress would use on unruly five year olds.

Fat cow.

"Hello. I am Barbara, your customer services manager. Please allow me to direct you to the checkouts. As you can see we have several free checkouts at this time and our team are happy to help you to pack your shopping. You should be aware that if any customer attempts to leave this store without paying for any items then we will most certainly prosecute. It is my duty to point out that right now we are recording all of you with our in store security cameras and we will not hesitate to pass on any such evidence to the police in the event of any theft taking place. That said, if any of you should decide that you might not actually have sufficient funds available to pay for your items, if you would like to leave your trolleys where they are, my team would be delighted to replace any items on the shelves. Obviously should any of you take such a course of action no offense will have been committed and *Tesco* . . ."

Bexx had heard enough. She could sense the resolve seeping out of a few of the women around her. It was time to step up to the plate.

"No you listen here you fat English cow. You either get out of the way or we're going straight through you. Got that? And I'm not about to miss you and hit the wall. Right? Now we're leaving now and you lot have a choice. It's step out of the way or A&E. Simple as."

She turned to her troops with a brick red face. The adrenalin was coursing through her.

"OK girls. We're leaving now. If any of these sad bastards try to get in our way then god help them. On three, OK? One . . . two . . . three!!"

And on three Bexx bent slightly and propelled her high stacked trolley straight at the open-mouthed Barbara. It had been many, many years since Barbara had been a quick-footed defender in her school hockey team and as she made a clumsy turn away from the wall of trolleys bearing down on her she lost footing on the polished floor. Even so, she very nearly made it, but at the last minute Bexx altered her course sufficiently to achieve a square on hit on customer services manager's not inconsiderable backside. By now Bexx's trolley was travelling at an impressive speed and the combined weight of angry dormitory woman and heavily-laden trolley was enough to propel Barbara headlong into a display of half-price crisps.

Just a few yards to go now. Time to give that Terry Phillips bastard a bit of the same. Except Terry Phillips wasn't there any more. None of them were. The huge front door was open and unguarded. With a sense of triumph Bexx led her charging troops out into the crisp brightness of the afternoon. They had done it. She had done it. Now they could . . .

An image of the last scene from Butch Cassidy and the Sundance Kid leapt into her head. How many do you think there are, Butch?

Seven police cars had deployed in a semi circle around the front door. The officers were out and waiting.

Shit.

Nightmare.
So near and yet so far.

Doogie stepped forward and confronted the break out column who had now stopped their charge and were bunched together in a tight group outside the main door.

"OK girls. Time to calm down a bit, don't you think?"

Silence.

"Here's the drill. You've all had a clear warning and you have ignored it. Each and every one of you has now committed a theft. There is clear CCTV evidence. You have also been warned that any attempt to leave the store with unpaid for goods will result in prosecution. So we now need to take all of you into custody, OK? There is no need for this to be ugly. I now need you to leave your trolleys and wait where you are. We will come over and process you one by one. Why don't we all try to be as civilised as we can here . . ."

The can of beans that Bexx hurled at him had a flat trajectory that would have done a World series pitcher proud. He managed to rock out of the way and felt a brush of air as the tin whistled by his nose and smashed into the car windscreen behind him. The rest of the women reacted with the aggressive efficiency of an SAS patrol. Within seconds every woman was launching shopping at the police.

Doogie felt a wave of weariness at the pitiful scene. But orders were orders and there was a job to be done.

"OK. Pick them up."

Jason thanked his lucky stars that he had brought his camera along. He had arrived at the store just in time to see the column of trolleys erupt through the front door only to be halted by the sight of the police lines facing them. He fired off shots of both sides and zoomed in on Doogie as he made his plea for common sense. Now Jason got into full war photographer mode as he snapped off image after image. A police woman was down with blood seeping through red hair. A large trolley-woman was pinned belly down on the ground by an equally large WPC. The air was filled with hurled shopping and screamed expletives. Already a small crowd had gather to watch the battle unfurl. A ketchup bottle smacked into the side of one of the police vans with an explosion of sauce. A thin-faced women with a demonic look in her eyes fired off a full carton of eggs into the bodies of two advancing officers. Two women at the back of the melee frantically guzzled at bottles of Vodka. A young policewoman tried frantically to wriggle away from an assailant who had a firm hold on her pony tail.

The battle was not a long one. It took less than five minutes for Doogie's officers to have all thirty three women lined up with their hands on the wall. Cuffs were snapped into place and mandatory cautions issued. A bus pulled onto the car park ready to take the prisoners three miles across town to the football ground. Jason walked over to his housemate and offered a cigarette which was gratefully accepted. By now his camera was safely tucked away in his pocket.

"What brings you here then?"

Jason nodded towards Bexx who was running through every profanity in her lexicon as the officer behind her struggled to apply handcuffs.

"Bexx hinted that something was about to go down."

"Nice story then?" There was an edge of bitterness to Doogie's voice.

Jason shrugged. "It's alright. Sad more than anything else. Don't sweat it mate. I'm not about to have a pop at you lads. You did pretty good I reckon. How on earth did you many to deploy so many female officers so quickly?"

Doogie shrugged. "There was a plan in place. This kind of thing has been going down all over the country. Called Operation Harvest."

"Is that on the record?"

"Why not? Nobody told me otherwise. As far as I am concerned you can tell it as it is. It might just stop it happening again. Do you want to follow the story through to the end? I can sort it if you like."

"How do you mean?"

Doogie nodded to the line of dejected women been loaded up onto a waiting bus. "Now we will take them to the football ground. There is a fast track system in place. You'll see."

"A fast track system?"

A grim smile. "Just come along. Today is day one for yet another Pendleton new beginning. Why not have the press along to record it. Come on. Hop in."

They climbed into Doogies Merc and left the car park.

"Did I ever tell you about that time when I had to go to Munich?"

Jason shook his head. "No. I don't think so."

"It was a few years back. A conference on terrorism. You know the kind of thing. All European police forces working together to foil the Islamic nut jobs."

"OK." There was a flat bitterness in Doogie's voice which Jason had never heard before.

"We got a day off on the Sunday. I took a bus out to the camp at Dachau. There are little signs saying 'KZ Gedenstatte Dachau'. It took me a while to clock on to the fact that KZ Gedenstatte meant concentration camp. It was a beautiful day. May. The mothers were out pushing prams and the kids had ice cream. Lots of family Sundays. I remember that getting to me a bit. It wasn't long after my break up you see. The camp was nothing like I thought it would be. It was quite small really. About ten football pitches. No more than that. The thing that hit me most was that it was in a nice leafy suburb. There were houses along the perimeter fence. Old houses. Easily old enough to have been there when the camp was running. The people who lived there could have had a barbeque on their front lawn and watched the pyjama people a few yards away. The thing that was really obvious was that the place wasn't hidden at all. Quite the opposite. It could not have been more open. They have a museum full of pictures. The ones that really got me were the newspapers from 1934 covering the official opening. It must have been a really big thing. It made all the front pages. You know, a real media fanfare. I can't read German but you could tell easily enough that all the coverage was really upbeat and positive. Give me a fag will you."

Jason lit two and passed one. Doogie carried on.

"It scared the shit out of me Jace. You see, for the first five years Dachau wasn't a death camp. Less than seven hundred guys died in the first six years. Think about it. That was in a camp that held up to 10,000 cons. Less than 100 deaths a year. Back in those days there would have been about 1000 banged up in Barlinnie and I am pretty sure there would have been more than ten deaths a years. So in terms of fatalities it was no different from any other prison. It wasn't designed to kill people. It was designed to completely break the spirit. It was for union men and socialists and Catholic priests and comedians, anyone who might be a thorn in Hitler's side. From dawn to dusk, every second of the day was dedicated to destroying the spirit. The average term was less than a year. That was all it took to break a problematic individual down into tiny, tiny pieces. Then it hit me. If a similar regime was introduced here for drug dealers and gang bangers and paedophiles *The Sun* and *The Record* and the *Daily Mail* would trumpet the place just like all of those German papers back in 1934. And in some ways I had to admit that I could see their point. There are many complete and utter amoral, vicious bastards I have lifted over the years who I would have loved to send to a place like Dachau for a year. No *Sky TV* and *Playstations* and playing the big man on the wing. That is why this kind of thing is so seductive. But then a much bigger thing hit me. They had the same sign over the entrance gate. 'Arbeit Mach Frei'. Just like Auschwitz. Just like every death a camp. You see mate, you need a Dachau before you can have your Auschwitz. You start with something that seems harsh but acceptable. Take away the human dignity from those who have no right to any. The scum. The lowest of the low. The pond life. Do that, and the majority will cheer you and vote for you. Who needs civil rights anyway. These kind of bastards don't deserve civil rights. So long as you have the press on board you can easily sell that idea to the public. And it gets them used to the idea. Before long it seems OK. Normal. Not a problem. Once you reach that point, the road to building your Auschwitz is wide open."

Jason blew out his cheeks. "Christ Doogie, you're giving me the bloody shivers."

Doogie said nothing. He just stared at the bus full of women fifty yards ahead.

All the fight and anger had drained out of Bexx. She had been a fool. A complete idiot. Like they were just going to let them waltz in and waltz out with full trolleys. As if. And she wasn't all that sure any more about her earlier assertions that there was nothing the bastards could do. It didn't feel that way. None of the other women were saying anything. They sat and stared out of the windows at the familiar streets of Rollerton. But nothing seemed familiar at all any more. They were on a bus with five police women and nobody was saying anything. There had been some talk that they were going to use the football ground if there were any mass arrests. Maybe that was where they were going now. It was the right road. Then what? Christ she could murder a bloody fag. She was so tired of craving nicotine. Maybe the best thing would be just to give up. Knowing there would never be another fag would surely be better that the desperate hope that some one might just crash her one. How many fags had she actually managed to smoke in the last week not counting the ones she had blagged off the journalist? It wasn't a hard sum to do. Three. Three smoked and hour after hour after hour of craving. Christ.

She could see the Rollerton Athletic floodlights now. So it was the football ground. She pulled her coat tight around herself and suddenly felt like crying. Nothing was fair any more.

The coach parked up in front of the main entrance and a WPC with a microphone instructed them to leave the bus. Once they were outside a line of officers ushered them through a door and guided them up a flight of steps to the main stand where a new looking sign said 'Women'. They were pointed to seats and told to wait. It was cold and she wondered how long they would be kept. Around her several of the women were now sobbing. Not fair.

Doogie showed Jason along a corridor which housed the manager's office and the small boardroom. A door at the end opened onto the corporate area. All dining tables had been moved to the side of the room and stacked against the wall. Old photos of what there was of Rollerton Athletic glory stared down at the surreal scene. There was a table complete with leather chair which was obviously waiting for the Sherrif. In front of it a couple of court officers shuffled papers and a clutch of gowned lawyers murmured to each other. Doogie gestured to some chairs at the back and they both sat. He spoke in a low matter-of-fact voice.

"Basically there is no difference to the Sheriff's Court in town. We are now in the public gallery. All the procedure is more or less the same. The only difference is that everything is speeded up. Right now the women will be getting a lecture on why it is a really good idea to plead guilty and be done with it."

"Then what?"

"You'll see."

Bexx was trying hard to focus on what the woman was saying. She wore a gown and had a posh voice and seemed to be looking down her nose at them. Something about her being their duty lawyer or some crap like that.

"Now please listen and listen carefully. Everything is designed for speed. I have had a chance to briefly review the CCTV footage from the store and the evidence is beyond dispute. Each and every one of you will be found guilty of theft. There is absolutely not a shadow of doubt about this. Now. The police are willing to drop any charges of assault or resisting arrest resulting from the affray outside the store. These of course are the most serious charges and the ones that will result in the most serious consequences. I can assure you that you absolutely DO NOT want to be charged with any of these offences. The deal has strings of course and there are two. Number one, you all tell me that you are willing to plead guilty to the charge of shoplifting. Number Two, any of you who are willing to do this must do so right now. Not in five minutes. Not in ten minutes. Now. That is the deal. As your lawyer, I urge you in the very strongest of terms to accept the offer. Should you do so I can guarantee that you can be back with your families as early as this evening. I have signed documents confirming this offer which you are more than welcome to take."

They were like a flock of worried sheep. Cold. Tearful. Completely disorientated and confused.

"Hands up those willing to accept the offer."

One by one every hand went up.

"Very good. Everything can now be arranged very quickly. Tea will be along in a minute. Be patient please."

"No chance of a photo I suppose?" Jason wasn't particularly hopeful but he asked anyway.

Doogie just smiled.

A side door opened and the trolley raiders were guided inside until they stood in front of the Sheriff in a long line. No handcuffs. No bravado. Just a line of miserable, cold-looking women in cheap coats.

"I gather that all of you will pleading guilty to the charge of shoplifting. Please confirm this individually starting at the left of the line."

Silence. The lawyer stepped up to the women at the left hand end of the line and whispered in her ear for a few seconds. A small voice.

"Guilty."

They got the hang of it and the plea was spoken by all.

The Sheriff removed his glasses and gave the women a stare. "I know that things have been difficult for you and I am going to take that into account. That said, we cannot tolerate this kind of attempt at mass-looting. And make no mistake, that is exactly what has happened this afternoon: an attempt to loot a superstore. It cannot happen ladies. It cannot happen under any circumstances. I am therefore going to sentence you to two pallets each. And if I should see any single one of you back in front of me again it will be ten pallets. Then twenty. Then forty. Be very, very clear. Looting is not going to be tolerated. That's all."

He rose to his feet and left through a door at the back of the room. The women were guided out through the same door they had entered through. The whole thing had lasted a little over seven minutes.

"Two pallets? What the bloody hell does that mean?"

Doogie stood. "Come on. I'll show you."

Once again the bus was all but silent as it worked its way out of town and onto unfamiliar country roads. The view outside made Bexx even more uneasy. She didn't like the countryside. It was alien. A place of posh people who looked down at her. Where were they being taken? By now the policewomen had been replaced by five different women in unfamiliar green uniforms. There were low nervous conversations around her. Where were they going? What did the Sheriff mean about two pallets? But Bexx was in no mood to talk. She just stared out at the wet fields and thin hedges.

After twenty minutes the bus stopped at a set of gates which were duly opened. There seemed to be three dormitory buildings the same as the ones in town. And some old wrecked buildings. The women in the green uniforms got them off the bus and lined them up in front of yet another woman in the same garb.

"Can everybody hear me?"

Nods from lowered heads.

"Very good. My name is Miss Spelling and I would like to welcome you to the Airfield. How long any of you stay with us is entirely up to you. This is where you will serve your punishment. I have been informed that each of you has been sentenced to two pallets. You will no doubt be wondering what this means. I will show you."

She waved over two forklift trucks which were waiting a few yards behind her. The drivers deposited their loads in front of the women.

"OK. This is the red pallet. As you can see it carries a load of 200 bricks. One tonne. This is the blue pallet which has no bricks. You will move the bricks from the red pallet to the blue pallet and stack them in exactly the same way as they are stacked now. You can see over there that there are already thirty four sets of red pallets each holding two hundred bricks each. You will find a card like this on one of the red pallets. The card with have your name written on it. Your sentence is to move the bricks from the two red pallets to the two blue pallets. Once you have completed this task you are free to leave. There is transport available to take you back to Rollerton. We will not force you to undertake this task. You are quite within your rights to refuse. Should you refuse, you will be accommodated in the dormitory over there. You will find that the dormitory is identical in all respects to the ones in town. There is also a feeding station which is also identical in all respects to the one in town. In fact there is only one difference. The Airfield is a secure area. As you can see it is fenced and guarded. The penalty for any prisoner who leaves without completing their sentence is 200 pallets. Ladies, the good news is this. If you would like to start your sentence right away it can be completed in a little more than an hour. The bus will remain for two hours. As soon as you move your two hundred bricks, you are free to go. There is no reason why you can't be back in Rollerton in time for your evening meal. If on the other hand you refuse to carry out your sentence you will remain with us, and you will stay with us until such a time as you have completed your task. So. As you can see. It is really all very straight forward. On the table here are gloves and warm coats should any of you require them. If you take my advice you will make a start straight away and be on your way. OK. Any who want to start their task please step forward for gloves and coats. Any who are unwilling, please remain where you are and we will escort you to the dormitory."

There was barely any hesitation. All thirty-four women stepped forward to collect their gloves and coats. Then they made their way to the old airstrip where thirty-four pairs of pallets waited for them, lined up neatly in alphabetical order. The last women to finish took a little over an hour and a quarter. Ninety minutes after their arrival the women left the airfield behind. There was not a lot of talk on the bus ride back into town. But they all shared the same thought. Two pallets had been a hard, miserable and degrading task. They were in no doubt what it would be like to have to tackle ten pallets. Or twenty. Or forty. It wasn't something any of them fancied at all.

A similar silence was in place in the Mercedes as it glided down quiet country lanes. Three miles short of the outskirts of Rollerton Doogie took a right turn and climbed a low hill until they reached a viewing area at the top. The place was familiar enough to both of them. Many years earlier when Doogie had been the first to pass his test and get a car, they had driven out here on weekend nights to pitch a tent and get drunk.

"Bloody hell Doogie, memory lane or what?"

Doogie climbed out and went to stand next to a graffiti covered picture which pointed out landmarks along the coast. Below them the town looked pretty much the same as it had all those years earlier. A quiet grey place squatting by a quiet grey sea.

"Got a fag?"

Jason had a fag. Jason always had a fag. "You OK mate?"

Doogie looked every inch the craggy faced Scot as he inhaled and blew out. "Can we go about a million miles off the record?"

"Of course."

A couple more draws.

"OK. You are familiar with the way Cobra is working?"

"In what way?"

"It is split in two, right? Cobra One does dorms and feeding stations. Cobra Two does security."

"Yeah. I heard a bit about that."

"Cobra Two is small. Tight knit. Pendleton, Hawkes and Taylor represent the politicians. Then there is police, MI5 and army. OK?"

"OK."

A long pause. A few last thoughts before stepping out over the line.

"The cops are represented by a man called Parker. He's number two at the Met. I don't know him, but I have heard about him. Hard as nails they say. I got a call from him the other night. Half past one in the bloody morning, straight through on the direct line. Know what he wanted? Full details on Nathaniel Pater Clarke. Your man Sponge."

"Sponge! What the hell would Cobra want with Sponge?"

"I haven't a bloody clue and I wasn't about to ask. I could tell that Parker was knackered. We're all knackered. I think he said more than he should have said. He let it slip that the information was for a man called Dyson. Sebastian Dyson. Parker was pretty pissed off with him. Said he is flavour of the month with the PM. Sometimes attends meetings, sometimes he doesn't. Parker tried to run him and came up with zip. Now that it is serious shit. When a man like Parker runs someone, something always comes up. Always."

"So who is he?"

Doogie shrugged. "Parker said he was a man who defended the Realm. A shadows man. He said even the 100 year rule wouldn't turn him up."

"Right. One of those."

"Yeah. One of those. I heard his name again the other day. I was talking with a pal who is a chief super down in Derby at a conference about what we have just seen today. You know, the whole pallets of bricks thing. My mate had worked under Parker a few years back and they had got pally. Golf. Anyway. Parker had mentioned to him that the pallet thing came from this man Dyson."

"Right."

They both stood and stared out at the sea for a while with their hands deep in coat pockets for warmth. Both knew full well that the chill they felt wasn't entirely down to the autumn wind that swept in from the sea. After a while Doogie broke the silence.

"Most of the guys at the conference thought the bricks thing was pure genius. No messing. Fast track. Get them in, give them some hard graft and get them out again. Plenty said it should have been done years ago. My guess is that the press will see it the same way.

There is going to be a big media shindig out at the Airfield next week. I'm not going to tell you what to do mate, but it would obviously be best if you didn't write about what you have seen today. If you do then it will be crystal clear how you know about it. That's not why I took you out there."

"So why?"

"Dachau. The public are going to love the whole pallets of bricks thing. Just like the German public were all on board with Dachau when it opened. I saw it myself, Jace. All those senior cops laughing and getting off on the idea of coming down hard on the toe-rags."

A passed cigarette. A shared light.

"They didn't have any gas chambers at Dachau. It was never a death camp. But they had the ovens. They're still there. Typical German engineering. They still look as good as new. I reckon with a half-day service they could be up and running again. There is a plaque on the wall. Four British women. They had parachuted into France to work with the resistance and got caught. The Gestapo tortured the shite out of them and got nothing. So they packed them off to Dachau. They hanged all four of them from these hooks on the ceiling. Right by the ovens. Efficient, yeah. Hang them, cut them down and toss them in the oven. Bastards. Just imagine the courage they must have had. What they must have gone through. And at the end of it, all they would have seen those hooks, the nooses, the open doors.."

He wiped angrily at his face as tears trickled onto his cheeks. Jason felt hollowed out by the sight. He had never ever seen his friend like this. By now there was new hardness in Doogie's voice.

"I got a few of the lads to look about for Sponge. There's no sign of him. Maybe he's just laying low. Maybe not. I think something bad is happening Jace. Really bad. And I can't get that plaque out of my head. Those women. Those sodding ovens. You know that Edmund Burke quote, right?"

"All that is necessary for the triumph of evil is that good men do nothing?"

Doogie nodded. "I think there is something evil about this Dyson. I can't tell you why? I just feel it. Obviously the fact that Sponge seems to have vanished off the face of the earth a couple of days after I send his details down to Parker stinks to high heaven. But more than that it is the pallet thing that frightens me. You can't get away from the fact that there is genius in the idea. Cheap, quick and effective. Designed to erode the spirit. To humiliate and degrade. Designed to appeal to the public. Do you see where I'm coming from?"

Jason nodded. "So what should I do?"

"Flush out Sebastian Dyson. Shine a light on him. Drag the bastard out of the shadows."

"OK. I can do that."

Doogie nodded. "Just to be clear Jason, you know what this means?"

"In what way?"

"You will need to go into the ultimate no go areas. The place where people disappear without trace. Defence of the Realm."

Jason gave a crooked smile. "Remember all the crap we used to talk Doogie? You know, when we were kids. When we used to camp out here. Light a fire and get pissed out of our heads. We were always going to change the bloody world weren't we? Looks like it's time to get on with it. We've put it off for long enough."

"I reckon."

Sponge was in a bad place. A really bad place. During his years of hopeless addiction he had been to many bad places. Twice he had overdosed and floated to the gates of death only to be dragged back by ambulance crews. He had done time in Scotland's grimmest jails. He had lived in filthy, litter-strewn squats. He had been beaten black and blue by enforcers doling out punishment for unpaid debts.

But none of the bad places he had known came close to this bad place.

Not that he had any idea where he was.

One minute he had been walking along a pavement in Greenfield. More floating than walking. All wrapped up in the bottomless bliss of the best tenner bag of smack he had known in years. Then there had been a van. And then he had been inside the back of the van with a bag over his head. Held down by hands that felt like steel clamps. And at last he had been brought to the room where he now sat. They had stripped him and pushed him onto a hard wooden chair and tied his wrists and ankles. The bag had stayed and when he had begged and screamed nobody had said a word. He had pissed himself and shat himself and cried until there were no tears left. How long? Hours? Days? Weeks? Centuries? Long enough for the effects of the bag to have disappeared over the horizon. Long enough for the rattle to have taken a hold. Cold, endless agony. His bowels seemed to have been wedged open. The stink made him vomit into the bag. At first he had been convinced that he was about to choke but the end was open and the sick slipped out and onto his chest.

Sponge had lived a life that was mainly despair. But now he knew that the despair he had come to know was as nothing to this despair. This was the bottomless pit.

This was the essence of hell.

A brush of cold air on his ankles told him that a door had opened. Eye-burning light as the bag was yanked from his head. Hard to focus.

Two men. One about seventy with thin white hair. The other in his forties with the hardest eyes Sponge had ever seen. The older one spoke in a quiet sort of voice.

"Oh deary, deary me. What an awful state you are in Sponge. You must be feeling absolutely horrid. Would you like a drink of water?"

Sponge nodded and the quiet one poured water between his dry lips. "Better?"

Sponge nodded.

"Very good. Now. This is my colleague Mr Atwood. We have worked together for some time. When I really need to know something I tend to get Mr Atwood here to ask the questions. He really is very good at it. I won't pretend that the process is particularly pleasant. Quite the contrary I'm afraid. It is extremely unpleasant. But I always hear what I need to hear? Do you understand Sponge? I am talking about torture here. Pain the likes of which you have never dreamed of. Very, very nasty indeed. I rather think that it would be much better if we could avoid all that unpleasantness, don't you agree Sponge?"

Sponge shat himself yet again and nodded.

"Splendid. This won't take very long. You have been giving out pills Sponge. Lots and lots of pills. Who asked you do that?"

A desperate pleading voice. "Donnie Baldini."

"Donnie Baldini, and who may I ask is Donnie Baldini?"

"A dealer. His ma Dot was the main smack dealer in Rollerton. But she's pissed off to Italy and Donnie is the man now."

"Is he indeed? How very interesting. What reason did he give you when he asked you do give these pills away? Do you know what they are by the way?"

"Donnie calls them *Anarchy*. He says they are a new brand like. Told me it was like those women in supermarkets who give away free samples like. Tasters like."

"I see. And tell me Sponge, was there anyone with Donnie when you had this little chat?"

"Aye. A bloke called Mikhail. A real hard bastard. Donnie said that if I grassed this Mikhail would kill me. He never said nothing to me but I heard him take a call. He was foreign like."

"What kind of foreign?"

"Dunnae ken. Russian? Polish? Something like that?"

"Russian or Polish. My goodness me Sponge, what a very exiting time you have been having of it. Now tell me, when did you have your last little chat with Donnie?"

"Yesterday."

"And what did he have to say?"

Sponge swallowed hard and Atwood dribbled more water down his throat.

"Well. We were all told to give out as many *Anarchy* as we could for two weeks. Then he told us to stop and keep out of the way. The kids have started to go mental. I mean seriously mental like. Climbing the walls like. They're all completely habited up. Then Donnie says that I need to pass the word. He wants them to attack the feeding station. And the tanker wagon when it comes along to fill up. He said they should do the wagon first. Then the feeding station. The word was that anyone who was in the attack would get some Anarchy."

"And are there many more like you Sponge? Distributors?"

"Aye. I think so. Donnie said there were."

"Well thank you Sponge. I must say I have found this little chat to be extremely interesting. And no need for any unpleasantness after all. Mr Atwood, maybe you could give our friend here something to cheer him up a bit."

Atwood nodded and took a needle from a small bag.

Sponge watched with frantic hope as the hard-looking man slid the needle into one of his veins with surprising efficiency. And in a second the nightmares were fading away and out of sight. He closed his eyes and felt his lips shape into a smile of utter nirvana. Complete and absolute and perfect peace. Complete and absolute and perfect.

Fifty-five seconds later he was dead.

Sebastian stood with hands in pockets and studied the look of contentment on Sponge's ravaged face. Not a bad way to go. Maybe the best way to go. Maybe it would be a way he might even choose himself one day. To die. To sleep. No more. "OK. Sort him out and get rid of the body. Call me when it's done."

"No problem boss."

"We are going to need the team I think Atwood. Can I leave it to you to get them up here?"

"Sure. How many?"

"Your call. I think we will pick up Mr Baldini and the mysterious

Mikhail at the same time. I will leave it you to get something in place. It sounds like Mikhail might be something of a handful."

"Details?"

"Give me a few hours. I will e mail you."

"Fine."

Sponge's corpse was quietly dumped in a disused factory a few hours later. A litter of used needles advertised the place as a popular shooting gallery. The body was found the next day and taken to the mortuary.

Doogie got the news a little after six and put in a call to the forensic pathologist who was an old football pal.

"Hi Bob, it's Doogie."

"Alright Doogie. You well?"

"Aye. Grand thanks. Can I ask a wee favour?"

"You can ask."

"Nathaniel Clarke. He's just come in, right?"

"Aye. That he has. What of it?"

"Just make sure you dot all the I's and cross all the T's. Know what I mean?"

"I do. Looks pretty open and shut to me at first glance though. Massive overdose. I'd put a tenner on it."

"You're probably right. But if there is anything odd you'll let me know, OK?"

"Sure."

"Only me though. By my mobile. It will be between us. That OK?"

A silence suggested that it wasn't.

"Is there something I should know here Doogie?"

"Best you know as little as possible. All can ask is that you trust me."

"All right. I suppose I can do that. I'll try and rush the toxicology through. Tomorrow morning soon enough?"

"Aye, that's fine. I owe you one."

Doogie's mobile rang a little after ten the next day.

"That's the cleanest smack I have ever seen in Rollerton. We're talking close to 100% pure. Only one place you get smack like that."

"Where?"

"The NHS."

"Shit."

"Aye."

"Can you put the thing through as death by overdose and nothing else?"

"Christ Doogie."

"I know. But if I hadn't given you the nod you would never have looked. I want to nail the bastards who did this and I don't want them to be tipped off."

"OK, OK. It's done. I really don't want to know any more about it."

"You're right enough about that."

Darren felt like he was about to go completely insane. Shit. Maybe he was already completely insane. He couldn't sit still. He couldn't sleep. He couldn't hold his head on one thing for more than a second. All around him faces were staring into his brain. Eyes like lasers. Mocking. Laughing. Plotting. The small room in the dormitory was like a matchbox. The sound of his younger brothers messing about made him feel like murdering them. Smashing their heads like egg shells. Putting their eyes out. Slashing their throats.

He tried to eat something at mealtimes but gave up after a few mouthfuls. The food tasted disgusting. His mouth tasted disgusting. He couldn't stand all the eyes. Millions and millions and millions of staring eyes. Mocking eyes. Judging eyes. Hating eyes. Plotting eyes. Evil eyes.

And so he walked. Sometimes on his own. Sometimes with others in the same state. They were like a pack of hungry dogs as they walked. The banter of old was all gone. No more talk of football and who battered who. Just sets of hungry eyes as they walked and walked. Unable to stay still. Unable to settle with the demons that had seeded inside them.

By now they all knew full well that the *Anarchy* was the reason. Darren had thought about it and thought about it and thought about it. He had taken three *Anarchy* on the night of the last D-Zed gig. Course he had. They all had. Obviously they had. The bastards were free weren't they? And it had been banging. Bloody pure brilliant. Especially when they had piled into those FCNS wankers. That had been the best ever. And for days after that Sponge and a bunch of other smackheads had been doling out the Anarchy like sweeties. Just tasters like. Freebie tasters. Plenty more. Dunnae worry. Plenty more. The man is in a good mood, right?

And then nothing.

Fair enough he had thought. There was no way it was ever going to last forever no matter what that tosser Sponge said. Pity like. *Anarchy* was the business. Maybe they would be back?

None of them saw the crazy time coming. The lack of sleep and the constant gnawing hunger. At first they all talked about it. Shared their experience. On and on and on as they walked. But after a while there seemed like there was no point.

But now at last it looked like the cavalry were on the way. Not that Sponge had anything to do with it. That waster had turned up deader than dead in the old factory on Troon Street. Served the junkie bastard right. Nobody gave a shite. There were plenty more like Sponge. And now they were passing the word that the Anarchy was coming back. Loads. Handfuls. Bucketfuls. But this time they were not freebies. This time there was some work to be done.

The man wanted something.

And the man was ready to reward those who gave.

The man wanted the feeding station doing. He wanted it smashed into pieces. He wanted it taking apart. But first he wanted the tanker bringing in the lunch-hour soup to be done. Stopped and set on fire. Once the tanker was done the word would come down. And when the word came down it would be time to take out the feeding station.

And they had been told that the man was going to be watching. He was all seeing. He had cameras everywhere. He was hacked into the CCTV. He had his guys out and about with their cameras. He would see who got in there and did the biz. And he would see who tried to hang back. He would know who shat it and stayed clear. Only the ones who got in there and got stuck in would get their *Anarchy*.

A few weeks earlier Darren would had seen the whole thing as a pile of shite. He wasn't that stupid. He would have laughed at all the talk of the bloody man and his all seeing cameras. But now his brain was a tangled ball of string. And the string was on fire. And the fire was burning the backs of his eyeballs. And nothing made any sense any more. Only *Anarchy*.

Only *Anarchy*.

He was one of six. They had been the same six for years. At Primary school and High School and on the streets of Greenfield and in the dorm. And now they were a unit. Ready to roll. Ready for the news that the tanker had been taken down. Ready to please the man.

Ready to do whatever it took.

When he thought about it later, Jason realised that he had been lucky. If he had arrived at the feeding station a few minutes earlier he would have been caught up in the madness. Instead he was a hundred yards away when a swarm of youngsters came from all sides and attacked the centre. The air was filled with a mixture of screaming. There were the battle cries of the kids who poured into the giant tent like an army of invading ants. And there was the screaming of those inside who streamed out with terrified eyes. Like images from old wars. Mothers running with babies. Small children howling for lost parents. Old men trying to run and finding themselves unable to do so. Dazed looking victims of blood-pumping head wounds.

All the while the noise from the inside of the tent never eased until, with a kind of inevitability, smoke started to ease its way up into the sky.

Jason was frozen. The front line instincts that had served him so well on the car park at *Tescos* had deserted him. His camera stayed in his pocket. The scene before him was simply too crazy for him to react properly. It was complete madness.

The sight of Bexx blundering towards him with her two youngest boys in tow snapped him out of it. One of the kids had a gash across the forehead. Jason ran to her and pushed his handkerchief hard into the wound to staunch the bleeding. Bexx was incoherent. Mumbling and shaking.

By now the air was filled with the sound of approaching sirens. Figures were now streaming out of the blazing tent and dispersing. A few gathered in a group of around fifty to confront the arriving police. An officer climbed from the first squad car and he was immediately engulfed by a swarm of bodies. A second car drew up. Then a third. Six officers and about thirty kids. Batons cracked heads. Bodies hit the concrete. The kids fought much longer than they should have fought. They fought until over half were down on the floor. And Jason could see the growing rage and panic on the faces of the policemen as they fought with all the ferocity they could muster. New cars were arriving all the time now and soon the numbers were balanced. The policemen were bigger. Older. Stronger. Better armed with their heavy batons. But still the kids refused to take a backward step.

By now more and more of the kids were returning to the scene to throw themselves at the makeshift police lines. There seemed to be fighting everywhere. Jason remembered what Sheena had said about the German Stormtroopers who had raged through the Ardennes. No fear. Complete rage. Berserkers.

It took the police over half-an-hour to clear the area around the blazing tent. Only then could the firemen start their work. Only then could a fleet of ambulances get to the injured. Now the sounds of rage were fading away down the streets that led away from the battleground.

How long had it all taken? Just a few minutes really. But the damage was huge. The feeding centre had clearly had it. It was a complete wreck. By now paramedics were rushing stretchers out from inside the smouldering tent. There had been people trapped inside. Christ. Some stretchers carried bodies writhing in agony. Other carried bodies completely covered by red blankets.

Corpses.

Surely not. Please no. Not corpses. And now two policemen were laying a jacket over the face of the first officer to get out of his car to confront the mob. And his partner was leaning against the roof of the squad car and crying and crying.

Beside him Bexx had taken over with the handkerchief. She was still mumbling to herself in deep shock. Jason picked up threads of sense here and there. Her Darren had been there. Like a madman. Like a psycho. Like a complete lunatic.

Jason lit two cigarettes and passed one to Bexx. It was hard. His hands were shaking.

By now there was a desperate quiet. Something truly terrible had just happened. It was merely a question of how terrible. How many bodies?

How many?

And why?

The Prime Minister stormed into the room where the Cobra Two committee waited and hurled a packet of cigarettes down onto the table.

"Give me a bloody light will you John."

Taylor obliged, conscious of raised eyebrows. The PM lit and dragged and then drummed his fingers angrily. "This best be as important as you lot are making out. I was in with the German Chancellor for Christ's sake. The cocky bastard must be loving every minute. What's going on John?"

Taylor kept his voice even. "Looks like we have a problem boss. A big one."

"Go on."

"We are getting reports of attacks on the feeding stations. Mainly up in Scotland but its kicking off down here as well in places."

"Attacks? What the hell do you mean, attacks?"

"Not that clear yet. It seems like it's mainly kids. Big groups of them. They just seem to have gone crazy. There seems to be a kind of pattern. Tankers get hit first. Stopped and burned. Two drivers have been killed."

"Killed!"

Taylor nodded. "Fraid so. The attacks on the tankers seem to be a trigger for a much bigger attacks on the feeding stations."

"Slow down a bit. Attacks? What do you mean by attacks?"

"I can't think of a better word to be honest. Gangs of kids are smashing everything they can find, including people. Most of the time they are setting the tents on fire. They're not backing off when the cops land either. Quite the opposite. We've got pitched battles all over the place. Lots of casualties I'm afraid. Look. Maybe it's best if you watch this. CCTV footage from Airdrie."

The Home Secretary snapped off the lights with a remote control and set a video rolling on the wall mounted screen. Pendleton's face drained off colour as he watched a full scale battle between a mob of youths and an embattled force of policemen. At times close ups revealed the naked aggression on the faces of the rioters. It was impossible not to notice how many bodies there were on the ground. It was impossible not to notice how many of them didn't seem to be moving at all.

"Jesus Christ. How many towns?"

"Twenty-five so far."

"Casualties?"

"Over sixty dead so far. It's going to go up boss. It's going to go up a lot."

Now the PM rubbed at his face like a man trying to clear everything away.

"Ideas?"

Parker of the Met cleared his throat. "Remember that article in the Enquirer? That Jason Marsh wrote it. You know, the Rollerton guy?"

"Yeah, I remember."

"He reckoned the riot in Rollerton was down to free Methamphetamine pills being handed out. We checked into it of course. Collected a few samples here and there. Marsh was right. The pills were Methamphetamine. They are calling them Anarchy. We've never had a big problem with Crystal Meth here in the UK. It looks like that just changed. The behaviour you've just seen has Crystal Meth written all over it."

"Look. Am I being thick here, but why in the name of Christ would anyone want to dole out free drugs to a bunch of bloody yobs?"

Nobody seemed to have much of an answer to that. Pendleton sighed and lit another. At this rate he would be doing four packs a day in a month or two. "Anyway, where the hell is Dyson?"

"Rollerton."

"Well get the useless bastard on the line."

A couple of minutes later Sebastian's voice drifted out of the speaker in the centre of the table.

"Good morning Prime Minister. I gather you are wanting a chat."

"Of course I'm wanting a chat you bloody idiot. The damn country is going up in flames for Christ's sake."

"Yes. It does seem as things are getting a touch exciting. What do you want from me?"

"I want to bloody well know why."

"I see. Well I have to point out that it is still early days, so to speak. That said, I have a few ideas. I suggest that you refer to Jason Marsh's article about the Heroin addict. You will find that he makes some interesting points. I always think it is a good idea to follow the money. Read the article and have a think about how your new changes have affected the illegal drugs industry. I think it is fair to say they are probably not the happiest of campers at the moment. I dare say they are not the kind of chaps to take things lying down. Maybe today is the day they have started to fight back? I certainly seems that way."

"Well that is all very well and good, but what exactly are you going to do about it?"

"That Prime Minister is something that you really do not want to know. What you do need to agree right now is that my fee has just doubled. Agreed?"

"Now wait one minute . . ."

"I asked you a question, Prime Minister. Are we agreed?"

Pendleton looked across the table to John Taylor and John Taylor gave a small nod.

"Yes damm it. We are agreed."

"How very splendid. Give me a few days and I am sure I will be able to give you a clearer picture. Must be off now. Tootle pip."

For a moment it seemed like the Prime Minister of great Britain and Northern Ireland was about to attack the speaker phone in front of him. But he didn't. Just.

4.10 a.m. A favourite time for men of the night. A time when dark deeds would go unnoticed. Steve Atwood drew steered an old transit van quietly around a corner and parked up. Silence. A quiet seep of rain. Dull orange light. A line of grey boxy houses. So called social housing though what the hell made it social he had never got his head around. He came from a place like this. An estate in a small Yorkshire mining town rendered obsolete after the great strike if 1984. Maybe in another life he might have followed his dad and granddad down the pit. Instead he had taken the only option other than the dole and signed on the dotted line for the infantry. This was the kind of place where his new life had started back in the late eighties. Then it had been the social housing of Ulster where the Giro terrorists had patiently waited to put a round through the back of a patrolling squaddie's head. Newry and Derry and Ballymurphy. He had moved up the chain on rainy streets just like this one. First as an infantryman. Then as SAS. Then as 14th Intelligence. After the peace he had spent his days in very different landscapes, almost all of then parched and dusty. Only with the War on Terror did he return, this time in social housing schemes in West Yorkshire and East Lancashire where a different kind of Giro-terrorist hatched their internet plans to burn everything down.

He had never been a man much given to philosophical depths. He was a man who took a task at face value and got it done. He had never done niceties which of course had always made him an A Grade soldier. Once upon a time he had patrolled the streets of Northern Ireland for a little over £2 an hour. Now he banked £2000 a day. But the job had never really changed. He had joined Rutland International eight years earlier after a stint with an American security outfit working out of Baghdad. It was a good gig, no doubt about it. When they had interviewed him in a London hotel it was soon clear that they knew more about him than his own mother. Lots of homework done and done well. Some suit from the foreign office had shown him proof that the vast majority of the work Rutland was involved with was in the service of the Crown. Not that it made any difference. Atwood had never been a patriot. They said that they wanted him to put together a small team. No more than six. They would need to be able to operate in a variety of areas. Snatch squad stuff. Surveillance. Forced interrogation. Maybe assassination. The dark arts and the going rate was £2000 a day for him and £1500 for the lads.

Fair enough.

Over the course of a few months he recruited his guys. He had worked with all of them at one time or another. Two had been with him in the Regiment. One, the only woman, was an ex 14th Intelligence operative who had joined from the RUC. The final two were South Africans who had got out of Dodge fast when Apartheid had crashed and burned in the early nineties. Between them they ticked all the boxes. The team had expertise in all areas where expertise was needed. Computers, communications, bugging, wiring, sniping, blowing up and torture. They were anybody's worst nightmare.

Oddly enough he had become a very rich man. He had a gaff in the Caribbean and a pile of cash in the bank. Maybe one day he should think of retiring, but it was hard to the see the point. He had never married and his family was a thing of the past. All he really had was the work. And Stevie Atwood had always liked the work. It gave him a buzz. It got him out bed in the morning. It pushed him every yard of his daily five-mile run. It was the only sport he had ever played.

A hundred yards ahead Trish was watching the target from the upstairs window of one of the newly-vacant houses. She had been there for three days taking notes and crapping in plastic bags. In an ideal world they would all have preferred to have gone in when only the two targets were in residence. For three nights the kid had taken a bird back, each time a different one. Dirty little bastard. Typical Wop. At the start of things it had seemed like time had been on their side, but that had all changed once the town centre had gone up like an Iraqi marketplace.

Dyson had called him in for a meet at a *Little Chef*. They needed to move things along. The clock was ticking at a faster rate. It had to be tonight, bird or no bird. Did they have any Rohypnol? They did. Good. Go that route then.

He buzzed Trish.

"Any change?"

A familiar Ulster voice. "No change. Three targets, one female. They're all spark out. Target one and the women in front room south. Target two is back room west. Clear?"

"Clear. We go in three."

"OK. I'll watch your backs."

"Team two. All good?"

This time a familiar Boer twang. "Ya. All good chief. We take target two, ya?"

"Affirmative. On my word, OK?"

"Roger that chief."

He eased the van to the kerb and three sets of rubber soled boots hit the pavement without a sound. Front door. A man either side scanning the empty street. One man on the door.

Door open.

"OK. Go."

Stairs. Door. A double bed with two sprawled figures coming awake in a panic. A dart fired from a range of three feet. A figure rendered inert. Now just a pair of frantic teenage eyes staring from a mop of tousled bleach blond hair. Any scream stifled by a calloused hand over her mouth.

"No need to panic lass. Open wide and swallow."

The calloused mouth opened her mouth and popped in a pill.

Closed the mouth. Pinched the nose. Forced the swallow. Good lass. Be calm now. Give me your arm."

A thin pale arm. An inserted needle. A few seconds for the sedative to take hold. A second inert figure.

"Team Two. Status?"

"Target 2 is down."

"Trish. All clear?"

"All clear."

"OK. Let's go."

A few seconds later two bodies were hauled fireman style out of the front door. One was naked and slight. The other was in boxer shorts and huge. Into the van and down the street and into the empty night. Ten minutes later a last figure emerged from the house across the road and walked away.

Sebastian listened as Donny Baldini poured it all out. All Atwood had needed to do was to show him a hammer. Now the budding gangster looked like the child he was. Tearful, terrified eyes. Shivering pale limbs. Desperate to please. He told them all about his mum and the Russian called Yuri who had supplied all the kit for the last five years. He told of how Yuri was pissed off with how everything was turning out and how he wanted to screw it all up. Yes, Yuri had given him the Anarchy. Yes, Yuri had told him to give them away. Yes, Yuri had paid him. No, he had never met Yuri at his home, always hotels and service stations. Yes, it had been Yuri who gave him Mikhail as a minder. No, he didn't know Mikhail's second name, only that he was a hard bastard. Really hard. Yes, of course he could give the names of all the junkies he had signed up to give away the pills. No point in them checking Sponge's address. That junkie loser was dead. No, he didn't know the names of any of Yuri's dealers in any other towns. Yes, Yuri had ordered the attack on the feeding station. No, he hadn't been given any new orders. Only to keep dishing out the *Anarchy*.

Atwood kept it going for three hours. The same questions again and again. The same answers again and again. At last Sebastian nodded and left the room, followed every inch of the way by Donnie's terrified puppy eyes. Atwood walked round the back of the chair where Donnie was trussed and shot the teenager through the back of his head from a distance of nine inches. It wasn't much of a gun. It had been bought for £500 a week earlier from an address in Glasgow. It was in dire need of a proper clean but to clean it would have given the game away. It wasn't a gun Atwood would have ever wanted to trust in a contact. But it was good enough to put Donnie Baldini's lights out from a distance of nine inches.

They dressed him in clothes from his wardrobe and took him to the van. The following night they dumped his corpse on a landfill site that took in the rubbish of the good folk of Paisley.

When they had studied Mikhail's inert figure it had been immediately apparent that they would need to do rather more than show him a hammer to encourage him to spill the beans. A tattoo on his forearm marked him as ex-Spetsnaz. Gunshot scars on the shoulder and thigh spoke of time in combat. The Russian Mafia had found an abundant supply of Mikhails in the Yeltsin era when the Red Army had gone hungry and unpaid. It meant that the job would go one of two ways. That all depended on Mikhail. Was he a realist or had he watched too much TV? They decided it would be best to dress him before he came round. The humiliation of nakedness would only make him more stubborn.

It took a couple of hours longer than they had expected for him to wake up. Maybe they shouldn't have been so surprised. Trish had suggested they use as much of the immobilising sedative in the dart gun as they could get away with. Her assessment was that Mikhail was one big, dangerous looking bastard. The tranquiliser they had used was from South Africa where is was used to drop elephant and rhino. Mikhail was a big lad, but in the end he was not a rhino.

He came awake in degrees over a period of ten minutes. For an instant there was terror in his eyes, but he managed to control it and put it away.

Stevie decided it was as good a time as any to make a start.

"Speak English?"

A nod.

"That helps. Right. We know a bit about you. You're called Mikhail and the tattoo says Spetsnaz. Which means you're a hard bastard. Fair enough. You've taken two bullets and you're still in the game. You work for a lad called Yuri who is Russian Mafia. He obviously thinks enough of you to have you work alone. Which means you probably have a brain in your head. So we can be civilised. So here's the deal. Three of us are SAS. Two South African Special Forces. One 14th Intelligence. OK? Get the picture. We're all hard bastards as well. So we all come from the same place, right? Maybe you're a patriot, but we're not. We're in it for the money and my guess is that you are the same. This isn't about taking out Chechnyan nutters who are planning to blow up shopping centres in Moscow is it Mikhail? This is about selling drugs for cash. Simple as that. Is it worth getting hurt for? I don't think so. So let's look at the facts. Nobody has a clue where you are and they never will have. You're on foreign soil and you have no backup. We've scanned you for any GPS implants and there are none. You're on your own Mikhail. No rescue, no nothing. So what are you going to do? You can do the resisting interrogation thing if you like. And maybe you might just buy this Yuri enough time to get away. Aye, I reckon you can do that. But is it worth it? All that pain. I reckon you're a lad who knows a bit about pain. It's not good is it? It's a complete bastard. I'm hoping that this Yuri isn't your dad or anything. Because if he isn't, I don't reckon he's worth it. This here is my boss. Mr Dyson. Know what Mikhail? I wouldn't bother taking a slap in the face for him. He pays me well but he's not worth going through the shit for. Know where I'm coming from?"

A nod.

"Good lad. So here is where we are. Option One. Tell us what we need to know. Answer the phone when Yuri calls and I give you my word as a soldier that I will personally put your lights out with a clean shot to the back of the head. Option two? You know Option Two. Option Two is an absolute bastard. Is Yuri worth Option Two?"

A pause. Barely a flicker of expression in Yuri's dead eyes. And then a slow, deliberate shake of the head. "No. Not worth it."

"Good lad. Option One, right?"

A nod.

Three hours later they had what Mikhail knew and it was a lot. The Mafia group based in Moscow. A sense of the UK operation. An address for the man in charge in England. And the address of a rather fine new property on the shores of Loch Lomond where Yuri Bonderenko laid his head most nights. And that was all good. What was not so good was the news of the huge quantities of Methamphetamine pills that were already on the streets of Britain.

Christopher Pendleton knew that everything was suddenly in the balance. He could feel it in his bones. Only a week earlier he had been well on course to becoming the next *Time Life* man of the year. Not any more. The sudden eruptions in towns and cities across Britain had come from nowhere. Once the dust had settled on the day of attacks on the feeding stations, it emerged that there had been over two hundred fatalities. In Rollerton eight had lost their lives including a mother of four, a toddler and a police officer. Thankfully there had been no more concerted attacks but the streets were no longer quiet. Police forces all over the country were fighting running battles with gangs of youths. And time and again the reports read the same: the kids were refusing to back off. The kids were acting like they had been possessed. A reasonably clear picture was emerging. A plague of Methamphetamine pills had hit the streets. Nobody had a clue where they had come from. Nobody had a clue why on earth they were being given away free of charge. Everybody was making noises about having harder information soon.

The media was split. A day earlier, the Lester Gall papers had gushed with enthusiasm at the official opening of the new Airfield site outside Rollerton. Early soundings from focus groups indicated that the public liked the idea of punishment by pallets of bricks. In fact it looked like they liked it a lot. Which of course was good. Bloody good. And as more and more areas descended into anarchy, the pallets of bricks thing became even more appealing to the law-abiding majority. Already over fifty punishment centres had opened up and business was brisk as unruly teenagers were delivered by the busload. Staffing levels were being increased all the time as many of the younger prisoners were proving to be particularly difficult to manage. But at least the system was working. Just.

Other papers were raising huge and difficult questions. Was this only the beginning of the violence? Was this the beginning of the end for the Pendleton experiment? Was the country about to descend into anarchy? Where was the Crystal Meth coming from? Why was it free? Was this an attack from a foreign power? Conspiracy theories abounded and the internet was alive with chatter. The French and Germans were loving every minute. Bastards.

He took in the faces around the Cobra Two table. Tired. Many, many more lines than there had been a few weeks earlier. Even Taylor was showing the strain. He half listened to reports and statistics. Riots and arrests. Damage estimates and numbers detained. Plans to protect tankers. Plans to re-build wrecked feeding stations. Planned to guard feeding stations. Plans to guard dormitories. Options for new restrain equipment for the staff at the punishment centres. Plans for upgraded anti-riot equipment for the police. Casualty lists. Last ditch plans for the deployment of troops onto the worst affected streets . . .

"Where the hell is Dyson?"

Why even ask? The bloody man hadn't been near Cobra Two in over a week.

"Never mind that. Just get him on the line."

It took a few seconds and then the voice which had got so infuriating was in the speakers.

"Where the bloody hell are you Dyson?"

"Scotland."

"Don't you think it's about time you showed your face and gave us a report. In case you hadn't noticed the sodding country is burning to the ground."

"I had noticed actually Prime Minister. I expect to be with you in three or four days. Then I will give you the report you are clearly so keen to hear."

"Look Dyson, I've had about enough of this. I'm not standing for your three or four days crap. You need to get your arse in here now. Hear me Dyson? Now."

"That would be plain silly Prime Minister. You are obviously upset at the course of events and it is impairing your judgement. That is entirely understandable. You are paying me very well to resolve the problems at hand and that is what I am in the process of doing. In three to four days I will have a clear picture of exactly where we all stand and some recommendations as to how we might proceed. In the meantime I suggest the best approach is to stay calm. Is that OK, Prime Minister?"

Pendleton didn't bother to reply. He killed the call and grabbed for his cigarettes.

Bastard.

Bastard, bastard, bastard.

Sebastian smiled at the killed call and popped his phone back into his pocket. Before pulling out of the lay-by he had drawn into, he called up Trish who was watching Boderenko's house from a small wood on the edge of his property.

"Any developments?"

"Not really. When he stays the night there is a guard team of four. They work four hour shifts: two at a time. I have found motion sensors, but nothing we can't handle. I can't see any great problem."

"Is Vince there?"

"Sure."

"Put him on will you."

"Vince here."

"Where are you up to?"

The South African kept his voice low just in case there were any unnoticed dog walkers in the wood.

"Straight forward enough. The guards meet every five minutes or so as they do their patrol. We'll snipe them with the dart guns. Then it should be easy enough. Disable the security systems, go in and do the other two guards. Then we take Bonderenko. None of them look particularly on their toes. Ten minutes, tops. Want me to tell Stevie when you want it done?"

"Yes please. Best get in there tonight. Things are hotting up."

"Yeah. We're all watching the news. Do you need any more or shall we just get on with it?"

"No. I'll leave it with you."

Sebastian checked his appearance in the mirror. Today was a suit day. A day to give the respectable Sebastian Dyson an outing. A man with and easy smile and smooth manners. A man he might have become had he so wished. A lawyer? A banker? A Chief Executive Officer? How different life would have been. No doubt there would have been a wife and children and by now grandchildren as well. Family photos on the living room wall. A dog to walk. Golf clubs to swing.

The thought of it made him smile. He had never come close to such a reality. His watch told him that he had twelve minutes to cover the five miles to his appointment. Fine. He had never been a man who was ever late. The only time he was late was when he wanted to be late. When he wanted people to sweat on his arrival. Today was a day to be on time.

The appointment promised to be routine. His role for the day was to play the part of Colin Jarvis, an independent consultant who specialised in helping businesses to take over other businesses. Two weeks earlier he had been granted an appointment to meet Mr Charles Peacock, the sole and outright owner of *Supa-Vit Ltd*. An in-house Rutland International account had trawled records held in Companies House and turned up Mr Peacock and his Northampton based vitamin business. They appeared to tick all the boxes. The business had been established by Peacock himself back in the early Eighties on the back of a redundancy payment from *Glaxo*. For twenty years the business had gone from strength to strength, specialising mainly in producing jazzily-packaged multi-vitamins for concerned parents to purchase for their pampered children. Then slowly but surely the profit margins had been squeezed by the Supermarkets until there were barely any profits left at all. The most recently posted accounts showed profits down to the bare bones. By now Peacock was sixty-six and the register of Directors showed no hint of any sons or daughters following him into the family business.

Sebastian AKA Colin Jarvis had spun a line about representing a Korean company who needed to get a presence in the EU Market as soon as possible. They needed a manufacturing base and they needed it in a hurry. Their hurry was so great in fact that they were willing to offer Charles Peacock a price for his business that was quite frankly ridiculously generous. As soon as he mentioned the figure Sebastian knew that he had his man. Of course checks had to be made and by now the *Supa-Vit Ltd* accountants would have completed a confusing journey of discovery which ended with a holding company in Luxembourg. No matter. The cash that was lodged in a UK holding account was real enough. All that remained now was for the dotted line to be signed on and the cash would flow magically into Peacock's personal account.

There seemed no likelihood of any hitches. Telling the Prime Minister that he had just invested seven million pounds of tax payer's funds in a failing vitamin business would be interesting of course. No doubt the man would be less than happy but it couldn't be helped.

The real moment for the gallant Christopher Pendleton would come when Sebastian explained that there was in fact a nuclear option. Only a month earlier such a proposition had seemed to be hugely unlikely. Not any more. The realm was descending into anarchy and nobody seemed able to do much to stop it by conventional means.

The time was fast approaching where more drastic action would be needed. Would Pendleton have the nerve to take it? Maybe. Maybe not.

Jason and Sally had been locked in conversation for well over three hours. He had driven to Edinburgh after his disturbing talk with Doogie at the viewing point. The Dachau day. The day when everything started to feel scary. He told her about the whispered name. A name that Google had no knowledge of. A name with no history. And yet a name that was sitting at the top table in the land. He told her that the man with the whispered name had been the one to come up with the idea of punishment by pallets of bricks. He told her that the country's most powerful policeman had asked Doogie for a file on behalf of the man with the whispered name. Sponge's file. And now Sponge was dead.

In the days that followed more threads emerged. Sally asked around quietly and twice more the name was whispered. Then Doogie dropped the bombshell about a toxicology report that proved that Nathaniel Peter Clarke had overdosed on the purest Heroin ever seen on the streets of Rollerton. Heroin so pure that it could only have come of production line of a maker of licensed pharmaceuticals.

Conclusion? There was only one conclusion to be had. The man with the whispered name had asked for files telling all there was to tell about Sponge and had then used the information to stage manage his death.

But why?

Why would a man nobody had ever heard of be invited to sit at the table where the shots were called?

Why would such a man order the execution of a hopeless, low-level heroin addict from an inconsequential Scottish town?

It all seemed far too fanciful to be true, but the facts refused to be re-arranged. They had agreed to pool their resources and to try and find out more about the whispered name. And they had come up with nothing.

So now they were discussing a Plan B. Jason's Plan B. And they knew all too well that Plan B was very much of the wing and a prayer variety. It was a plan that offered no guarantees whatsoever of success. However, it was also a plan that would ensure that they would be squarely in the spotlight. Maybe the plan might take them to the man with the whispered name. Or maybe not. What was for certain was that the man with the whispered name would be very much aware of their names. Only the day before, the body of Donnie Baldini had been discovered at a landfill site of the outskirts of Paisley. He had been executed. A single shot to the back of his head. The killing bore the familiar fingerprints of a gangland affair. And maybe it was exactly that. But could it really be pure coincidence that Donnie and Sponge had been killed with such apparent expertise within a few days of each other? Two rather inconsequential figures from the drug world of Rollerton. At least one of them was directly connected to the man with the whispered name. And now Sponge was dead.

As in dead. Not beaten up. Not threatened. Dead.

They both knew well enough that the line they were considering taking a step over was ultimately serious. The country was teetering on the brink. It was the kind of time when the gloves would be taken off. But no matter how they tried they could find no alternative to Plan B. Doogie had already signed on the dotted line. Now it was their turn.

In the end they took the plunge.

It was a mark of Jason's new status as star reporter that Amelie suggested that they meet for lunch at one of her favourite places. Jason arrived first and ordered himself a beer. It was another indication of the new state of things. A few months earlier he would never have dared order a beer when the Fridge was about to sweep into the room. No chance. Then it would have been mineral water and nervous sips. Beer might have been enough to give her the excuse she needed for some dinosaur downsizing. Well the dinosaur had earned himself enough a stay of execution to turn into an asset to the paper. It really should have felt better. Just a week or two earlier it had felt better. It had felt bloody great. But now somehow the dark clouds had swept in from the sea. The world suddenly felt cold and dark and frightening. He had spent the train journey south from Edinburgh gazing glumly out of the window. It had all seemed so much the right thing to do when he had talked with Sally and Doogie. When they had made their pact with each other. It had seemed so much better at the time.

Not any more.

Now he was just plain scared.

Amelie shimmered across the room. A woman at the top of her game. Heads turned as she breezed by tables of power-lunching city types.

"On time Jason. I'm impressed. I seemed to be impressed quite a lot these days. Isn't it just super, don't you agree?"

She eased into the seat opposite and picked up a menu.

"Actually, Amelie. Are you really hungry?"

"Well. Peckish I suppose. Why do you ask?"

"Maybe we could go for a walk. You know. Fresh air and all that."

"A walk?"

"Mmm. Open spaces and traffic and pedestrians."

She got it. It never took Amelie very long to get anything. Jason decided it was a high-flier thing.

He left money on the table for his half-finished beer and they walked out into a crisp afternoon. She hooked her hand through his arm and lowered her voice somewhat theatrically.

"This is all jolly exciting Jason. I rather wish I had a Gabardine raincoat. Where to? The park?"

"That will be fine."

He had no clue how surveillance equipment worked. In fact he had no clue as to whether or not they were being surveilled at all. Doogie had suggested it would be good to play safe. Choose a very open space. The very open space was a stretch of carefully mown grass at the centre of Hyde Park. Apart from two joggers and a solitary dog-walker they had the space to themselves.

"Are we safe now?"

He shrugged. "Hopefully. I don't pretend to be an expert."

"You seem very troubled Jason."

"I am." He breathed out a plume of smoke which wandered up into the clear blue of the sky.

"Something bad seems to be happening. Really bad. To be honest, I'm beginning to feel a long way out of my depth."

Her usual mocking tone was now gone. "I always believe it is rather a good idea to start at the beginning and take it from there. OK?"

He did as he was bid. Sponge. Donny Baldini. Nazi Crank. An overdose on the purest Heroin Rollerton had ever seen. An executed corpse on a Paisley landfill. A late night call from the high up cop from Cobra Two. Why would such a man want the life and times of a low-life like Sponge? And why just two days after the call was made and the information sent did Sponge end up so very dead? And more than anything else, who the hell was Sebastian Dyson? Nobody knew. Even Google didn't know. The man was a ghost, and yet it seemed he was a ghost who had the ear of the Prime Minister of Great Britain and Northern Ireland. He was a ghost who came up with the idea of punishment by pallets of bricks. And he was a ghost who could possibly make people very dead indeed just hours after receiving their files.

"Have you any theories?"

He shook his head. "Not really. Well nothing I could begin to back up. I have some ideas."

"Go on."

"OK. We know that this Dyson is on Cobra Two. You don't get any higher than that. Look at the other guys: PM, Leader of the Opposition, Home Secretary and top men from the police, army and MI5. So this guy has to be a big player. Right?"

"Agreed."

"But despite this, nobody seems to have ever heard of him. You have to have a lot of clout to be on Cobra Two and not on Google. He has to be some sort of spy or something. We know that the role of Cobra Two is to maintain security. That much is obvious. Politicians, a soldier, a copper and a spook. And Dyson. The pallets of bricks thing came down from Cobra Two and Dyson thought it up. So. The Pendleton changes kick-in and much to everyone's surprise they are a mega success. The silent majority are chuffed to bits. And why wouldn't they be? Less tax to pay. A chance for their kids to get an affordable place of their own and free bed and board when they go to university. And best of all, at long last someone has come along to crack down on the free-loading poor and get the foreigners out. All fact, agreed?"

"Agreed."

"So who are the losers? The poor of course. The ones who have lost their season tickets for the gravy train. Fine. We know this. But then we need to think about who else has lost? Where did the benefits get spent? The thing is, I have already written it down and you have already printed it. The Drugs Industry. Just think of the loss of turnover they must have had to deal with. 300,000 heroin users in the UK and almost all of them spending every penny of their benefits on the next tenner bag. Do the maths. 300,000 times by about a hundred quid a week. We're talking north of thirty million a week. So who are the biggest losers? Organised crime. Not the two-bit tenner bag merchants in the schemes. We're talking bloody cartels with yachts and helicopters and bank accounts measured in billions. Stay with me. What do the cartels do about it? Do they lie down and die and find some other crime to commit? Not their style. Instead they are going to fight it. How? They need to stop Pendleton's New Order from taking root. They need to kill all those Lester Gall good news stories that the whole world was starting to buy into."

Amelie's brow was furrowed in concentration. "I think I can see where this is going. They need to stop the changes in their tracks. Discredit Pendleton. Set the streets alight. Yes?"

"Did you ever read any WB Yeats?"

"I did."

" 'Turning and turning in a widening gyre, the falcon can no longer hear the falconer . . .'"

" ' . . . things fall apart, the centre cannot hold, mere anarchy is loosed upon the world'. Yes. I think I can see. The drugs industry wants to destroy Pendleton and his new system. How would they go about this? Obvious. They use the tools they have to hand. Drugs. It is what they do after all. And I expect you think that is the reason why millions of methamphetamine pills are being doled out free of charge?"

"Yes. I also think the attacks on the feeding stations were ordered and co-ordinated by the drugs industry. Maybe Sponge was one of the ones who handed out pills. Maybe Donny Baldini was involved as well. Since his mum went to Italy, he is pretty much top dog in Rollerton. How about this. As soon as the shit starts to hit the fan, the PM looks to this Dyson to make it stop. Dyson needs to find out what the hell is happening. More to the point, he needs to find out who is making it happen. So he gets into the chain at the bottom end. Sponge.

Who is next? Donny Baldini. Why them? Why Rollerton? I don't know. But maybe there is in fact a really simple answer. We decided to run the Rollerton series because it had the highest number of citizens drawing benefits or working for the state of any town in Britain with a population of over 100,000. Yeah?"

"Correct."

"Well maybe this Dyson has done exactly the same maths. Maybe he is working on the theory that if they can stop the rot in Rollerton, then they can stop the rot anywhere. Think about it. Where was the first punishment centre opened?"

"Rollerton."

"Exactly."

They walked for a while in silence. "What do you propose we do?"

"We need to find out who Sebastian Dyson is."

"I can agree with that. Any idea how?"

"We ask the public."

"What?"

"If you agree, this is how things can play. The Parliament in Edinburgh is due to sit late tonight. Sally can place an emergency question. Basically she asks for more information on a man called Sebastian Dyson who is a member of the Cobra Two team. It means that the question is put into the public domain under the protection of Parliamentary privilege. Sally is an MSP and enjoys protection as such. We obviously have prior warning and we have our lead story ready to roll for the midnight internet posting. The headline is simple. "Does anyone out there know who Sebastian Dyson is?" The story is basically what we have just talked about. It will quickly put Doogie, Sally and I in the spotlight, but surely there will not be much anyone can do about it. Once the secret is out, it is out."

"And what do we hope will happen next?"

"There has to be someone out there who knows who the man is. Maybe they will make contact? Maybe we will get enough to shine a light on him?"

"You are suggesting that we play in a very big league here Jason."

"I know. In the end it is your call. I don't suppose the top brass would back it anyway."

She smiled. "If they knew about it I am sure that you would be quiet correct in your assessment. But they will not know about it. They can read about it in the paper along with everyone else. You see Jason, I am their blue-eyed girl. I have taken *The Enquirer* from being a loss-making basket case to a veritable cash cow. They trust me. They love me to bits. They have given me a free hand. And do you know what Jason, I do believe that I was born to play in a big league. Stuff it. Tell Sally to do it. You have your story ready?"

He passed her a memory key. "Good. We'll run at midnight."

Sally had addressed the Parliament on several occasions during her time as an MSP. At first she had been almost liquefied with nerves. But the fear hadn't lasted very long. At times she found it almost pathetic, times when her collective audience was less than ten. She had been picked to fire a question at the First Minister three times when the chamber was full. That had been a little better, a little closer to what she had thought it would be all about when she decided to embark on her political career. What novelty there was soon worn off. Soon she spent little time in the debating chamber. What was the point? Her time was far better spent helping her constituents on a case by case basis.

Luckily she had always enjoyed a good relationship with the Presiding Officer. He had been clearly pleased to see her when she visited his office during a break in proceedings. He made coffee and they discussed the turn events were taking. The late night debate was a state of the nation thing and the temperature promised to run high. For weeks London had been calling all the shots and it seemed as if Devolution had been more or less canned. Emotions were running high. Noses were out of joint. It promised to be a lively evening. She hadn't been the first member to beg for a chance to make a point. Almost every MSP in the house wanted to have their say. The Presiding Officer however promised to get her on.

Now the debate had been ongoing for well over two hours. Not that it was much of a debate. It was more like a collective moan. The message for the executive down in London was fairly clear. Don't you dare ignore us all the time. As she listened to her colleagues huff and puff through their statements, she had a picture of Christopher Pendleton watching it all on TV and laughing his socks off.

Well. Maybe that was about to change.

A question ended and she shot her hand in the air along with fifty others. The Presiding Officer caught her eye and gave the nod. Show time.

She stood. She took a moment. She took a breath.

"My fellow members, we have heard a continuous theme this evening. Whatever happened to devolution? Just a few short weeks ago, law and order and crime and punishment were a devolved issue.

A few weeks ago it was down to this house to decide on such issues. Well, all that seems to have changed. What I would like to know is who is really calling the shots? From what we read in the papers, it seems that all the power is now concentrated around the Cobra Two emergency committee. What they say goes in Scotland just as it does every other corner of the land. Are the men who sit around that murky table elected? Well, three of then are. The Prime Minister, the Leader of the Opposition and the Home Secretary. Not that any of them were elected by the people of Scotland. But who are the other men who are tasked with shaping our destiny? Well, we have Philip Parker from the Metropolitan Police. Fair enough. It is clear to all of us that the police have an enormous role to play as our streets descend into chaos. Next we have General Alistair Lockhead. This of course begs a question. Are troops about to be deployed onto the streets of Scotland? More to the point, is anybody going to have the courtesy to consult this house should they decide to do so? And then we have Mr Dominic West of MI5. It would be very nice to know just what Mr West has in mind for all of us and whether that is bound by the constitution. And finally we have one last member of the committee. Mr Sebastian Dyson. I recommend that each and every one of you should type the name into Google when this sitting is over. I can tell you what you will discover. Nothing. Not a word, not a whisper. It seems that Mr Sebastian Dyson doesn't exist. And yet the Prime Minister has chosen to give him a seat at the top table. My question is simple and my question is this. Who on earth is Sebastian Dyson? What is his area of expertise? And what right does he have to make decisions about the people of Scotland?"

There was a kind of collective shiver around the chamber as Sally sat down. Everyone in the room knew that she had stepped into a dark and dangerous place. And yet they also knew that she had done so wearing the protective cloak of Parliamentary privilege. Would it be enough? Almost every MSP in the house secretly wished they had been the one to have made such a huge play in the glare of the cameras. And almost every MSP in the house secretly thanked their lucky stars that it had been Sally and not themselves who had stepped out into the cold.

John Taylor seldom got nervous about anything much. He never had. What was the point? But he was nervous now. Nervous as a spotty teenager asking a dream bird out on a date. This was not going to be good.

He tapped at the PM's door and was shouted in. Christopher Pendleton was working his way down a pile of papers. In front of him sat a tumbler of scotch and a full ashtray. Business as usual.

"Hi John. Grab a pew. Won't be a sec."

He skip read the paper in front of him and then signed.

"OK. That'll do. What's happening?"

"Nothing good boss."

A dry sort of laugh. "Why am I not surprised? Go on."

Taylor cleared his throat and lit up. "We've got a problem. You know there was a debate up in Edinburgh tonight?"

Another sardonic laugh. "Yeah, yeah. The Celtic Fringe met up for a good old whinge. Twats."

Another clearing of a tired old throat. "The thing is boss, it got to a bit more than the usual whinging. A LibDem MSP has caused a bit of a problem. Sally Webster."

"Who in the name of Christ is Sally Webster? I've never even heard of Sally Webster. I couldn't give a shit about Sally Webster."

Taylor could see that he would have to tell it straight.

"She demanded to know who Sebastian Dyson is."

"She what!"

"You heard it right I'm afraid. That was it basically. Who the hell is Sebastian Dyson? Google him and come up blank. How can a man who does not exist on Google be calling the shots on the lives of her Scottish twat constituents?"

"Shit."

"Exactly."

"At least it was Edinburgh. Who the hell gives a damn what they say up there? We should have a bit of time to get our ducks in line."

"Sorry boss."

Taylor laid down a printout of the midnight online edition of *The Enquirer*. The front cover was dominated by a black silhouette of a man's head on a white background. The mystery guest. The headline was straight forward enough. "Who is Sebastian Dyson?"

The last vestiges of colour seeped from Pendleton's face. "Bastards. They knew it was coming. What is going on here John?"

"We've found some links boss. Sally Webster was at school with the Chief Superintendent up in Rollerton. Douglas Jameson. Seems like they were an item once upon a time. She was also at school with Jason Marsh."

"The journo on *The Enquirer*?"

"The very same."

"I don't believe this."

He was about to ask what they were going to do about it when the phone rang. At the other end of the line was a voice he fervently wished he had never heard.

"Good evening Prime Minister."

"Have you seen *The Enquirer*, Dyson?"

"Of course. Quite flattered actually. Super to be a media star, wouldn't you say?"

"Don't you get flippant with me Dyson."

"So sorry. I'll make a note. No more flippancy. Got it boss."

"Are you ringing to show what a complete and utter twat you are, or is there a point here somewhere?"

"Just keeping you in the loop boss. I hope to be down for the meeting tomorrow afternoon. I anticipate being in a position to give you a clearer picture."

"A clearer picture of what exactly?"

"A clearer picture of why the Realm is breaking up by the hour. And I might just have an idea or two as to how you might be able to make it stop. Anyway. It has been lovely to chat. Must go now. See you all tomorrow. Have the kettle on. Bye-eee."

The Prime Minister stared down at the suddenly silent speaker in front of him.

"The man is insane. He's a bloody lunatic. Christ John, what the hell have we got ourselves into?"

Taylor shrugged. "I reckon that if anyone is going to get us out of all this shite, it's probably going to be Dyson. Couldn't tell you why. It just feels that way."

The PM couldn't think of anything to say. Instead he drained his tumbler and stared off into space.

Yuri Bonderenko felt tired. Worse than that, he felt tired and old. It was hard to believe that only a few months earlier his life had seemed to be so well appointed. The golf courses of the world had been beckoning. His journey from the KGB to the Mafia had been both long and dangerous but he had completed it. He had proved himself to be one of life's survivors. A winner. And at long last the finish line had been in sight.

Then everything had changed the day the Right Honourable Christopher Pendleton MP had appeared in prime time TV. From that moment the voice in Moscow had started to change in tone. Things had been relatively normal to start with. Of course they hadn't been happy with the collapse of UK income. And of course they had been determined to fight it. That had been normal. It had also been normal for them to expect their man on the spot to run the show. What had been troubling him was the new intensity that had grown by the day. There was something different in the voice. Somehow he sensed it wasn't just about business any more. Now it was more. To Yuri it all felt like the half-forgotten days of the Cold War when a blind, unthinking hatred of the West governed most of what they did. And of course in those days the voice on the phone from Moscow had been a real top-floor man. A hard-liner. The kind of man who would have happily sacrificed a hundred million for the joy of nuking Washington.

Over the past weeks the voice had steadily become more demanding. More threatening. More demonic. All of a sudden there was a threat of Siberia in the air. Did the Mafia have camps in the East? Yuri wouldn't have put it past them. Most of what they did was shaped by the old days.

The voice had informed Yuri that people in Moscow were very pleased with the effect the Methamphetamine was having. Very pleased indeed. So pleased in fact that they wanted more. The factory in Kaliningrad had been switched on to twenty-four hours a day. The voice rattled out production figures with similar glee to the old Party lags who had once reported to the Politburo on how many tractors had rolled off the lines in factories in the Urals. The decision had been made at the highest level to crank up the operation. A wagon was to be sent with a load of five tonnes. It was ridiculous. Utter madness. Far, far too many eggs in one basket.

It wasn't how they did things. Yuri had hinted at this and been told with a voice that cracked like a whip that he was showing the kind of attitude that would have allowed Hitler to prevail at Stalingrad.

That was when the penny dropped. When men like the voice on the phone started to bang on about Stalingrad it only tended to mean one thing. The hawks had gained sway.

Five tonnes on a single load. Unbelievable. How much of an investment did that represent? Yuri had no real idea. But he knew that it had to be huge. Maybe too huge. The organisation was hardly short of money, but even so. This must be costing a king's ransom. The maths didn't add up at all. Even if the plot did indeed derail Pendleton, there was no guarantee that business would return to normal. Britain had been plainly bankrupt before all of this had started. The Government had been unable to borrow any more money and it had gone cap in hand to the IMF. That of course had been the whole point. If the new changes were to fail, then what then? The Pound would collapse and the next government would find it even harder to raise cash. They would be very unlikely to be able to re-instate benefits.

So why?

To Yuri there seemed to be only one logical explanation. Maybe there were new men in charge in Moscow. Maybe the company was merely the means, not the end. And that could only mean one thing: the Kremlin.

Relations between Russia and Britain had been disintegrating for years. Yuri knew only too well that the men in charge in the Kremlin would love nothing better than to find a way to bring Britain to its knees. Maybe they had just found it. Why else would anyone want to take the crazy risk of sending five tonnes of Methamphetamine on a single truck?

That afternoon he had driven down to Hull to watch the truck as it emerged through Customs. He had experienced a gnawing terror he hadn't known for years. Had the truck been stopped, the buck would have stopped with him. No one would have cared that it not been his idea. They never did. It was always the man on the spot who took the bullet in the back of the head. It always had been.

The truck hadn't been stopped. The truck had made an uneventful journey to a warehouse on the outskirts of Rotherham where the consignment had been broken up. Nineteen operatives had loaded boxes of pills into their car boots and headed off to every corner of Britain to bring more mayhem to the streets. One operative failed to show: Mikhail. Mikhail who hadn't answered his phone for nearly 24 hours and Yuri had a bad feeling in his guts. He had kept this development to himself. The voice on the phone was clearly in no mood for any kind of failure. If there was no news by the morning he would send a couple of the guys down to Rollerton to find out what was going on. Maybe Mikhail had taken a bag of cash and headed for some place sunny. It happened. Not often, but it did happen. But Mikhail? Yuri didn't think so. He really didn't know what to think.

It had been almost midnight by the time he got back home to his house by the lake. The night was rotten; windy and wet and dark. He changed into comfortable clothes and poured himself a huge scotch. The news online did little to ease his anxiety. *The National Enquirer* was demanding to know who a man called Sebastian Dyson was. There was little else to the story. A man *Google* had no notion of, was a part of the Cobra Two committee. How could a man with no history have such a huge say on how the shots were called? How indeed? Yuri's instincts sensed a man from the world he had always lived in. A man like the voice on the phone from Moscow. As the situation cartwheeled into violence and chaos, the men from the dark side were starting to pull the strings.

Not good.

He had just finished reading the article for a second time when the door to his study flew open and two soaking wet figures clad from head to toe in black stormed into his life. He made no effort to resist. What was the point? They were years younger than him and he had never been a soldier anyway. He allowed them to lift him to his feet and lead him from the room. In the corridor outside there were two corpses with lifeless eyes staring into infinity with two neat holes in the centre of each of their foreheads. Double tap.

So this was how it ended. It had always been the most likely outcome. The dream of rolling fairways and manicured greens had been an old man's fantasy all along.

They handled him gently once it was obvious that he had no intention of putting up a fight. They drove him through the night for two hours. The wipers thumped across the windscreen. Small lifeless towns came and went. If he had tried he could have gained an idea of where they were, but he didn't have the energy.

It was a small farm, a few hundred yards up a track strewn with puddles. The clock on the dashboard told him that it was nearly four. Of course it was. The darkest time of life. The time when the knock on the door would always come. The time when the nightmare would start.

They took him into a tired kitchen and tied him to a chair. They weren't rough about it. Merely efficient. Almost bored. A little deflated now the effects of the adrenalin had worn off.

After a few minutes had passed the door opened and two men joined him. They sat at the far side of a pine table that had seen better days. One was in his late forties with hard edges and lifeless eyes. The other was nearer his age, maybe older. His eyes carried a sense of bleak amusement. An old sweater. Jeans. Well worn brogues. A mug of what smelt like hot chocolate.

At ease. And all of a sudden Yuri knew exactly who the man was.

"You must be this Sebastian Dyson I think?"

A smile. "Very good Yuri. Very good indeed. Jolly well done. I am not at all surprised. I have been reading your files you see. You would be surprised at ho many files we have. Not new files of course. Old files from different times. You were quite a player in your day. And then of course things went a bit quiet when everything crashed to the floor. We have never spent enough time keeping an eye on the Mafias. Silly really. Never enough resources. Every penny was allocated to chasing the Mad Mullahs. But in the end, here we are again. Old adversaries and all that. I actually feel rather nostalgic. They were better times Yuri. Far better times. We all had so much of a better idea as to where we stood. Anyway. Enough of my senile ramblings. This gentleman is called Atwood. He is the same sort of chap as the ones you used to employ to work in the basement at the Lubyanka. Need I say more?"

Yuri smiled and shook his head. "No. There is no need to say more. And there will be no need for your Mr Atwood to deploy his skills. I can tell you all you need to know. It is OK. I am not a fool. I think you can promise that when the time comes it can be quick?"

Sebastian smiled. "Of course I can Yuri. To do otherwise wouldn't be cricket at all."

And so Yuri told him. The whole thing. The plan to use Methamphetamine to bring chaos to the streets. The new tone from Moscow. He suspicions that the whole thing was moving to a new level. His gut feeling that it was now the Kremlin that was calling the shots. The fact that the five tonne consignment of pills was already broken-up and distributed. The details of the next stage of the operation which demanded that the dormitories should be attacked.

An the exact co-ordinates of the factory in Kaliningrad.

It was mid-morning by the time that a bullet entered the back of Yuri's head. Not that it had seemed to have got light at all. The world was grey and wet. A couple of bedraggled crows flapped up from a hawthorn bush when the gun popped. Otherwise neither man nor beast either noticed nor cared.

Sebastian was not present to wave Yuri off to the next world. He was already on his way to London.

At first Bexx had told them all to get stuffed. No way was she going back to the Airfield to stack any more bloody bricks. Not a chance. But she had sat with the rest of them to watch the news. It was Falkirk first. Then Ayr. Then Kirkaldy. And then just about every town in Scotland and the North of England. The basic theory was the same as Bexx had come up with when she had led the abortive raid on *Tesco*. The difference was sheer numbers. In Falkirk an estimated three hundred women stormed the town's Asda store. And then there was another key difference, for in Falkirk the kids had joined in.

When the cops had lined up outside *Tesco*, Bexx and her fellow raiders had gone fairly quietly. There was no such quietness in Falkirk. The kids were obviously off their heads on the new pills and their demonic will to fight seemed to seep into the women. Tear gas was fired and there was a cavalry charge of mounted police. Most of the loot in the trolleys was used as missiles. But not all. The TV pictures clearly showed a large number of raiders escaping from the fighting with armfuls of goods.

This was what had got the women around her in the feeding station going. For weeks now they had spent hours on end dreaming of things they had lost over endless cups of tea: cannabis, big Saturday nights out, bacon rolls, Pizza, make up, new clothes, magazines, fags. Fags,fags,fags.

A few women had found some work, usually cleaning for a pound an hour. Enough for a ten pack. Not that they ever risked a smoke anywhere near the feeding station. To have done so would have meant being stared at by a hundred sets of resentful eyes. Worse still was the fact that the kids always seemed to have fags, usually robbed from the few small shops that continued to ply their trade.

As the weeks of dormitory life drifted by, resentment levels had escalated and hardened. To start with the news channels had trumpeted the stunning successes of Pendleton's New Britain. There were the smiling faces of the foreign backpackers taking pictures of each other in Trafalgar Square and then telling the camera how great it was in the London Dorms. There were the students who made the dorms in the big university towns into places of bouncing optimism. There were the young people who had taken the subsidised train south to free accommodation, plentiful work and a taste of the fast lane life of the capital. The camera teams seemed to have little interest in the places like Rollerton where the Pendleton losers eked out their dismal existence with endless cups of tea.

Then the pictures on the news started to change. First it was the kids. Wild-eyed and possessed, trashing everything in their path, just like they had done in Rollerton. They were the trailblazers. They had set a new tone. A mood of defiance. A militancy that was then taken up by the three hundred women who had stormed the gates of *Asda,* Falkirk.

Now the women of the Rollerton dorm were determined to follow the Falkirk lead. They were dead set on raiding *Tesco* at eleven that morning. At first Bexx had told them they were crazy. She had tried it and wound up humping bricks. It was loser's alley. But nobody was in the mood to listen to what she had to say. They didn't care about

MERE ANARCHY

humping bricks. They had seen those Falkirk trolleys. They wanted crisps and chocolate and make up and hair dye and decent shampoo. And they didn't give a shite if they got lifted.

By ten o'clock on the morning of the planned attack it was becoming clear to Bexx that this was going to be very a different operation to her abortive raid. Hardly a woman in the dorm was opting out. They would be a trolley army of over two hundred. And they would not be alone. The kids had heard of the operation and were planning to join it. The mysterious *Anarchy* pills had once again disappeared from the streets four days earlier and once again the youngsters who had come to so depend on them were becoming almost deranged. At least the *Tesco* raid would distract them from screaming at their frightened and beleaguered parents. Surely they would be the main focus for the coppers to deal with, especially when they were all in such a hyped up mood. Maybe that would give the trolley women the chance to break the cordon and get clear.

And so when the time to move out arrived Bexx duly joined the two hundred strong army that made its way through the streets of Rollerton. How many pallets of bricks had that posh bastard Sheriff threatened her with if he ever saw her again? Five? Ten? Well, so what. She was beyond caring about it. She was sick of having nothing.

Doogie had forgotten what an regular night's sleep looked like. For four nights in a row he had snatched a couple of hours here and a couple of nights there on the newly-purchased camp bed in his office. Scattered pieces of intelligence suggested that the Anarchy pills had once again vanished from the streets creating ever more fury among the youngsters who had become so dependent on them. The police were dealing with constant frantic calls from the desperate victims of the marauding gangs. Small shops and pensioners living alone and stay-at-home mums from the leafier side of town. It was an endless cycle. Units would be deployed and there would be violence. The kids constantly refused to back down and run away. Every time they stood their ground and fought. Over seventy officers were now hospitalised with an array of injuries, many serious. The Airfield was filled to overflowing and a new dormitory was being erected to accommodate the ever increasing numbers who were being processed through the temporary court at the football stadium.

As well as the calls for help there were an equal number of calls reporting unacceptable levels of violence and brutality being employed by his officers as they fought to control the roving gangs.

231

It was quite impossible to employ normal procedures to deal with this. Had they done so, there would barely have been a policeman or woman on the streets: they would all have been suspended on full pay pending investigation. It was getting harder and harder to hold the line whilst sticking to the letter and spirit of the law. Doogie was damned if he was going to come down hard on his officers if they overstepped the line. What the hell were they supposed to do? They were all shattered. Nobody was getting any time off. And the constant level of violence they were trying to deal with was taking a heavy toll on morale.

Already the morning had brought more of the same. A disused factory was ablaze and a mob of about thirty was pelting the firemen with half bricks. A newsagents on Peninsular Rd had been attacked with a gang of fifteen and a pitched battle with the police was now in full swing. He could feel his lines become more and more stretched. He just didn't have enough people.

A tap on the door. A face creased with fatigue and worry.

"Sorry boss. Looks like we have a problem."

Doogie couldn't help but smile. "That makes a change then. What's up?"

"There's a group of about 200 women who seem to be headed for *Tesco*. They left the dorm about ten minutes ago."

"Shit!" Doogie slammed his pen down on the top of his desk and snapped it in two. He had been dreading this development. Ever since the women of Falkirk had marshalled their forces he had known the same thing would come to Rollerton. Operation Harvest had worked well enough the first time around. But things had been very different then. Then he had had a full force of well motivated officers at his disposal. And there had only been thirty women. Now his lines were stretched to breaking point and there were two hundred.

"Gets worse I'm afraid boss."

"Go on."

"We've already got gangs of kids assembling on the car park."

"Bloody brilliant. OK. Get me the store manager on the phone."

A couple minutes later a nervous voice came onto the line. "Margorie Hindle here."

"Hello Margorie. Superintendant Jameson here. We have a problem I'm afraid. There is a group of over 200 women on route to you and it seems as if there are groups of youngsters gathering on your car park. I need you to close the store right now. Evacuate all customers with immediate effect please. We will deploy as many of our people as we can. Get all your staff away except security. You need to act now, understand? There isn't much time."

"Of course. I will do it right away."

Doogie concentrated. "OK. Is the helicopter in the air?"

"Yes."

"How far away are they now?"

"Not far. Maybe ten minutes."

Ten minutes. Not enough time. Not nearly enough time. "OK. There is no way we'll ever be able to get enough people in place to stop them on the street. Best thing is to give them free passage to the car park. Hopefully most of the public will be away by the time they get there. I anticipate that they will attempt to smash their way in, especially if the kids are with them. We will deploy all of our people in line in front of the main entrance. Make sure we have tear gas available. I will be there to take command as soon as I can. Just get who ever has seniority to sort things until I get there, OK?"

"Boss."

Bexx could feel that everything was wrong. A helicopter had been hanging in the air above them for five minutes and the party mood of the women was fading fast. As they reached the car park it was obvious that something was very different. There was barely a car to be seen. A clutch of squad cars had gathered in front of the main entrance and already there was standoff developing between the officers and a crowd of about fifty teenagers. As they drew nearer she could see a line of scared faces behind the glass of the entrance doors. Security. The doors were clearly locked. The bastards had closed the store.

Now there was anger in the crowd. Built up hopes had been dashed yet again. They were close now, a natural angry momentum driving them towards the police line. A hail of bricks was crashing into the glass doors turning them into a spider's web of cracks. There was no need for a leader to make a decision on tactics. It was obvious what they were going to do. They were going smash through the police line and break in.

Already fights between teenagers and policemen had broken out. The crowd pressed forward and Bexx could feel they were making progress. She felt a surge of optimism. There weren't enough cops. Not nearly enough. And one or two were getting an absolute battering. The women were empowered by their numbers and nothing was about to stop them this time. Nothing.

Suddenly she couldn't breathe properly any more. Her eyes seemed to be on fire and her lungs were in a vice. All around her everyone was the same. What was it? Gas? Oh my God.

She sank to her knees and tried to cover her face. Beside her a youth was in the process of throwing a petrol bomb when a screaming woman crashed into him as she desperately tried to run away from the gas. The collision dislodged the bottle from his hand and it fell to the ground.

The tarmac.

The hard, hard tarmac.

The tarmac that was much too hard for the glass. Basic physics kicked in. The glass broke. The petrol splashed out onto the crouching form of Bexx. And a fraction of a second later the petrol ignited with a soft thumping sound that was completely lost in the noise of the battle.

Within seconds Bexx was alight and her screams were loud enough to stop everyone around her in their tracks. The fighting died away in an instant as horrified faces turned to stare at the thrashing, running, burning figure that made a sound that would bring nightmares for years to come. Soon every bit of Bexx was ablaze and an unimaginable pain poured through every inch of her being.

Her brain was beyond computing the fact that she had collapsed to the floor. It was beyond her realisation that Doogie and three fellow officers had managed to put out the flames with their jackets.

Unconsciousness arrived three minutes before death.

Doogie stood over the charred remains and felt like he was hyperventilating. All around him the faces of police officers, dormitory women and anarchy craving teens stared down at a horror beyond imagination. There was no need to order the crowd to disperse. People just drifted away in silence.

They had to spray Bexx's corpse with foam before the paramedics could wrap it in blankets and get it onto an ambulance.

Doogie sat in his car for a long, long time before he felt able to switch on and drive away.

Jason sat and stared at the phone on his desk and tried to pull himself together. He didn't really know how he felt. Only that it was beyond bad, probably beyond any bad he had ever felt before. The bleakness in Doogie's voice completely mirrored the place he found himself in. Just a few weeks earlier life had seemed to be filled with such promise. But now he didn't want to be in the game any more. Now the game had turned into something terrible.

Was any of it his fault? Or was it co-incidence? His Rollerton series was becoming a death list. Sponge. Donnie. And now Bexx. He hadn't particularly liked any of them, particularly Donnie. They had been subjects. Case studies. Words on the page. Part of his ticket out of festering middle-aged obscurity.

And now they were all dead.

One in a disused factory with his veins filled with super, pure Heroin.

One on a landfill site in Paisley with a bullet through the back of the head.

And now Bexx had been burned to death on the *Tesco* car park. Doogie hadn't gone into much detail. He hadn't needed to. The detail was in his voice.

For some reason Jason couldn't really explain, it seemed all wrong that he was sitting at his desk in the London office. It was almost as if he was hiding. There were still very few riots in London. There had been a couple of incidents in Hackney and Peckham, but by and large the capital was still thriving on the new era. The country seemed to be inexorably breaking in two. In the South there was a new hope and a vibrant confidence. Everywhere else things were falling apart. Doogie had told how his men were finding it harder and harder to hold the line. Every day more officers were being hospitalised. Every day he had less bodies to deploy to the constant outbreaks of trouble. Morale was collapsing and no amount of overtime was going to restore it. He didn't know how long they could continue if things stayed the same. But it wasn't long.

Yet there seemed little sign of anything abating. Every day the news carried stories of escalation. It was becoming very clear that the Government would have to move to some sort of next stage if it was to keep any kind of control.

No doubt that stage would be down to men like the mysterious Sebastian Dyson. A day had passed since *The Enquirer* had asked its readership if they knew the man from Cobra Two. Bits and pieces had drifted in, but nothing of any substance. Jason's confidence in the plan was starting to drain away.

His phone buzzed.

"Yes."

"Hello Jason. Could you spare me a minute?"

Amelie. All business.

"Sure."

She was with Rogers. Rogers the fifty-something Welshman complete with fierce red moustache. Amelie had hired him in on the morning they had popped the Dyson question. Rogers was ex-Special Branch and now he ran his own ship. He did internal security. He swept for electronic devices. He helped his clients to be able to conduct their business in private. Not that he had been particularly optimistic about the chances of *The Enquirer* being able to keep itself clear of the gaze of those who would now be watching. The Government was in a league of its own when it came to being nosey. There was little anyone could do to escape the attention of GCHQ. But he had promised to do what he could. Now he sat in the corner of the room with a pained expression on his face.

"Hello Jason. Do sit. Coffee?"

"No thanks."

"Are you OK?"

"Not really."

"Has something happened?"

He nodded. He told her of how Bexx had been burned to death.

"Oh Christ, that's appalling."

"Yes it is."

They shared a few seconds of silence whilst Rogers picked at a fingernail with a match. Then Amelie squared herself.

"This letter has just arrived by courier. Mr Rogers isn't very happy about it. I can understand why. He feels it might well be some kind of trap. I am not so sure. My gut feeling tells me it is real. Here. Have a read. See what you think."

Roger's chipped in. "Don't comment aloud on any of the detail You know . . ." He waved a finger at the walls around them.

She passed over a single sheet of paper.

> *You want to know about Dyson. I can tell you. I will be in the café at Watford Gap service station at 2 p.m. on Wednesday. Northbound side. I will wear a green cord jacket and I will have a copy of The Enquirer. I will wait for ten minutes. I will only talk to Marsh.*

"What do you think?"

Jason shrugged. "We can't ignore it."

She nodded and mouthed 'will you go?'

He nodded.

Another line crossed.

Rogers passed him a hand written piece of paper.

*There is a delivery van leaving the loading dock at 11 a.m.
You will go out in the back. It will drop you at a tube station.
Take four tubes to North Harrow. Turn right out of the station
and walk 300 yards. There is a multi-storey car park. On the
second level there is a green Toyota. Here are the keys and
the registration details.*

Jason read and then nodded.

10.42 a.m.

Eighteen minutes and then a step over another line.

His first experience of escape and evasion actually turned out to be
rather dull. He dutifully tried to check if he was alone on the journey
to North Harrow, but he had little confidence that he would have spotted anyone had they indeed been there.

He arrived at the Service Area with a quarter of an hour to spare
and killed some time browsing books in the shop. At exactly 2 p.m. he
strolled into the café area and collected a coffee. He spotted the man
by the window straight away. Green cord jacket. Probably in his seventies, but still straight-backed and fit-looking. A folded copy of *The
Enquirer* in front of him.

Jason took the spare chair at the window table. There was nobody
else sitting close.

"You're Marsh?"

"Yes."

"Reckon you're on your own?"

"I think so. We have a security consultant. Ex-Special Branch guy.
He made the arrangements. It seems to have worked."

The man nodded and stared out across the car park. Jason could see
that he was also bracing himself to cross a line.

"My name is McGee. Hamish McGee. Fifty years ago I was a
Lieutenant in the Argyll and Sutherland Highlanders. We were stationed in Aden."

In a matter of fact voice little weakened by age, he went on to tell
the story of a small village on the edge of the desert called El Kebir.
Of how there would be a riot every afternoon as regular as clockwork.
And then a stranger in a Panama hat turned up and told them to blow
up the village well and make it look like the insurgents had done it.
He told of how the army had brought along a tanker to keep the vil-
lagers watered until the well was repaired. He told of how the rioting
had at first eased and then ceased altogether. He told of how young
men who had been fuelled with anger became like zombies.

"God alone knows what we put in that water, but it had a profound effect. I found it quite terrifying. The man in the Panama hat introduced himself as Sebastian Dyson. I suppose he would have been in his early twenties. When I asked him who he worked for he just smiled and said he was a cloak and dagger type. After Aden I transferred to Military Intelligence. Stayed there for twenty years. Most of the time I was in Ireland. I met a lot of men like Dyson in those days. Too many. They were never bound by the same rules as the rest of us. They worked directly to offices in Whitehall nobody had ever heard of.

'They were not good times Mr Marsh. Not good times at all. We did things that were quite unacceptable and it was always men like Dyson who pulled the strings. Anyway. I have drawn a few conclusions. As I said before, this is an area where I have some expertise. If you check my record I hope you will conclude that I am no basket case. Personally, I never came across Dyson again after Aden. However if he is still in the game to the extent that he sits on Cobra Two, I think we can safely conclude that he has risen very high. Maybe he moved away from the darker end of things, but I personally doubt it. Had he done so there is no way that he would be such a *Google Ghost* as you so aptly put it.

'I suggest you consider this. The country is falling apart. That could not be any clearer. The situation is deteriorating every day. The police are clearly finding it harder and harder to maintain order. Remember, this is something that I know about. I saw it at first hand for many years in Ulster. However I only ever saw it suddenly stop once. El Kebir. Whatever it was that they put in that water tank will still be out there somewhere. El Kebir was not an important place. It was irrelevant. A nothing little village in a colony we were about to leave. It doesn't take much of a stretch of the imagination to conclude that what happened at El Kebir was some kind of a trial. Somebody sent Dyson out to Aden to see if whatever it was actually worked on human beings. I have no doubt that they must have tried it out on rats and monkeys.

'Well, it did work Mr Marsh. And Dyson watched it all very carefully and took copious notes.

'I do not need to tell you to watch what is happening on the news. You have seen what is happening at first hand. I have read all of your pieces. The country is on the brink Mr Marsh. If the decision is taken to deploy the army onto the streets we will never recover. Pendleton will know this. He will want to avoid it at any cost. I cannot help but wonder whether Mr Dyson might bring up the El Kebir experiment and other experiments like it that I am not aware of."

He stared out of the window for a few more moments. Very still. Then he continued.

"Something else has struck me Mr Marsh. It was a water tanker that Dyson brought into El Kebir. Look at how we are supplying the feeding stations. With me?"

Jason nodded. He felt as if he was being sucked ever deeper into a place he dreaded. The old soldier continued.

"Who is rioting? Where do they live? What do they eat? Can they be controlled? Think about that Mr Marsh. I suggest you watch very carefully for a town where the trouble dies down very suddenly with no apparent explanation. That will be the trial. Then who knows. You need to think how whatever it was that was used in El Kebir could be added to the food. If I am right, then arrangements will already be in place. If you find anything, then it is for you to make the decision on what to do with the information. Do you allow the country to fall apart by exposing Dyson and Pendleton if they take this action? Or do you allow them to do to the people of Britain what was once done to the people of El Kebir? It is too great a question for an old man like me. I shall leave it to you Mr Marsh. Now. There is one more thing.

'At the very end of my time in Ulster a strange thing happened. There was a firebrand lawyer called Patrick O'Leary who was raising all kinds of hell. He was a genuine thorn in the side. Then something changed. One night he was due to make a keynote speech in front of a large audience of Republicans. Oh he turned up. But it was like he was in some kind of trance. He stood at the lectern and couldn't speak a word. His political career never recovered. I learned about this from a colleague. Colonel Peter Anderson. In those days he commanded the Forced Research Unit. You can *Google* them if you like. They are not a secret any more. James lives in Nuneaton now. I have spoken to him and he assures me that he will be in this afternoon. Maybe you might like to call on him. Here is his address."

McGee gave Jason a small smile. "Thank you for coming Mr Marsh. I apologise for passing the torch so to speak. I am too old to be of any real use. Go and see Anderson. Hear his story. Then you must decide what to do next."

Jason remained at the table after McGee got up and left. He fired up his laptop and duly Googled the Forced Research Unit and spent half an hour learning about how the army had tried to crawl under the skin of the IRA by recruiting and paying informers. A search on Colonel Peter Anderson revealed a long army career which ended with a CBE. A similar search on Hamish McGee revealed a similar story without a CBE. Both Kosher. Both what they said on the tin.

His sat nav found the house on the outskirts of Nuneaton easily enough. The front door was opened by a tiny white-haired woman who twinkled with hospitality. Of course they were expecting him. Hamish had called earlier. Such a lovely man. A true friend. She took him into the front room where her husband waited. Peter Anderson was clad in tweed and had the red face of a long-term drinker, a fact that was rather confirmed by the tumbler of whisky he had sitting on a table by his chair. Mrs Anderson asked if Jason would like anything to drink and Jason said that coffee would be very nice thank you. Coffee came accompanied by cakes which Mrs Anderson had baked only that morning. She left the room and Jason sugared and stirred.

"Hamish called an hour ago. He seems to think you are all right. Take his word for it I suppose. Been reading your stuff. Not bad. Not an *Enquirer* man myself. *Telegraph* man. Always have been. Sure you don't want anything stronger?"

"No thanks. Coffee is great."

"Right. Patrick O'Leary. Man was a bloody stone in our shoe. Wouldn't keep his nose out. He was getting far too close to stuff we didn't want in the public eye. There was a bit of a flap on, I don't mind telling you. Careers were on the line. My career was on the line. So I asked about a bit and someone told me to get on to Dyson. Gave me a number. Got knows where he worked. All I had was a number. Called him and we met in the Adelphi Hotel in Liverpool. Back in '88 it was. The bastard had done his homework alright. Knew all about me and my problem with O'Leary. I asked him what he was going to do but he just smiled at me. Couldn't stand the cut of the man's gib to be frank. A few weeks later O'Leary was due to address a rally. Ballymurphy if I remember right. It was a big deal, especially in Republican circles. We had a camera in place. Up on the ceiling looking down at the stage. I got to watch the whole thing. Damnedest thing I ever saw. O'Leary was like a zombie. Bugger could hardly stand up. Just stood there and stared. God alone knows what Dyson did to him but it bloody well worked, I can tell you.

'Hamish has told me all about El Kebir. We agree that Dyson must have used the same stuff on both occasions, whatever the hell it was. He seems to think it might get used again. I have no idea. Maybe it would be a good thing. Bloody country's going to the dogs. He said you'd need to hear it from a second source. Well. You've heard it. Rather you than me."

Deeper and deeper.

Anderson's twinkling little wife waved him off from the front porch. He hooked into the M1 and headed north. The radio news was wall-to-wall bad. Riots and casualties and fatalities. The sounds of a country in full on collapse. Breaking glass and bricks crashing into plastic riot shields. Experts analysed and admitted that there really were no experts. This was a place where Britain had never been before. No one had a clue what would come next.

It started to rain and the traffic thinned out. Sheffield. Newcastle. Berwick. He was just thirty miles short of Edinburgh when the heaviness of his eyes got the better of him. He considered finding a hotel but chose a lay by instead. Sleep came in snatches and brought no relief from the raw fear that was running through him. For years he had privately dreamed of reaching this moment. No doubt all journalists were the same. The Watergate moment. The moment when the fearless journalist risks all to expose the dark deeds of the state.

The dream had always had a glowing Holywood quality about it. It had certainly never involved trying to sleep in a borrowed car whilst the rain hammered down on the roof. It had never involved being so completely terrified. He finally drifted into a coma-like doze just after four and enjoyed two hours of welcome oblivion.

The dawn was as grey as any he had ever seen. Wagons rolled by throwing up clouds of spray. The news told of more of the same. The pound was on the slide. The airports were eerily quiet. The French were having a field day. He stopped ten miles shy of Edinburgh to shave in a service area toilet and drink three black coffees, one after another.

Just after nine he parked up in a multi-storey at the foot of the Castle and walked along Princes Street to Waverley Station where it should have been the rush hour but wasn't. Finding a vacant payphone couldn't have been easier. He dialled up the number that Rogers had supplied him. It answered on the second ring. A nothing sort of a voice. Female and from the south.

"Yeah?"

"It's Marsh. You ready?"

"Go on."

"I'm seeing S in a few minutes. Be back on the road by 11. Back at base early evening. That's all."

"Got that."

A dial tone. Rogers had explained the system to Jason before he had left the day before. The number belonged to a person with no traceable connection to his company. She was available to take any message from Jason. The key was to keep everything low tech. The unconnected woman would write down the message and have it sent by courier to the arts desk at *The Enquirer*. Untraceable unless the Government stopped and searched everyone entering the building. It was communication beyond the reach of GCHQ.

In the Gents he fitted on a blond wig, also care of Rogers. It made him look like a geeky nerd once he donned a pair of thick glasses.

Good enough.

A ten minute walk took him to the main entrance of the Scottish Parliament. He had nothing on his person to alarm the metal detectors and require a body search. At the reception desk he informed a bored looking operative that he had an appointment with Jim McCrae. She showed no signs of caring much about this and told him to sit and wait without looking up.

He sat and waited. Five minutes later a pale-faced young woman collected him and took him along a series of corridors to McRae's office.

"He won't be long."

He wasn't. The old warhorse of the hard left breezed in and sat down heavily behind his desk.

"Coffee?"

"Please." Jason waved a hand at the walls and then pointed to his ear with a questioning expression. McCrae shrugged. "I'm fairly sure we're all clean. I don't represent a threat any more. The buggers have bigger fish to fry. I guess you must have reached shark-size by now. You holding up?"

"Just about."

"Scary isn't it?"

Jason nodded.

"Sally should be along in a couple of minutes."

She was. She looked tired. She looked frightened. Out of her depth.

"Hi Jason. Everything OK?"

"Not particularly, but I think we are getting closer. None of it is good though."

The pale-faced woman brought in coffee and digestive biscuits. Jason ran them through his interviews with the two old soldiers and the skin on Sally's face seemed to stretch a little tighter. McCrae took it better. He was older. More used to this kind of thing.

"So where now?"

"Sally told me that one of your contacts is a shift foreman in one of the factories supplying the feeding stations."

McRae nodded.

"I need you to fix up for me to meet him. If Hamish is correct they will feed this stuff into the system through the feeding stations. That means there will have to be some way of mixing it in at source. Maybe you're man will be able to come up with some ideas? It's worth an ask. It was Lincolnshire wasn't it?"

"Aye. When do you want to see him?"

"This afternoon would be good. I could catch him on my way back down the road."

McRae nodded and picked up his mobile. He got lucky first time and arranged a meet at a *Little Chef* in the early evening. "Do you really think they'll use this stuff? Whatever the hell is?"

Jason shrugged. "Who the hell knows? Maybe they will have no choice. From what Doogie tells me the police are all but done in. If nothing improves he reckons it will only be a matter of days before they are forced to deploy troops. The general view is that they will want to avoid that at all costs. So, yes. I reckon they just might do it. I reckon they might just do anything."

Sally reached a hand out across the desk and Jason took it in his. They held. The squeezed gently. They were bound by promises they had made to themselves many years before; promises they never dreamed for a minute they would have to keep. Jason disengaged after a few seconds and bid his farewells.

South.

South on a clear autumn morning on the A1. Everywhere flat with lines of hills on the horizon. Ploughed wheat fields gleaming from days of rain. Lines of starlings on telephone lines. Three columns of smoke rising high into the sky from the Benwell district of Newcastle. The Angel of the North. And all the while rolling news telling the same story over and over and over again. Riots. Fatalities. Fires. Looting.

Mere anarchy

An academic mused that the veneer of civilisation was never as thick as people assumed. One moment life was about shopping in *Tesco* and watching soaps. The next minute you could have Kigali or Srebrenica. Politicians promised the tide was turning. Chief Constables assured one and all that levels of professionalism and morale were sky high. Economists feared the run on the pound had a way to go yet. And American gap year student at Gatwick said she was trying Italy instead. A mother from Daventry focused her screaming grief on the riot policemen who had fatally fractured her fourteen-year-old son's skull.

Mere anarchy.

More smoke hanging in the sky above Sheffield. And Doncaster. The centre cannot hold.

The car park at the back of the *Little Chef* was all but empty. Inside the restaurant a figure by the window sipped at a mug of tea and met Jason's eye.

The inside man. Jason joined him and ordered coffee and a burger which looked so huge in the menu that it could hardly fit on the page. The man said he was called Tommy. There was no need for a second name. He explained that basically everything in the plant was more or less the same. The produce still arrived in bulk tipper wagons, full of vegetables mainly. Meat came in shrink-packed blocks, but they weren't using much in the way of meat. The big changes had come at the far end of the line. The canning line had been disconnected. Now all the finished soup and stew flowed into thirty-tonne holding tanks from which the delivery vehicles could draw their loads. They were running flat out and producing over 700 tonnes of food a day. Where could something be added? Something small? Powder or liquid? In a discreet manner? Tommy thought for a moment. Not for long. Only one place really. Via the vitamin system. Vitamins arrived in liquid form on 10 tonne tankers. Ever since the changes the choice of vitamins had been made away from the factory. They merely received instructions about how much to add in to the mix. Had the supplier changed? No. Same place as ever. Would anyone in the plant know if there had been any sort of change made to the vitamin formula? No. They simply added as required. All nutritional testing was done in Government labs.

"So if you wanted to add something to the mix you would use the vitamin system?"

Tommy shrugged. "In theory, yes. But I couldn't do any thing in practice. The system is closed. It could only been done by the vitamin supplier. Nowhere else. Look. Is there something I need to know here?"

"No. Believe me. You don't want to know a damned thing. Maybe you'll read all about it one day. I appreciate your time. I'll get the tab. Be seeing you."

Questioning eyes. Troubled eyes. Eyes with a hint of fear.

South.

South with a racing mind and a dry mouth. South to the capital. The enclave. The calm zone.

It was late by the time he back tracked his route to *The Enquirer* headquarters. Unsurprisingly Amelie seemed as fresh as someone who had stepped into work an hour earlier having enjoyed a long weekend away in Cornwall. Ridiculous.

No such luck for Rogers. The Welshman had been camped out on a sofa in one of the meeting rooms and his appearance was borderline tramp.

Jason brought them up to speed on what he had learned from the old soldiers and the site foreman. They said little. Rogers displayed the body language of a man who wished he had taken another job whilst Amelie took careful sips from a bottle of water. When Jason finished she smiled.

"Well. Once again you have excelled yourself Jason. But of course we have problems. I am under no illusions that this is the biggest story *The Enquirer* has ever been party to. The problem is that we can't possibly write any of it. Do you agree Jason?"

He nodded. This was an issue that he gone over again and again on his long journeys north and south. It was the story to end stories. The thing was that it hadn't happened yet. The stuff from Aden and Ballymurphy would never make it near the printed page until the story moved along to the next level. Until Christopher Pendleton pushed the button.

Amelie took another careful sip. "Do you think they will really do it?"

"It's impossible to say. It seems pretty clear that things are deteriorating fast. The experts seem to think that troops on the streets would send the pound down into Zimbabweland. He might feel like any gamble is worth it. So. Like the old boy said. We need to sit and wait and watch for some kind of trial run."

"Do you have any ideas about further background?"

"Sure. The vitamins. I reckon my man from Lincolnshire has it right on that front. It is the obvious route. Maybe they have already got sort of provision in place. Everything would have to appear normal on the surface of things. Which probably means that two things will happen. One, a new vitamin supplier will appear on the scene. Two, something will have happened with that company. You know. A takeover or something. They would need absolute control of that side of things. If this thing goes down, it will be the biggest secret in the kingdom."

"Agreed. Leave that side to me. I could do with something to get on with. Your plans?"

"I'm going to head back up to Rollerton for a couple of days. Knock out some sort of holding piece."

"Good idea."

"OK then. I'll hitch a ride out on the midnight delivery van and use the car again. I quite like the idea of staying under the radar as much as I can."

There wasn't much more to say. *The National Enquirer* was in possession of the story to end all stories. But for now it was completely unprintable.

Doogie was beginning to understand how the German generals must have felt as the Red Army rolled over the flatlands of Pomerania to the gates of Berlin in the spring of 1945. Every day his forces were being depleted a little further. His officers were bone tired and morale was hanging on by a thread. The holding stand at the football ground was full. The detention centre out at the Airfield was full. Every ward in the infirmary was full. And yet there seemed to be no sign of the constant street violence easing. For some reason the giant *Tesco* store had become a constant target. The place hadn't opened its doors since Bexx had burned to death on the car park. It was hard to imagine it ever opening again. There was barely a shop open in Rollerton. Most of the population was relying on the feeding station for sustenance. Every day saw the queues for soup and stew grow longer.

By now it had become routine for a mixed mob to start to gather close to *Tesco* in the early afternoon. Doogie would deploy whatever forces he could muster in a line across the car park. Then the mob would attack. Every day the line wore a little thinner. Every day the mob got a little closer. Every day his snatch squads would drag bodies from the crowd and send them to the football ground. But it never seemed to make a dent. Every day the mob would be back again.

He couldn't remember when he had last slept for more than three hours. What time was it now? Almost one. No reports of trouble for a couple of hours. Time to get home for a shower and the first sleep in a bed for five days.

Outside the streets were completely empty apart from patrolling squad cars. Maybe the rioters were beginning to feel the same kind of exhaustion. Scratchy intelligence reports suggested that the methamphetamine pills had dried up for a while. At first this drought had provoked a spike in violence levels. Then there had been something of an easing. Then the reports once again came in that the pills were back on the street and within hours the youngsters were re-energised and spoiling for a fight.

Like most senior policemen he was pinning his hopes on a new initiative which allow a fast track entry into the force for part-time officers. The pay was good and there were plenty of applicants; ex-doormen and infantry soldiers, rugby-playing students and gym built wannabes. Not exactly the best material to work with but everything was coming down to numbers. Boots on the street. Riot shields in the line. He had as many officers in hospital as he had on duty. Soon it would be impossible to field any kind of effective force. So if they had to welcome a few mercenary thugs into the line, then so be it. The afternoon riot at *Tesco* had seen the first deployment of a coach-load of the new specials. It hadn't been pretty. A group of five Corsicans who had come over on the Eurostar for money and action had behaved like madmen and almost killed a seventeen-year-old. Doogie had paid off the Corsicans and had them driven to the station. And once again the line had held. The locked doors of *Tesco* had stayed locked. A semblance of order had been maintained.

There was a light on in the kitchen when he arrived home. Jason? It was. His old friend looked dreadful.

"Christ, I thought I looked bad."

"Cheers Doogie. Drink?"

"Too sodding right."

Whisky was poured and downed in one. Refilled glasses, lit cigarettes. An easing of tension.

"So what's fresh?"

"On the record or off?"

Jason grinned. "Does it really matter any more?"

"Not really. Getting suspended would be like a holiday in the Seychelles."

"Don't sweat. We're off. We're always off, unless you tell me otherwise."

Doogie told how bad things were getting. Not just in Rollerton. Everywhere outside of the South East. He painted a picture of a line about to break. How long would things hold? Maybe a fortnight? Maybe less. And then Jason brought him up to speed on the hunt for the mysterious Sebastian Dyson. The accounts from El Kebir and Belfast accelerated Doogie's attack on the bottle.

"Think they'll do it?"

Jason shrugged. "Not possible to say. From everything you've been saying it seems like they might feel like they have to."

Doogie stared at the table. "Go on. Ask me."

"Ask you what?"

"Come on Jace. The bloody great elephant in the room."

"Fair enough. I'll ask you. Would you like them to use this stuff. Have things got that far out of control?"

"Honest answer? Don't know. Not today. Today it still seems like an idea from hell. In a week's time. Christ Jace, I don't know."

"Me neither."

Sebastian was struck by how very different the faces around the Cobra Table now looked. It had only been a matter of weeks since they had first convened, but a heavy toll had been taken. His partners in crime looked like men who hadn't breathed fresh air for a long time. They had the grey-skinned look of cave dwellers. Or the long term inhabitants of post nuclear strike bunkers. The table was a mess of papers. An overflowing ashtray sat squarely in front of the brooding Prime Minister who fixed Sebastian with a look of pure malevolence.

"Bloody hell. The wanderer returns."

Sebastian gave the man a smile. Why not? He was paying enough.

"Good evening Prime Minister. Bit chilly out, don't you think?"

"Just sit down."

He sat. Only General Woodhead had bothered to keep up appearances. He was all straight back and gleaming buttons. No doubt his shoes under the table were polished within an inch of their lives. Parker the cop looked like he had been dragged through a hedge. West from MI5 was rumpled in a venerable tweed suit and his eyes were ringed black. Obviously he wasn't coming up with the answers to all the questions he was being asked. The three politicians all looked ten years older, none more so than Pendleton who was a shadow of the man who had so confidently announced the birth of a New Britain. Sebastian could see a man on the brink. Red eyes and a slight shake to his hands. Hitler in the bunker with the distant sound of the Red Army artillery shaking concrete dust from the ceiling.

The man was spoiling for a fight.

"There's no point in beating about the bush here Dyson. Your behaviour has been beyond contempt. In case you hadn't noticed the bloody country is falling apart and you are being paid a king's ransom to make it stop. Not to bloody disappear off the map. I tell you what . . ."

"Look. Let's fast forward shall we?" Sebastian allowed a snap to his voice. "You are angry at me. Fair enough. I really am very, very sorry. OK? That good enough? Would you like me to writhe around on the floor in anguish? No? Splendid. You might like to listen to what I have found out. Yes?"

Pendleton almost dragged a cigarette from an all but smoked packet. "Go on."

"I have been finding out about the pills. Unfortunately the news is not good."

He ran them through how Yuri Bonderenko had been tasked by his superiors in Moscow to take whatever steps needed to be taken in order to derail the new changes which so threatened their lucrative UK operation. Faces visibly tightened when he passed on Bonderenko's suspicions that the Kremlin had become involved in the affair. They tightened to tearing point when they learned that five tonnes of pills were already on the streets of Britain.

"Obviously there is nothing we can do about the consignment that has already landed. The so called War on Drugs has been a complete and utter waste of time and treasure for fifty years. We are unable to stem the flow of drugs when the sun is shining. Now with every policeman in the land on riot duty there is no chance whatsoever."

He took a pause so see if they were in the mood for what he was going to say next. Maybe. Probably.

"We can however buy a little time. A window if you like. I have deployed a team into Poland. They are at the border with the Kaliningrad enclave right now. With your consent, they can hit the factory this evening. It will be nothing subtle. If things go well, they will get in and blow the place up. We have no time for frills. The Russians will hate it of course but in reality there is little that they can do about it. They can hardly go howling to the UN Security Council that the Brits have sneaked onto their sovereign territory and blown up their drugs factory. I doubt if they will launch a pre-emptive nuclear strike either. They won't forget of course. They never do. It is for you to consider the diplomatic fallout. If you want Rutland International to get the job done, it will cost you £50 million. No ifs, no buts. It's a take it or leave it offer. There will be no British nationals involved. My team leader is Russian himself. The majority of his men are South African. They are completely deniable and expendable. And expensive. It is entirely you call. There is no guarantee of success but we don't tend to fail very often."

When they got over being appalled by the idea they talked it through for two hours until Sebastian pointed out that make their mind up time had arrived. Then they were unanimous.

Sebastian left the room to make calls from the corridor. A screen was fired up which gave them a satellite view of a non descript looking warehouse on the outskirts of the city that had once been called Konigsberg.

"OK. All done. They are due to kick things off at 0300 GMT."

"How will we know if they have been successful?" Asked James Hawkes.

"There will be a bang. A very big bang."

And at 0301 there was a very big bang indeed which shook the cold night air. The population of Kaliningrad were drawn to the windows of their high rise blocks to look at the orange glow on the horizon of the city. Soon the night was filled with sound of wailing sirens and a crowd gathered in the road outside the warehouse to watch the towering flames. In the end it took the fire-fighters over nine hours to put down the blaze and by that time the factory was a shell. Nobody seemed to be able to make contact with any kind of person in charge and there was no shift foreman to advise how many workers had been inside. Over the days that followed, over forty charred bodies were picked out of the ashes, but by this stage none of the local media were in the mood to talk about it much. The word was the factory was a Mafia place. And it was never healthy to talk much about Mafia places. Instead they talked about football and what was going on in Britain.

Sebastian hadn't bothered to stay to watch the show. A sudden orange flash on a screen was hardly *Doctor Zhivago*. He found an armchair in one of the state rooms and napped for a few hours. The alarm on his phone brought him awake at 0310 and he made his way back to the Cobra Two room.

"Ah. Wonderful. Coffee. And biscuits. What a treat."

Pendleton was in much better spirits. For days he had been itching to take it out on someone or something. The factory in Kaliningrad had done nicely. Only Woodhead was in something of a sulk. He would have liked to have made the call to Hereford. Parker was grinning around a fat cigar. Everyone was obviously feeling rather pleased with themselves. They had pressed the button and hit the bad guys where it hurt. Time to pop the balloon.

"OK chaps. All done. But it is important that we stay realistic. Our friends in Russia are not known for giving up at the first hurdle. 1941, right? Give them a week or two and they will be back up and running and next time it will be ten tonnes. They are going to be very cross indeed. So. We have a window, no more than that. Some respite. What are we going to do?"

Nobody seemed to know. They were clearly miffed at having cold water poured onto their moment of triumph. Sebastian had the stage.

"Gentlemen, I am going to tell you a story. It is the story of a secret. In fact it is the story of one of the very secretist secrets in the Realm."

And he did. How a reconnaissance company of the Third Armoured Brigade had entered a forced labour camp in the forests outside Kassel in February 1945. How over four hundred half-starved Red Army prisoners of war had worked away in a factory even though the camp guards were all long gone. How a file had been discovered in the case of a dead civilian. A series of carefully compiled test results describing the effectiveness of a substance known as Hyrdacol 5. And then the story moved from the Forties to the Fifties. Secret experiments at Porton Down. Mice, monkeys and dogs. And finally time human beings. Human beings in an internment camp in the emptiness of Northern Kenya. Then El Kebir. A Community Centre in Ballymurphy. A brothel favoured by the Serb Militia Commanders in Bihac. A rebel camp in Sierra Leone. A notorious Madrassa in Karachi. An oil negotiation in Tsavo West. And every time the Hydracol 5 had achieved its task. Completed its mission.

Then there was the story of the takeover of a small vitamin manufacturer on the outskirts of Northampton. New management. New staff. Local discontent. An electric fence and maximum security. Alterations to the production line. Another bill from Rutland International of many millions. A place made ready for the last throw of the dice.

"So gentlemen, there you have it. You have the ability to mix Hydracol 5 into the porridge, soup and stew in every feeding station in the land. What will happen? We don't really know. All indications are that the population will become calm and compliant. That is what has always happened before. What then? It is impossible to say. Maybe it will give us some time to take a breath. Let the policemen have some time off to watch the tele and eat pizza. Take the sting out of the situation. Once any fire is damped down it is very hard to re-kindle. Hopefully we can do something similar with the rioting. Then Hydracol 5 can always be re-introduced to targeted areas as and when required."

'So. There we are. Who would have ever thought it would all come to this. I can see in your eyes that you hate me for bringing you this story. Of course you do. This is the land of our worst nightmares. That is OK gentlemen. I can understand that. It really doesn't matter. What is important is that you do not allow your dislike of me and what I do to cloud your judgement. It is important to bear in mind that the situation we now find ourselves in is actually none of my doing. Is it important for us to allocate blame? I can't see that it is. If we are to look for a scapegoat, then maybe we should go all the way back to

Clement Atlee who gave us a Welfare State which was never going to be affordable once the Empire was gone. Or maybe we should blame Thatcher for squandering our North Sea oil treasure on silly wars and breaking the unions. Or Blair for so completely wasting the window of opportunity. Or the casino bankers who set us on course for bankruptcy. For what it is worth Prime Minister, I personally do not see any of this as your fault. You found yourself in an impossible place. It happens. You have given it your best shot and for a while it looked like it might work out. Sadly the Russians have found a vulnerability. History has taught us time and again that the veneer of civilisation is never all that robust. It does not take a great deal to unleash the forces of anarchy. Germany in the 30's, Bosnia, Rwanda . . . you all know the case studies. We are merely the latest on a long list. My job description when I joined you at this table was crystal clear. I am the one who has to think the unthinkable. And let us be in no doubt, the widespread dosing of the population with Hydracol 5 is an appalling prospect. Unthinkable. Of course it is. It isn't for me to voice an opinion. I merely present you with the option. You have things to consider. Can we contain the situation in the country with the police force alone? If not, do you deploy soldiers onto the streets? Have you got enough soldiers? How will the rest of the world accept this? What happens if the policemen and soldiers are incapable of restoring a semblance of order? How long can we go on with no shops open? How long until the old and the infirm start to starve?"

He took a pause to sip at a glass of water.

"Hard questions gentlemen. And questions that I have no answers for. I merely offer you an unthinkable option if you feel that all else is about to fail. Will Hydracol 5 work? I expect it will. It always has before. Can you try it on a small scale first? Of course. I have that option set up and ready. Where? Rollerton of course. Our little Scottish guinea pig town. When? Whenever you like. I can have the Rollerton feeding stations churning out fully-dosed meals by this evening. Everything is set up. Quite frankly gentlemen, it is as simple as that. Your call."

He saw the hatred in their wrecked eyes. Pale, ashen faces. Men at their limit. Men cursing the fact that they had been landed with the impossible. He knew what would happen next and it duly happened. The policeman and the soldier and the spy backed away. They said that the Hydracol 5 option was a hundred percent political. It wasn't for them to make such a call. It was just too big. They had no democratic mandate for such a thing.

MERE ANARCHY

Which left it down to three. Three men at the limit of their endurance. Bone tired and frightened and tasked with halting a slide into uncontrolled anarchy. They would have loved to have passed the buck to the whole of the Parliament, but to do so would have been unthinkable. They found themselves in the darkest of corners. They realised they had entered the same place as many politicians who had gone before them who had signed off on the dark deeds that had put the Great into Great Britain. Slavery, peddling drugs, the concentration camps of the Boer War and Mau Mau, the massacres of Wexford and Drogheda and Amritsar, the thousand bomber raids that killed three million German civilians whilst barely touching industrial output, the sanctions that wiped out half a million Iraqi children. It was a list that went on and on down the centuries. Dark, dark deeds covered by the fact that Great Britain had most of the time managed to win. And history was always written by the victors. And of course there had always been men like Sebastian Dyson offering their unthinkable options. Victory would ensure secrets could be quietly kept. Defeat would put them out in the light.

And Great Britain had always managed to win.

But now, in the year of Our Lord 2016, it appeared that time had at last run out. Night was falling fast.

They came to their decision in the hour before a dismal December dawn. The Hydracol 5 option was to be trialled in Rollerton.

With immediate effect.

A few hours later General Phillip Woodhead had a long standing arrangement in the world of normality. A lunch with his daughter in a favourite family Italian restaurant. He had been putting off the call to cancel. But obviously he would cancel. How could he not? There was no time for family birthdays. To have gone along would have been tantamount to deserting his post. Leaving the line. Shirking his duty.

Duty.

He had devoted his life to duty just as his father and grandfather had devoted theirs before him. He had served his Queen for thirty-two years and he had given her all he had to give. He had served her on the streets of Belfast as a young Guards Lieutenant. He had served her when her forces had swept across the Saudi border to liberate Kuwait. He had served her in the death zones of the Balkans and the parched moonscape of Afghanistan. And he had served he well. Very well.

And of course his service had been recognised by three decades worth of steady promotions which had taken him all the way to a seat at the most powerful table in the Realm.

And Sebastian Dyson.

He wasn't naïve of course. He had been there when bad things had been done. He had issued orders he wasn't proud of. But never had he felt that he had stepped over any sort of line. He had always stayed within the bounds of what was acceptable.

Not any more.

Like the other two non-politicians he had sat mute with astonishment at the story that Dyson had told them. Almost paralysed. And silent. Disgracefully silent. When the three politicians had decided that Hydracol 5 was the only solution, he had buttoned his lip and let them do it. He had convinced himself that such a decision was political, not military. He had accepted the wisdom that soldiers on the streets could mean a terminal decline for the nation. He had taken the easy way.

And when the meeting had broken up he had gone back to his house and showered and prepared to call his daughter to say that he simply could not get away for their lunch date. And of course she would understand. No doubt she would be fully expecting the call. Cynthia was no fool.

He had made some coffee and taken a seat at his desk and reached for the phone. And then his hand had hesitated.

Pictures of the old Wehrmacht generals at Nuremburg jumped into his mind. Cropped hair and shining boots and all of them so desperately earnest in their claims that they had only applied themselves to military matters. Not their fault. They had only followed orders. Maybe they had. After all, what else was a soldier to do? It was an article of faith that was hammered into every young soldier from day one. The very bedrock that every army in history had depended on. The chain of command.

And it was a creed that he had never once questioned during all his long years in uniform.

Until now.

Until Dyson.

Until Hydracol 5.

And still he had sat there all straight back and obedience and said nothing.

Just like those grey-faced German generals at Nuremburg.

Could he live with that?

No. He couldn't. And so instead of picking up the phone he started to write.

Amelie was running out of gas. Forty-three hours had passed since she had grabbed any sleep. Caffeine and adrenalin had kept her going at full tilt, but now the words on her computer screen were starting to wobble. No matter. She felt certain that she discovered her haystack-hidden needle.

Supa-Vit Ltd of Northampton. Sold by a Mr Charles Peacock to a South Korean Pharmaceutical company from Pusan that didn't seem to exist. She had enlisted the help of a freelance hacker to follow the money and the money had been particularly well hidden. They had taken a virtual journey through the firewalls of banks in Luxemburg and the Cayman Islands until two magical words had appeared on the screen.

Rutland International.

Security and corporate advice. And a turnover more appropriate for a car plant than a private security firm working out of a PO Box in Bedford.

More firewalls and more money-chasing. Cash that had gone through one-hundred-and-fifty accounts before finally arriving at its destination. Down and down through the labyrinth until the truth slowly started to take shape. The source of the vast majority of the cash was Whitehall.

Unknown departments in anonymous offices. Nondescript Civil Service backwaters tasked with disbursing EU regeneration funds and transport upgrades and environmental improvement projects. Places where the money was quietly washed and ironed and sent on its complex electronic journey to Rutland International.

More firewalls. Huge firewalls. Top end security systems. And for while she had worried that her hired genius might finally have met his match. But at last he had found a crack in the wall and worried at it until he had managed to wriggle through.

And on the far side of the wall was the name that she had put on her front page.

Dyson.

Sebastian Dyson.

And Sebastian Dyson had spent over the odds to buy a vitamin factory in a hurry.

Her office door opened and a secretary apologised for disturbing her. There was a visitor waiting. Could she spare a moment?

The visitor was a young woman in jeans and duffel coat. Over coffee the visitor explained that she was a friend and colleague of Cynthia Woodhead. They worked together for a charity that supported the families of children suffering from terminal diseases. But that wasn't why she was here. She was merely a messenger. She explained that Cynthia's father was General Philip Woodhead. He had written a letter which needed to be delivered discreetly.

By hand.

In person to the news editor of *The Enquirer*. Amelie duly accepted and was effusive in her thanks.

Another layer of the onion. Another mile down the road. An account of that morning's Cobra Two meeting. A decision taken that was sufficiently desperate for the soldier to break his code. The greatest secret of them all. The greatest scoop in the paper's history. A close up view of an unimaginable nightmare. And finally details of the next scheduled meeting that was arranged for eight o'clock the following morning. And the location of a secret door to a discreet government office half a mile from Downing Street. The basement of the office gave access to the Downing Street tunnel system where Churchill had once called down hell on the cities of The Reich. It was the door that Dyson would use to gain entry. There was a matter of fact description of the man *The Enquirer* had asked its readers to shed some light on. Early-seventies. Just under six feet tall. Mainly bald with a band of white hair. Lean. Usually dressed down in casual clothes. A creased leather shoulder bag. He would arrive at door sometime after seven o'clock the next morning.

It would be a photo opportunity.

The letter ended with a promise to go public and back the story if *The Enquirer* chose to run it.

Time?

Seven-thirty. The night was young. She called up a car from a limousine service which duly arrived at the front door twenty minutes later. The driver couldn't help a flicker of surprise when she asked him to take her to Rollerton. But it was only a flicker. He was a man who prided himself on his professionalism. Amelie was asleep well before they entered the strange quietness of the M1. The driver woke her five hours later as they cruised through the outskirts of a town she felt she knew to the last brick.

"Where would you like to go madam?"

"Give me a minute please." She dialled up Jason and got him on the second ring.

"Jason. It's Amelie. I'm in Rollerton. Where can we meet?"

"Rollerton? Bloody hell. Right. The house is as good as anywhere. You have the address?"

"I do. Expect me in a few minutes."

The streets were horribly quiet. They passed three blazing houses complete with attendant fire engines. A fleeing group of youths chased by flashing blue lights. Broken glass everywhere. Torched cars. Shuttered shops. A kind of undistilled violence hanging in the air.

It took ten minutes for the Sat Nav to locate Doogie's house on a quiet street where most of the windows were hidden by thick boards.

"Would you like to come in?"

"No thank you ma'am. I will stay with the car."

"OK"

Jason opened the door and let her in. Paler. Older. Fear in his eyes.

"Come on through. We're in the kitchen. This is Doogie."

Doogie was still in his uniform although the tie had been tossed. He stood and shook her hand. The table was a mess of half-eaten food complete with a well-filled ashtray.

"Coffee? Drink? We're on the scotch."

She rewarded him with a smile of expensively white teeth.

"Oh I think it's a case of 'when in Rome' don't you? A splash of water please."

Doogie did the honours whilst Jason lit up his sixty-seventh cigarette of the day.

"I can't believe this. I was going to be heading down to see you later. I have a development. My man from the factory in Lincolnshire has been in touch. They have taken a delivery from a new vitamin supplier he's never heard of before . . ."

"*Supa-Vit Ltd.*"

His eyes widened. "You know?"

"I know. Told you I was decent journalist as well as a staunch defender of the bottom line. Go on."

"The delivery came in on a van. They had to reset the line so that it could be added into a single load. A complete clean down was ordered once the batch was processed. But here's the thing . . ."

"The destination was Rollerton."

Wider eyes. "Christ. You've been busy."

"I have indeed. As busy as a bee. And if we manage to stay alive for the next twenty-four hours we are about to become the most famous journalists in the world. Are you both sitting comfortably? Then I shall begin. But one question first. When did the batch arrive in Rollerton?"

"We can't be completely sure. This afternoon probably."

She nodded and held her glass out to Doogie for a refill. "So. Going on what Hamish McGee told us about the trial in Aden, there will be few signs of change today. It will be tomorrow. However as soon as people ate their evening meal this evening the clock started ticking. The time frame is good for us. Very good in fact. We will go public at midnight tomorrow."

"You mean you have confirmation?"

"Oh yes Jason. I have confirmation. Lots and lots of it. Are you both sitting comfortably? Good. Then I shall begin."

She didn't draw it out. Instead she rattled through the facts. The well protected cyber trial that had taken her from *Supa-Vit Ltd.* to Rutland International. The place where the whispered name of Sebastian Dyson had finally taken shape and formed into letters on the screen. Then she gave them the General's letter to read.

Confirmation. The sum of all their fears. A wicked fairytale come true. And now the mystery substance had a name. Hydracol 5. An evil born in the dying days of the Nazis and lovingly kept on ice by the British for seventy-one years. Tested and tried on laboratory animals and human beings in hidden corners of the world. And now it was to be Christopher Pendleton's final throw of the dice. The frantic gamble of a man almost deranged with fear and panic.

And they had it all. Every last piece of a jigsaw made in hell.

By the time she had finished Jason and Doogie had polished off the bottle and opened another.

"So what now?"

She smiled. "You come back to London with me. With luck we will have our photograph by the time we arrive. Then we write it. You write it. You will write like you have never written before. And at the stroke of midnight the world will know. It is as simple as that. It is what we do Jason."

"It is?"

"Absolutely it is."

"Are you scared?"

"Petrified."

"That's all right then. What time will we leave?"

"Whenever you are ready."

He said he needed a shower and a shave. Was half-an-hour OK? Half-an-hour was fine.

They were about to take their leave when Doogie's radio bleeped. The look on his face spoke of yet more bad tidings. He said nothing and listened until he had taken it on board.

"Jesus."

"What?"

"Something bad is happening. Really bad."

"Go on?"

"People are sick. A&E is already overflowing. It is like they have been poisoned. Twelve dead already and the doctors haven't a clue what to do. They are stomach pumping them as fast as they can. It sounds like a complete nightmare down there."

Amelie started to compute the news.

"It has to be the Hydracol 5. The batch must have arrived in time for the evening meal. This has obviously never happened before. There has to be something different. Maybe they are using a stronger dose? I can't see it though. Woodhead said the plan was to play safe and dose low and only raise the levels if necessary. Did they say if the victims had anything in common?"

Doogie nodded. "They are on the methadone programme."

They digested this for a moment. Predictably enough Amelie was the first to reach the obvious conclusion.

"Some sort of adverse reaction. Think about it. All the trials. First rats and monkeys. Then Aden and the Irishman. No doubt there were others we haven't heard about. But it is highly unlikely that anyone who was ever given Hydracol 5 was using Methadone. Doogie, how many Methadone users will there be in Rollerton?"

He shrugged. "I don't know exactly. Over a thousand I think."

"And by definition these are people are unlikely to have jobs and houses. Which means that a very high proportion will be living in the dorms and using the feeding station."

Suddenly the penny dropped with Jason. "Oh no. Sheena. What about Sheena? We have to get to her."

Doogie drove. The streets were unusually quiet. They all wondered if Dyson's potion was already taking effect. Or was the terrible news from the infirmary beginning to seep out across the town? The speed with which the victims were dying was terrifying. Doogie spent most of the journey gathering information from his radio. The death toll had now passed two hundred and it was rising by the minute. Some of those who had been stomach pumped were hanging on, but it didn't look good.

Sheena had kept her job at the youth centre and therefore had been able to keep her flat. Hers was not a street that had attracted the working young. By and large it lay vacant and semi derelict. A third of the empty houses had been burnt out during the riots. One or two windows showed lights. Most were dark squares.

The pavement was strewn with broken glass and general garbage. Already the less attractive parts of Greenfield were beginning to resemble to doomed suburbs of Detroit where clapperboard houses had collapsed all the way down in value to a dollar a go in the wake of the 2008 sub prime crisis.

They hammered at Sheena's door. Nothing. Just an echoing emptiness. Jason and Doogie exchanged glances. Doogie nodded, took a step back, and kicked the tired front door off its hinges. Inside Sheena's small flat was mainly dark. The low sound of a TV wandered from the room at the back.

"Sheena! Are you there?"

Nothing. None of them felt much like opening the door. There was an overpowering sense of doom that was almost suffocating.

Doogie pushed open the sitting room door and his shoulders sagged. Jason stepped to his side and understood the body language.

Sheena was spread across the threadbare carpet, her stick like arms and legs making unlikely angles. The side of her face was resting in a pile of vomit whilst her unblinking eyes stared through and beyond the damp walls into a billion miles of nothing.

Sebastian took a tube and then walked. The morning was fresh and bright. Faces on the pavements were lost in their own thoughts. The world was in the process of going mad and millions upon millions of people were trying to work out where they stood. All night the news channels had carried live updates from Rollerton where over a thousand people young and old had died from some unknown poison. Was it a terror attack? Was it a bad batch of Methadone? Scientists had never seen anything like it. At nine o clock in the morning, a grave Prime Minister had announced that early indications suggested there must have been a terrible malfunction in the plant where the Heroin substitute was manufactured. He promised that the Government would not rest until answers had been found.

By dawn, the town of Rollerton had joined a list of other previously inconsequential places where something truly terrible had happened. Bhopal, Chernobyl, Aberfan.

It wasn't the best cover story Sebastian had ever heard. Maybe it might last a week. Maybe even a fortnight if they were lucky. But the Methadone would be exonerated in the end. And then it would be very hard indeed to come up with any kind of plausible alternative.

The whole thing was unravelling. It had probably been inevitable. They had been far too ambitious. Almost all plans developed problems and gliches. Only the most simple tended to stay on script.

And there was no plan B. Hydracol 5 had been the last resort. All night he had trawled for answers. By dawn it was clear enough there could only be two choices. They could either drop the whole idea and instigate the mother of cover-ups or come clean and withdraw all Methadone prescriptions. There was another option of course. They could all get out of Dodge and leave the country to burn to the ground.

He paused outside the door and turned his face to the sun for a moment and enjoyed a last few lungfuls of clean air before descending to the tomb that was Cobra Two. It was an action that made the job of *The Enquirer* freelancer easier than he could have ever hoped. A zoom lens fashioned with Japanese precision brought Sebastian's face into close focus. The motor whirred. The image was perfect. An ordinary-looking man in his seventies. Eyes closed for a moment. A half-smile.

The atmosphere in the Cobra Two room was terrible. Pendleton was slumped in his chair staring at the clutter on the table. Hawkes was leaning forward slightly with his fingers intertwined. Taylor had his ruddy hands behind his head. Only Woodhead sat up straight.

The Prime Minister lacked the energy for anger. He gave Sebastian a half-hearted wave to a chair.

"Sit down Dyson. Sit down and please tell us just how the hell we are going to get out of this."

Sebastian sat and folded his arms. "Possibly it might be a good idea to get a few CCTV images from Rollerton on the screen. Mr West? Could you maybe facilitate that?"

It took ten minutes. Then pictures of early morning Rollerton started to appear. Empty streets washed in pale sunshine. Light traffic in the town centre. It was all very ordinary. A sunny December morning in a small Scottish town. Then the screen showed the inside of the feeding centre. Every seat seemed to be taken. Long, long lines of people, all sitting very still. Young and middle-aged and old. There was no sound to go with the picture but there was no need for any. It was clear enough that nobody was talking. They were mechanically spooning porridge into their mouths. And once a bowl was finished it was taken to the table designated for used crockery. All six men watched the utterly boring scene with a kind of appalled fascination. Sebastian gave it ten minutes and then broke the spell.

"So. Gentlemen. There you have it. Hydracol 5. I think we can safely say that these are not people who are about to riot today. Order had been restored in Rollerton. But of course we have a problem. The unfortunate effect the drug has had on Methadone users means that it will be rather hard to keep what we have done secret. So we have a decision to make. More accurately, you have a decision to make. My part in this rather tawdry affair is complete. You can withdraw Hydracol 5 and do all you can to cover up what has happened in Rollerton. That course of action will ensure that the descent into uncontrolled anarchy will continue unchecked. On the other hand, you can find a way to carry on and introduce the Hydracol 5 more widely. Essentially this is a problem of presentation. A political problem. Your problem. I have done all I can. You now have the means to keep control for as long as you wish. So. I think is high time for me to bid you all adieu. Jolly good luck with it all."

"You can't just walk out!"

Pendleton looked appalled.

"Oh but I can. More to the point, that is exactly what I am going to do. Please don't do anything silly like having me detained. You can probably imagine the kind of files we hold at Rutland International. Unless my solicitor hears from me very four hours for the next few weeks, copies of the files will be released to people you really wouldn't want to see them. So let's not be childish here. My role was to ensure the lid could be kept firmly in place. I believe the situation on the streets of Rollerton offers ample proof that I have carried out my part. There is no more for me to do. So goodbye gentlemen."

He left them and started along the corridors that always felt like a time warp. It was as if he closed his eyes he would be able to here the wail of air raid sirens in the world above. For some reason he found he was counting his steps, all the time fully expecting to be halted by strong arms. Forty nine, fifty . . .

Still walking.

Maybe they would actually let him go. There were no arranged calls with his solicitor. He was far to old for any of that nonsense. If they took him then so be it. At last he reached the old metal spiral staircase that would take him back up into the light.

Into the light. About time. He had been hiding away in the dark world for longer than he cared to remember. With a shock it hit him that half a century had passed since he had been tasked to take Hydracol 5 to El Kebir. With hindsight it had become clear that Aden had been his point of no return. Once he had become a party of the Hydacol 5 secret they were never going to allow him to go his own way. There had only been two options on the table. Carry on or end it.

He had chosen to carry on. No. That was wrong. He had been happy to carry on. What on earth would he have done instead? And he had been one of the better defenders of the Realm. Maybe even the best of his generation. Victories had been secured which had seemed significant at the time. Now he wasn't so sure. The Soviet Empire had imploded. A kind of peace had come to the mean streets of West Belfast, though the recent Methamphetamine fuelled riots in the Province had been pure and simple sectarianism. Coal was no longer mined in any significant quantities. Many of towns in the North and Midlands where immigrants from the Indian Subcontinent had chosen to settle had become the CCTV capitals of the planet. Age had brought realism. The bottom line was that the rich had stayed rich. They had got richer. Wealth had moved from the bottom 50% to the top 1% at a rate not seen since the days of William the Conqueror and he had eased its passage.

He took the stairs steadily, slowly rising up to the light. At least it was finally over. Not that there was a great deal of time left. As he stepped out onto the pavement he wondered how long it might be. Would they give a younger version of himself the task of rubbing out every vestige of Sebastian Dyson? Maybe they would. Or maybe they would find that they had much bigger fish to fry. He decided the best thing to do was simply to enjoy the day in front of him.

Leisure time.

He took a long bracing walk through Hyde Park and did old man things. He watched the ducks on the Serpentine. He watched young mothers pushing prams. He strolled without hurry along straight pathways covered in leaves. He ate an ice cream.

A half-remembered pub for a pint of bitter and steak and kidney pudding.

A matinee at the Royal Court.

Three gin and tonics in the Ritz bar.

A film in Leicester Square.

A bowl of pasta.

A bottle of Chianti.

Then back to his hotel feeling more free than he could ever remember. Firing up his laptop was a pure ingrained habit. Logging onto *The Enquirer* was a pure ingrained habit. He had come to feel almost paternal about Jason Marsh. The reporter was almost an alter ego. A different version of Sebastian that might have taken shape had things been different.

The page opened up and for a moment Sebastian's eyes widened in surprise for the screen was filled by a large picture of himself. His eyes were half closed and a smile played on his lips. He recognised the door in the background: the gateway to the tunnel system. When? That very morning.

Good Lord.

Under the large photo was an extended headline.

Here he is Sebastian Dyson. The mystery man from the Cobra Two Committee. The man responsible for bringing a long-hidden Nazi drug to the streets of Britain, a drug that maybe lies behind over a thousand deaths in Rollerton. This paper is proud to expose the secret. The drug is called Hydracol 5. It is designed to turn people into compliant zombies. It has been deployed to stop the riots. It has been kept on ice for seventy-one years, the greatest secret in the Realm. And now Sebastian Dyson has delivered it from hiding. It is the last throw of the dice for our desperate Prime Minister.

He couldn't help but smile. They had certainly decided to call a spade a spade. He clicked through the pages that followed and speed read. Extraordinary. It seemed that they had almost all of it. The camp in Kassel complete with grainy black and white pictures. Old images of the Argyles patrolling the dusty alleys of Aden. Ballymurphy. Rutland International. *Supa-Vit Ltd.* They had truly excelled themselves. Without doubt it was the greatest journalistic triumph since the *Washington Post* had shone a spotlight on Watergate.

He stood up from the small desk and pulled on his anorak. Time? Almost one. Would they still be there? Of course they would.

The night porter called up a taxi and the taxi took less than ten minutes to reach its destination. It took a while for him to persuade the night people to let him in. But when they at last agreed to buzz upstairs the reaction was instant. Three minutes after the call was finally made the door of the lift slid open and the creased figure of Jason Marsh stepped out.

"Good evening Jason. It seems to be high time we met face-to-face, face don't you think?"

Jason's eyes flicked nervously from side to side.

Sebastian smiled. "No need to be alarmed. I am quite alone."

"Right. Well. We best go up then."

They rode the lift in silence to the fourth floor. The door opened to reveal the statuesque figure of Amelie waiting in the corridor outside. She was power-dressed in a charcoal suit and her eyes glittered.

"Good evening Mr Dyson. Would you like to follow me?"

She took him through the newsroom where every eye watched him every step of the way. It felt strange. For years he had been one of the most anonymous men in the land and now he was probably about to become the most famous.

Infamous.

Amelie took them into her office and offered chairs. Jason took out cigarettes and lit one. He hesitated for a second and then offered the pack to Sebastian with a raised eyebrow?

"No thank you, but I must say that I am delighted to see that the old traditions of the Press have survived the smoking ban. Most encouraging."

Amelie bristled slightly. "It isn't usual. Jason has earned himself a special dispensation."

"And quite right too. I hope you are paying him well."

"Of course we are. Anyway, I am sure that you are not here to discus Jason's remuneration package. Maybe you might get to whatever point you have come to raise. But I give you due warning Mr Dyson, I am not a woman who is easily intimidated."

Sebastian chuckled. "No. I can see that. But have no fear. I am not here to deliver any dark and evil threats. As of this morning I am no longer a servant of the state. Why am I here? It is actually rather odd. I suppose I have come as a fan."

"A fan?"

"Yes. You see, I have been following your work closely Jason. It always seemed such a co-incidence that we should both choose Rollerton as a focal point for our efforts. At first I was a little annoyed. Then it seemed that you were doing us a favour by making Rollerton into something of a sounding board. And of course it has now become our downfall. Which to be perfectly honest is a very good thing. I dare say you both will know that I have done very questionable things. I do not deny this. Am I ashamed? I suppose I am. But I realise that this is a bridge too far. What has been done deserves to be exposed and I am delighted that you are the man to have done so. You deserve it."

Jason scowled with suspicion. "Why not cut out all the bollocks and get to the bloody point."

"Of course. I come to offer you an exclusive. Me. It is rare these days that a newspaper has the opportunity, well, not without paying a ludicrous fee. I have no fee. I suggest an interview to be filmed and put onto your website as a video. No doubt the TV stations will pick it up soon enough, but at least you shall be the first. Let's see if we can give the people of Britain a taste of the truth for a change. I don't suppose they will like it much and it is hard to say that they deserve it. But they can have it. What do you think?"

Jason was speechless. Amelie wasn't. "No fee, right?"

"No fee."

"And you will answer all questions?"

"If you insist, then yes. There is one area that I feel we might be better leaving out, but you can decide."

"Go on."

He ran them through the likelihood of the Kremlin standing behind the flood of Methamphetamine that had hit the streets. Then he described the attack on the warehouse in Kaliningrad.

"It seems to me that we have problems enough at the moment. Re-igniting the Cold War is maybe not the best idea. But like I said. Your call. If you ask me the questions then I will answer them."

Amelie drummed her fingers for a moment and then gave a firm nod. "I agree entirely. We have enough. More than enough. What you did in Kaliningrad can stay secret. Anything else?"

"Actually, yes. One request. I would like us to do this with no make up. Let us be two normal looking men. Tired and frayed at the edges. If it is to be the truth, then let it be the whole truth."

"Jason?"

He shrugged and smiled. "Sod it. I'm long past caring."

And so they filmed it as they were. The screen made Sebastian look slightly frail in his tired looking anorak. Jason looked as if he had been dragged through a hedge. They took the story all the way back to El Kebir. A young man in a Panama hat high on the secret world. Not that he had been the first. A predecessor had taken Hydracol 5 to a secret camp in Northern Kenya during the Mau Mau uprising. They rubber stamped every word of the story that was now getting internet hits by the million. Sebastian filled in some gaps. Gave some detail. Pointed out how the final decision had been down to the three politicians. He confirmed that Cobra Two had reached a point where the deployment of troops was only a matter of days away. He pointed out that there was a genuine fear that the soldiers might not have been enough. Maybe things had already gone too far. Soon people would start to go hungry. Of course the decision to try out the Hydracol 5 option in Rollerton had not been taken lightly. It was a decision taken by men drinking in the last chance saloon. Obviously they had no clue that the Hydracol 5 was going to have such a catastrophic reaction to Methadone. They weren't monsters after all. Merely men. Tired men. Men working way beyond the boundaries of acceptable stress.

"So what comes now? Where next?"

Sebastian shrugged. "Well. Once this little film of ours finds its way onto the airwaves I can't see a great deal of point in the government trying to pretend that nothing has happened. It will be a time for brutal honesty. I expect you have heard all about the streets of Rollerton today. The streets are completely quiet. There have been no incidents whatsoever for the police to deal with. Hydracol 5 has worked. There is the brutal truth. Now that everything is out in the open it seems that the people of Britain might have a choice. They can give the nod for Hydracol 5 to be deployed in all areas where law and order has broken down. Or they can opt for it to be destroyed forever and ever amen."

"You say the British people. What do you mean by that?"

"What I say. Maybe we should ask them. I suggest a referendum. Democracy in it's very purest form. I think maybe the people have the right to chose between order and chaos, don't you think Jason?"

"I don't know."

There was little more to say. No more ground to cover. The red light on the camera winked off. Sebastian got up from his chair rather creakily. Now the deed was done everyone felt a little awkward. Sebastian smiled.

"All done then. I'll be off I think."

"Can we call you a taxi?"

"No. I think I will walk. It isn't far."

They saw him down to the front door and stood a while to watch him make his way down the empty pavement and out of sight.

Christopher Pendleton appeared on the nation's TV screens at the stroke of noon. He and Taylor had fallen out big time over the speech. The PM was beyond caring. Well beyond. He had angrily waved away the make up people and his wife had failed to persuade him to put a tie on. Most who watched thought he looked at least twenty years older. But it wasn't his appearance that lasted in the memory. It was his manner. He offered no semblance of a Prime Minister. Instead he brought his people up to speed like some bloke in the pub.

'Good afternoon. By now I dare say most of you will have listened to what Mr Dyson has had to say. Thanks a million Sebastian by the way. So. What of it? Well I can see no point in pretending. It's true. All of it. Lock, stock and barrel. Did we make the right call?

Well I don't suppose that is for me to say. It seemed like the best option at the time. Now I have well over a thousand deaths on my conscience and that is a thing I will have to learn to live with. It is water under the bridge for now. No doubt there will be endless enquiries in the months to come. The important thing is where on earth do we all go from here? As I speak, our country is on the slide. Barely a shop is open and most of our streets are war zones. Things here in London are OK of course, but elsewhere it is a very different story. So. What are the options? The police are almost at breaking point. Within days I will have to give the order to deploy the army onto the streets. It is not a decision to take lightly. You need to be aware of how the rest of the world will see us. A basket case. And will the army be able to restore order? We hope so, but there are no guarantees. How far will they have to go to make it happen? Will they be forced to use live ammunition? I can't answer that.

'Which all brings me to Plan B. At the bottom of the screen is a web address. Log on and you can watch live pictures from Rollerton today. You will find that the streets are calm. There is no rioting. No looting. Law and order has been fully restored. Why? Well I guess you all know the answer to that. Hydracol 5. It is as simple as that. It has worked. Of course there are a million moral issues which I should not have addressed on my own. That was wrong. That was out of line and I apologise. You should know that I have no wish whatsoever to carry on as your Prime Minister for very long. I have one last task to complete. In ten days time there will be a National Referendum. There will be two options to choose from. Option One, you give your consent for the government to deploy Hyrdracol 5 as and when it deems it necessary. Maybe this will mean using it only in the punishment centres. Maybe we will have to target particular trouble spots on a short basis. Or maybe we will have to use it on a permanent basis. Only time will tell. Should you vote for this option, then we will obviously withdraw all Methadone with immediate effect. That will of course be very hard for those on the programme but we have reached a time where hard choices need to be made.

Plan B will be an instruction to the Government to destroy all stocks of Hydracol 5 with immediate effect and a law to be duly passed by Parliament to ban its use in the future.

So there you are. It's your call. I will not be campaigning for either option. I will simply ensure that it happens. Thank you."

In the weeks, months, years and decades that followed Christopher Pendleton's address to the nation, the way his words were remembered and interpreted changed dramatically. At first there was a collective gasp of horror in the TV studios. A variety of experts and pundits queued up to voice their utter dismay. How could he have done such a thing? It was beyond comprehension. Psychiatrists were wheeled out to assess the PM's mental health. Image experts analysed his down trodden appearance. Doctors wondered aloud if the haggard grey face spoke of more than mere stress. Maybe he was terminally ill? Maybe he had completely lost the plot?

All were agreed that the idea of controlling the population of Britain with drugs was unthinkable. Unimaginable.

Un-British.

The very idea that a majority of the people would vote for such an appalling state of affairs was so far fetched as to be laughable. Option A was a non-starter. A crackpot idea wheeled-out by a man who had obviously lost it.

But then slowly but surely the tide started to turn. The pundits hadn't even started to get it. These were voices from a world that was speaking from the safety and calm of their Southern enclave. Britain had become a tale of two countries. The area around London remained a haven of normality whilst anarchy continued to grip the rest of the land. The pills from Kaliningrad continued to wreak their havoc and the police lines continued to thin out.

The first poll hit the news two days after the speech and it induced another collective gasp of amazement. 72% of a representative poll of the British people were opting for Option A. They cared not a jot for the philosophical niceties peddled out by a procession of pundits, panellists and priests. Instead they were desperate to end the constant terror of having their front doors stoved in by mobs of semi psychotic teenagers in the grip of Nazi Crank. All that most of the people of Britain wanted was to feel safe again. They wanted to be able to walk their dogs and go shopping and watch football and order takeaway pizza, and if that meant dosing up the poor on Hydracol 5, then so be it.

Once the first poll gave such an unexpected snapshot of the public mood everything changed. Lester Gall's papers and TV channels took up the torch and championed Christopher Pendleton as a visionary and a genius. It was on the day that a poll breached the 80% barrier for the first time that a pundit first compared Pendleton's words to those Churchill had spoken when the might of Hitler's armies were massing in Northern France.

Yet again a leader had taken to airwaves to give the people hope when it had seemed as if all was lost. Drug them in the dormitories became the new fight them on the beaches. And once the names of Pendleton and Churchill had been put next to each other it made the whole thing seem so much better.

When the great referendum was finally held, 83% of those who turned out voted for Option A.

Within days the streets of Britain were quiet again.

And they stayed quiet.

The Russians realised that the game was up and no more Methamphetamine pills were shipped. Without the demonic influence of the Nazi Crank. there was less and less need for Hydracol 5. Within a year it was only used in the prison system where it controlled the more unmanageable and violent inmates. Christopher Pendleton was true to his word and he stepped down despite the pleadings of his people. He followed the Blair route and amassed a tidy fortune giving speeches around the world at £250,000 a pop. A year after his death in 2032, his statue joined Churchill's in Parliament Square: minus a tie.

For a few heady days Jason Marsh, Sally Webster MSP and the *National Enquirer* were the undisputed heroes of the story. But not for long. Once it became clear that the vast majority of the people were going for the Prime Minister's Plan A, they faded from view. As ever Amelie was the smartest of the cookies. She cashed in her share options at the top of the market and emigrated to a villa in Tuscany where she established herself as a successful screenwriter. Jason hung around for a while but soon discovered that his dinosaur status had resumed. He found himself a happy ending in 2018 by marrying Sally and the pair of them emigrated to Australia. Doogie duly made Chief Constable and he was knighted in 2029.

On a frosty February morning Sebastian had risen early to try for the umpteenth time to try to paint the redness of the dawn. The air was vivid and clear and the heron was back. No doubt it had never been away. In the crazy months when Britain had almost tottered over the edge, the stately bird had remained oblivious to all of it.

He had just finished mixing his paints and was ready to start. Maybe today would be the day when he finally managed to put the familiar scene before him onto the canvas. Or maybe not.

Far below him the heron's beak snapped through the surface of the water in a grey blur. It tipped its head back and gobbled down a wriggling trout. For a fraction of a second the shiny skin of the fish glinted slightly in the crisp clean air.

So much had happened and yet the stream still delivered water to the sea. And the heron still went about its daily routine. In that moment he saw the glen millions of years in the future when man's brief term of office on planet earth had been long forgotten. The stream would still deliver water to the sea. Just like it always had done.

He closed his eyes and raised his face to the watery sun. His memory wandered back many years to a row of desks where generations of pupils had carved their names. English Lit. The poets of the Twentieth Century. T.S. Eliot. Or 'Toilets' as they had all called him. 'The Waste Land'. And lines on the page that had seemed to chime with his confused soul. He smiled at the memory and spoke the words softly into the wind. He spoke them into the utter endlessness all around him.

"This is the way the world ends, not with a bang but a whimper."

THE END

So.

Journey's end. The book that you have just read is of course pure fiction. Let's hope that it stays that way. There are however many elements of fact that underpin the story. Dumfries - where The First Base Agency is based - is half the size of fictional Rollerton with a population of just under 50,000: There are 500 hundred people on the local Methadone programme. There are many like Bexx, and yes the £400 a week is entirely true. There are many like Sponge, and yes they are given 'steal to order' shopping lists. There are many like Sheena trying to make their way back to some kind of normality. There are also one or two Donnies, though none have Italian roots.

Out of 'Broken Britain' come many broken people. Mostly they are good people who have been dealt a lousy hand of cards. At First Base we do our best to help them to put the bad times behind them and to move on to something better. We don't pretend to be miracle workers, but we do our best.

Want to give us some help?

Then send your friends along to:

www.justgiving.com/first-base-agency

Thanks,

Mark

MORE TITLES FROM
THE FIRST BASE AGENCY

We have four more books that you might like to read. You can find details on the following pages.

All of the books are free of charge but we charge between £3 and £4.50 for postage and packing.

If you would like copies of any or all of these titles, please drop me an email with your name and address to

mark@first-base.org

or call **07770 443 483**

We will send an invoice for the P&P out with the books

One book	**£3.00 P&P**
Two books	**£3.50 P&P**
Three books	**£4.00 P&P**
Four books	**£4.50 P&P**

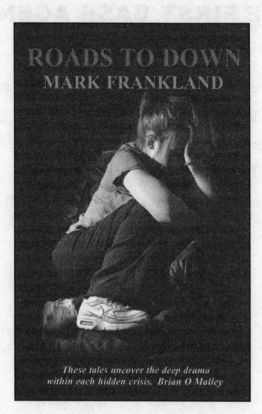

OTHER TITLES BY MARK FRANKLAND

One Man's Meat

Drums of Anfield

The Cull

Terrible Beauty

Red Zone

Target One

The Long and winding road to Istanbul

Poisonous Past

Bialystok

Threads

**TO FIND OUT MORE ABOUT
ANY OF THESE TITLES GO TO**

www.thecull.com

or call 07770 443 483

Afterwards by Mark Frankland

The battles our soldiers continue to fight once they have left the forces have been much in the news of late. For several weeks the Ghurkas dominated the front pages and captured the public mood.

The miserly payments made to grievously wounded men have caused widespread outrage, especially when they have been compared with compensation payments in other areas of the public sector.

There has also been a growing awareness of the huge problems many of our veterans are fighting whose wounds are in the brain rather than to the body.

Twenty years ago few of us had ever heard of PTSD. Not so now. But what does it actually mean in practice? How does it erode away a man's life like a malignant cancer? How does it destroy family bonds and careers and all that men hold dear? And is it really true that our Veterans fight help hard to find?

This book tells the stories of three Scottish Veterans who have shown huge courage in laying their stories on the line. They have done this in the hope that the veterans of the future will not have to suffer like they have suffered.

They want people to know how it has been for them. They want the politicians to know so that they can do the right thing and make more resources available. They want the public to know so that they can pressurise the politicians into doing the right thing. And they want fellow veterans to know that if you look hard enough there is help and things can get better.

The sights that our young soldiers are seeing every day in Helmand Province will come back to haunt them in years to come. We know this. Now we must make sure that the right help is there when they need it.

This is a responsibility that every one of us shares. And if every one of us makes enough noise, our politicians will do what is right.

Christmas Carroll by Mark Frankland

Over a hundred-and-sixty-five years have passed since Charles Dickens published 'A Christmas Carol' and my word hasn't it ever stood the test of time. The story not only gives us a lasting snapshot of grinding Victorian poverty, but also a view of the brutal harshness of a cruel and bleak Britain.

It is tempting to think that we have left those dark times tucked away deep in a dusty corner of the cupboard that is our country's history. Things have changed. Moved on. No longer can men like Ebenezer Scrooge have the power to spread pain and misery. Not with the minimum wage and the welfare state and the human rights act. Our gallant politicians promise us 'No child left behind!'

And of course for most of us Christmas is a time for telly and turkey and presents in warm houses. But not all of us. The terraced houses of Dickensian times have been replaced by the pebble-dashed sink estates none of us really likes to think about much.

And so it is that in this Noughties version of the old classic, the mantle of Ebenezer Scrooge is taken on by Eppy Scrounge. Eppy is a businessman with a heart as cold as a glacier. His business is heroin and his empire is a sink estate called Deepmire.

Eppy is a modern-day leper. A truly hateful figure. An outcast. A person to be loathed and reviled. But ghosts can show up just as surely in 2008 as 1843. And maybe, just maybe, nobody is a completely lost cause?

And so everyone at The First Base Agency invites you to take a journey into the dark and hidden world of Eppy Scrounge. It is a world we like to sweep under the carpet and avoid looking at as we speed past on the bypass. But Christmas is still Christmas, and so long as there is Christmas then there should always be hope. Even for Eppy Scrounge.

So you though Ebenezer Scrooge was bad . . .
Just wait until you get to meet Eppy Scrounge

To order a copy contact

mark@first-base.org

or call 07770 443 483

Stoppage Time by Mark Frankland

Danny McCann is a boy with the world at his feet. He's fifteen. He's just been selected for the Scotland Under 16's football team. Coaches from big clubs are coming to Dumfries to watch him play.

The road to the football dream lies open. But Danny starts to make the wrong choices.These are choices that involve cannabis and ecstasy and alcohol. And suddenly his football dreams are starting to crash and burn.

Now Danny finds himself on a different road. It is a road that leads him into a world of crime and addiction and prison. It is a road that takes him all the way to the gates of death.

'Stoppage Time' is all about how very easy it is for any young person to make the wrong choices. To take the wrong turn. To listen to the wrong people. It is about the consequences that come as a result of such choices. It is a hard, stark story that has come from the stories of many, many desperate young people who have come into The First Base Agency.

Danny McCann is a fictional character. But there are thousands and thousands of Dannys all over present day Scotland. 'Stoppage Time' is a book that can tell our young people where it all can lead. It is also a book that gives the older generation a look at just how very tough it can be being a teenager in today's world. How very easy it can be to come off the tracks.

To order a copy contact

mark@first-base.org

or call 07770 443 483

Roads to Down by Mark Frankland

Young people take drugs to get high.
That's the part they see on the T-shirts.
Sadly, all too often young people take drugs
and find themselves on the Road to Down.

Sometimes it leads them all the way down
to the place where life doesn't seem
to be worth living any more.

This book isn't about the stuff on T-shirts.

This is about the dark stuff that gets swept away
under the carpet. It isn't warm and fuzzy.